Frankie gave a long, quivering sigh.
"This is some fantasy," she said. "Wow."

"You are a beautiful and very complicated creature," he said. "And you will be even lovelier in the throes of pleasure. Let me show you, Francesca." Sunderlin untied the laces at the bodice of her dress, and she did nothing to stop him. She closed her eyes as she felt the dress part, felt the cool night air spread over her breasts, causing the nipples to jut against the thin silk of her camisole.

"Look at me," the Duke commanded as he caressed first one breast and then the other. She could not resist the order, could not move away or lift a hand to stop his sweet plundering. She met his eyes, entranced.

"What are you?" he asked, in a raspy voice. "Tell me now, be you angel or witch?"

—From "A Midsummer Day's Dream"
by LINDA LAEL MILLER,
New York Times bestselling author of *Forever and the Night* and *Yankee Wife*

TIMELESS

also includes

"Lovers of the Golden Drum"
by DIANA BANE,
Author of *Eyes of the Night*

"Out of Time"
by ANNA JENNET,
Author of *R...*

"Echoes of ...
by ELAINE CR...
Author of *Ca...*

TIMELESS

Linda Lael Miller
Diana Bane
Anna Jennet
Elaine Crawford

B

BERKLEY BOOKS, NEW YORK

"A Midsummer Day's Dream" by Linda Lael Miller copyright © 1994 by Linda Lael Miller.

"Lovers of the Golden Drum" by Diana Bane copyright © 1994 by Dianne Day.

"Out of Time" by Anna Jennet copyright © 1994 by Hannah Howell.

"Echoes of Love" by Elaine Crawford copyright © 1994 by Dianna Crawford.

TIMELESS

A Berkley Book / published by arrangement with
the authors

PRINTING HISTORY
Berkley edition / May 1994

All rights reserved.
Copyright © 1994 by The Berkley Publishing Group.
This book may not be reproduced in whole or in part,
by mimeograph or any other means, without permission.
For information address: The Berkley Publishing Group,
200 Madison Avenue, New York, New York 10016.

ISBN: 0-425-13701-5

BERKLEY®
Berkley Books are published by The Berkley Publishing Group,
200 Madison Avenue, New York, New York 10016.
BERKLEY and the "B" design
are trademarks belonging to Berkley Publishing Corporation.

PRINTED IN THE UNITED STATES OF AMERICA

10 9 8 7 6 5 4 3 2 1

Contents

A Midsummer Day's Dream

Linda Lael Miller

1

FRANKIE RAN ONE fingertip over the raised letters on her American Express Card—*Francesca Whittier*, it read—while she waited for the clerk to emerge from the back of the small, dusty costume shop at the end of Ainsley Lane.

If she ended up with nothing to wear to the Medieval Fair, an occasion she'd been looking forward to through a long and unusually gray Seattle winter, she would have no one to blame but herself. She might have phoned from the United States weeks ago and reserved something, or had a gown and headdress made by a local seamstress. Instead, she'd been so caught up in running her own small shop that she'd let some important vacation details slide.

For one, she'd counted on her cousin Brian to look after Cinderella's Closet, her store, while she was away, but at the last minute he'd landed a job waiting tables on a cruise ship.

When, she wondered, had a promise stopped being a promise?

Frankie flipped the credit card end over end on the counter top, listening hopefully to the sounds of bustling enterprise coming from the rear of the shop.

"Have you found anything?" she called out, unable to contain her eagerness any longer. There was no discernible reply, just more industrious noises.

Frankie sighed. She had seriously considered canceling her long-awaited trip to England, but in the end she'd taken a deep breath and dialed an employment agency specializing in temporary workers. They'd sent over Mrs. Cullywater, a retired schoolteacher who had once managed her nephew's hamburger franchise.

Mrs. Cullywater was no Lee Iacocca, obviously, but she seemed competent enough, and she was likable. She would hold things together until Frankie returned.

While Frankie was mulling that over, the clerk, a stout man with a monk's halo of graying brown hair and overlapping front teeth, burst into the main part of the shop again. He was carrying a plain muslin dress over one arm, and his expression conveyed both hope and chagrin.

"I'm afraid there's nothing, Miss Whittier, except for this. More seventeenth-century, really, with the lacing up the front of the bodice and all, but it could pass as medieval, I suppose. . . ."

Frankie surveyed the butternut gown in polite dismay, but she had few choices. She could return to London and spend her precious week sightseeing. She could hide out in her room just down the lane and feel sorry for herself because for the last eighteen months or so, everything had gone wrong for her.

Or, she reflected, she could do what her late-great dad would have recommended—rent the muslin dress, hie herself off to the fair, an event she'd been anticipating ever since she'd read about it in a travel magazine months before, and have the best possible time.

"Will it fit?" she asked, taking the gown from the clerk's hands and holding it up in front of her. She turned toward the full-length mirrors at one side of the shop, but her gaze stopped at the front window.

A man dressed in a wizard's flowing robes and high, pointed hat was hovering there, peering in at her. The shiny threads in the rich purple fabric of his clothing seemed to be spun from moonbeams, and his beard curled grandly down his chest, white laced through with silver.

For a moment, all of time seemed to stop.

Just a guy in a costume, the logical left side of her brain said. *There's a fair going on, remember?*

Frankie blinked, the magician was gone, and the sidewalk was filled with people who were purely ordinary, even in their costumes.

"That must have been the grandest outfit you had in stock," she said, feeling peculiarly off-balance.

The good-natured clerk squinted toward the window. "What? Oh, that knight who just passed? We have lots of those—"

"No," Frankie broke in. "It was Merlin. You must have seen him—he seemed to fill the whole windowpane—"

The clerk frowned. "Didn't see him. Say, are you feeling quite well, miss? You look a mite on the peaky side, if you ask me. It's a cuppa you need."

Frankie yearned for tea, strong, rich, English stuff, of the sort rarely found in the United States, with plenty of milk and sugar. Still, she would wait until she'd returned to her room at the inn, where she could sit down, catch her breath, and sort through her thoughts as she sipped.

"No, thanks," she said in bright tones that sounded brittle even to her.

Nothing unusual had happened, really, and yet Frankie had been moved on some deep level by the sight of the splendid wizard. He was probably just a solicitor from London or a vacationing dentist from Albuquerque, but dressed up in that costume he had seemed the personification of some private myth.

Frankie felt a twinge of the same mysterious enchantment she'd known as a child, when Christmas Eve came around.

She drew a deep breath, pushing her loosely curled blond hair back from her forehead with a slightly damp palm, and indicated the dress. "Will it fit?" she asked again.

The clerk still looked worried, but he smiled. "One size suits all," he said.

Frankie pushed her American Express card toward him. "Fine. Then I'll take it for the whole week of the fair, please," she said.

Approximately five minutes later she left the shop, carrying the muslin dress in a plastic garment bag. The narrow cobbled streets of Grimsley were brimming with happy tourists, most of whom wore medieval clothing.

Frankie hesitated on the narrow sidewalk and peered in every direction, searching for the wizard. She didn't catch so much as a glimpse of him, and her disappointment was out of all proportion to good sense.

She made her way back toward the inn, which, according to a brochure offered at the front desk, had stood on that very spot, in one incarnation or another, for over six hundred years. From Frankie's tiny second-floor room, tucked away at the rear, the ruins of Sunderlin Keep were visible in all their glorious, tragic grandeur.

While gazing at the castle, Frankie thought of its most illustrious inhabitant, a certain Braden Stuart-Ramsey, Duke of Sunderlin. He'd been so important, this fourteenth-century noble, that he had a whole chapter to himself in one of the guidebooks.

Frankie took a moment to indulge in romantic fantasy, imagining the Duke as a handsome, golden-haired knight clad in rich purple and carrying a jeweled sword. Then she smiled and shook the fancy off. True, the whole village resembled a scene from a beautiful fairy tale, but this was Real Life she was dealing with, and she'd keep that in mind.

After spreading the rented dress out on her bed, Frankie called downstairs and asked for raspberry scones and a pot of tea. It was midmorning and she had not taken the time for breakfast before rushing out to the costume shop. Maybe that, along with jetlag, explained her peculiar reaction to the man in the wizard suit.

She was still quite shaken, though at no time had she felt afraid. It was as if she stood on the precipice of a wonderful adventure, her toes curled over the edge, her arms spread in joyous abandon. The very air seemed to vibrate with some crazy magic just beyond the reach of normal sight and hearing.

The tea and scones arrived, brought by a cheerful middle-aged woman straight out of an English novel, with her mobcap, black dress, and pristine white apron. Frankie settled down at the small round table next to the leaded windows to revive herself.

She gazed out through the diamond-shaped panes as she ate. The food did not calm her, as it normally would have; in fact, Frankie was barely aware of taste or texture. The ancient keep held her full attention, and in her admittedly fruitful imagination, she saw guards walking the crumbling parapets. She saw the drawbridge lowered over the moat, pictured a company of horsemen in grand livery riding across.

The yearning to see the castle as it had once been, in the height of its glory days, swelled in Frankie's heart. So strong was her desire that, for a fraction of a moment, she thought she actually caught a glimpse of impenetrable walls and towers, instead of rock piles.

You're imagining things, scoffed a voice in her head. The words didn't come from her overvigilant left-brain, which had a lot to say about almost everything she did, but from Geoffrey Mason, her ex-husband.

She had been divorced from Geoffrey, a handsome and extremely egotistical airline pilot, for almost three years. Frankie, who had been a flight attendant at the time, had given up her job and returned to her hometown of Seattle, where, with a sizable loan from her dad, she'd started Cinderella's Closet.

Miraculously she'd been successful, selling antique jewelry and vintage clothing in her shop, and later recycled designer stuff on consignment as well. She'd even dated a few harmless types.

Still, Frankie had truly loved Geoffrey, and she'd been fragile for a long time, concentrating mainly on survival.

Fate had never seemed crueler than it did the day a year after the divorce, though, when Frankie's dad, her only living relative besides the capricious Brian, had died suddenly in an accident on the freeway.

After that she'd sunk into a sort of functional depression, eating, sleeping, working, doing those things and only those things, in endless succession.

Then she'd read about the yearly week-long medieval fair at Grimsley, just a short bus ride from London, and the idea of going had rolled into her mind and clattered to a stop, like a runaway hubcap. It was just what she needed to jolt herself back on track, she decided, a complete change of scene— even the *illusion* of a different century. Talk about getting away from it all!

Inspired, Frankie had made the decision to stop grieving,

to stop hiding, to venture out into the big world again and do something spectacular. Right away she'd been up to her eyeballs in preparations to fly to England and enjoy the fair.

Frankie brought her thoughts sharply back to the here and now and was surprised to find herself giving a little sniffle. Her eyes were filled with tears, and she angrily wiped them away with the heel of her palm.

She shook off the bittersweet reflections that had been quivering on the clear surface of her mind and tidied up the tea tray.

It was time to put the past out of her mind and follow through on a dream.

Frankie set the tray in the hallway, then took off her white shorts and coral tank top to put on the muslin dress. Her gray eyes widened as she looked at herself in the antique cheval mirror that stood in the corner of the room. Although she saw her own face, her own curly, chin-length blond hair, she also saw a hitherto unrecognized facet of Frankie Whittier. A saucy medieval wench gazed back at her, full of joy, adventure, and mischief.

For a moment the sun-washed dust speckles floating in the room seemed to sparkle, even to make a very faint sound, rather like the tinkle of wind chimes.

Then Geoffrey's influence struck again.

Get a grip, Frankie. You're always living in a fantasy world. That's your trouble.

Frankie smiled and held the muslin skirts wide, as if they were French silk instead, but it was the wench who replied aloud, "Go to hell—and take your opinions with you!"

Frankie laughed, tightened the ribbon laces on the bodice of the dress so that her modest cleavage looked more impressive, then tucked a packet of traveler's checks into her pocket, along with her room key. Her thin platinum watch, a life-goes-on gift from her father after the divorce, was Frankie's only other concession to modern times. She slipped it onto her wrist, where it was hidden by the cuff of her dress, and set out barefoot for the fair.

The sunshine seemed especially bright that day, and the sky was a memorable blue. It seemed to Frankie, as she

stopped to purchase a wreath of tiny delicate flowers and
trailing ribbons for her hair, that there was magic abroad;
sweet, dangerous magic.

She watched the puppeteers for a time and cheered the
jousting knights. She laughed and clapped as the mummers
put on an impromptu play, then bought a small "dove"
pie—which was really made with pheasant—and found a
place on the banks of the stream that flowed through the
center of the village. There she was, eating her lunch and
soaking her bare, dusty feet in the cool water, congratulating
herself on what a bold and modern woman she was, when
the air around her began to hum.

That excited feeling pooled in her stomach, that
Christmas-Eve sensation of old. But this was something
much, much bigger.

Frankie leaned back against the trunk of an ancient oak
tree and closed her eyes. Not a migraine, she thought, for
she hadn't had one of her headaches since before Geoffrey
left her. Too young for a stroke. And why do I feel so happy?

The humming sound grew to a roar, and Frankie waited.
Maybe she was having a nervous breakdown or some kind
of manic episode. That would explain her exhilaration—
wouldn't it?

When she opened her eyes again, she was stunned to see
that the world had altered itself during those tumultuous
seconds just past.

The stream was wider and deeper, and there was a
wooden bridge where the stone one had stood before. The
grass she sat upon was fragrantly verdant and quite un-
trampled. The village itself stood at a distance, and the brick
buildings had been replaced by cottages and huts of wattle
and daub, with thatched roofs. Though there were people
about as before, they weren't the *same* people. Their
clothing was rustic, rougher looking than before, and most
of them had bad skin and even worse teeth.

But what drew Frankie's attention was the spectacle of
Sunderlin Keep.

The castle loomed whole and sturdy and magnificent
against the soft blue of the English sky. The drawbridge
looked sturdy, and there was a moat, full of murky water.

Frankie stared in amazement, blinked, and stared again. The scene did not fade.

She climbed unsteadily to her feet, crumbling the pie in a nervous grip, and pressed her back to the oak tree. It too was different, a younger tree, hardly more than a sapling, and flexible.

One of the villagers pointed at her and spoke to a colleague, and some sort of stir began. Frankie was both terrified and intrigued as mummers and jugglers, merchants and minor nobles all stopped to stare.

The way they were acting, *she* might have been the hallucination, and not them. Fleetingly she wondered again if she was experiencing some kind of individual myth, a colorful gift from her subconscious mind, fraught with meaning.

The crowd began to press around her, pointing and gaping. The smell of them, coupled with the wild confusion she was feeling, nearly overwhelmed Frankie. They were babbling, questioning, but their language was like the Chaucer stuff she remembered from high school, and she could comprehend only a word here and there.

Just when Frankie thought her knees were sure to give out, that she would drop helpless to the ground, someone came pushing through the crowd, a tall, broad-shouldered someone with golden-brown hair and eyes of the same intriguing color. He wore gray leggings, leather shoes, and a purple tunic with a complicated image of a lion embroidered on the front. At his side swung a sword that might have been a cousin to Excalibur.

Frankie stared up into those sharply intelligent brown eyes, at the same time reaching behind her to clutch the supple oak with both hands, in an effort to stay on her feet.

"I don't know how you people managed to make this all seem so real," she blurted out, her tongue driven by nervousness rather than wisdom, "but I'm impressed."

The towering vision before her frowned, and his brow furrowed slightly. The crowd around them began to murmur again, and he stilled them with a gesture of one hand and a brusque, "Silence!"

One disjointed moment hobbled by before Frankie realized that he'd spoken in modern vernacular. She felt an odd certainty that her deeper mind was translating his Old English into words she could understand.

She put out one hand. "Hello, there," she said, her voice shaking only slightly. "I'm Francesca Whittier."

The giant looked at her hand, then gazed into her eyes for what seemed like a long time before grasping her fingers in greeting.

Frankie came close to fainting again, this time because his grip was so tight. "And you are—?" she managed to squeak.

He bowed slightly. "I am Braden Stuart-Ramsey, Duke of Sunderlin," he said. He ran his impudent gaze over her rented muslin dress. "Are your favors for hire? You look suitable for an afternoon's entertainment."

Frankie felt as though she'd been caught between two revolving doors, both turning in opposite directions. She was awestruck on the one hand, not only by the situation but by the Duke's title. On the other hand, she was outraged at his blatant presumption.

Her dignity prevailed. "You're not anything like I imagined you to be from what I read in the guidebooks. Furthermore, you will have to look elsewhere for your afternoon's amusements, I'm afraid, because I don't sing or dance."

The Duke threw back his head and laughed, and the rich, masculine abandon of the sound stirred Frankie on a level of her being she had not been aware of before. "Take her to the keep," he said to someone standing just outside the hazy edges of Frankie's vision.

"But, Your Grace—"

"Now," Sunderlin interrupted.

She felt someone grasp her arm as the Duke turned and walked away, parting the crowd like the waters of the Red Sea as he passed.

"Now, just a moment, you," Frankie protested. She took a step away from the tree. When she did, the sky did a quick spin, her stomach jumped, and then the ground seemed to rush toward her.

*   *   *

Braden paused when she dared to challenge him, turned,
and saw the wench crumpled in the summer grass. No one
came forward to offer her aid, and from the way all the
villagers hung back, staring and pointing, it was plain they
were afraid of her. Damn them and their incessant superstitions; their lives were ruled by fearful imaginings of all
sorts.

He went back, crouched, and lifted her into his arms. She
felt strong and at the same time fragile, and something
tugged at Braden's gut, deep down. Reaching his horse, he
swung up onto the gelding's back, hauling his captive along
with him.

A grin lifted one corner of his mouth as she opened her
stone-gray eyes, looked up at him, sighed, and then sank
against his chest again.

Braden turned his mount toward Sunderlin Keep and the
drawbridge, reflecting as he rode, leaving the midsummer
fair behind. She was a spectacular creature, this insensible
wench in his arms, unusually fine and strong, clearly a
misfit. He empathized with the loneliness of that, having
always felt strangely misplaced in the world himself.

The villagers surely thought this woman was an angel, or
a splendid witch.

She sighed again, looking up at him in a guileless way,
and said, "If you're wondering why I'm not kicking and
screaming right now, it's because I know I'm dreaming this.
You aren't real—none of this is real—it's probably all part
of some weird sexual fantasy."

Braden frowned. What an odd pronouncement. "Sexual
fantasy"? Why would anyone indulge in such fancies when
the real experience was so easily had?

He thought again of what the villagers were probably
saying by now, and shook his head. It could not be denied,
however, that this wench was different. She was bigger and
stronger than any woman he'd ever seen—God's breath but
she felt heavy on his arm, even though she was sleekly
made—and her skin and teeth *were* uncommonly good.
Still, Braden reasoned, he himself was of rare good health

and sturdy construction, and he was certainly neither angel nor warlock.

"What," he began as they crossed the drawbridge, the hooves of his charger making a rhythmic sound on the wood, "are you blathering about?"

She took a deep breath, wiping aside the two bright ribbons that dangled across her face from the halo of flowers, now sitting askew on her head. "Well," she replied, "it's not something I can explain easily. I've always had a thing for knights and castles, and I played Guinevere in our high school production of *Camelot*—"

They passed beneath the points of the iron portcullis and into the lower bailey. "Guinevere?" Braden asked, somewhat shortly. He'd heard the legends of King Arthur as a child, and loved them, but he couldn't see what they had to do with the afternoon's events. "I thought you said you were called Francesca."

She smiled, and the effect was startling; rather like sunlight flashing suddenly upon very clear water. Once again he felt a lurching sensation, much like the time in his boyhood when he'd nearly toppled off a cliff and a companion had caught hold of his tunic just in time to pull him back. "My friends call me Frankie," she said.

Braden couldn't help smiling back, even though he didn't approve of a woman having such a name—even if she was a lightskirt, selling her favors at a country fair. "Frankie" was better suited to a lad; to him, she would always be "Francesca."

Always? The word stretched through Braden's mind like a vine gone wild, making him distinctly uncomfortable.

"Are you traveling with the mummers or the puppeteers?" he asked. "I haven't seen you before."

She laughed, and the sound quivered in his heart like a lance, at once painful and sweet. "You know, it's just like me to have a fantasy where the man who is going to ravish me turns out to be a nice guy. You are nice, aren't you?"

He was baffled again, and at no behest from him, his arm tightened slightly around her. "I don't know," he replied thoughtfully. "No one has ever described me that way as far as I know." Braden felt his neck reddening, drew back on the reins, and swung one muscular leg over the saddle horn, at the same time lowering Francesca to the ground. "Furthermore," he said, "I've never *ravished* a woman in my life. They've always come to my bed quite willingly."

Francesca's flawless cheeks turned pink, and the gray eyes sparked. "Fantasy or no fantasy, buddy," she replied, "I'm not going to your bed, period. Willingly or otherwise."

Braden dismounted. "We'll see," he said. He tossed the reins to a stable boy and gripped Francesca's arm with his other hand, propelling her up the slope toward the keep.

2

SOLICITOUSLY THE DUKE straightened the beribboned floral wreath Frankie had bought earlier, in the real world. Then, with an air of amused ceremony, he squired her under a high archway and into the keep's Great Hall.

There were rushes on the floor, and knights lounged at long trestle tables, playing dice and arm wrestling. There was no hearth or chimney but instead a huge firepit in the center of the hall. Smoke meandered toward a large round hole in the roof, turning the air acrid before disappearing into the sky.

Frankie coughed, blinking because her eyes burned and because she couldn't believe what she was seeing. Surely this was the most elaborate hallucination anyone had ever had, without taking drugs first.

She rubbed her right temple nervously. Maybe the scones she'd had at the inn that morning had been laced with something. Or perhaps someone had slipped her a mickey at the fair.

Both scenarios seemed unlikely, but so did finding herself in a place she'd only read about, a time centuries in the past. Just then, not much of anything was making sense to

Frankie—including the staggering and surely ill-advised attraction she felt toward the Duke.

The men-at-arms looked up from their mugs and games to leer at Frankie in earnest, but one quelling glance from the Duke made them all subside again.

"What year is this?" Frankie asked, squinting up at Sunderlin's daunting profile as he double-stepped her over the rushes toward a wide stone stairway lined with unlit torches.

He looked down at her and frowned, but he didn't slacken his pace. "It is the year of our Lord thirteen hundred and sixty-seven," he answered. "Where have you been that you had to ask such a question? Even in nunneries, they mark the passage of time."

Frankie's head was spinning, and she felt a peculiar mix of desire and utter terror. They were taking the stairs at a good clip; evidently, this fantasy was going to reach its dramatic crescendo soon.

"If I told you where I'd been, you'd never believe me," she replied. "Suffice it to say, it wasn't a 'nunnery,' as you put it." She dug in her heels, or tried to, but the Duke just kept walking. "Wait a second! Could we just stop and talk, please? I mean, I know this is all a production of my subconscious mind, starring me, with a guest appearance by you, but I'm not ready to play out the big scene."

Sunderlin finally halted, square in the middle of the upper hallway, and stared at Frankie as if completely confounded. It was all so real—the dank stone walls of the castle, the burnt-pitch smell of the torches, the remarkable muscular man standing beside her. She marveled at the power of the human imagination; clearly, her yearnings for adventure and romance had run much deeper than she'd ever guessed. Now her mind was producing the whole dream like some elaborate play, though she must remember that it was all taking place inside her head.

"What in the name of God are you talking about?" he demanded. Even in his consternation, the Duke exuded self-confidence and personal strength.

Frankie reached out and pressed one palm to the cold rock wall, to steady herself. She was ready to wake up now, ready to go home to Kansas, so to speak, and yet the idea of never seeing Sunderlin again struck a resonant note of sorrow in her heart. It was a sensation she couldn't have explained, as mystical as the experience in general.

"I don't feel so good," she said.

Sunderlin bent his knees and peered into her face, which was probably quite pale by then. "You don't have the plague, I hope," he replied.

Frankie could only shake her head.

"Here, then, you're probably starving, and it's plain that you've come from some far place." He lifted her into his arms again, just as he had at the fair, when she'd been surrounded by curious villagers. "I'll send for some food and wine, and when you've had a rest, I'll bed you."

Frankie's temper flared, even though she knew she was only dreaming. "That's very generous of you, my lord," she said tartly. Sunderlin carried her into yet another large, drafty chamber and dumped her onto a bed roughly the size of her whole apartment back home. "Now, what on earth does *this* symbolize?" she muttered, distracted for a moment, as she patted the thick feather mattress with both hands.

"Enough of your strange chatter," Sunderlin growled, bending over her and forcing her backward until she was lying flat. His arms were like stone pillars on either side of her as he leaned on the bed. "God's kneecaps, woman, the villagers are sure to think you're either a witch or an angel. There's something very different about you, and to their minds, anyone who is different is dangerous. If they decide you're a sorceress, they might very well stone you or burn you at the stake!"

Frankie was completely undone, but not by the delusion she was having or even by the prospect of being executed for sorcery. No, it was the proximity of Braden Stuart-Ramsey, Duke of Sunderlin, that was making her so wildly nervous.

She reached up, with a trembling hand, to touch his tanned, clean-shaven face. "You seem so real, so solid."

He made an exasperated sound, then leaned closer still

and brushed his lips across hers. His mouth felt soft and warm, and a hot shiver rushed through Frankie's system.

"I am definitely 'real,'" Sunderlin said, his voice hoarse. Then, just when Frankie wanted the fantasy to continue, he pushed himself away from her and stood straight beside the bed. Never taking his eyes from hers, he unbuckled his sword belt and laid it aside, weapon and all. "Who are you, Francesca?" he asked. "Where did you come from?"

Frankie knew she should have bounded off that bed immediately—everything she believed as a modern, right-thinking female demanded it—but she was possessed of an odd lethargy. She yawned. "This is not going to compute," she said, "but since you insist, here goes. My name is Francesca Whittier, and I'm from the United States."

Sunderlin pulled his tunic off over the top of his head, revealing a broad, hairy chest and powerful shoulders. His glorious caramel-colored hair was rumpled by the process. "The United States?" he asked, giving a braided bellpull a hard wrench and then reaching for a ewer of water sitting on a nearby table. "I've never heard of that place. Where is it?"

"On the other side of the Atlantic Ocean," Frankie said, watching him. As hallucinations went, the Duke of Sunderlin was downright delicious. "At this point you could only describe it as—underdeveloped."

A servant entered the room, probably in reply to Sunderlin's yank on the bellpull, a bow-legged little man in leggings and a tunic that looked as though it might have been made of especially coarse burlap.

The Duke spoke to him in an undertone, and he disappeared again. Even though the servant had not so much as glanced in Frankie's direction, his curiosity had been palpable.

"Mordag will bring you bread and wine," Sunderlin said. He'd washed his face and upper body and was now drying himself with his discarded tunic. "As I said, you may eat and sleep for a reasonable time. Then you and I will work out an agreement."

Frankie felt her cheeks turn hot again. "I very much appreciate your hospitality," she said in measured tones.

"However, there's no need for us to 'work out an agreement.' As I told you before, I am not a prostitute."

Sunderlin's white teeth flashed in a grin so lethal it should have been registered somewhere. He folded his arms, which Frankie now noticed were scarred in places, and tilted his magnificent head to one side. "I see," he teased. "Then you must be a lady—one who's fallen upon unfortunate circumstances." He sketched a deep bow, and Frankie was flushed with fury, knowing he was mocking her.

At last she found the strength to scramble into a sitting position; not an easy task, since the mattress was so deep and soft. "I'd have *been* a lady if I'd gotten to the costume shop on time," she blurted.

"What?" he asked, frowning again.

"Never mind!" Frankie floundered around on the mattress for a while, making no progress. She finally turned over onto her belly and wriggled until she reached the side, where she swung her legs over and stood. "My point is," she went on, while Sunderlin stood grinning at her, "you shouldn't assume that I'm a loose woman just because of my clothes!"

Sunderlin approached, hooked one finger through the laces that held Frankie's bodice together. Underneath, she was wearing only a thin camisole of sand-washed silk. "Witch or angel," he said, his voice low and throaty, "you are fascinating."

Frankie swallowed and retreated a step. "Don't touch me," she said, without conviction.

Sunderlin reached out and pulled her against him. "Fascinating," he repeated.

She stiffened. "Are you planning to force me?" she demanded. "Because if you are, I'm warning you, I'll knee you where it hurts, and I'll scream my head off, too. Your reputation will be completely ruined!"

He threw back his head and laughed, and when he looked into her eyes again, a moment later, she saw kindness in his gaze, along with desire and amusement. "My reputation will be ruined," he corrected, "if the servants do not hear you crying out in passion." Sunderlin paused, sighed philosophically. "Didn't I tell you before, little witch? I have never in my life taken a woman who did not want my attentions." He held her loosely, his arms linked behind the small of her back, and bent to kiss the pulse point at the base of her throat.

Frankie felt faint. "Good," she replied when she could manage to speak. "I'm—I'm glad."

Sunderlin touched her breast, very gently, his thumb passing over one muslin-covered nipple and causing it to blossom. "Of course," he went on, idly entangling a finger in the laces that held her bodice closed, "I have no doubt that I can rouse a fever in you."

His arrogance was like a snowball in the face, and Frankie jerked back out of his arms just as the servant reappeared, carrying a tray. She turned away, embarrassed, and when she looked in Sunderlin's direction again, he had pulled on a clean tunic and the servant was gone.

"Refresh yourself," the Duke commanded, pausing in front of a looking glass to run splayed fingers through his hair. "I will return later." He paused as Frankie inspected the items on the tray. "Just in case you're thinking of escaping," he added, in grave tones, "don't. My men would find you before sunset, and honor would require that I punish you."

Frankie was too confused and scared to think about escape just then, but she meant to entertain the notion later, when she'd had a little time to gather her wits. She sketched a curtsy every bit as mocking as his bow had been earlier. "Your word is my command, O Pompous and Arrogant One," she said. Then she took a piece of dark bread from the trencher and examined it for weevils and other moving violations.

Sunderlin only grinned, strapped on Excalibur again, and walked out of the massive room, leaving Frankie quite alone.

She bit into the bread and reached for a brass bottle, which contained a bitter and very potent red wine. Normally, Frankie didn't drink, but on that day all the other rules of the universe seemed to be suspended—why not that one?

Having eaten, and consumed the wine, Frankie began to

feel light-headed and sleepy again. Good, she thought. I'll wake up in my bed at the Grimsley Inn, or even back in Seattle, in my apartment, and all this will be over. A dream and nothing more.

As before, the thought of leaving Sunderlin left her strangely bereft, and close to tears.

She sniffled once as she stretched out on the featherbed.

Hours later she awakened to the same room, the same stone walls, and her shock was exceeded only by her relief. The dream or delusion had not yet ended, and she was glad, though she couldn't have offered a rational explanation for her attitude. Luckily, no one was asking for one.

"Mr. Stuart-Ramsey?" she called tentatively. "My lord?"

There was no response, but in the distance she heard the sounds of raucous male laughter and the music of some sort of pipe, as well as a stringed instrument or two. Frankie rolled to the side of the bed and struggled to her feet, smoothing her hair and her muslin skirts.

By the light of the moon, which came in through narrow windows empty of glass, Frankie found the bellpull, stared at it for a few moments, and then gripped the cord in both hands and gave it a good jerk.

The spindly servant appeared almost instantly, and Frankie wondered if the poor man was compelled to work at night as well as during the day. He carried a flickering candle, which he used to light oil lamps set around the room.

"You may tell the Duke that I will see him now," Frankie announced, with great dignity. Never mind that it was mostly pretense; she *sounded* sure of herself even if she wasn't.

Mordag merely looked at her in bewilderment and something like awe. His Adam's apple traveled the length of his scrawny, unwashed neck as he stood there, apparently at a complete loss to understand her instructions.

She drew a deep breath and very patiently began again. "I said—"

"He won't speak to you," a familiar voice interrupted. "He probably fears you'll either cast a spell over him or strike him dead for some secret sin."

Frankie turned and saw Sunderlin standing in the doorway. He said something unintelligible to Mordag, and the servant rushed from the room, plainly eager to be gone.

"Couldn't you just tell these people that I'm an ordinary woman?" she asked, exasperated.

Sunderlin smiled and ran his gaze over her in a leisurely way. "They wouldn't believe me," he replied after a moment's reflection. "And why should they? It's plain to any man with eyes that you're no 'ordinary woman.'"

Frankie felt dizzying confusion, as well as a terrible attraction to this strange and powerful man. She averted her eyes for a moment, wondering that a mere delusion, a figment of her imagination, could stir her the way Sunderlin did.

"Have you rested?" the Duke asked when she failed to continue the conversation, sitting down at a rough-hewn table near the bed and putting his feet up.

Unconsciously Frankie tightened the laces on her rented dress. "Yes," she said. "If you would just take me to a hotel now, I would appreciate it very much."

"Take you where?"

"An inn," Frankie said in frustration. "A tavern—"

Sunderlin swung his powerful legs down from the tabletop and rose to his feet in a graceful surge of rage. "You would prefer such a place to my bed?" he demanded, breathing the words more than speaking them.

Frankie figured since this was a fantasy, she might as well be honest. "No," she said. "I guess not."

He approached her slowly. "You are a beautiful and very complicated creature," he said. "And you will be even lovelier in the throes of pleasure. Let me show you, Francesca." Sunderlin untied the laces at the bodice of her dress, and she did nothing to stop him.

"If—if I want you to stop—then—?"

"Then I shall stop," the Duke said.

Frankie closed her eyes as she felt the dress part, felt the cool night air spread over her breasts, causing the nipples to jut against the thin silk of her camisole.

"Lovely," Sunderlin said. He smoothed the dress down

over her shoulders with excruciating gentleness, then removed the camisole, too. "So lovely."

Frankie trembled, afraid to meet his gaze even though his words and his tone held quiet reverence. He made her feel like a fallen goddess, too beautiful to be real.

"Look at me," the Duke commanded as he caressed first one breast and then the other. His touch had the weight of a moonbeam, the fierce heat of a newly spawned star.

She could not resist the order, could not move away or lift a hand to stop his sweet plundering. She met his eyes, entranced.

"What are you?" he asked in a raspy voice. "Tell me now, be you angel or witch?"

Frankie gave a long, quivering sigh as he fondled an eager nipple. "This is some fantasy," she said. "Wow."

Sunderlin bent, took the morsel he'd been caressing into his mouth, and suckled, wringing a cry of startled pleasure from Frankie's lips.

"Answer me," he said when he'd raised his head again.

Frankie wanted to press him back to her bosom, to nourish him, to set his senses ablaze as he had hers. "I'm whatever you want me to be," she replied, and she was rewarded by a low groan and the conquest of her other breast.

God only knew what would have happened if the clanging sound of metal striking stone hadn't sounded from the passage outside Sunderlin's chamber, along with a good-natured and exuberant male voice.

"Braden!" the visitor called as the Duke swore and Frankie dived for the shadowy end of the chamber, struggling to right her dress. The clang sounded again, louder and closer. "Are you in there wenching, like Mordag says?"

Frankie heard Sunderlin swear and peered out of the gloom, holding the bodice of her dress closed, her breathing still fast and very shallow. A handsome man, younger than the Duke and much darker in coloring, swaggered into the room, sheathing his sword as he entered. Apparently, it had been the blade of that weapon that Frankie had heard striking the stone walls.

Sunderlin shrugged, adjusting his tunic. "Alaric," he greeted the other man, and there was an undercurrent of humor flowing beneath his irritation. "I thought you were in London Town, pandering at court."

Alaric laughed, ignoring the Duke's jibe and looking around with an expression of impudent curiosity. "Come now, Brother, where is she? I must see the creature or perish of wondering. Mordag says she's too beautiful and too perfect to be a human woman."

"Mordag talks too much," Sunderlin answered. He went to a side table, though it couldn't have been plainer that he didn't welcome company, and poured wine into two ornate silver chalices. "Show yourself, Francesca, or my brother will seek you out. He's just brazen enough to do it."

Frankie would have preferred to remain in the shadows, since she'd never found her camisole and, even though she'd pulled up her dress and tied the laces, there was still a lot of skin showing through. She came out of her hiding place anyway, her arms crossed demurely across her chest.

Alaric was definitely a new development, and she wondered where he fit into her fantasy.

He studied her with dark, shrewd eyes. Clearly, Alaric had the same forthright, supremely confident nature as his brother. Frankie was both relieved and puzzled to realize that she understood him clearly, as she did Braden.

"Neither angel nor witch," he said in a speculative tone, the hint of a smile lifting one corner of his mouth. "No, Brother, this is surely a wood nymph, or a mermaid weary of the sea."

What a line, Frankie thought, but she liked Alaric. It would have been impossible not to, for he was charming. She smiled as he took her hand and lightly kissed her knuckles. Out of the corner of her eye, she saw Sunderlin frowning ominously.

"Do not become too enchanted," he warned in a quiet voice. "Nymph or mermaid, angel or witch, Francesca is mine."

Frankie's proud heart pumped hot crimson color into her

cheeks. "Unlike your favorite horse and your hunting dogs," she said, "I am not 'yours'! I'm my own."

Sunderlin's jaw tightened, and Alaric chuckled, obviously amused by his brother's annoyance. "Such a quick tongue," he said.

"'How sharper than a serpent's tooth,'" Frankie quoted, getting into the spirit of things. She might as well enjoy this delusion to the hilt; there was no telling when or if she'd be able to work up another one like it.

"That's very good," said Alaric, waggling an index finger. "Someone should write it down."

"Someone will, someday," Frankie assured him.

Sunderlin narrowed his eyes again. "Witch talk," he said. "Have you no sense at all?"

The words stung. "Yes," Frankie snapped. "I also have a sense of humor—a claim *you* certainly can't make!"

"Sparks!" Alaric cried, spreading his arms in a gesture of expansive delight. "The air is blue with them!"

"Silence!" Sunderlin boomed, but it was Frankie he was glowering at, not his brother.

"In your dreams," Frankie answered, folding her arms and lifting her chin. Okay, so she was having a fantasy. Okay, so it was probably a *sexual* fantasy. That didn't mean she was going to let a man push her around, no matter how attractive she found him.

Alaric laughed again, bracing himself against a table edge with both hands. "At last," he said. "A woman who doesn't tremble before you like a blade of grass in a high wind. Brother, your fate is sealed. You are doomed. Congratulations!"

"Out," Sunderlin said. His gaze rested on the pulse point at the base of Frankie's throat, or so it seemed to her, but there was no doubt that he was addressing Alaric.

The younger brother bowed, but his good spirits were as evident as before. "As you wish," he said graciously. "Never fear, Braden. I will carry the news of your conquering to every part of England."

At last Sunderlin's stare shifted from Frankie to his sibling, and she let out an involuntary sigh of relief. The expression on the Duke's face could only have been called ferocious. "We will speak privately," he said to Alaric. "Now."

Frankie watched, a little nettled that she'd been forgotten so easily, as both men left the chamber.

3

IT WAS THAT night, while she waited in vain in Sunderlin's bedchamber, alternately cursing Braden and praying for his return, that Frankie started to accept the possibility that the experience she was having was not a flight of fancy at all, but some new facet of reality.

A delusion, she reasoned as she lay beneath the covers on Braden's bed, clad only in her silk camisole and tap pants, would surely have faded by this time. Furthermore, while no sensible person would ever have described Frankie as a hardheaded realist, she wasn't given to wild imaginings, either. She wasn't insane, and her surroundings were simply too solid for a hallucination. The only other explanation was that she had slipped through some unseen doorway, into another time.

How could such a thing happen? Frankie had no answers, only questions. What seemed most remarkable to her was her own resilience—nervous breakdowns are made of such stuff as she was experiencing, and yet she had a sense of well being and belonging now that had eluded her since childhood.

The first pink light of dawn was just creeping across the stone floor when Braden reappeared, looking rumpled and somewhat bleary-eyed.

Frankie sat bolt upright in bed, heedless of her near-naked state, furious jealousy flowing through her. Even with Geoffrey, she had never felt any emotion so intense. "Where have you been?" she demanded.

To her infinite exasperation, Braden grinned. "Not with a

wench," he replied, "so calm yourself." He went to a table uncomfortably near the bed and poured water from a ewer into a waiting basin. He made a great production of stripping off his tunic and washing.

That done, he removed his soft leather shoes and woolen leggings as well. He loomed beside the bed, gloriously naked and utterly without self-consciousness.

Frankie's arousal was complete, and unbidden, and she was mortified by it. Blushing, she wriggled down under the bedclothes.

Braden promptly tossed back the thick fur coverings and surveyed her. "Such a strange manner of dress," he said, clearly confounded by her lingerie. "Still, I imagine you're a regular woman underneath."

Frankie's cheeks burned. She was two women, all of a sudden—one sensible and modest, one wanting nothing so much as to thrash beneath this man in noisy abandon. "Why is this happening?" she murmured. "Why me?"

The Duke bent over her, hooked his big thumbs under the waistband of Frankie's tap pants, and slid them deftly down over her thighs. She could only watch, stunned at the depths of her own feminine need, as he frowned, apparently more interested in watching the elastic stretch when he pulled, then snap back into place.

Finally he tossed the tap pants aside and looked at Frankie with a possessiveness and hunger that made her blood heat. With one hand he parted her thighs; with the other he tugged upward on her camisole.

Frankie closed her eyes and groaned softly as Braden's fingers claimed the most private part of her. It did no good, telling herself that this was no fantasy after all, that what was happening was real and would have its consequences. This was more than a mere encounter; Frankie felt as though she and Braden had been drawn together from separate parts of the universe.

She thrilled to his weight and warmth as he stretched out beside her. He bent his head to nibble at her breasts, one and then the other, all the while gently caressing her most feminine place.

He made a low, sighlike sound as Frankie began to twist

and writhe under his attentions. Although she had thought she'd known pleasure before, with Geoffrey, the fitful realization came to her that she had instead been entirely innocent until this man, Braden Stuart-Ramsey, Duke of Sunderlin, touched her.

Braden nipped lightly at Frankie's nipple while at the same moment plunging his fingers deep inside her, and she arched her back and gave a strangled, joyous cry of welcome.

"Braden," she pleaded, not precisely sure what she was begging for, clutching at his bare shoulders with both hands. "Oh, dear God—Braden—"

He raised his head from her breast to look straight into her eyes. "This is what you were made for," he said, "and what I was made for. No, no—don't close your eyes, witch. Let me see your magic."

Frankie was practically out of her mind with need by that point, and Braden showed her no quarter. While his thumb made an endless, tantalizing circle, his fingers alternately teased and conquered.

She began to toss her head from side to side on the pillow while the incomprehensible ecstasy carried her higher and higher. Braden was choreographing her every move, and he would not let her look away, yet she had never known a greater sense of freedom. She was, in those fiery moments, more truly herself than she had ever been.

Frankie arched high off the mattress, a long, high, keening cry spilling from her throat as wild spasms of pleasure seized her. Again and again, her body buckled in fierce release, and Braden held her entranced the whole time, not only physically, but emotionally as well.

When at last she was sated, and she lay breathless and quivering, her flesh moist from her exertions, Braden caressed her, all over, with his big, gentle hands. He spoke soothingly and kissed places that still trembled with the aftershocks of cataclysmic pleasure, and then he held her. The holding, in its way, was as fulfilling as her repeated climaxes had been.

Frankie could not have said how much time had passed

by the time Braden mounted her; she was only half-conscious, lost in bliss.

Braden took her wrists in his hands, frowning a little when he felt the band of her watch but not pausing to examine it, and raised her arms high over her head so that his body lay flush with hers.

"As I told you," he said, kissing her jaw as he spoke, "I have never taken a woman against her will. I want to be part of you, Francesca, to make you a part of me. Will you allow that?"

She whimpered softly, sleepily, feeling her nipples harden against his hairy chest and her feminine passage expand to receive him. "Please," she said, opening her legs. She was still intoxicated, and sleep beckoned seductively. "But—you will forgive me, won't you—if I drift off—?"

He chuckled. "You will be wide wake in a moment, witch," he said. "What happened before was only a preparation for this."

Truer words had never been spoken.

Frankie's heavy eyelids flew up as Braden entered her in one strong stroke, arousing her sated body all over again, bringing every nerve ending to frantic awareness.

Braden glided in and out of her a few times, still holding her wrists above her head, though gently, watching her face as though he found every changing expression fascinating. He was a modern lover, ahead of his violent, uncaring time.

When he knew she was wild with need, he withdrew and whispered raspily, "Tell me, beautiful Francesca—are you angel or witch?"

"Witch," she half-sobbed, and Braden lunged deep into her, covering her mouth with his own in the same instant and swallowing her shouts of passion.

It was dizzying, like riding some cosmic roller coaster. Every moment, every nuance had to be experienced; there was no going back.

Until that morning Frankie had considered herself a knowledgeable woman. Admittedly, her past was unspectacular when it came to romance; she'd been intimate with Geoffrey and before him, a guy she'd dated in high school and college. She'd been aroused and, yes, satisfied, in a sweetly innocuous sort of way.

Now the Duke of Sunderlin, a man who might not even exist, had shown her that there were whole universes yet to be discovered and explored. He'd turned her inside out and outside in, and somehow, in a way she couldn't define, he'd given her a totally new sense of herself.

Braden held her for a long time, like before, then rose whistling from the bed to don a fresh tunic and woolen leggings. "I have things to attend to today," he said, pausing to pat Frankie solicitously on the bottom. "You can explore the keep if you want, and the grounds, too. Just don't wander into the village."

Frankie sat up, her sense of challenge stirred. "Why not?"

Braden shrugged. "Do as you wish, then. Be advised, though, that the villagers are saying you appeared out of nowhere—one moment, nothing, the next, there you were. Half of them want to declare you a saint and worship you accordingly, and the others lean toward roasting you on a spit, like a pig."

Frankie's eyes went wide, and her throat constricted as she imagined a martyr's death. "I'm scared!"

He kissed the tip of her nose. "Wise woman. I don't suppose I have to tell you that from the beginning, saints have fared even worse than witches. People can't bear the contrast, you see, between what they are and what they believe they should be."

"Thanks for trying to reassure me," Frankie snapped as Braden straightened and began strapping on his sword belt.

Braden grinned. "You're most welcome, milady. I'll have Mordag bring you one of my sister's gowns, as well as some breakfast."

Frankie brightened at the prospect of female companionship. "You have a sister, then. I would enjoy meeting her."

Braden's expression had turned stony, all in the space of a few moments. "That is impossible," he said. Then, without further explanation, he turned and walked out of the chamber, leaving Frankie alone.

True to his word, however, Braden sent Mordag with an underskirt and kirtle of the softest blue wool, brown bread and spotted pears for breakfast, and a ewer of clean water for washing.

Within half an hour Frankie had eaten, given herself a bath of sorts, and gotten dressed. The underskirt and kirtle were delightful; just what she'd hoped to find in the costume shop, the morning after her arrival in England.

Frankie stopped on the stone stairway, pressing one hand to the cold wall as if to test its substance. Odd, but her "memories" of a world six centuries in the future seemed to be fading, like a random dream.

It was real, she told herself, as real as this. Seattle, the inn, the costume shop, all of it was real. I mustn't forget.

She proceeded, after a moment, keeping to the rear passageways. She paused and hid in the shadows when she heard voices, not wanting to encounter superstitious servants or men-at-arms who might well consider her fair game.

Alas, Frankie had little or no experience at sneaking out of castles. She had almost gained the kitchen, and was looking back over one shoulder to make sure no one was following her, when she collided hard with Alaric.

He steadied her by gripping her shoulders. "Please, lovely one," he pleaded in a teasing voice, "tell me you've found the strength of soul to spurn my legendary brother."

Frankie was uneasy, even though Alaric's smile was ready and his touch was gentle. She sensed that he harbored some dangerous fury behind those bright, mirthful eyes. She shook her head. "Sorry," she responded, somewhat gravely. "I've never met anyone like Braden, and I rather enjoy his company."

That was certainly an understatement, she thought, as memories of just how intensely she'd enjoyed the Duke's company filled her mind. She was grateful for the dim light of the hallway, not wanting Alaric to see her blush.

For a fraction of a moment, a time so brief that Frankie would always wonder if she'd imagined it, Alaric's grasp on her shoulders tightened. His dazzling grin seemed slightly brittle as he released her.

"You shouldn't be wandering through the keep alone, milady," he said with a courtly bow of his head. "I'm

surprised Braden allowed such a breach, as a matter of fact."
Alaric paused, shrugged. "He leaves me no choice but to
uphold the family honor by escorting you myself."

Frankie was still troubled by something in Alaric's
manner, but she had to agree that it was safer to have a
companion. "I'm happy to know that chivalry is not dead
after all," she said.

They crossed the kitchen, a massive room empty except
for two great hounds that lay sleeping on the hearth. When
Alaric led her into a grassy sideyard, where sunlight played
golden, like visible music, Frankie's spirits rose a notch.

Like all natives of Seattle, Frankie was reverently fond of
sunshine. She raised her face to the light and spent a
moment just soaking up the glorious stuff. When she opened
her eyes, Alaric was smiling at her.

"I'm told that you arrived—er—quite suddenly yesterday, at the village fair," he said. "Is that true?"

Frankie lifted the skirts of her cloud-soft woolen dress
and set off across the grass, headed for a copse of trees she'd
spotted earlier, from Braden's window. She wondered if the
branches of the maple were sturdy enough to support her,
and if she'd be able to see over the castle wall if she climbed
high.

"Of course not," she lied blithely, sensing that it would
not be wise to tell Alaric what had really happened. "I
arrived with a mummers' troupe and simply took my place
in the crowd without being noticed."

Alaric kept up, taking long strides. His build was similar
to Braden's, except that he was smaller, and his bone
structure seemed fragile by comparison. "Of course I
wouldn't think of questioning your word, milady, but it's
hard to imagine you passing unnoticed anywhere. You seem
to glow, and there's a knowingness in your manner, as if you
might be privy to secrets the rest of us could never grasp."

They passed through tall grass, moving between stone
outbuildings that looked deserted, while Frankie considered
her reply. She saw the maple trees up ahead, beckoning,
offering her solace in their fragrant green leaves.

In the end she decided to respond by countering with a
question. "What does it matter where I came from? Surely

you don't believe that superstitious rot about my being a witch or an angel."

Frankie thought she saw a muscle tighten in Alaric's jaw, though she couldn't be certain. "Of course I don't believe that. Like my brother, I am an educated man, but I know how dangerous the beliefs of simple people can be."

They had reached the copse, and Frankie inspected a promising tree with a fork in its trunk and a great many sturdy branches. "I've had this lecture already," she said, without looking at her companion. Instead, Frankie was recalling her happy childhood in Seattle, and the big elm that had stood in the backyard. "Don't worry, Alaric. I have no intention of wandering off to the village and getting everyone all worked up again."

With that, Frankie hiked her skirts a little, gripped the trunk of the tree in both hands, and hoisted herself up into the fork.

"Here, now," Alaric protested. "You'll break a limb!"

Frankie proceeded upward, rustling leaves as she went. "Since I know you meant that in only the kindest sense of the word," she called down cheerfully, "I won't take offense." Clinging to the gnarled old tree, she fixed her gaze on the world beyond the orchard, beyond the castle grounds.

The village, made up of tiny daub-and-wattle structures with thatch roofs, stood in much the same place as it would six hundred years in the future, but the forests to the west looked denser and far more primordial. The remaining three directions were choked with fields, and narrow cow paths served as roads. Far out, beyond the thriving crops, Frankie saw a croft or two, but it was plain enough that Braden was pretty much master of all she surveyed.

"Come down," Alaric wheedled, a thread of irritation vibrating in his voice. "It's not ladylike, climbing about like that!"

"Surely you've guessed by now that I'm not a lady," Frankie replied sunnily, settling herself on a thick branch and smoothing her borrowed skirts. In doing that, she remembered Braden's sudden mood change when he'd mentioned having a sister. "Is it just you and Braden, Alaric, or are there more Stuart-Ramseys running around the countryside?"

"We have a sister," Alaric answered. "Now get yourself down here before I'm forced to climb up after you."

We *have* a sister, he'd said. When Braden had spoken of a female sibling that morning, he'd used the past tense. "Calm down—I'm an expert tree-climber. Tell me about your sister. What is her name? Where does she live?"

Alaric's sigh rose through the maple leaves with a soft summer breeze. "Her name is Rianne, she's seventeen, and Braden sold her off to a distant cousin in Scotland. Furthermore, he'll have me chained to a wall and whipped if he finds out I've been talking about the matter. Now—please come down."

Frankie lingered, swinging her legs and thinking. "You don't mean he forced her to marry someone she didn't love?"

"Love." Alaric practically spat the word. "Now, there's a fatuous notion." He gripped the trunk of the tree and gave it a slight shake. "Love didn't enter into the bargain, Francesca. Braden caught Rianne kissing the chandler's boy, and he was outraged. He gave her a choice between our esteemed cousin and a long stay in a nunnery and—and I can't imagine why I'm telling you all this."

"Did she choose the cousin over the nunnery, then?"

"No. She said she was going to travel all the way to London and then throw herself into the Thames. *Braden* chose the cousin. He believed Rianne would be better off with a man to keep her out of trouble, and he was probably right."

Frankie was horrified to comprehend just how wide the breach of time and custom between herself and Braden really was. "She should have spit in his eye—he had no right to make such a decree!"

When Alaric replied, which wasn't until several moments of vibrant silence had passed, he sounded confused, nervous, and not a little exasperated. "Braden is a duke. Everyone obeys him, except for the King and the Almighty Himself. Rianne was foolish to anger him in the first place."

Just as Frankie opened her mouth to announce that, in her

opinion, the Duke was long overdue for some consciousness raising, a very strange thing happened. A loud thrumming sound filled Frankie's ears, and she felt dizzy, as if she might topple out of the tree. Her vision was blurred and her stomach lurched.

Looking down, she barely made out the figure of Alaric. He was standing eerily still and staring up at her with his mouth open, one hand outspread in a conversational gesture.

Frankie wrapped one arm tightly around the tree trunk and held on. "All right," she said aloud, "what's going on here?"

She heard a rustling sound, saw a glimmer of blue silk out of the corner of one eye. When she made herself turn her head and look, she was flabbergasted.

Sitting on a branch in the next tree was the wizard she'd seen the day before, peering through the window of the costume shop in Grimsley. He was a tall man, obviously not at home in the high regions of a maple, and he held on to his splendid, pointed hat with one bejeweled hand. His white beard was filled with twigs and parts of leaves, and ice-blue eyes snapped behind round glass spectacles as he glared at Frankie.

"Who are you?" she demanded.

"My name is Merlin, not that it's important," he replied with a distinct lack of enthusiasm. Plainly, he had not situated himself in the branches of a tree, decked out in full wizard gear, to make small talk. "Kindly listen, Miss Whittier, and listen well. We don't have much time."

Frankie swallowed. Merlin, she thought skeptically. Right. She couldn't think why the sudden appearance of a wizard surprised her so much, given all that had gone before, but she was definitely in shock. "Wh-what did you do to him?" she asked, looking down at Alaric, who was still standing down there with his mouth open.

Merlin made a dismissive gesture with one hand and nearly fell out of the tree. "He'll be perfectly all right, more's the pity. It's his job, in fact, to run the Stuart-Ramsey estates into rack and ruin."

Frankie thought of Braden, and how much his small kingdom probably meant to him, and felt wounded. "What about Bra—the Duke? He's the firstborn son. The title and the estates are his."

The wizard sighed. "Not for long," he replied regretfully. "There's a tournament coming up, about a week hence. Sunderlin will be killed, run through with an opponent's blade when sport turns to deadly combat."

"No," Frankie breathed. In that instant, of all instants, she realized that, as incredible as it seemed, she loved Braden. If he died, she might well perish from the grief, no matter how she fought to stay alive. "No, it can't be—I'll warn him!"

"He won't listen."

Frankie was desperate. "Isn't there some way—?"

"Perhaps," Merlin answered grudgingly, and his expression was grim. "I wasn't in favor of your coming here, but since a mistake had been made in the Beginning—"

"A mistake?" Frankie held on tighter to the tree, and her voice came out in a squeak. "What are you talking about? And why *did* I end up here in Merry Old England?"

"You and Sunderlin were matched, long ago, before the tapestry of time was woven. There was an error, and somehow he was born in the wrong century, to the wrong parents. On some level of your being, you must have known, and come in search of him."

"Impossible," Frankie breathed. It was no comfort that the wizard's remarks rang true, somewhere deep inside her. "I don't know how I made the trip, but I didn't do it on purpose. The whole thing came as a big shock."

"I understand that," Merlin answered, somewhat brusquely. "Well, there's nothing for it. You'll just have to think long and hard of your own time. That should put you back where you belong, though I can't promise you won't find yourself an old woman or a very young child. These matters are not precise, you know. You can only be sure of landing somewhere in your original life span."

Frankie heard the vaguest humming sound, and she sensed that the magician would disappear in a moment, and that Alaric was already beginning to stir from his enchantment. "Never mind all that," she blurted. "Just tell me how to help Braden!"

For the first time Merlin smiled, but the expression in his eyes was regretful. "Love is the answer to every question," he said, and then, between one instant and the next, he was gone. He didn't even take the time to do a fade-out.

Frankie hesitated a few moments, collecting herself, then shinnied quickly down the tree, practically landing on a befuddled Alaric, who had just started to climb up after her. Gaining the ground, she lifted her skirts, without pausing to offer even a word of explanation, and ran toward the castle as if all eternity hinged on haste.

4

FRANKIE FOUND BRADEN on the other side of the castle, his upper body protected by chain mail, wielding his fancy sword. His opponent was a young knight, obviously eager to prove his prowess on the field of battle.

Thinking only of what Merlin, the magician, had just told her—that Braden would die by the sword in a week's time—Frankie hesitated just briefly. She would have marched right into the center of the large circle of loose dirt if Alaric hadn't crooked an arm around her waist and stopped her.

The small fracas drew Braden's attention, and in that brief moment of distraction, his adversary struck, reckless in his enthusiasm. Bringing his sword downward, from shoulder height, he made a deep gash in the Duke's right thigh.

There were eight or ten men crowded around, watching the morning exercise, and a shout of outrage went up as blood stained Braden's gray leggings to crimson.

For Frankie, all of this took place in a pounding haze, rather like a slow-motion sequence in a movie. In reality, of course, it happened in the space of seconds. She screamed and struggled so violently that Alaric could not hold her.

Braden was still standing when she fought her way

through the crowd of men pressed close around him, but she was alarmed by the ghastly paleness of his face. He looked at her as though she were an enemy, as though she herself had wounded him.

There were mutterings in the small assembly, and Frankie heard the word *witch*, but she didn't think of the implications. All that mattered then was Braden, that he be well and whole, and somehow saved from the fate that awaited him.

A rotund bearded man in coarse robes took charge. "Steady him," he ordered, crouching at Braden's feet. Two men immediately came forward to stand close, lest their leader need them. The big man tied a band of cloth around the Duke's upper thigh, just above the deep cut, and pulled it tight.

Braden flinched and swayed slightly, but remained on his feet. His gaze, accusatory and bewildered, had never left Frankie's face. "Continue with your practice," he said to his men, and then he limped toward her.

Only when Braden was standing close did Frankie realize that her cheeks were wet with tears.

"I'm sorry," she said brokenly. "I didn't mean—"

"Come along, Your Lordship," the heavy man interceded. "You'll be in need of some looking after."

Braden raised one hand and, with the rough side of his thumb, wiped Frankie's cheek. Then one corner of his mouth rose in the merest hint of a smile. "What was so important, Francesca, that you would burst into the middle of swordplay like that?"

Frankie shouldered aside the man who'd been hovering close to Braden and slipped under the Duke's arm to help support him. She couldn't very well explain about Merlin, not with so many superstitious ears about. Besides, she was more concerned, for the moment, with the state of Braden's health. Her thoughts had shifted to medieval medical practices.

"Never mind," she said, feeling injured because Braden was. "We can discuss that later. You're not going to let these yokels put leeches on you, I hope—you've lost enough blood as it is, and the possibility of infection—"

The heavy man, who was supporting Braden on the other

side, leaned around the Duke's chest to glower at Frankie. "Yokels?"

An exasperated sigh burst from Braden's lips. "Perhaps you two could argue this out later, when I may be spared the pleasure of listening."

Alaric, who had been following the small party, sprinted ahead to walk backward in front of Braden, talking a mile a minute. "I tried to stop her," he said, taking care not to meet Frankie's gaze. "God's knees, Braden, but you look like a walking corpse—"

Frankie tuned him out, concentrating instead on the Duke's needs. She was no doctor, of course, but she'd had intensive instruction in first aid while being trained as a flight attendant. She wasn't about to leave Braden to the mercies of people who might pack his wound with sheep dung or drain away still more of his blood.

They entered the Great Hall, and the smoky atmosphere made Frankie's eyes burn. Braden stumbled once as they moved toward the stairs, and then his knees buckled.

"No farther," ordered the heavy man, who had taken charge from the first. "You must lie down, milord."

"You make much of little, Gilford," Braden said, and Frankie heard affection in his voice, as well as impatience and no small amount of pain.

Nevertheless, one of the great trestle tables lining the Hall was cleared of salt cellars and wine ewers, and Braden lay down on the surface without further protest.

Gilford looked across the table at Frankie, who stood staunchly on the other side, keeping her stubborn vigil. "You are in the way, wench. Leave us."

"Not on your life," Frankie replied.

Braden chuckled, but he was looking worse with every passing moment, even though the tourniquet had slowed the bleeding from his thigh. "Don't waste your breath arguing with her," he warned his friend. "Francesca's opinions are as immovable as the walls of this castle."

Gilford treated her to a scathing glare. "Then perhaps she can make herself useful in other ways. By fetching wine, and my herbal kit."

Frankie tightened her grip on Braden's hand. "Alaric can

do those things, or one of the servants. I'm staying right here."

Alaric needed no urging; he rushed off to get the things Gilford wanted. In the meantime, the castle medicine man took a knife from the folds of his robe and began cutting away Braden's bloody leggings.

Frankie swayed slightly when she saw just how bad the wound was, but she willed new strength into her knees and somehow stilled the tempest in her stomach. "Shouldn't someone be boiling water?" she asked shakily.

"The water is filthy," Gilford said. "I will clean the area with wine."

His statement jarred Frankie, and she lifted her gaze to his face again. "You know about antisepsis?" she asked.

"You," Gilford replied, "are not the only stranger in these here parts, young woman."

Frankie's mouth fell open. Automatically she stroked Braden's sweat-dampened forehead with one hand, but it was the castle physician who held her attention. "When?" she asked in barely a whisper. There was no one else close by, since Alaric had gone off on his errand and the sword practice had continued outside, per Braden's orders.

"Seventy-two," Gilford said. "I came here to get away from my practice in London for a while—I was suffering from what you Americans call burnout. Went to sleep there, woke up here. For a long time I thought I'd lost my mind."

Frankie nodded her understanding, but could say nothing. Merlin hadn't mentioned that there were other time-travelers abroad, but then, they hadn't talked for very long.

"What in the name of God's Great Aunt are you two talking about?" Braden asked, slurring his words. He was waxen, and although his flesh felt cold, he was sweating.

"Cabbages and kings," Gilford told the Duke. "Just lie there, please, and conserve your strength." Alaric returned with the wine and the doctor's herbal kit, and Gilford used the alcohol to clean the wound. Braden drifted in and out of consciousness, and the physician talked to Frankie in even tones as he worked. "I've never wanted to go back, you know. Strange as it seems, I feel I belong here. What about you? What part of the Rebel Colonies do you hail from?"

Frankie was trying to funnel her own strength into Braden, and she didn't look up from his face when she answered. "It was nineteen-ninety-three when I left," she said. "And I'm from Seattle, in Washington State."

"Hmmmm," said Gilford, packing Braden's wound with an herbal concoction. "He's going to have a nasty scar, here, but I've no catgut to stitch him up with. I was in Seattle once, on a holiday tour. My wife and I flew there by way of New York and Chicago and took a sailing ship up the coast to Alaska. Spectacular experience."

Braden laughed stupidly. "Flying," he said. "There's a picture, Gilford—you, flying. Didn't your arms get tired?"

Despite the fact that her eyes were red and puffy from crying, Frankie laughed, too. "Do you miss your life in the twentieth century?" she asked Gilford when she'd had a few moments to regain her composure. "Your wife must be very worried."

Gilford sighed. "I suppose I'm on some police roster," he said. "One of those pesky people who've just disappeared from the face of the earth without leaving a trace behind. As for my wife's state of mind, well, Zenobia is the resilient type. By now, she's probably sold my practice and remarried."

"You've been here a long time, then?"

"Roughly twenty years, now," Gilford answered, binding Braden's thigh with clean cloth taken from his own supply kit. "I've been happy the whole while, too."

Frankie studied the doctor closely. "How did you know I was a time-traveler like you?"

At last Gilford favored her with a smile. A rather nice one, as a matter of fact. "I'm a doctor. After only one look at you, I knew you'd grown up in a world where there was relatively clean water to drink, healthy nutrition, excellent medical care, and the like. Most of the people around us, in case you haven't noticed, are rather fragile creatures."

Frankie still held Braden's hand, and unconsciously she cradled it between her breasts. "What of the Duke? He's certainly nothing like them."

Gilford smiled at Braden, who had drifted off to sleep. No doubt the herbs the doctor had administered were responsible for that. "No, he isn't. He's a misfit, like you and me."

Frankie liked Gilford, despite their getting off on the wrong foot earlier, and it was a great comfort to know she was not the only one who'd ever found herself in the wrong century. "Are there others?" she asked.

"Other time-travelers?" Gilford was using the last of the wine to wash Braden's blood from his hands. "Almost certainly. If it happened to us, then surely someone else has experienced the same phenomenon. You, however, are the first such sojourner I've had the good fortune to meet." He summoned Alaric, who had been hovering at a little distance throughout the procedure, and sent him off for men fit to carry Braden upstairs. "You've been very careless so far, Francesca," the medical man scolded after Alaric hurried away on his mission. "These people fear what they do not understand, and what they fear, they destroy. You must guard your tongue, in the future, and try not to be so brazen."

Frankie felt faint and gripped the edge of the table to steady herself. "I'm no fool, Doctor—I don't want to be hanged, or burned at the stake, and I promise I'll be more careful. At the moment, though, it's Braden I'm worried about—is he going to make it? How long will he be laid up with this injury?" She held her breath while she waited for Gilford's answer.

The portly time-traveler sighed again and folded his bulky arms. "Sunderlin will recover, I'm sure—he has the personal tenacity and physical strength of a mountain goat. And my guess is, he'll be up and walking about on that leg within a day or two, though I'd much prefer that he rest."

Frankie was torn, feeling both joy and terrible desolation. Braden would get well, that was wonderful. But if he truly was back on his feet in a matter of days, he would still participate in the tournament in a week's time. And that meant he would die.

"You're his doctor! Can't you order him to stay in bed until he's had a chance to mend?"

Sadly Gilford shook his head. "No one keeps this man from doing exactly as he wishes," he said.

Frankie confided in him about her encounter with Merlin

that day, and told of the dire prediction the magician had made, but only in the barest detail. She felt drained; so much had happened, just since she'd opened her eyes that morning, that it seemed she'd lived a whole decade without taking a breath.

Alaric returned with two big men, and they carried Braden to his room. Frankie sat with Braden until midafternoon, then, satisfied that he was sleeping comfortably, went off to get some fresh air and some perspective on the situation.

She was drawn to the chapel, which she found by trial and error on the ground floor of the castle, well away from the Great Hall and the usually busy kitchen. She was not a particularly religious person, but a spiritual one, and sitting in that small chamber, with its rough-hewn benches, rows of unlit candles, and towering wooden cross, was like nestling in the soul of God.

"Show me what to do," she whispered, clasping her hands together tightly in her lap. "Please. Show me how to save Braden from the sword."

No ready answer came to Frankie, and yet she was restored by the mystical peace of the place. It seemed then that there was indeed a solution, and that she would find it.

After an hour she went back to Braden's chamber and found him sitting up in bed, drinking ale from a wooden mug. His color was better, but his mood was sour indeed.

"Why, Francesca?" he demanded hoarsely, virtually impaling her with his sharp gaze. "Why did you interfere with the fighting that way? The distraction could have gotten me killed."

Frankie kept her distance, even though she knew instinctively that Braden would never hurt her. "I told you I was sorry. And I was coming to—to warn you about something."

Braden's brows knitted together for a moment as he frowned. "Warn me? About what?"

She swallowed. This was not going to be easy. Braden probably wouldn't believe her story, and she didn't blame him. "I met a wizard today—his name was Merlin. He said you were going to be killed a week from now, fighting in a tournament."

Braden refilled his cup from a jug on the table next to his bed and took an audible gulp, then filled his mouth again, so that his cheeks bulged. He swallowed once more, and his voice came out sounding raspy when he spoke. "A wizard," he repeated with irony.

Frankie's temper flared when she heard the quiet annoyance and thinly veiled pity in his tone. "Yes."

The Duke was not looking at her when he spoke again. "Alaric was with you. Did he see this man of magic, too?"

Braden's manner told Frankie it was Alaric's presence he was concerned about, not the wizard's. Despite her frustration, and her fear, she felt a little thrill of pleasure at the realization that Braden was jealous.

"No," she answered, gaining confidence. "Alaric didn't see anything. He was frozen, between one heartbeat and the next, and freed only when Merlin permitted it."

Braden reached out suddenly, grasped her hand, and squeezed. His face was filled with an anguish Frankie suspected was unrelated to the wound in his thigh. "Francesca," he whispered, "promise me, please, that you will not speak thus, of wizards and the like, to anyone but me."

She sat down on the edge of his bed and smiled softly. In those moments Frankie was filled with immeasurable joy and equally unfathomable sorrow, for it was then that she grasped the terrible, wonderful miracle that had occurred. She was in love with Sunderlin, and that love was an eternal thing, meant to outlive both of them.

She smoothed Sunderlin's rumpled, dusty hair back from his forehead. "I do promise to try, Braden," she said gently. "But I'm impulsive, and sometimes words are out of my mouth before I know I was even thinking them."

Braden lifted her hand to his lips, sent a charge of emotion through her merely by kissing her knuckles. "You and Gilford were saying very strange things today," he recalled after some moments had passed. "He has always refused to explain his odd talents and beliefs. Will you refuse as well?"

Careful not to bump Braden's injured leg, Frankie made a place for herself beside him, resting her back against his shoulder, turning her face into his neck. "I'll tell you everything," she said. "But I'm so afraid, Braden. So very afraid."

"Why?" He entangled a finger in one of her curls, twisted with an idle gentleness that somehow stirred her heart. "I know there's something different about you, but I'll not declare you angel *or* witch, and I promise I'll protect you from the whole of the world if need be."

Frankie was touched to the core of her spirit. Why, she wondered sadly, couldn't she have met this man in her own time, where they might have had a happy life together? Here, they had a mere week to share.

She sighed, settled closer to Braden, and began to talk. She told him about Seattle, and other modern cities. She described flying to New York in a jumbo jet, and then crossing the Atlantic the same way, to land in London. Braden listened to the whole story, in what was probably a stunned silence, never interrupting.

Frankie spoke of her trip to the village of Grimsley, the Medieval Fair that was held there every year, for the tourists, her attempt to rent a costume, the glimpse she'd caught of Merlin through the shop window, her unscheduled trip through time.

When it was over, Braden shifted both himself and Frankie, so that he could look deep into her eyes. "How could one person devise such a tale?"

Tears brimmed along her lower lashes. "I'm not making anything up, Braden," she said. "It's all true. And I saw that same wizard again this morning, like I told you. He said you were supposed to be born in my time, the future, but there was some sort of mistake and you ended up here. And you're going to be killed in a tournament next week, unless you call it off."

His face hardened, and Frankie saw in his light brown eyes both bewilderment and the desire to trust her. "I cannot do such a thing. I am not a coward, and I won't have the whole of England saying I heeded the words of a witch!"

Frankie wriggled off the bed and stood, disappointed and

stung even though she'd known he wouldn't readily believe her story. "All right. You're a hardheaded, arrogant, opinionated *male*, and as such you aren't about to listen to reason. Well, that's just fine, but I don't intend to hang around here, caring more with every day that passes, only to see you run through with a sword!"

She would have turned and fled the room then, and maybe the castle and the village, too, but Braden caught hold of her hand and held it fast.

"'Caring more with every day that passes,' is it?" he asked in a low, teasing voice. "Confess, witch—are you falling in love with me?"

It was worse, Frankie admitted to herself. She'd already fallen. But that didn't mean she had to let Braden know. "Of course not." She thought fast. "Alaric is more my type."

"What?" Braden snapped the word, and his color, so good a moment before, had gone waxen again.

Frankie looked away, biting her lip. She couldn't say any more; the lie was too profound, the truth too holy.

"Look at me, Francesca," Braden ordered gravely.

She looked, not because of his command, but because she was hungry for the sight of him. And she despised that hunger, even as she succumbed to it.

"Whatever you are, witch or angel," Braden said, "you've managed to cast an enchantment over me. I must have you, no matter what else I gain or lose. In you I will plant my children, and all my hopes of joy and passion."

Frankie stared at him, dumbfounded, wondering at the new universe that had sprung to life inside her, a vast expanse of love for this one man.

He smiled and caressed her cheek, then pushed her off the bed, where she scrambled to get and keep her footing.

"Summon Mordag," he said, gesturing toward the bell-pull. "I would have him fetch a priest."

5

FRANKIE RECOVERED SOME of her aplomb only after she'd given the bellrope a good yank. "Braden, stop and think. We can't be married—we're from different universes! Besides, you don't even know me, really, and I don't know you, either."

"Happens all the time," Braden said, settling back on the pillows and folding his great arms. "My mother came from the North to be wed to my father—the first time they laid eyes on each other was at the ceremony." He hoisted himself from the bed, and Frankie winced as he flexed his injured leg. "That marriage went well enough."

Frankie ignored the comment. "Shouldn't you be lying down?"

Braden was walking back and forth over the rushes, his jaw set, his face colorless as he dealt with the inevitable pain. He did not reply, except to pinion her with a brief, fierce glare.

Mordag appeared soon enough, bowing and scraping and plainly alarmed that his master was up and about so soon after sustaining a wound. He chattered away in Old English and distractedly Frankie wondered why she could understand Braden and Alaric, but not the ordinary people.

Braden told Mordag to go into the village and bring back the priest, but before that, he was to send up women servants to groom "the lady" for a wedding.

"I haven't agreed to your proposal yet, you know," Frankie pointed out, somewhat shakily. "You're being a bit hasty, don't you think?"

"No," Sunderlin answered succinctly. His color was returning now, and he moved more easily. "Even now my son and heir may already nestle in your womb. There will be no question of his legitimacy."

"It's equally possible that there is no child," Frankie reasoned. "We've only—we've only been together once, you know."

Sunderlin smiled. "Once is often enough. I'm sure that's true even in your faraway world."

Frankie gaped at him for a moment, then blurted out, "You believe me, then?"

He came to her, fondly lifted a tendril of her chin-length hair, rubbed it between his fingers, and let it fall back into place. "At first," he reflected with a bemused grin, "I thought you had been shorn in some asylum while suffering from a brain fever. But reason tells me that you are too sound, not only of body but of disposition, to have been through such an illness." Braden paused, sighed, kissed her forehead. "Yes, I think I believe you, Francesca, though I don't claim to understand how such a thing could happen."

Frankie laid her head against Braden's chest, felt his hands come to rest lightly on her shoulder blades. She was almost as confused by the suddenness and depth of her feelings for Sunderlin as she was by the knowledge that she had indeed traveled through time.

"Take me to London," she said in a desperate bid to spirit Braden away from Sunderlin Keep and the tournament. "Please, darling—as soon as we're married."

Braden curved a finger under her chin, lifted her head so that he could look directly into her face. "I will be happy to take you to London, there to present you at court. *After* the tournament."

An overwhelming grief surged up inside Frankie, and she marveled because at the same time she felt a powerful, greedy joy. "Do you wish to die?" she demanded angrily, leaning back in his arms but not quite able to leave his embrace. "Why else would you ignore such a warning?"

He sighed, and she saw the pain of his physical injury flicker in his eyes. "I cannot run away from what has been given me to do," he said with gentle reason. "It is a matter of honor. Besides, if my death has been ordained by the powers of heaven, as it would seem, it will do no good for me to flee to London."

Before Frankie could offer further argument—and even

then she knew it would be fruitless to try anyway—several
female servants came to collect her. She was taken to a
smaller chamber down the hall, where a large copper tub
had been set before the fire.

Frankie had a bath, her hair was washed and brushed, and
then the women dressed her in a slightly musty-smelling but
nonetheless beautiful white velvet gown. She went back to
the master chamber to fetch the wreath of dried flowers
she'd brought with her from the other time, and there was no
sign of Braden.

He awaited her in the chapel, pale and grim, and yet with
a fire burning in his caramel eyes as he watched her come
toward him. He had to be in serious pain, but he'd learned
to transcend it, probably through his training as a knight.

What are you doing, Francesca Whittier? Frankie's good
sense demanded, even as she hurried up the narrow aisle to
stand beside her future husband. This man isn't real—he's
a ghost, a pile of moldering dust lying in some crypt!

Frankie shook her head slightly and sent the ghoulish
thoughts scattering. Braden was a miracle, and he might
well be taken from her all too soon, either by the sword or
by her own unexpected return to the modern world. She
would live breath by breath and heartbeat by heartbeat,
cherishing every moment she was given to spend with
Braden.

The priest was a friar, straight out of a storybook, and
Frankie didn't understand a word he said. She simply
mumbled and gave a slight nod whenever he turned an
expectant look on her. All too soon the romantic, strangely
magical ceremony was over, and Braden bent his head to
place a light kiss on Frankie's mouth.

She lifted her eyes to meet his, inwardly stunned at the
power and breadth of her love for him. It was as if it had
always existed within her, a vast plain of the spirit, infinite
and rich, only now discovered.

Tears brimmed along her lashes; she gave a little cry of
mingled sorrow and joy, and threw her arms around his
neck. This caused a twittering among the few guests, but
Frankie didn't care. Every second was a pearl of great price;
not one would be wasted.

Braden smiled, shook his head, as if marveling at something too amazing to mention aloud, and tugged gently at one of the ribbons trailing from her crown of flowers.

Frankie had expected that she and her groom would return to the bridal chamber straightaway, and she was unabashedly ready. Instead, however, a celebration of sorts was to be held in the Great Hall; musicians and mummers and jesters had been commandeered from the village fair, and there were mountains of food.

Despite the festive air of the place, Frankie had no illusions that the people of Braden's world accepted her as their mistress. She saw in more than one pair of eyes that she was still feared, still suspected.

While Braden held court at the head table, enjoying the toasts and guarded congratulations of his men-at-arms, Gilford approached Frankie and took her elbow lightly in one hand.

"Come with me," he whispered urgently. "Now."

Frankie didn't want to stray too far from Braden's side, but she was alarmed by the doctor's earnestness. They slipped into a small courtyard, tucked away behind the Great Hall, where bees bumbled and buzzed among blowsy red and yellow roses.

"If you know a way to get back to the twentieth century," Gilford whispered after making certain they were alone, "you'd best be about it. There's talk among the servants and the others that you've bewitched the Duke somehow— they're blaming you for his wound, and they say no power less than the devil's own could have made him marry you." The doctor took both her hands in his own and squeezed. "Please—do not tarry in this place. If you can't will yourself home somehow, then we must smuggle you out of the keep and hide you somewhere."

She opened her mouth to protest, but Gilford never gave her a chance.

"Frankie," he said, "these people are terrified of you. They want to burn you as a witch."

"Braden would never allow it!" Frankie said, but she was cold with fear there in that warm, fragrant garden.

"Sunderlin may not be around after the tournament, if

your wizard is to be believed. I beg of you, Frankie, save
yourself both heartache and a truly terrible death if you
can."

She pulled her hands free of his and hugged herself, but
that did not still the trembling. "Merlin did say something
about thinking long and hard of my own time, as if that
would make me go back. He also said I could end up at any
stage of my life—"

"Do it, then."

Frankie shook her head. "No," she said. "I'm here now,
and there must be some reason for that. I'm going to see it
through."

Gilford sighed heavily and gestured toward the west. "At
least let me take you to the nunnery, just beyond the fells,
where you'll be safe. I can enter and leave the keep
whenever I wish, and you could hide in my cart, under some
straw or blankets."

For a moment Frankie considered the idea. In the end,
however, she discarded it because it meant being parted
from Braden, even by a short distance.

"I'm staying," she said, starting around Gilford to return
to the celebration. After all, she was the bride, and her
handsome groom awaited.

Gilford caught her arm. "That is a very foolish decision,"
he bit out. His fingers cut into the tender flesh on the inside
of her elbow. "I beg you to reconsider."

Frankie looked down at her white velvet dress, and when
she raised her eyes again, her vision was blurred with tears.
"I must get back to my husband," she said softly. Then,
reluctantly, Gilford freed her, and she hurried back into the
Great Hall.

Strong as he was, Braden had had an especially hard day.
After only a few boisterous toasts, each followed by a
tankard of ale, he began to yawn. It was a relief to Frankie,
who had been feeling more alienated from the guests with
every passing moment, when he signaled that it was time for
them to leave the festivities.

Once they were in their chamber, and the ever-present
Mordag had been sent away, Frankie gave her bridegroom
an unceremonious push toward the bed. Her reason was

anything but romantic. "You need to rest," she scolded. "You're dead on your feet."

Braden limped to the bedside, sat down gingerly on its edge, then stretched out with a low groan of mingled relief and suffering. "Now, there's a memorable saying. I suppose someone is going to write that one down someday, as well as the remark about the serpent's tooth."

Frankie smiled and bent over her husband to kiss his forehead. He looked very handsome in his clean blue leggings and purple silk tunic, even though the bandages on his thigh made for an unsightly bulge.

"Someday," she agreed. "I love you, Braden. Whatever happens to us, please remember that."

The groom reached up, touched the side of the bride's nose with a fingertip, then yawned again. "I'll just rest a while now, Duchess, then we'll enjoy the traditional consummation."

Frankie laughed, though she felt as much like crying. "What a poet you are, Braden Stuart-Ramsey, Duke of Sunderlin."

He grinned, though his eyes were closed, and only moments later he was snoring.

Frankie sat beside him for a time, trying to assimilate his presence somehow, as if it were medicine to her soul, and then went out onto the crude stone terrace. There, she had a view of the village, and the stream flowing through it like a wide ribbon of shining foil in the sunshine.

Standing high above the moat, which was filled with stinking, stagnate water, Frankie again considered her plight. Never before had she had a keener sense of what was meant by the phrase, *living for the moment.* She had nothing else—no past and, perhaps, no future. Just this precious wrinkle in time, where she and Braden were tucked away together.

When Braden stirred, after an hour or so, Frankie went back inside the chamber, removed her improvised wedding dress and the wreath of dried flowers, and lay down with her husband. Slowly, and with great reverence, the Duke introduced his Duchess to pleasures even sweeter and more fiery than those she had known before.

It was the next morning, when Braden had gone back to oversee the sword practice despite his wounded leg, that Frankie saw the wizard again. She was sitting in the hidden garden, the one off the Great Hall that Gilford had taken her to the day before, when she suddenly looked up and found Merlin standing in front of her.

On a man of less commanding presence, the magician's robes and pointed hat might have looked silly, but he carried them off with a flourish.

"So you've married the Duke," he said, arms folded. "That was very foolish, indeed."

Frankie's heart had shinnied up her rib cage and made the leap to her throat, she'd been so startled by the magician's sudden materialization in the garden. Now the organ sank back to its normal place—or perhaps a little lower. At the same time she lifted her chin in a gesture of polite defiance.

"I love Braden."

"Perhaps," Merlin conceded, "but as I told you before, this is not meant to be. An error was made at the Beginning, yes, but what is done is done. Sunderlin shall perish, ere the week is out, and you must go back where you belong before you are executed for sorcery."

"By thinking long and hard of home?" Frankie sounded sarcastic, she knew, but she couldn't help it. She was terrified and confused, and those elements combined to make her tongue sharp. "What is this, the Land of Oz? Shouldn't I just click my heels together and say—"

"Enough," Merlin broke in, exasperated. "Time is a creation of the mind. Your other life is not at the end of the universe; indeed, it is so close you could reach out and touch it. Think of your own world, Francesca. Think of it!"

His words enchanted her somehow; she recalled Seattle, with its hills, its busy harbor, its bustle and energy. For the merest fraction of a moment, she saw flashes of old brick around her, heard the horns of taxicabs as they bumped over the streets in Pioneer Square. For one tiny portion of a single heartbeat, she was back there, standing on the corner of Yesler Way and First Avenue South, only a stone's throw from her shop. A little more concentration, just a little, and she would truly have been there, as solid and real as the old brick building she knew so well.

Still, Frankie's heart was with Braden, and she followed it back in a single cosmic leap. She was perspiring, cold and sick, as she sat clutching the edge of the ancient stone bench in the garden of old roses, struggling to stay long after the need had passed.

"Fool," Merlin said, but in a kind tone. Then, as quickly as he'd appeared, he vanished into the soft, misty air of the morning.

Frankie braved the kitchen after that, there purloining a basketful of various foods from beneath the cook's disapproving nose, and ventured cautiously to the practice grounds. This time, heaven be thanked, she did not surprise Braden into being stabbed. In fact, he was on the sidelines, calling out instructions to other combatants, and when he sensed Frankie's presence, he tossed a smile in her direction and then came hobbling after it.

Even with a limp, she thought, he was a magnificent man. She pictured him in jeans and a half-shirt as he moved toward her, then in a perfectly tailored three-piece suit. Both prospects were delicious.

"I've brought the stuff for a picnic," she said. "We can sit under those maple trees on the far side of the grounds."

Frankie had half expected Braden to refuse her invitation, but instead he took the basket from her and started toward the place she'd chosen for their picnic.

An idea was forming in her mind, and as they ate, she told Braden more about modern-day Seattle. While keeping herself as detached as possible, lest she be snatched back, she tried to make her husband see the buses and cars, the paved roadways, the concrete and steel buildings that loomed against the sky. Her theory was that, if he could imagine the place, perhaps he could also go there somehow, with her. After all, Merlin had once said that Braden truly belonged in that other world, and not in the much cruder and more dangerous one around them.

They lay side by side in the grass for a time, once they'd eaten, and Braden plucked a dandelion from the grass and tickled Frankie's chin with its ghostly down. "I wish I could make love to you right here," he said hoarsely. "We are, of course, being watched."

"Of course," Frankie agreed sadly, catching his hand in hers, squeezing tightly. "Oh, Braden, won't you please call off the tournament? For me?"

He raised her knuckles to his mouth, brushed his lips across them in a caress as light as the passage of a butterfly. "I'm sorry, Francesca. I would do almost anything for you, but I cannot abandon my honor as a man."

Frankie was suddenly flushed with conviction, frustration, and fear. "Your *honor*? Good Lord, Braden, what is honorable about suicide? That's what this is, you know, because you've been warned and you still insist on fighting!"

He smoothed her wind-tousled hair back from her face. "I can do nothing else, beloved—this is who I am. Besides, I am among the best swordsmen in England."

She closed her eyes tightly, seeking some inner balance, and then nodded. There was no use in arguing; that was clear. Braden was as set on following his path as she was on following her own.

They finished their meal of cold venison, dried fruit, and even drier bread, and then Braden insisted on going back to the field of practice. While Frankie could certainly see the sense in his desire to be as expert a swordsman as possible, she wished there were no need for fighting.

It was a brutal time in history, she thought as they walked back together, her hand tucked into his. And yet, Frankie had to admit, her own era was fraught with peril, too. Each had its pestilences, its widespread poverty, its violence and prejudice. The differences were really pretty superficial.

Now that she'd had a chance to compare the two, however, Frankie knew with a certainty that she preferred her own niche, far away in the tempestuous nineteen-nineties. The only hitch was that she would have to leave Braden to get back there.

Frankie stopped, shading her eyes from the sun and watching as her husband moved haltingly, and yet with that profound confidence of his, toward the field of practice. He must have felt Frankie's gaze, for, although he did not look back, he raised one hand in a gesture she knew was meant for her.

Inside the keep Frankie made her way through cool, shadowy passageways until she reached the chapel. There she sat alone on the bench closest to the wooden cross beside the altar, her hands folded.

The next few days passed in much the same manner as that one had. Braden practiced incessantly, refusing to rest, and Frankie prepared a picnic meal for their noon repast. In the afternoons she sat in the quiet sanctuary of the chapel, offering wordless petitions, prayers of presence rather than pleading.

The nights, ah, the nights. Those were the most delicious, the most bittersweet, the most glorious and tragic times of all.

Braden and Frankie loved until they were gasping and exhausted, until their bodies rebelled and tumbled into the dark, bottomless well of sleep. Always, when the morning came, they loved again.

Day by day, knights and nobles from other parts of the country arrived, with pageantry and fanfare, some housed within the keep, others pitching brightly colored tents outside the walls. The summer fair would soon culminate in a tournament that, according to Gilford, had been a local tradition since the time of William the Conqueror. It was even rumored that the king himself, His Royal Majesty, Edward III, might put in an appearance.

Frankie cared about none of this. When she awakened to the sound of trumpets that morning just a week after her arrival, she knew her own personal Judgment Day had arrived.

6

THE MAIDSERVANTS MURMURED among themselves as they attended Frankie that morning of the tournament. She was decked out in a lovely gown of rose-colored silk, trimmed at cuff and hem with fine lace. Her hair was brushed and then pulled into a French braid, with ribbon to match the dress woven in for ornamentation.

Frankie was not seeing her reflection in the looking glass affixed to the wall behind the dressing table. The sounds of the trumpets echoed in her ears, and her heart was pounding with a steadily rising fear.

This day, unless she found some way to prevent it, the man she loved more than her own soul would die. He would no longer exist, either in this world or the one she knew, and she found the thought unbearable.

It was a word snagged from the conversation of the sulky maids attending her that caught Frankie's attention.

"—witch—"

She rose from the bench where she'd sat and turned on the two women. Both lowered their eyes.

"What are you saying about me?" she demanded.

The reply came not from the servants, but from Alaric, who had entered the chamber unannounced and was now helping himself to a piece of fruit from a clay bowl on a table just inside the door.

"They're certain you're the devil's mistress," he said idly, his hand hovering over one piece of fruit and then another. Finally he settled on a speckled pear. "God be thanked for the Italians and their sunny orchards." Despite his cheerful manner, he spoke sternly to the maids, and they vanished, but not before casting looks of mingled terror and resentment in Frankie's direction.

Frankie was only slightly more comfortable in Alaric's

presence. He, after all, was slated by the fates to take over the estates following Braden's death and destroy everything the family had built over the centuries.

"Braden isn't here," she said, keeping the breadth of Sunderlin's writing desk between them.

Alaric ran his dark gaze over her, then sighed. "What a lovely, lovely thing you are, Francesca. My brother is a fortunate man."

Frankie said nothing; she knew Alaric had not come to praise Braden. Perhaps he'd even known all along that his elder brother was already out greeting visiting nobles and their knights.

After taking a bite from the pear and wiping the juice from his mouth and chin with a forearm, Alaric set the core aside and regarded Frankie in silence for a time. Then, hands resting on his hips, he said solicitously, "Poor Francesca. This, I fear, will not be a good day for either you or my dear brother."

She clutched the table's edge, felt herself go pale, and yet kept her chin high and her eyes fiery with rebellion. "Why do you say that, Alaric?" she dared to ask. "Are you plotting against Braden, and thus against me?"

Alaric chuckled. "There is no plot," he said. "But I sense danger, the way one sometimes senses the approach of a storm in otherwise perfect weather. I have a cart ready and waiting at the south gate, Francesca. It's not too late to escape."

"And leave my husband? Never."

"How is it that you've become so attached to him in such a short time?" Alaric inquired with what sounded like genuine puzzlement. He shrugged when she didn't reply, and went on. "True, Braden is much-praised as a lover. But he is not the only man in the world who knows how to give a woman pleasure."

Frankie felt her cheeks turn crimson. As far as she was concerned, Braden *was* the only man in the world, period, for she wanted no other. And she wasn't about to discuss something so personal as her husband's sexual prowess with Alaric or anyone else. "I love him," she said honestly and with a certain quiet ferocity. "Now, please leave me. It's time I joined my husband."

Alaric did not leave; instead, he crooked one arm. "I know, milady," he answered. "I have been sent to escort you. The Duke is busy welcoming his guests, you see, and as a younger son, I am expected to serve as his emissary."

Frankie glared at her brother-in-law for a moment, keeping her distance. "There must be no more talk of my sneaking away in a cart," she warned. "No matter what happens, I will not leave Braden's side."

"Rash words," Alaric replied, not unkindly. "I hope you do not come to regret them."

With the greatest reluctance Frankie took Alaric's arm and allowed him to squire her out of the bedroom, along the wide passageway, and down the enormous staircase to the Great Hall. There, an enormous crowd had gathered, the women chattering, the children running in every direction, the men laughing together and hoisting pints of ale.

At Frankie's appearance, however, a buzz moved through the group, and then there was utter silence. It took all her courage not to cower against Alaric's side when every person raised their eyes to stare.

Alaric called out something to the people, and Frankie knew he was presenting her as the new mistress of Sunderlin Keep even though she didn't comprehend the actual words. The room seemed to quiver for a moment, with that special kind of silence that indicates strong emotion. Then, here and there, a tradesman or a knight or a squire dropped to one knee and lowered his head in deference to the Duke's bride.

The women eyed her narrowly, far more suspicious than the men, but some of them executed grudging curtsies as she passed with Alaric.

It was something of a relief when they passed beneath the high archway and onto the castle grounds.

Colorful tents dotted the landscape, inside the walls as well as out, and one could not turn around without seeing a juggler or a pie merchant or a musician or a nobleman in grand clothes. Frankie took in the spectacle—that could not be helped—but she was too nervous to really appreciate what she was seeing and hearing.

Where was Braden?

Alaric took her to the field of practice, where a long, fencelike structure had been set up, along with a grandstand of sorts and still more tents. Keeping Frankie close to his side with a certain subtle force, Alaric explained that the wooden wall was called a tilt, and that it was designed to keep the horses from colliding during the joust.

Frankie was shading her eyes from the morning sun and searching the crowd for Braden. She thirsted for the sight of him, yearned for the sound of his voice.

But Alaric did not seem anxious to find his brother. He gestured toward the drawbridge, which lay open across the moat. It was packed with travelers coming in and out, on foot, in carts, and on horseback.

"It would be easy to pass through unnoticed, milady," he said. "We have only to exchange those rich silks of yours for a peasant's rags and muss up your lovely hair a bit—"

Just then Frankie spotted Braden. He was standing in a circle of men, smiling, and as she watched, he threw back his magnificent head in a burst of happy laughter. The sound struck Frankie's spirit like one of the spiked steel balls she'd seen in the chamber where weapons were kept.

She pulled free of Alaric, despite his attempt to hold her, and set off toward her husband. It was probably a breach of some masculine code for her to stride right up to him that way, but Frankie was past caring about such things, if she ever had. Her only plan—and a pitifully thin plan it was, too—was to hover close to Braden throughout the day and somehow protect him.

On some level Frankie knew this would probably turn out to be an impossible feat, but she had no other choice but to try. She could not simply abandon Braden to the death the fates had assigned him, even to save her own hide. If the worst happened, she wanted to hold her love in her arms as he passed from this world into the next, and give him whatever comfort she could.

Just the thought filled her eyes with tears.

Braden saw her and pulled away from his circle of friends

to greet her with a husbandly kiss on the forehead. With one hand he held her shoulder, with the thumb of the other, he brushed the wetness from her cheek.

"This day will pass, beloved," he told her quietly. "Tonight, you and I will celebrate my victory together."

Conscious of Alaric standing nearby, Frankie shivered. "Who is your opponent?"

Braden lowered his hands to his sides. "I don't know. Lots will be drawn before the competition begins." He offered her his arm as the trumpets sounded, evidently to mark the beginning of the first event. They were settled on a high wooden dias, in straight-back chairs, before he spoke to her again. "First, the joust."

Frankie sat stiffly, biting her lip, as men in heavy armor, mounted on spectacular horses, took their places at either end of the field. The tilt protected the animals to breast-height, but the knights themselves were exposed to their onrushing opponent's lance.

Nothing in Frankie's high school performance of *Camelot* had prepared her for the sight of two men riding toward each other at the top speed their burdened horses could manage, long spearlike weapons in hand. The sound was even worse, and she bit her lip throughout, and only kept her breakfast down by the greatest self-control.

The events seemed interminable, but finally, in midafternoon, Braden left the dias to take the field, wearing his sword and a chain-mail vest. Frankie wished he were in full armor or, better yet, that he'd been born in the right time period in the first place and avoided this moment forever.

The people cheered as he took his place in the center of the action and unsheathed his sword. Sunderlin ignored the adulation; his gaze locked with Frankie's, and he seemed to be making a silent promise that he wouldn't let anything separate them.

Frankie's vision blurred; she lifted her hand. *I love you,* she told him in the language of the heart. *Forever and always, no matter what happens, Braden Stuart-Ramsey, Duke of Sunderlin, my soul is mated to yours.*

Braden's opponent was a large man, not as solidly built

but clearly strong. He had a red beard and a Nordic look, and Frankie thought uneasily of the Viking god Thor.

She rose out of her chair when the blades were drawn, stepped off the dias, and moved through the crowd as the swords were struck together in a sort of warrior's salute.

The cheers and calls of the spectators seemed to Frankie to roll from some great, hollow cave, and the air pounded like a giant heartbeat. Over this, always, always, rang the cruel sound of steel on steel.

She might have stepped right onto the field if Gilford hadn't grabbed her and hauled her back against his rotund torso.

"Are you trying to get him killed?" the doctor rasped, his breath whistling past her ear. "Did you learn nothing before, when Sunderlin was wounded because of your reckless-ness?"

The thrumming in her ears stopped; suddenly everything was clear as crystal. Something had passed between the warriors, and the crowd sensed the change and fell silent. The match had turned, between one moment and its successor, from sport to warfare.

Frankie almost screamed, so great and uncontrollable was her terror, but Gilford stopped her by pressing one meaty hand over her mouth and shaking her.

"You must not distract him!" he breathed.

Someone else did that, as it happened. Alaric rushed onto the field, shouting, and in that fragment of time Braden hesitated. It was enough for Thor, who plunged his sword straight into the Duke's abdomen.

Frankie felt the blow as surely as if it had been dealt to her. She shrieked in protest and furious grief, and somehow twisted free of Gilford's hold, stumbling as she raced onto the field and threw herself down beside Braden in the bloody dirt.

She was wailing softly, speaking senseless words, as she gathered him into her arms.

Remarkably he smiled at her, reached up to touch her face. "So you were right," he said softly. "It ends here. I'm sorry, my love, for not believing you."

Frankie sobbed when he closed his eyes, tried to shake

him awake. It was no use, and she was like a wild creature when Gilford and another man took her arms and hauled her off Braden so he could be carried away.

The crowd had been stirred to rage by the spectacle, by the unthinkable fall of their legendary leader, but it wasn't Thor they turned upon.

No.

One of the women pointed at Frankie. "Witch," she said. Others took up the cry. "Witch—witch—witch—"

"God in heaven," Gilford gasped, "it's happening. Come, Francesca, we must be away from here, quickly!"

Frankie was prostrate with grief; the damning words of the crowd meant nothing to her. She wanted only to sit with Braden, to tell him all the things she'd stored up in her heart, to hold his hand in case he would know somehow that she was there.

Alaric moved to join the others, who had encircled Frankie and the physician now.

"She knew this day would come," Braden's brother said clearly, gesturing toward Frankie. "She predicted it. Maybe she even made it happen with chants and magic!"

"Are you insane?" Gilford demanded of Alaric, holding tightly to Frankie, who was only half-conscious. He raised his voice, addressing the witch-hunters who surrounded them, looming closer and closer. "This is a mere woman, not a witch!" he cried. "She has a heart and soul, blood and breath, like any one of you!"

Frankie fainted at that point, only to revive a few moments later and find herself being forcefully separated from Gilford, her only defender.

"In the name of all that's holy," her friend begged, his face wet with sweat and perhaps tears, "release her! She has done nothing wrong!"

"Silence!" Alaric shouted. "Why do you defend her, Gilford? Are you in league with this—this mistress of the devil?"

"You are a traitor!" Gilford accused in return. "Mark my words, Judas Iscariot, the Duke will avenge this wrong, and God Himself will come to his aid!"

Someone came forward from the seething crowd and

struck Gilford hard with a staff. The big man's knees buckled and he went down, and the sight shook Frankie partially out of her stupor. At last she realized what was happening.

She was dragged, kicking and scratching, to the whipping post, a horror she had not seen before, and thrust against it with cruel force. Her arms were wrenched behind her and tightly tied with narrow strips that bit into the flesh of her wrists.

For a few moments Frankie honestly didn't care whether she lived or died. After all, Braden was dead—he'd perished in her arms. If there was an afterlife, she might see him there.

As the villagers began stacking twigs around her feet, however, and as their eyes filled with unfounded hatred, it occurred to Frankie that she might be carrying Braden's child. It didn't seem fair that the infant should die before living.

Frankie fought hysteria as she searched the mob for one friendly face, one person who might dare to speak for her. There was no sign of Gilford—he had been overcome and perhaps even arrested—but Alaric soon approached, as if drawn by her thoughts.

"I warned you, Francesca," he scolded. No one would ever have guessed from his manner that he'd just seen his only brother die, that he was about to watch another human being burned alive. "You should have listened to me. I would have taken you away."

"You did it on purpose," Frankie accused, as the terrible realization dawned. "You weren't going to help Braden on the field; you only wanted to distract him so that his opponent could run him through!"

Unbelievably, Alaric smiled. "You might have been my duchess, after a decent interval had passed," he said. "How sad that you would never listen to reason."

Frankie spat at him, though until then her mouth had felt painfully dry. "I'll burn for a few minutes," she hissed, causing the mob to gasp in fear and draw back, "but you, Alaric Stuart-Ramsey, will suffer the flames of eternity for what you've done! *You are cursed!*"

Alaric paled, then his jaw hardened. "Bring the torches!" he cried.

Frankie watched in stricken horror as the pitch-soaked torches were lit and then laid to the dry twigs at her feet. She heard the crackle of burning wood, smelled the acrid smoke, saw the shifting mirage of heat rising in front of her like a wall.

Then she heard Merlin's voice, though she could not see him.

"Think of Seattle, Francesca," he said urgently. "Think of the big white ferryboats crossing Puget Sound. Think of those wonderful snowcapped mountains, and the hillsides carpeted with green, green trees. Remember your shop, and your cousin Brian, and your friends. Remember the Space Needle, and Pioneer Square, and the Pike Place Market—"

Tears rolled down Frankie's cheeks as she tilted her head back and remembered with all her might, with all her being. She felt the flames begin to catch at her skirts, felt the horrible, choking heat . . .

"Seattle," said Merlin. "Seattle, Seattle—"

"Witch!" screamed Alaric, his voice hoarse and fading. Slowly fading, into the heat, beyond it. *"Witch . . ."*

There was no explosion, no sprinkling of magic dust. The shift was graceful and quiet.

Frankie's first realization was that it was cooler, that her hands were no longer bound. She opened her eyes and found herself staring into a shop window at her own reflection.

She was wearing a silk dress, torn and singed, and her face and hair were dark with soot. Taxis and pedestrians moved past, also mirrored in the dusty glass, and Frankie turned slowly to look.

Pioneer Square.

Frankie began to weep, stumbling through staring, whispering tourists, street people, and office workers, making her way around the corner.

The sign above her shop still read CINDERELLA'S CLOSET. Frankie sagged against the door, sliding downward until she was sitting on the worn brick step.

Passersby stopped and made a semicircle around her; Mrs. Cullywater pushed through, carrying a bag from a nearby bakery in one hand and wearing the key to the shop on her wrist, dangling from a pink plastic bracelet.

"Why, Miss Whittier!" the friendly old woman cried, dropping the bag and crouching. "What's happened? Merciful heavens, how did your clothes get into such a state. . . ."

Frankie drew up her knees, wrapped her arms around them, and shook her head from side to side, unable to offer a sensible explanation.

She spent that night in Harborview Hospital, under observation, but was released in the morning. A friend, Sheila Hendrix, brought jeans and a T-shirt and drove Frankie back to her apartment.

"I'll stay if you want," Sheila said. She was obviously worried, but Frankie didn't want to keep her. Sheila had a good job with a local advertising firm, and she had better things to do than play nursemaid.

"I'll be all right," Frankie insisted, and Sheila left.

The apartment was unchanged, except that everything was covered with a fine layer of dust and the plants were all desperate for water. Frankie made a ritual of small chores, but the place was small, only a studio, though it was attractive, and all too soon there was nothing to do.

Frankie sank onto her couch, gnawing at her lower lip. It was only a matter of time before the police would show up, wanting to know what she'd been doing, staggering through the streets in such a state, with her dress half burned off and her hair and face covered in soot. Given the bohemian nature of Pioneer Square, she could probably convince them that she'd been practicing to become a street performer.

What would be harder to explain, however, was her total lack of identification. Her passport, driver's license, and credit cards were all still in England, in the Grimsley Inn, where she'd left them before going to the medieval fair that first day.

She splayed her fingers and plunged them into her hair. Braden, she thought, with a sorrow so desperate, so all-encompassing, that it was crushing her. Oh, Braden. What do I do now? How do I go on without you?

Somehow, though it seemed an impossible thing to do, Frankie did manage to go on with her life. After a few days the police casually stopped by to ask what had happened, why she'd been wandering in the streets in a charred dress, and she told them she was into performance art. She didn't think for a moment that they believed her, but they had other concerns and didn't press.

Mrs. Cullywater stayed on to help run the shop, since Frankie was in a daze of grief most of the time, and it was that kind woman who called the inn in Grimsley and asked them to send back Miss Whittier's identification, along with her suitcase. Yes, the older woman assured the clerk on the other end of the line, Miss Whittier was fine. She'd left Great Britain under special circumstances and apologized sincerely for any concern her disappearance might have caused.

A month had passed since her dramatic return from England, and Frankie was sitting in her shop, watching lovers pass by on the sidewalk, hand in hand. She was sipping strong tea and feeling sorry for herself when a terrible crash sounded from the back of the shop.

Mrs. Cullywater, normally unflappable, was back there sorting a shipment of antique buttons, and she let out a scream that all but cracked the window glass. Frankie spilled her tea and overturned her stool in her haste to get to her employee.

The shop was small, and very narrow, and Frankie had to make her way between counters of old jewelry, racks of both vintage and used designer clothing, and pyramids of hatboxes. When she burst into the storeroom, she screamed, too—not for fear, but for joy.

Braden was sitting on the floor, clad in his usual leggings and tunic, looking dazed and very pleased with himself. "God's knees," he said. "I finally managed it."

Mrs. Cullywater had collapsed into a chair and was fanning herself with an old copy of *Photoplay*. "Out of nowhere," she muttered. "I swear, he just appeared out of nowhere."

Frankie was kneeling on the floor, laughing and crying, fearing to close her eyes lest Braden disappear again. She flung her arms around him, held on tight, and sobbed because he was real, and because it was no dream.

"How—?" she finally managed to choke out. "Oh, Braden, I thought you were dead!"

He got to his feet, bringing Frankie with him. "Gilford was there to take care of me." Braden put his arms around her, held her loosely, so that he could look down into her eyes. "You should have heard the uproar, Duchess, after you disappeared right out of your bonds the way you did!"

Frankie reached up, tentatively touched Braden's face. "How did you get here?"

"Your wizard came to my room one night and told me to remember all the things you'd told me about your world. He said I might be able to get to you, since I was supposed to be born here in the first place. I failed any number of times, but I'm glad I kept trying."

Mrs. Cullywater edged around them and fled the shop. Frankie hoped the poor dear wasn't too frightened, but she did not go after the older woman. Any attempt to explain would, of course, have only made matters worse.

Braden bent his head, kissed Frankie lightly on the mouth, the way he always did before he made slow, sweet, thorough love to her. "For a time there," he confessed a moment later, "I thought the villagers might have been right about you. Who else but a witch could vanish the way you did? It was Gilford who set me straight and said you'd come back here."

Frankie remembered the insane anger of the mob and shivered, and Braden held her a little closer. "I thought they were going to kill him, too, because he tried so hard to save me."

Braden shook his head. "They gave him some bruises and scrapes, all right, but he was a healer. They needed him, and they knew it."

Frankie laughed, even though her eyes were glistening with tears. "How are we going to explain you to the modern world, Braden Stuart-Ramsey?"

He gathered her to him and kissed her in the way she'd dreamed of, remembered, mourned during the long weeks since their parting. "We'll worry about that later," he said. "For now, Duchess, I just want to hold you in my arms."

Not wanting to confront Braden with the strange sights and sounds of the nineteen nineties without some preparation, Frankie took him by the hand and led him through the alleyways to the rear entrance of her apartment building. They climbed the inside stairway and hurried along the hall to Frankie's door.

They were inside before Braden really began to absorb his surroundings. He touched the television set in curious bewilderment, and Frankie smiled. She would show him how it worked later; with the twentieth century rushing at him from every direction, his senses were surely approaching overload as it was.

"Where do you sleep?" Braden asked when he'd checked out the bathroom, where he immediately flushed the toilet, and given the kitchenette a quick examination.

Frankie was just standing there, leaning against the door and silently rejoicing. She was all but blinded by tears, and yet she couldn't stop smiling. That is, until she remembered that he'd suffered two grievous sword wounds in the space of a week.

She thrust herself away from the door and hurried over to him. "You're hurt—good heavens, in all the excitement, I'd forgotten—"

Quickly she removed the sofa cushions and folded out the hidden bed.

Braden stared for a moment, then crossed himself.

Frankie took his hand. "You need to lie down," she said.

He smiled. "What I need, Duchess, is for you to lie down with me." He pulled her close and kissed her in his old, knee-melting way. Gently he lifted her T-shirt off over her head and tossed it aside. "Strange clothes again," he teased, but he had no trouble removing her bra.

"Braden," she whimpered joyously as he cupped her breast in his hand, chafing a ready nipple with his thumb.

Sunderlin was fumbling with the snap on her jeans by then. "What manner of leggings are these?" he asked, but he didn't wait for an answer. Instead, he gently stripped away the last of Frankie's clothes and lowered her to the bed.

Frankie watched as her husband removed his own garments, things that probably belonged in a British museum, saw the scars on his belly and his right thigh. If anything, these imperfections made Braden even more magnificent. She held out her arms, and he fell to her with a low, hoarse groan of need.

"Your wounds?" Frankie asked, searching his eyes for some sign of the pain he had to be feeling.

Braden kissed her hungrily and at great length before answering. "My wounds will heal, now that I am with you again. For the moment, let there be no more talk of suffering, Francesca, or of trouble. We can think about our problems later."

Frankie arched her hips and deftly received him, delighting in the way he tilted his head back and moaned. "Much later," she agreed.

In that moment, somewhere far away and yet very nearby, a passageway between two eras closed without even a whisper of sound.

Lovers of the
Golden Drum

Diana Bane

AUTHOR'S NOTE:
In this novella I have made use of a real
Outer Banks legend as the framework for fiction.
I have not altered the legend insofar as I
know it, but I have changed the names of
those involved to protect their descendants
who still live on the Outer Banks.

ACKNOWLEDGMENTS
I am indebted to Clare Baum, whose research on
North Carolina Christmas traditions first brought
the Golden Drum to my attention; and to Mary Ishaq,
Margaret Pfaff, and Virginia Powell for assistance
with materials.

D.B.

The Dream Begins . . .

"YOU'RE CRYING," said Margaret.

"Nay," said the boy vigorously, "I'm not."

"Aye, you are, and too proud to admit it. Does your wound pain you?"

"Nay," he said again. He would not look at her but stared at the flames that danced in the fireplace.

She approached him, curious, with greater caution than she did most things. "If you are not in pain, then why are you crying? Don't bother to deny again what I can see with my own eyes."

Slowly the boy turned his face to her. Large tears rolled silently down his cheeks. He could do nothing to stop their progress, for one arm was bandaged tightly against his chest, and the other he had wrapped about his fabulous drum.

He was a handsome lad, even though he was pale and sick. Margaret's heart went out to him. She stepped close, lifted a corner of her overskirt, and wiped the dampness from his face. The tears stopped flowing. "Well, then?"

"Our Bonnie Prince has gone," said the boy, "and left me behind. I wanted to go with him."

"Hah. You're just a boy—"

"So what? I wager I'm older than you, and what's more I've been to battle, which is more than you'll ever do because *you're* just a *girl!*"

Margaret tossed her head. Her hair, a tangled mass of curls the color of new-fired brick, bounced about her shoulders. "Don't be so sure! I could disguise myself, wear the kilt. I'd be a good warrior. I can heft my father's claymore, while your wrists are thin as sticks. Drumsticks. Don't boast, drummer boy!"

"I'm thirteen. When I'm older, next time—"

"I'm thirteen, too." Margaret sank down next to him. "My name is Margaret, of the clan Macquarrie. This is my father's house. What's your name, drummer boy?"

"Douglas, of clan Douglas."

"My father says you are to stay here until your wound is healed, Douglas of clan Douglas. We may as well be friends." She eyed the drum he clutched so tightly. Its golden bands glowed in the light from the fire. "So tell me about your drum."

January 8, 1993

"I know, I'm up, I'm up!" Without opening her eyes, Maggie flung her left arm out, fingers groping for the button that would shut off the rude blast of her clock radio's alarm. She found it, but too late: the dream was gone.

"Rats!" she groused at no one; Maggie Ross lived alone. She opened her eyes, swung her legs out from under the covers, and sat on the side of the bed. She glared at the clock radio, which innocently played morning music. A bad sign, sleeping through the music, having to be awakened by the alarm—it was happening more and more often, and she knew it meant she was exhausted. Physically, mentally, maybe both. Maggie shoved her feet into her slippers and padded off to start the coffee, then finish waking up in the shower.

As she stood under the spray with her eyes closed, a piece of the dream returned. Just a glint of something gold, and a feeling . . .

Maggie turned carefully, eyes still closed, and let the spray fall upon her upturned face. The dream-feeling clung to her, the feel of a place that was familiar—haunting, tantalizing. She yearned to go back, back into the dream.

Dumb, she told herself, *dumb, dumb, dumb!* She was awake now, no more silly thoughts about dreams, there's work to do, life goes on . . . whether you want it to or not.

She turned off the shower, rubbed her skin with a towel until it tingled, then blew her hair dry.

Maggie's hair was an unusual dark red and so thick that it tended to shagginess if she didn't keep a good cut. Her skin was milky-pale like that of most natural redheads, and her eyes were hazel-green. Her self-image had been fixed during a skinny, hypercritical adolescence, so she didn't much like looking in mirrors. That was one good thing about the job she had so much trouble getting herself to these days: She was a behind-the-scenes person; she didn't have to be all polished and perfect. She liked long, slouchy sweaters—wool in winter, cotton in summer—over narrow trousers, an acceptable look for a commercial artist who worked behind the scenes in an Atlanta advertising firm, which was what Maggie did for a living.

She'd liked the job, and had liked Atlanta, when she started fresh out of college eight years ago. Eight years ago she'd been able to drive to work in ten minutes; now she sat stuck in near-gridlock traffic, the kind of traffic she'd thought to escape by moving South. *It could be worse,* she told herself as she inched her Saab along. She'd been telling herself that a lot lately.

Suddenly Maggie wanted to jump right out and run through the lines of cars, tearing her hair and ripping at her clothes until she was bare-breasted, screaming like a Fury. *God, I really do have to get hold of myself!* she thought. She hung on to the steering wheel so hard that her knuckles turned white.

At lunch she confided these things to her friend Rita. Rita was an account executive now, very much on her way up the corporate ladder. Maggie had made it to senior illustrator, which was as far up as a commercial artist could go. Twenty-nine years old, and already she was stuck.

"Bare-breasted Fury?" Rita rolled her eyes. "*You,* meek Maggie?"

Maggie shrugged and pushed her salad around on her plate. She wasn't really hungry. "I'm not all that meek. I'm just—I've just learned to keep myself under control. But I think my control is cracking—I mean, so much of the time

I just feel like I want *out*. But I'm not sure out of what. It sort of scares me."

"Hmmm." Rita had sleek black hair, dark brown eyes, and long fingers, which she now laced under her chin, elbows on the table. "I always wondered what goes on beneath that quiet surface of yours. Could it be that you have a personality like a sleeping volcano and now you're about to erupt?"

Maggie grinned. "Nothing that dramatic. I've probably just got some kind of depression left over from the holidays. Christmas and New Year's are always kind of hard for me—maybe I didn't get over it yet."

"How boring. I like my volcano theory better. But seriously, Maggie, I think what you need is a vacation. Or a new man. How long has it been since—"

"Not long enough! Vacation, yes—man, no. New man, maybe never—"

"Never say never!"

Maggie stuck out her tongue and made a face in reply.

"Same to you, I'm sure," said Rita. "What is it with you, Maggie? You don't let people get close, you never date anybody for more than a few months at a time—"

"Knock it off, Reet. Stick with the vacation concept. I have some time coming up soon. In a couple of months."

"Think you can hold out that long?"

"I think I have to. You should see the pile of stuff on my desk!"

"I know what you mean, and speaking of piles of stuff, we'd best get back to it."

Halfway through the afternoon, completely unbidden, the dream-feeling enveloped Maggie as she sat on a high stool, sketching at the drafting table in her office. A golden glint flickered at her eyelids, and she closed her eyes. Her hand holding the pencil went still.

In her mind's eye a picture formed: a fabulous drum, banded top and bottom in gold, crisscrossed by gold laces, the drum's red-and-black-painted body all but obscured by the shining gold.

"The Golden Drum," she murmured, opening her eyes. In

a flash of illumination she remembered: A couple of days ago she'd read a newspaper feature article about some out-of-the-way place where they still celebrated "Old Christmas" on the date that's now called Epiphany, January sixth. Something about a procession, and a legendary drum . . .

How odd! she thought. *What a strange thing to dream about, and even now I can see it so clearly.* Maggie gave herself a shake—this was ridiculous, she'd never seen such a drum in her life, never heard its story before reading the article, and couldn't even recall the whole thing now. There was work to be done—she couldn't sit wasting time like this. She dismissed the drum from her mind.

But not from her dreams: That night she dreamed again, and the dream picked up precisely where it had left off the previous night.

June 29, 1746

"So tell me about your drum."

At Margaret's request a light came into Douglas's gray eyes, and they shone in his too-pale face. His voice, still youthfully high-pitched, sank to an awed near-whisper. "The Prince himself gave the drum to me. He called it the Golden Drum, and me, his brave drummer lad. He said the drum was blessed for battle."

"But we lost anyway," said Margaret glumly, resting her chin in her hands, her elbows on bent knees. "More than a thousand men fell on Drummossie's Moor, at the place called Culloden. Or so I heard from Cousin Flora."

"Aye, that's so." Douglas matched her for glumness. "The clans will never be the same again."

"I guess your drum was blessed for the wrong battle."

"'Tis not my drum, 'tis Bonnie Prince Charlie's drum, and you'll do well not to make light of it, lassie!"

Margaret tossed her head and folded her arms across her chest where breasts had recently begun to form. "I'll make a deal with ye, Douglas Douglas. I'll not call you laddie if you'll not call me lassie. Only my father can call me lassie to my face, for since my mother died last year I'm mistress in this house! And by the way, I did not intend to make light of the Prince's drum. Though to my way of thinking, it's more yours than his now that he's gone."

"I accept your deal, Margaret Macquarrie, it's fair enough. After that battle I'm nobody's laddie, that's for sure. My own father died at Drummossie. I wonder yet that I still live."

"I'm sorry," Margaret sympathized. She looked into the fire, thinking about death and war and Highlanders' pride. "My father said the Macdonalds, for all that they're our kin, were daft to follow the Young Pretender. But then in the end, even if he didn't fight himself, Father sent money."

"The money was needed, as much as the fighting men," said Douglas graciously. He cocked his head and regarded Margaret with interest. "Did I hear you say that Flora Macdonald is your cousin?"

"Aye!" Margaret smiled.

Douglas lowered his voice to a near-whisper; it was dangerous to speak of this, but who could resist? "A brave woman, Flora Macdonald! How clever she was to help the Prince get away, dressing him up as her serving maid!"

Margaret nodded, her eyes shining. "My cousin is both brave and clever, but I'm sure you know that what she did is a great secret." Deftly she changed the subject. "I'd rather know about you. Is it true that the golden drum saved your life?"

"Aye"—he nodded solemnly—"'tis true enough. The shot that went through my shoulder and broke the bone would have hit me in the chest, but for glancing off the golden band round the top of the drum." Awkwardly, having only one hand to work with, he turned the drum upon his knee and indicated with a sharp nod. "See, look here where the band is dented. The drum and I, we will both bear scars."

Margaret moved closer so that she could better examine the dent. "I think you have got the worst of it," she declared, raising her eyes to Douglas's, "for that's only a wee ding on the drum."

She was leaning too close to him, and she knew she should resume her former place. But she could not. His eyes attracted and held her—they were gray, with an outer rim of black. So unusual, so deep and calm. Not the eyes of a mere boy, oh, no! Her heart beat faster, and she was suddenly short of breath, pierced by a feeling that was new, wild and sweet.

"Your hair is brighter than the fire, Margaret," he said.

In that moment she knew she loved him. He was a boy yet, but she could see the man he would become. Margaret said softly, "You have a flattering tongue, Douglas Douglas."

He started to smile, but even as his fine lips curved up at the corners, beads of sweat popped out upon his brow, and the smile turned into a grimace of pain. He swayed on his stool, lost his grip on the drum, and instinctively tried to reach for it with his wounded arm. "Aagh!" he cried, then bit his lips to keep silent.

Margaret leapt to her feet, ignoring the drum which hit the floor with a resonant thump. She wrapped her arms around Douglas's chest and helped him to stand, chiding gently, "You should be lying down, resting, not sitting on a stool in front of the fire. No wonder you're in pain! Come, let me help you back to bed."

"Mmf," said Douglas, suddenly too woozy to speak. He clung to Margaret. Sweat poured from his hot skin.

Margaret knew it was not heat from the fire that made the boy sweat so. Nor was it mere pain from his broken shoulder bone. She had seen this before: the sweating, the sudden raging fever that meant torn flesh was not healing right and had become tainted. People died from such tainted wounds, more often than not.

Douglas burned, but she was cold with fear for him. Her fear made her sound angry: "Walk with me, Douglas of clan Douglas, you great heavy lump of a boy! Were you trying to kill yourself by getting out of bed too soon? More likely you were trying to make everyone think you're some kind of hero—"

"Don't—unnh," he grunted, every step toward the bed on the other side of the small room an effort. "Don't fuss at me so, Margaret. I—unnh—I know I'm no hero."

"Don't talk. Walk!"

Locked side by side, lurching and swaying, they made their way to the bed. Margaret bent her knees, every muscle straining, and tried to deposit Douglas upon it gently. Moaning, barely conscious now, he toppled from her arms. Bustling, blinking back tears, she worked a pillow under his head, put up his feet, covered him with a woolen blanket, and on top of that, his own plaid.

Douglas thrashed, reaching out with his good arm. "The Golden Drum—" he cried hoarsely.

"Oh, all right, I'll get you your precious drum!" She flew across the room and swept up the drum from where it had fallen in front of the fire. When she returned, Douglas had lost consciousness. His black hair clung to his forehead in damp tendrils, his thick eyelashes lay like furry crescents upon cheeks flaming scarlet with fever.

"Don't you dare die on me, drummer boy!" Margaret commanded fiercely. She hugged his drum to her breast. The thing felt alive, seemed to beat as if it marked the beating of Douglas's heart.

Oh, Blessed Mother and all the Saints in Heaven, let him live, please let him live, Margaret prayed. Her tears rained upon the drumhead and trickled down the golden bands.

January 9, 1993

Maggie Ross whimpered and turned her face back and forth upon her pillow. Her eyes were wet with tears, but she did not awaken.

January 23, 1993

"Newspapers from the beginning of this month?" asked the librarian. "Daily or Sunday?"

"Both," said Maggie. "I don't really know the exact date I'm looking for, but it would have to be somewhere around the sixth. You see, there was this article—" She stopped abruptly, running a nervous hand through her thick hair. If she told the librarian that she was looking for a newspaper article about a Golden Drum because it was haunting her dreams, the woman would be bound to think she was nuts. She was beginning to think so herself.

"Ah, you're doing research." The librarian jumped to her own conclusion, eyes twinkling behind her glasses. "In that case, you probably won't mind the inconvenience of going down to the basement. You see, we only have space up here for a month's worth of Sunday papers and the current week of the dailies. We keep the rest downstairs for three months before putting them on microfiche. Come with me, I'll show you."

Maggie felt a rush of gratitude that loosened a tight place in her chest. "Thank you so much!" She followed as the librarian chattered on.

"There are plans to scan the newspapers onto laser disk instead of the microfiche, but that technology is changing so fast, and we really haven't any money to spare, so the powers that be are arguing about it. Here, we'll take the stairs rather than the elevator, if you don't mind."

"That's fine," said Maggie. Her mind and her body were impatient so near their goal, silently urging, *Hurry, hurry!*

"So anyway," the woman chattered, "it looks like we won't be getting the laser disks any time soon. Library politics, you understand. Storage of old newspapers is unfortunately a low priority for the people who set the budget." With a glance and a warm smile over her shoulder she added, "Not everyone, even in the library field, can appreciate the value of such things for people doing research."

"Mm-hm," said Maggie with a thin grin, hoping that her impatience didn't show. They walked through a dimly lit narrow corridor lined with shelves of untidy books and papers in all sizes and thicknesses. Their footsteps ticked on a cement floor, and the air felt damp—true basement atmosphere.

"Lucky for you that what you need is so recent—this way, we're almost there—because you won't have to deal with the microfiche reader. Those things are so hard on the eyes!"

"Mm-hm," said Maggie again, nodding as expected

although she wouldn't know a microfiche reader if she stepped on one.

"All right, here we are!" The librarian flipped a switch that instantly bathed their section of shelves in light. She pointed and said, "The Atlanta papers are here. If you should want to check the others—*Washington Post, New York Times,* and so on—for comparison, you'll find them over there. There are tables down yonder, against the wall, where you can sit. I'm sure you'll want to take notes."

"Yes." Maggie nodded. "Thank you so much."

"So I'll leave you alone now. You can find your way back all right?"

Maggie assured her that she could, then bent to the Atlanta shelves. The librarian's footsteps grew fainter, and soon Maggie was left in welcome silence.

She crouched and began to pull out newspapers, going back and back through the days. Her fingertips were soon black with old newsprint. January 7, 6, 5 . . . She folded her legs and sat down on the cold cement floor right where she was and began to scan the pages.

A few minutes later Maggie dropped a newspaper, and it rustled to the floor. She sat stunned by the paucity of what she'd found.

The feature article was tucked away at the bottom of a page in the January sixth paper. It was a mere two column inches of text under a head that said EPIPHANY=OLD CHRISTMAS. The article began by saying that before the introduction of the Gregorian Calendar in 1752, Christmas was celebrated on January sixth rather than December twenty-fifth. Then it went on to tell of isolated places in the United States that keep the old date and call it "Old Christmas." The part that mentioned the Golden Drum was a single paragraph:

In the tiny town of Rodanthe on the Outer Banks of North Carolina, they celebrate Old Christmas with an oyster feast and a procession featuring the legendary Christmas Drum. This drum, sometimes called the Golden Drum, is said to have magical powers due to the fact that it saved the life of a man shipwrecked off the coast of Cape Hatteras in the Great Hurricane of 1757.

That was all. It wasn't nearly enough. Where was the detailed description of the Golden Drum? The black and red lacquer, the crisscrosses, the golden bands? What about all the Scotland stuff?

"That's it, I've gone right over the edge. In my dreams, yet!" Maggie grumbled as she folded the papers neatly and restored them to the shelves.

July 15, 1746

Douglas Douglas was fighting for his life. Margaret Macquarrie, whose skills as a nurse had been learned a year earlier, when she was only twelve and tending her mother's deathbed, insisted on taking care of him herself. She had made a pallet in his bedchamber over her father's objections, and there she snatched what little sleep she could. Her red hair was tangled and matted; her hazel-green eyes, dark-shadowed with fatigue, made smudges in her young face.

For days upon days and nights upon endless nights, Douglas tossed and moaned and babbled and cried out in delirium. Margaret bathed his face and body with cool, damp cloths; she forced water and clear broth between lips that were cracked by fever; she cleansed his stinking wound. But he got no better.

Finally, desperate and half-delirious herself from exhaustion, Margaret harangued the Golden Drum. "You stupid, stupid drum! You sit there all bright and shining and perfect while your Master Douglas is coming apart. Is this what you saved him for? To die like this, when he could have died in the glory of battle if not for you? Do something, Drum, help me! You saved him once, help me to save him now!"

The sound of her own furious voice sobered her, and she sank to her pallet feeling ashamed. She should have been praying, not yelling at Douglas's drum. She was so tired . . . her mind went completely blank.

The drum began to beat by itself: Rat, tat, tat. Rat, tatta, tat. In her trance she did not hear it; or if she heard, she did so unaware.

Soon Margaret roused herself, got up from her pallet and

went to the door. She called a servant and said, "Bring me
whiskey." The old servant looked surprised but did as she
was told. Margaret took the bottle, thanked her, and closed
the door. Then she uncorked it, sniffed, and took a sip. On
its way down her throat the whiskey burned like fire, and a
look of satisfaction came upon Margaret's face. Yes, the
whiskey burned, and that was what she wanted. Where the
inspiration had come from she did not know, but her actions
were now swift and sure.

Margaret removed the bandage from the wound in
Douglas's shoulder. Once again, though she had changed it
not long before, the cloth was sodden with ugly pus.
Douglas did not stir; he had neither moved nor moaned for
a long time, and Margaret was sure that death was near.

She touched his hot face with cool, loving fingers and
whispered, "This will hurt, but you're going to live. The
whiskey will burn the poison out, I swear it!" She poured
the fiery liquid into the angry open wound.

Douglas groaned heavily and long; he twisted his torso,
but he was too weak to move much. With a grim smile on
her face, Margaret kept on pouring.

February 1, 1993

"Outer Banks? What Outer Banks—you mean Nova
Scotia? In the wintertime?" Rita's eyebrows arched up as far
as they could go in disbelief.

"Not Nova Scotia," explained Maggie quietly. "I think
that's the Grand Banks. The Outer Banks are in North
Carolina. And yes, that's where I'm going. Now, in the
wintertime. I leave tomorrow, and I'm taking two weeks."
She smiled. Now that her decision was made, she felt
relaxed and sure of herself for the first time in ages.

Rita took a sip of coffee, regarding Maggie over the rim
of her mug. They were taking a break in Maggie's office,
and both sat on high stools at her drafting table.

Rita was still not convinced. "I agree that you need a
vacation. Lord knows, you've been looking like death
warmed over ever since the first of the year. But you always
go to Florida. If you want something different, something

more interesting, why not Jamaica? Or Bermuda? Come on, Mags, you could afford it! *Nobody* goes to *North Carolina* for vacation; and *everybody* knows you go south in the cold months, not north!"

"So"—Maggie shrugged, looking away—"I'm different. We knew that already." She wished she could just tell Rita the truth, but she didn't dare. In the first place, confiding in people was difficult for her at the best of times. Secondly, now was not the best of times, and she just didn't want to get Rita recalling that old volcano theory.

The truth was that Maggie was being haunted by dreams, dreams that fascinated her, although upon waking she could recall only pieces of them, dreams that were somehow connected to the legendary drum that was supposed to have come to shore near a place with the mysterious-sounding name of Rodanthe, on North Carolina's Outer Banks. So she was going there, to see with her own eyes. It was a crazy thing to do, completely unlike anything Maggie had ever done in her whole life. And she was sure it was absolutely right.

Rita didn't give up easily. She said, "Yeah, but—"

Maggie interrupted as if she hadn't heard. "I'm going to the Outer Banks because that's where *I* want to go. Not Florida, not Jamaica, not Bermuda. I'm going to drive, and I have reservations in a town called Manteo. Sounds romantic, don't you think?"

February 2, 1993

Maggie drove north through undulating hills that were brown and sere with winter. The sky held a high white haze. There was no snow, but it was cold. At Charlotte the interstate bent eastward, and traffic increased. Six hours she drove; seven. Then she stopped for the night, as the auto club's map-giver had suggested, in Raleigh.

July 17, 1746

"Well," said Alexander Macquarrie, Lord of Dunkellen on the Isle of Skye, to his daughter, "I see ye didn't kill him with yer odd ministrations. Aye, he'll live now. Though like as not with what's to come, he may oft wish himself dead!"

"Father!" Margaret tugged the burly, gray-headed old man away from the bedside and hissed in a whisper. "You mustn't say such a thing. He might hear you!"

Douglas of clan Douglas slumbered on, his pale face gaunt but peaceful, his talisman drum at the bedfoot.

"The English will hunt the lad if they find out that he's still alive," said Alexander, "as they hunt all the Scots who survived the Battle of Culloden. He might be better off dead, and that's the God's own truth! The poor laddie has nae home to go to—did ye not know that, daughter? The English have seized the lands of the old Douglas that was the boy's father. I presume this lad's the heir, which makes him now the head of his clan, and survivors who are heads of clans are being captured and imprisoned. Executed, the most of them. Executed or not, his land's already forfeit."

"Does he, young Douglas, know that?"

"Nay, I doubt it. Word is only just beginning to reach us here on Skye, of the terrible reprisals against all who fought at Culloden. It hurts all the clans, lassie. They say there's an oath all Scots will have to take, swearing that we will never again bear arms except in the service of the King of England. What's worse, the clans are forbidden to wear the kilt or the plaid, or to play the pipes, ever again."

Margaret was aghast. Her mouth dropped open, and her eyebrows shot up. "Surely that canna be true! The bagpipes and the plaid, they make us who we are, Father!"

"Right, lassie!" her father growled, "Which is why they'd forbid them. The English would take the very souls of the Scots if they could!"

He threw back his broad shoulders and cleared his throat, recovering his composure. "Enough of that now. Young Douglas can stay here until he's recovered. But then he'll have to leave. We canna have him bringing more trouble on this house than what we have already. Come away, Margaret. You've saved the boy's life, but you've neglected your other duties for far too long."

"Yes, Father," she said obediently.

*   *   *

Later, deep in the night, Margaret stole back to Douglas's room and sat once more by his bed, watching him sleep. She reached out and smoothed the plaid that covered him—the muted greens and black of the Douglas clan. She looked down at the faded old plaid that she wore like a shawl over her shoulders, in the red and green of the Macquarries. She set her lips in a grim line. Mere laws could not separate a Scot from his tartan, never!

Douglas stirred. Margaret grasped his hand and leaned eagerly toward him. He opened his eyes and looked right at her. She stared into those eyes and saw that they were clear now, for the first time in weeks; she saw recognition of her own face hesitantly gather in their black-rimmed gray depths.

"Margaret!" Douglas exclaimed, and slowly, slowly, his mouth grew a smile.

"Aye, Douglas." She felt her own face alight with joy.

February 3, 1993

Maggie Ross woke smiling. She stretched luxuriously. No alarm-clock noises to jar her waking. How wonderful! She stretched again and then turned on her side, snuggling the soft blanket up to her chin.

Blanket, blanket . . . something about a plaid blanket. Different shades of green squares, with a black stripe; what do they call it? Sett, yes, that was it. Yes, there was a blanket in her dream, and last night for a change the dream had been good. He was going to live, whoever he was, the boy with the drum. So maybe she had finally dreamed her way to the end of it, this strange continuing story that had been coming to her almost every night for weeks. Not that she was ever able to remember much detail—she couldn't, which continued to be frustrating.

Anyway, thought Maggie, turning on her back once more and looking up at the ceiling of her motel room, *I'm glad he's going to live, whoever he is.* Or was: The dreams had an atmosphere of the past, of something that happened a long time ago.

But not my past, thought Maggie, wrinkling her brow. She knew perfectly well that she had never spent night after night tending a very sick young man!

Maggie's second day of driving was much different from the first. Route 64 out of Raleigh soon became a two-lane highway with none of the purposeful feel of an interstate. At first its rural meandering irritated Maggie, with her city-conditioned driving habits—especially if she happened to get stuck behind a slow-moving farm truck. But gradually she surrendered to the slower pace. She could feel herself letting go, letting go, letting go . . .

As she drove, Maggie worked on a theory that had occurred to her about her dreams: Maybe she'd seen a movie or TV show based on the Golden Drum tale and stored it in her subconscious mind. The newspaper had triggered it, and now the story was moving from the subconscious into her dreams. She liked the theory—it beat the heck out of worrying that there was something wrong with her mind!

Maggie stopped theorizing and started to pay attention to the countryside. It was getting interesting: Small towns with great colonial architecture began to crop up with regularity. Historical markers by the road suggested intriguing side trips, but Maggie would not be lured. The landscape became increasingly flat, sparsely treed, stark in the bleakness of winter.

When she had been driving for about four hours, Maggie sensed a subtle change in the air. She rolled down her car window and sniffed. Took a deep breath. It was sharp and clean and tangy, with a hint of the sea.

"Yes, yes!" Maggie cried. Her skin tingled, and her whole body came alive with anticipation. Soon the road became a long causeway, and then a bridge. She was crossing the Alligator River, which is not a true river but an inlet of the Albemarle Sound. To her left stretched the vast waters of the Albemarle, as far as her eye could see.

Maggie could not explain why she, a native Midwest-erner, became so entranced by the sea. She only knew that she could never get enough of it, and the more isolated was the beach, the more she loved it. Once again, she felt that she was going to the right place.

Now she was on a long, long bridge with water all around her. Though the water was choppy and gray due to the overcast sky, its wide majesty made Maggie shiver. She remembered names from her study of the map: the Albemarle Sound on her left, the Croatan Sound on her right. And just ahead, her first destination: Roanoke Island, and the town of Manteo, where she had a reservation at the Elizabethan Inn.

Rodanthe, the place mentioned in the article about the Golden Drum, was her final destination, but she could not stay there in the off-season. When she'd located Rodanthe on her map, she understood why: it was on Hatteras Island, at the spot where the spinelike curve of the Outer Banks bent farthest out into the Atlantic. Only the hardiest souls would want to be out there, exposed to winter storms.

The same map showed that Roanoke Island was sheltered between the spine of the Outer Banks and the mainland, and now as she left the bridge and drove onto Roanoke, she saw the benefits of that shelter: trees that were green even in winter. In just a few minutes she was in Manteo, where a small forest of masts rose up from the boats in another kind of shelter, the harbor.

The Elizabethan Inn, from the outside, lived up to its name with whitewash and crossbeams; on the inside it was as promised, a full-service hotel complete with restaurant, indoor heated pool, and fitness center. Maggie located her room, saw with approval that it was comfortable and even had a small refrigerator. She decided that she would stock it later so that she wouldn't have to depend on the restaurant for all her meals, but at the moment she was hungry—she'd eaten nothing since breakfast—and she headed back downstairs.

As Maggie ate a late lunch in the inn's dining room, outside the sky darkened, and the wind picked up. Driving across yet another bridge and on down to Rodanthe in what remained of the afternoon light didn't seem like a good idea. So she changed her plans and went to explore Manteo on foot instead.

*   *   *

The small-paned windows of a shop on a side street
glowed with light and drew Maggie like a beacon. She
approached and saw books on display in one window,
paintings of land and seascapes, mostly watercolors, in
another. She was intrigued, cold, and wind-battered, and the
shop offered shelter. She went inside. A bell tinkled as she
opened and quickly closed the door against the blast.

Her dark red hair, tossed by the wind and dampened by
the heavy mist, curled about her head in disarray. Her
cheeks burned, and she was slightly breathless, even a bit
dizzy in the sudden stillness of the shop. She tightened the
belt of her trench coat but loosened the green wool scarf at
her throat. She was the only person in the place, which did
not surprise her since there had been few people on the
street and no one else in the dining room at the inn while she
was eating lunch. The shopkeeper must have heard the bell
and would appear sooner or later. Maggie looked around,
appreciating the cozy atmosphere, and started to browse the
bookshelves along the walls.

A male voice said, "If you need any help, let me know."

The voice came from nearby. Maggie turned and saw a
man about ten feet away. He was tall and dark-haired, with
dark arches of eyebrows and a wonderful full beard that was
also dark, but streaked with gray on each side. He wore a
white turtleneck under a navy-blue-and-gray-plaid flannel
shirt, and dark gray trousers. He did not have the body or the
face of a person she'd picture to be a shopkeeper. He was a
big man who looked as if he had been carved by the
Elements, as if he belonged to Nature, to wind and water—
like a sailor or a fisherman.

"I, ah," said Maggie, suddenly self-conscious, "I mostly
came in here just to get out of the wind."

He came closer. She saw that he was smiling: The lips
that curved within the frame of beard and mustache were
full, sensual. He said politely, "You're welcome to stay as
long as you like."

"D-do you think this is the beginning of a storm? I was
driving all day, and I didn't have the radio on, so I haven't

the slightest idea about what the forecast is . . . or anything. . . ." Maggie moved closer, drawn to him.

"Might be. Nothing big though, maybe a day or so of hard rain, nothing to worry about. Is this your first time in Manteo? I don't recall seeing you here before." She could almost hear what he didn't say: "I'm sure I would remember."

Maggie nodded. "Yes. First time. My name's Maggie Ross. I'm from Atlanta." She shoved her hands down into the pockets of her coat, because she'd been about to offer a handshake, and that didn't seem the right thing to do. Yet she wanted to touch him.

"James Gentry." He did offer his hand, and after a moment's hesitation she took it. His clasp was firm, warm, brief. He said, "Your hands are freezing. I keep a pot of coffee on, for myself and customers. Would you like some? It'll warm you up."

"Yes, thank you. That would be very nice." Maggie followed him to the back of the shop, where a multicolored braided rag rug covered the floor in front of an old-fashioned wood-burning cookstove. There was a mottled blue enamel coffee pot on top of the stove and a couple of high-backed old wooden chairs on either side. She sat in one of the chairs and loosened her coat—the stove radiated warmth.

"This is half-caf," explained her host. "You know, half decaf and half the real stuff. You like sugar and cream?"

"Just black, thank you."

He poured, his back to her, then turned and handed her a pottery mug. She took it with both hands, gratefully. He turned back to the stove and poured a mug of coffee for himself; then pulled over a chair and sat near her, studying her as he sipped.

Maggie stared at the eyes that regarded her so steadily. They were calm, and kind, the most extraordinary eyes she had ever seen: the irises gray, ringed around their outer edges with black. Maggie felt dizzy again, as she had on first entering the shop. She gulped at her coffee, felt its heat down her throat, then looked again into his eyes. He smiled.

She said his name, as if she had known him all her life, unconsciously choosing the Scots diminutive: "Jamie."

His smile grew broader, touching those extraordinary eyes. He said, "If you like."

Then Maggie realized what she had done; she'd called a complete stranger by some kind of a pet version of his first name. How could she have done such a thing? Her cheeks flamed with embarrassment, and she floundered, making up an excuse. "I'm sorry, I guess I-I must have known somebody, or maybe you remind me of somebody who was a James, but we called him Jamie, I didn't mean—"

"I know you didn't," he said softly. Kindly. "I think I like Jamie. It's much better than Jim. You know, Maggie—you don't mind if I call you Maggie?" She shook her head, still blushing. "I know we've never met before, but I feel as if I know you from somewhere. That sounds like a line," he said, shrugging his big shoulders, "like I'm trying to be too familiar, but it's the truth."

"M-maybe we did . . . when we were children or something?"

Jamie shook his head. He leaned forward and put his elbows on his knees, holding his coffee mug in his hands. "Not possible, unless you came here for vacations when you were a kid. And it's not too likely even then. I come from a family of fishermen down in Wanchese. That's on the other end of the island. I didn't see much of the summer people—I was helping out on the boat summers, almost as far back as I can remember."

"Oh." She drank coffee. Her blush faded, and she felt wonderfully at ease, basking in his kindness. She was enjoying the silence, yet felt she should keep the conversation going. She ventured, "So this isn't your shop. You're a fisherman?"

Jamie leaned back in his chair, set his coffee cup on the floor, and laced his hands together over his flat stomach. "It's my shop—mine and the Dare Savings and Loan's."

Maggie was confused. "Dare what?"

"Dare as in Dare County. You really haven't been here before, have you?"

"I said I hadn't."

"Yeah, you did, it's just so damn hard to believe." He shook his head for emphasis and fell silent for a moment, seeming to stare at a spot on the braided rug. He said as if to himself, "You don't know the history of Roanoke Island, or you'd have recognized where the 'Dare' comes from. It's for Virginia Dare."

"Ah!" Maggie interjected. "Her I know about. Virginia Dare was the first English baby born in the colonies. I remember that from school. And I do know, of course I do, about Sir Walter Raleigh founding the first colony here on Roanoke Island in fifteen-whatever and they all disappeared."

"The Lost Colony."

"Yes. The lost colony. The baby was lost, too, Virginia Dare, I guess. It's sad."

"Yes, it is. Some people say that Virginia Dare survived and was raised by the Indians."

"Do you believe that?"

"No. None of the old families around here believe that, any more than they believe that silly business about Virginia Dare's ghost haunting the island in the form of a white deer. That kind of thing is for attracting tourists, such as yourself." He winked, not a suggestive wink but quick, playful.

"I guess I am a tourist. I don't feel much like one even though I just got here." Maggie set her now empty mug on the floor. "But anyway, you were telling me when we got off on the subject of Dares that this is your bookshop. But your family are all fishermen?"

"Yeah, my bookshop and art gallery. The art's upstairs in the loft. I keep it roped off in the winter. Art moves better in the summertime." He shifted his gaze again, as if this were a difficult subject. "I love the sea, but . . . If you just got here today, you can't have been down to Wanchese. It's interesting, you'll want to go there. Still a real fishing town, and there aren't too many of those left. For good reason. It never was easy to earn a living from the sea, but in my lifetime it's become damn near impossible.

"I have two brothers, and I was always the oddball. I liked school, loved to read from the first time I had a book in my hand and discovered that the letters made words and the words became stories. I used to sneak books onto the boat—I'd take them back to the library with the pages all puckered from salt spray." Jamie laughed softly at himself and with one hand rubbed his beard, fingers tracing down the silver lines. Then he continued.

"So when I saw which way the wind was blowing—economically, that is, when I was older—I decided to quit the sea. There was more money to be made from the tourists. I moved up here to Manteo, worked at this and that, and pretty soon the book-loving misfit former fisherman had a dream. This"—he gestured roundly with both arms—"is my dream. My own store, filled with books!"

Maggie was enchanted, and her eyes were shining. "It's wonderful."

James rubbed his beard, and his mouth curved in a rueful grin. "I think I just told you the story of my life. So. Now it's your turn."

Suddenly all Maggie's customary reticence rushed in and tied her tongue. "I, ah, I'm originally from the Midwest, but now I live in Atlanta—" she managed to say and found she couldn't go on. She tried to smile with something of his rueful touch, but her lips felt paralyzed. Cinching the belt of her trench coat, she stood up and did not notice that her green scarf fell to the floor. "I really have to go now. Thank you for the coffee and the company, and for letting me stay here long enough to get warm."

"The least you can do after letting me blabber on about myself," said Jamie, also getting to his feet, "is to tell me what brings you to the Outer Banks in the dead of winter."

Maggie wanted to tell him: the dreams, the Golden Drum, the desperate feeling that her life was going nowhere yet was at the same time running out of control. He was kind, she could tell, and understanding. He would listen. But she couldn't do it. A long, long habit of not trusting, of holding back for fear of being devastated by a relationship, stood in the way. So she strode purposefully toward the front of the shop, saying over her shoulder, "I just came for a vacation. I needed a complete change of pace. That's all."

Behind her Jamie chuckled—a wonderful low, intimate sound. "You'll get it, that's for certain." He reached out and closed his fingers over Maggie's shoulder, their pressure halting her and urging her to turn to him. She did. He looped her wool scarf about her neck, saying, "You forgot this. You'll need it."

"Thank you." She looked up into his eyes. His hand lingered at her throat.

In a husky voice he said, "I suppose it's too much to hope that you came to Manteo alone."

Maggie blinked. Her heart seemed to stop as she replied in a voice that matched his for huskiness, "I came alone."

October 2, 1746

"Those hills yonder," said Margaret, pointing, "are the Black Cuillins."

Douglas nodded obediently and wrapped his plaid more tightly around himself. The wind was fierce here on the cliff near Dunkellen Castle, but it didn't seem to bother Margaret. Nothing bothered Margaret; she was invincible, he was sure of it, and he was full of admiration as he gazed at her lithe form silhouetted against a cloud-filled sky. She wore a heavy black cloak that flapped about her, its hood uselessly down her back leaving her head bare, her magnificent mane of hair whipping about her head.

Margaret turned, brushed long red strands from in front of her eyes with an impatient hand, and continued Douglas's instruction. "And beyond that lie the Red Cuillins. They look higher because they have more of a pointed shape, but I think they're the same height, really. I prefer the Black because they're closer, they seem more like our very own mountains." She placed her hands on her hips. "Are you paying attention, Douglas?"

"Aye," he said, grinning up at her. He was quite content to sit at her feet. The climb up here had been embarrassingly difficult. His wound was well healed now, but his muscles were still weak from disuse. His convalescence had been long and hard. He urged, "Pray, continue."

"I will. If you're to go off on your own, walking to build up your strength, you need to know the lay of the land."

"That I do."

"Well, then. We Macquarries don't have much of a place, really. Just the house and this cliff and down to the sea, that's all. But on the other side, across the glen and up the hill—there, you see?" Douglas nodded, and she was satisfied, so she continued. "You come to the seat of the Macleods, Dunvegan. There's Dunvegan Loch, and on the other side is their castle. Did you ever hear about their flag?"

"I dinna think so, but I'm sure you're going to tell me."

This was one of Margaret's favorite stories. She sat down beside Douglas, scrutinized him for a minute, and decided that he looked cold. She scrunched closer to him and opened her cloak, wrapping it around the both of them. She began her tale:

"The flag of the Macleods is magic. It's a fairy flag."

Douglas chuckled. "Fairies, now!" He grasped the edge of the cloak and held it tightly, enjoying its warmth but enjoying more the warmth of Margaret's body so close to his.

"This is a true story, Douglas Douglas," she said, eyes flashing. "The fourth chieftain of the Macleods was married to a woman of the fairy folk. She lived with him there at Castle Dunvegan for twenty years, and when she left to go back to fairyland, she gave him the flag. She said if ever the Macleods should be in trouble, the clan's chief had but to raise the flag and all the fairies would fly to their aid. They say that twice since the Macleod has raised the flag, and the fairies have saved the clan from disaster."

"Are you a fairy woman, Margaret?" Douglas asked softly.

"Don't be daft, Douglas!" She turned her face to him, and their eyes locked—hers hazel—warm brown shot through with green—his calm gray ringed with black.

"I'm not daft," he said, moistening his lips, feeling a hot stab of rising desire that filled him with joy. Her face was close, so close; her lips looked soft, moist, inviting. Haltingly he declared as he inched his lips toward hers, "I think you must be a fairy, for you are magic and you have already saved me from disaster."

He kissed her: their first kiss, a kiss of fiery sweetness, a yearning and burning joining of young lips and wild hearts; a meeting of souls in a troubled, terrible time.

February 6, 1993

It had been raining on the Outer Banks for two days and was still raining. But at least the wind no longer howled and beat upon the inn's windows, or pushed at her body when she went outside. Maggie couldn't wait any longer. She set off to find Rodanthe—driving her car, driven by a dream.

Through the closed car windows, over the *thwack-thwack* of the windshield wipers, she heard the sea. She couldn't see it yet, but she heard the boom and shuss of surf. Maggie's heartbeat quickened. She had driven over yet another bridge from Manteo, and now she was on the real Outer Banks, on Bodie Island.

Boom, shuss, boom, shuss, a steady drone bass; over that, in counterpoint pranced the sharp, staccato beat of Maggie's heart. At Whalebone Junction the horizon opened up beyond her rain-spotted windshield, vast and gray. She turned south, stopped her car by the side of the road, and got out.

Maggie didn't notice the cold or the wind or the rain. She didn't notice how her booted feet slipped as she walked across the sand, or hear the seabirds cry overhead. The great Atlantic Ocean filled her eyes, her ears, her heart, and her soul.

"Ah-h-h-h!" Finally she let out a long, awestruck sigh. She felt all the knotted places inside herself loosen and dissolve. The ocean was disturbed, incoming waves swollen and frothed with foam, but Maggie Ross had found peace.

After a while she realized that her nose, hands, and feet were numb, and she returned to her car. She drove on south, reassured by the immense presence of the sea always at her left shoulder. The Bodie Island Lighthouse, with its black-and-white horizontal stripes, loomed ahead and to the right. She didn't turn off. Instead she went on across the Oregon Inlet on a bridge and now was on Hatteras Island.

Raindrops thinned out and became mere drizzle. Maggie drove on and on; for a good thirty of Hatteras Island's fifty-mile length, the only living beings she saw were four wild horses, standing in a miserable clump with their heads bowed against the drizzling cold. The landscape was wild and harsh; the unrelenting solitude unsettling. But at last she found Rodanthe, identified by a black-lettered sign over the post office building.

"If you don't mind me saying so, young woman, you look a bit bedraggled and forlorn."

Maggie jumped a foot. "I—I didn't hear you come up. I thought I was all alone out here." That was an understatement; she had seriously never felt more alone in her life than when she'd left Rodanthe a few minutes earlier. Her first wave of fear subsided; the man was old, looked harmless, and, judging by the gear he carried, she realized he was going to or coming from surf fishing.

He smiled. "My name's John Fortune. I thought I'd get in some fishing before nightfall, since the rain's stopped. If you want company, you can come along, and if not—well, there's plenty of beach out here for the both of us."

He had a wonderful face, pink-cheeked, seamed about the mouth, and crinkled around deep blue eyes that sparkled when he smiled. "I'll come along," said Maggie, "if you're not going far. I left my car up there at that lifesaving station—I'm sorry, I can't possibly pronounce its name."

"It's Chick-a-Mack-o-Meeko. Chicamacomico," said John, "and I'm just going up that way a few yards."

"Chicamacomico." Maggie tried it and liked the way the syllables rolled off her tongue. She also liked the old man. He had a comfortable bulky presence and walked with an easy gait. His clothes were not the clothes of a real fisherman—he wore one of those indestructible tweed hats with a wavy, turned-down brim, and a long, long scarf with horizontal stripes of many colors: red, purple, green, gold, brown, blue.

"You have a name, young woman?" he asked, setting his pail down in the sand.

"Maggie Ross."

The tide was out. "Maggie Ross. A lass of Scottish

heritage, by the sound of it," he said as with effortless grace he cast his line in a long arc, far out over the waves.

"I guess. My family doesn't much go in for searching out their roots and all that. They're salt-of-the-earth type Midwesterners."

"And what would you be doing all by yourself on the beach of Hatteras Island on such a desolate afternoon, Maggie Ross?" he asked with a wink.

Maggie grinned and shrugged. "Enjoying the desolation, I guess. What about you?"

"Me? I live here. Well, not *here* exactly. Like most people who live on the Banks year round, my cottage is over on the other side of the island. Not far from the Chicamacomico Station, across the road and down about a quarter of a mile."

"Oh!" Maggie was instantly hopeful. "You live here? I thought—I mean, you don't exactly look like a—what do they call themselves—a Banker."

John chuckled. "No, I'm not a true Banker, although I've been living on Hatteras a long time now. I retired here. I'm an eccentric old bachelor professor. I guess the professor part still shows, huh?"

"Yes, I guess it does." Maggie smiled, but she was disappointed again, as she had been in the town. She kept silent and watched the old man fish. Seagulls, attracted by the possibility of food caught by someone other than themselves, squawked and swooped over John's line out past the breaking surf. The drizzle had stopped. The waves, while still far from gentle, had settled down to a steady, majestic roll.

John said, as if picking up without a break in conversation, "Chicamacomico is, obviously, an Indian name. The Indians used to come here to fish, but they had more sense than to try to live on the barrier islands. The white folks—I mean the original Bankers—having less sense or maybe being more desperate, did settle here as far back as the late seventeenth century. They took the Indian name and called their settlement Chicamacomico. There wasn't a Rodanthe until the U.S. Government decided the Indian word was too difficult to use on a post office. So, when they started delivering mail here, they renamed the town Rodanthe.

Fortunately the old lifesaving station had the Indian name
and kept it for posterity."

Maggie glanced at John. He wasn't looking at her any
more than he was catching fish; he simply used his fishing
as an excuse to stand with the ocean breaking over the toes
of his rubber boots. He had an air of contentment so vast
that it reached out and enclosed her, too. She wanted to trust
him. And maybe there was still hope—if he knew that much
Outer Banks history. . . .

"That's interesting," said Maggie. "I was in Rodanthe just
now, before I came down to the beach. I, ah . . . there's
not much open in Rodanthe in the wintertime. But I went in
that kind of general store, and I tried to talk to the people,
asked a few questions." She ducked her head and dug the
toe of her leather boot in the sand. "I think they thought I
was a little crazy."

"Don't let it worry you. Folks are always cautious with
strangers in the winter. I think they feel like having to be
nice to tourists all summer is enough."

Water rose up in the hole she'd dug with her toe. Maggie
stepped back, shoving her hands into her pockets. "Well,
anyway, they were no help, said they didn't know what I
was talking about. And it was disappointing because I came
a long way. I don't know what I expected, but
something—"

"You know, Maggie, you're being awfully oblique. Tell
me straight out what it was you wanted, and maybe I can
help."

"I wanted to find out about the Golden Drum." Maggie's
lips quivered, but she forced herself to look straight at John.
"I read a story in a newspaper, in Atlanta where I live, about
how Old Christmas is celebrated on Epiphany in Rodanthe,
how there's a procession and they carry the Golden Drum.
That was all; it wasn't enough. So I came—" She stopped
short, biting her lip, afraid of revealing how insanely
important this had become to her.

"I've heard of the drum," said John. He reeled in his line
absently, not taking his eyes off Maggie. "But I think your
newspaper may have exaggerated. I don't know about any
processions, but that's not to say they don't happen. I stay to

myself in my cottage, one day's like another day to me. Thanksgiving, Christmas, *Old* Christmas, whatever."

"It's not the procession that's important to me, it's the *drum!* I-I want to find it, to see it again with my own eyes!" She could not keep the anguish from her voice or from showing on her face.

"Again?" John watched her intently.

"What? No, not *again.* I'm looking for the Golden Drum, I've never seen it. Except, except—" Maggie flung her hands out in a gesture of desperation. She could not say *"in my dreams."* She whipped her body away from the old man, and the sudden movement tore the green wool scarf from her head. The wind buffeted her ears and lifted her hair in a dark red halo.

A moment later Maggie felt a warm arm around her shoulders. John Fortune said, "I don't know for certain if the Golden Drum really exists, but I'd say it probably does. Or did. Don't lose heart, Maggie Ross. What you want is the truth. I can see it in your eyes. Here on the Outer Banks, where people were so isolated for centuries that the native speech pattern still sounds a little like Elizabethan English, the old stories were preserved pretty much intact. It's quite likely that the legends are grounded in truth."

"Tell me everything you know," Maggie begged, struggling to wrap the scarf around her neck. "Please."

"It's gotten too cold out here to fish. Let's walk back while I tell you." John picked up his still-empty bucket and started off. "There was a great hurricane in seventeen-something. I forgot the exact date, but it was a big enough storm that it shifted the banks, opened a new inlet. They had to change the maps—that's one reason why the storm is remembered. Another one is that a ship was wrecked off Cape Hatteras in that hurricane. The legend says that there was only one survivor of the shipwreck: a man who was washed ashore, clinging to that Golden Drum. He didn't drown, you see, because of it. So the drum became famous, got the reputation of being some sort of good luck charm."

Maggie could hardly breathe. The figures from her dream, the boy and the girl, seemed to hover just beyond the range of her vision. "What was the man's name? Where did he come from? What happened to him?"

John studied her face intently. His dark blue eyes probed deep, deep, until he seemed satisfied—he seemed to understand something that Maggie herself did not understand. Then he said, "I don't know. I've told you all I can. But don't give up, Maggie. There's a good reason this drum is so important to you. Don't give up until you find it."

"I won't," said Maggie, her mouth suddenly dry. She moistened her lips with the tip of her tongue. "I can't."

John Fortune smiled, a smile that came from his eyes as well as his lips, a smile of such warmth that Maggie's wind-chilled body felt enveloped by its rosy glow. Then without a word he turned and trudged on up the dunes to the lifesaving station. Maggie trudged at his side with a lighter heart.

As they reached her car, John asked casually, "Do you remember your dreams, Maggie?"

She pushed the hair out of her eyes, surprised. Wary. "Yes. No. I mean, why do you ask?"

He ignored her question and persisted, rephrasing his. "After you wake up, not briefly in the middle of the night, but when you get up in the morning, are you able to remember your dreams in any detail?"

Maggie opened the car door quickly and ducked inside. Why was the old man asking all these questions about dreams? He was making her nervous, ruining an otherwise pleasant end to her day. Unwilling to deal with the subject, she retrieved the car key from her pocket and shoved it into the ignition. "I have to go now."

John dropped his fishing rod and grabbed the car door, detaining her. "You can make yourself remember your dreams in their entirety, Maggie. All you have to do is tell yourself before going to sleep that you will remember them, and you will. If you wake up in the middle of the night, write them down before going back to sleep. Do it, and I promise you'll learn things about yourself that are important. And come back and see me again before you leave the Outer Banks. I'll be down on the beach or at my cottage. I'm easy to find."

Maggie made promises that she was not sure she would keep. She had liked John Fortune at first, but now, as she drove back to Manteo, the more she thought about him the more uncomfortable she became.

November 11, 1746

"Wake up, Douglas! And be quiet! You have to hide," said Margaret in an urgent whisper.

It was dark in the room Douglas had occupied since coming to Castle Dunkellen on the Isle of Skye. The fire had died to glowing embers; the only light was from the candle in Margaret's trembling hand. Douglas was not used to danger here, and his head was slow to clear. He blinked and rubbed his eyes. Already she snatched his plaid from atop his blankets and thrust it at him. Then she snatched it back.

"What am I thinking? You can't wear this anymore, it's forbidden! And if they should catch you—oh, dear God! Hurry!"

"You'll not take my plaid," he growled, slowly comprehending.

"All right, but you can't wear it. Get dressed quickly. I'll find you a cloak." Margaret flew from the room.

When she returned, Douglas had dressed haphazardly in the dark. His black hair was tousled, but by the light of the candle she could see that his eyes were alert. He asked, "What's happened? And where are you taking me?"

Margaret gave him her mother's old gray cloak—she'd been a tall woman, so it should cover him well enough. "There's a secret room—only the family knows about it. I'll tell you more when we're there. Come on, hurry!"

She bustled him to the door, but in the doorway Douglas stopped. "I'll not go anywhere without the drum."

Margaret stamped her foot. "That damn drum!" One look at the stubborn set of his jaw told her that argument would only waste time. "Get it, then."

The golden bands winked at Douglas as he seized the drum and wrapped it in the plaid of his clan. He secured the bundle firmly in the crook of one arm and allowed Margaret to grab his other hand. She pulled him along with her down the darkened stone corridors of her large house, the candle flickering in the gust of their rapid progress.

The secret room was dank and cold and cramped, a mere hole hidden beneath a turning of the stair in the old stone tower. Neither of them could stand; there was barely enough room for them to sit facing each other. Douglas held the drum between his knees. Margaret set the candle on the floor between them. Its tiny flame steadied; in its glow Douglas saw that Margaret's hair was wildly disheveled and her face looked raw, as if she had been crying.

He asked softly, "What has happened, Margaret?"

Tears pricked at her eyes again. "The English came to the Macdonalds' seat, Castle Armadale, on the eastern end of the island. They arrested Cousin Flora. They'll take her to London, to the Tower!"

Douglas was shocked. He had felt safe on the Isle of Skye as the months went by, and Flora was a heroine, well loved and protected by the people. He'd thought nothing could happen to her. "Och!" he said.

"That means they've learned that Flora helped the Prince escape. If they know that, then they may also know about you—that you survived the Battle of Culloden, that you were in South Uist with the Prince until the Macdonalds persuaded my father to take you in. He says you can't stay here any longer. You have to go, by boat, as soon as it's light. And oh, Douglas, Father says you have to go alone. He won't send anyone, not even one of the servants. I begged him, but he has set himself against you, because he fears you bring only trouble, Douglas." Margaret could not keep her tears from brimming over. She was frightened, and her heart was breaking.

"Hush, lassie," said Douglas, reaching out to smooth her wild red hair. "Don't cry."

"I can't help it. I'm so afraid. They could execute Flora—Father says they probably will. She's a woman, but she's a Scot. And you know Flora—she won't cooperate, she won't be a docile prisoner, she won't keep her mouth shut. She's so proud and strong-willed!"

"If that's so," said Douglas, smiling, still stroking Margaret's hair, "then she's very much like you."

This caused Margaret to wail, "Oh, Douglas! I can't lose both you and Flora! I can't bear it!"

"Hush, lassie. Don't cry anymore." Douglas moved the drum aside, and the candle, and held out his arms. "Come and sit by me. We'll keep each other warm until the light comes."

Margaret let him wrap her in his arms, but she refused to take comfort. Aloud, Douglas began to make plans. He would sail down to Iona, where the priests would help him. Margaret protested that he was a Highlander; he couldn't handle a boat. He had to remind her that Highlanders did indeed sail upon the lochs. She said it wasn't the same, he would be dashed upon the rocks. And in like manner she countered every plan he ventured until Douglas gave up and simply held her.

Chinks of gray light seeping around the door of the secret room told them it was morning. Their candle had long since guttered out. Margaret heard the steps of the servant who would lead Douglas down the cliff to where the boat was hidden. From there, he would go on alone. Douglas also heard. He planted a kiss on Margaret's cheek, unwound his arms from about her, and reached for the Golden Drum.

"You can't take the drum with you, Douglas," said Margaret in alarm. "It would be like wearing a sign around your neck: Here stands Bonnie Prince Charlie's drummer boy!"

Douglas set his mouth in a grim line. "I will not part with the Golden Drum, Margaret, not even for you. This drum is my talisman, and it's also a symbol to those who still support the cause of the Stewarts. There are more of us out there, I know it, and I will find them. You haven't paid attention to a word I've said!"

"No! Oh, no!" Margaret's fingers scrabbled at the drum's slick surface and caught in a crisscross of golden cord. The servant's footsteps were near. Margaret said in a hoarse whisper, "Don't do this. I fear for you. I-I love you, Douglas."

"We are both too young to speak of love," he said, forcing his heart to harden, for he knew that he went into danger. "Let go of the drum, Margaret."

She shook her head and closed her fingers tighter. The door opened, and Douglas wrenched the drum from her grasp. He stepped out of the secret room.

"You care more about that stupid, stupid drum than you do about me!" Margaret screamed, shaking her fists at Douglas from where she still sat.

He turned and said, "No, I don't. You'll hear from me."

She saw his lips move but didn't hear the words he said, for the sound of her own hysterical sobbing filled her ears. Anger and despair were tearing her to pieces.

February 7–12, 1993

When Maggie Ross woke, she remembered it all.

"That's what I get for listening to that strange old man," she mumbled. She sat, miserable, on the side of her bed with her head in her hands. Her pillow was damp from the tears she'd shed, right along with the girl—what was her name? *Margaret!*—in her dream. Maggie shivered; her own name, technically, was Margaret, though no one ever called her that.

Maggie showered and dressed and munched her way through a breakfast of cold cereal and orange juice from the small refrigerator in her room. By the time she was done eating, she'd convinced herself that she no longer wanted to know anything more about the Golden Drum. Not only that, but she'd forget what she already knew! The drum was bad, an ill omen, as last night's dream had clearly showed. That dream was a good place to stop all this nonsense, this obsession. As for John Fortune—well, maybe he did know what he was talking about where dreams were concerned— he'd said that if she told herself that she would remember, she would, and he'd been right. To her sorrow, for some things it was better to know nothing about.

"It should work just as well in the opposite way," Maggie mused as she rinsed her bowl and glass in the bathroom sink. "If I tell myself that I will *not* remember, then I won't. So that's what I'll do. I don't have to see John Fortune again. I just won't go back there. Enough is enough!"

Maggie looked up into the bathroom mirror. For a split

second she saw *her*, Margaret. She blinked, frowning, and there was her own face. She touched its contours in the cool glass, murmuring, "I don't look a thing like her. My hair is short and a much darker red, my face is a different shape, and I'm more than twice as old."

She watched her image blush as she realized what she was doing, then turned away from the mirror. Maggie screwed her eyes shut, clenched her hands into fists, and swore an inner oath: *I will not give in to this obsession, never again. NO MORE GOLDEN DRUM!*

There. She felt much, much better. Now she could get on with her vacation, enjoy herself, get the real rest that vacations are all about. With any luck, Jamie would be waiting for her downstairs, just as he had been every day since they'd first met.

He was waiting. In their short acquaintance they had fallen into an easy routine: Since he didn't open the bookshop until noon during the winter months, Jamie spent mornings being Maggie's guide to Roanoke Island and the Outer Banks. He showed her the Museum of the Outer Banks; the *Elizabeth II*, a replica of Sir Walter Raleigh's ship anchored in Manteo's harbor; the Elizabethan Gardens, where in summer the outdoor drama *The Lost Colony* was performed. He drove her to Nags Head, to the great sand dunes of Kitty Hawk, where even on a blustery cold day some idiots with Wright Brothers' disease were hang gliding; he promised in future days to take her to all the lighthouses on the Outer Banks, and up to a place with the odd yet charming name of Duck. But Jamie said no more of Wanchese, where his family lived, and he apparently did not intend to take her there.

Afternoons Maggie was on her own, but in the evenings she met Jamie at his bookshop when he closed up at six, and they went somewhere for dinner. After dinner they wandered, on foot usually, sometimes in his car or hers. They walked the beach by moonlight if the wind was not too stiff. More often than not they ended up back at his shop, Jamie poking up the fire in the old wood-burning cookstove, then searching for some special book he wanted to read to her.

Jamie had a beautiful reading voice, a baritone measured

and cadenced but without pretense, and most often he read poetry. He never took her to his house; she didn't even know where he lived, and though she sometimes wondered why, she thought it was probably for the best. He seldom touched her, beyond holding hands as they walked; he had never kissed her. But there was an unmistakable light in his eyes when he read to her, and his voice was like a caress.

On her afternoons alone Maggie Ross could almost feel herself growing, opening up like a flower. She was painting again, overjoyed to find that her creativity had not died during the eight years she'd intentionally strangled it in order to earn a living at commercial art. She worked in oil pastels on a large, rigid-backed sketchbook. She'd purchased both in an art supply store she had seen in Nags Head on an early outing with Jamie. When she went back to the store alone, she'd wanted to equip herself with an easel and canvas and scads of tubes of oil paints, but that wasn't practical. She had no studio space here, she'd be working outside in the wind, so the pastels were a good compromise. The weather held good after those first two days of rain, and every afternoon Maggie chose her spot, sat down on the sand or a wooden pier or a handy rock, and worked until the light faded.

She had one special painting that she saved for those last precious minutes of light, and each day she added to it: it was a sunset seascape, in which she tried to capture the exquisite shadings from gold to orange, then rose, then purple, and finally magenta, reflected up onto low-lying clouds and down onto the water by the setting sun. As the days passed, Maggie gradually became aware that she was painting this for Jamie. She would give it to him when she left on the fourteenth of February. On the eleventh she realized that the sunset painting—Jamie's painting—had become a labor of love.

On the twelfth of February, Maggie had to stop earlier than usual and go back to the inn to change clothes before dinner. The previous night, Jamie had fought down embarrassment to ask her if she had brought a dress with her. The restaurant he wanted to take her to on her next-to-last night in the Outer Banks was a coat-and-tie kind of place, he'd explained. Fortunately she'd stuck a dress in her bag at the last minute, just in case. Now she was glad she had.

Maggie seldom wore dresses, so when she acquired one she didn't mind making an investment. This was her favorite, although she hadn't brought it for that reason, but because it packed well: a pure cashmere knit, with long sleeves, scarf neckline, and a gently flaring mid-calf skirt, in a soft shade of green that brought out the green flecks in her hazel eyes. She'd forgotten the gold pin that she usually wore with it, but no matter; the dress itself was elegant enough without the touch of gold.

As Maggie critically surveyed her appearance in the mirror and thought about a touch of gold, something flashed behind her eyelids, just out of sight, at the edge of awareness. She ignored it, leaning toward her image to brush a little color on her cheekbones. They didn't really need it, since she was already slightly flushed with excitement. She stepped back, a flutter of panic in her stomach.

It's okay, she told herself, *just two more nights and one more day, and you'll be gone. You won't have to see him again, so you can't mess it up! Or mess myself up,* she thought, reaching for her purse. She definitely did not want to mess herself up now that she had finally begun to feel so much better! She took one last glance in the mirror, then threw her trench coat over her arm and went downstairs.

Maggie's heart caught in her throat when she saw him. The dark suit Jamie wore gave him an air of immense masculine power held under civilized constraint. He saw her, smiled, and began to walk toward her, and Maggie felt a rush of physical pleasure simply looking at him. The handsome beard, the incredible dark-lashed eyes, the sheer size of him, the animal grace with which he moved—

"Hi," said Maggie, before she got any more carried away, "don't we look gorgeous all dressed up!"

Jamie's glance swept her from head to foot, his lips curved appreciatively within the framing beard, and he reached for her coat. "I don't know about we, but you're more than gorgeous. You're beautiful."

Maggie rolled her eyes, glad she could turn her back as

she slipped into her coat. By the heat that was furiously burning up her neck and into her cheeks, to the very crown of her head, she knew that she was caught in just about her worst blush ever. She had always hated blushing; it made her feel somehow guilty even when there was nothing to be guilty about.

Jamie looked down at her, amused, as he ushered her through the inn's door. On the quiet street, in air that blessedly cooled Maggie's cheeks, Jamie tucked her under his arm and said, "I love it when you blush like that."

"I don't, I hate it!"

Jamie gave his low, intimate chuckle. It sent chills down her spine. Maggie felt she was coming apart with the pleasure of being near him—hot one minute, chills the next—and wondered what she would do if he ever made love to her. She would probably die of sheer joy.

The restaurant was in Nags Head on the water, a small, discreetly elegant place. The atmosphere, the food, everything was as special as Jamie had said it would be. Maggie wondered, as she toyed with an after-dinner brandy that she didn't need and probably shouldn't drink, if she dared invite him up to her room tonight. She wanted him, desired him. She had never been in this situation before; usually she was trying to find a graceful way to say no to men, yet here was Jamie who wouldn't even ask her!

"I can't believe that we have only one day left," he said.

"And two nights," she said quickly, then wished she hadn't, and gulped at her brandy.

"Yes, and two nights." A slow smile spread over Jamie's face. "But it's still not enough."

"I know," she agreed unhappily.

"You seem to like the Outer Banks, to have a real feel for this place. In fact, I think it agrees with you. You've changed since coming here, Maggie, you've kind of . . . opened up. Blossomed."

He was right, of course; she hadn't realized that it showed. Yet out of habit she shrugged, discounting. "That's what vacations are for, isn't it? I was exhausted when I came, and I'm not anymore. That's all."

Jamie was silent. He gazed out of the window next to

their table, although there was nothing but the night and an invisible dark sea beyond their dim reflections. Maggie sensed that he was gathering something inside himself. She felt it, and felt a thrill of her own expectation rising in response.

He turned back to her and stretched out his hand, palm up on the table. He looked into her eyes, fingers beckoning, and she placed her hand in his waiting palm. "Do you really want to go back to Atlanta?" he asked.

"I—" Her words stuck in her throat. She didn't want to think about going back, she wanted only now, only tonight, with him. . . . Yet she felt the desires within her die even as Jamie's hand tightened over her fingers. She forced herself to say what she truly believed. "I don't have a choice. I have to go back."

"Is there—are you committed to someone there, Maggie? A man? Or a woman, even? A—what do you call it—significant other?"

"N-no." She could no longer bear his touch. She took her hand back, clasped both hands tightly in her lap. "It's just my job. I have to work, Jamie. I've pretty much painted myself into a corner with that job. It's the only thing I know how to do to support myself."

He leaned back and let out a long breath through his nostrils while a huge grin spread across his face. "A job! Is that all? I was afraid there was someone else."

"There's no one else," said Maggie, puzzled. How could he have thought that?

He answered the unspoken question. "You seem so reticent, so skittish. Just when I think you're about to come close, you shy away. Over and over again."

"I didn't realize—" Maggie swallowed hard and took a terrific risk. "I don't want to shy away from you, Jamie. In fact, just the opposite."

"Maggie!" His voice stroked her with the way he said her name, a luxurious, yearning stroke that matched the desire in his gray eyes.

And Maggie, quivering inside, saw out of the corner of her eye a figure approach their table. By his many-colored scarf, which tonight trailed to his knees over a suit of Harris tweed, she knew him: John Fortune.

"Hello, hello!" he hailed, coming to a halt at tableside. "What great luck finding you two here together. I should have known, should have known. Hello, James. Maggie, I'm glad to see you're still in the area. I thought you'd forgotten your promise."

"Do you men know each other?" Maggie asked Jamie, incredulous.

"I was going to ask you the same thing," Jamie replied, then remembered his manners, rising. "Sit with us, John. We've eaten, but you could join us in coffee and a brandy."

"No, thanks." John beamed, his eyes twinkling in their network of cheery lines. "I was on my way out when I caught a glimpse of you. I just came over to say how nice it is to see two of my favorite people together." He winked at Maggie. "You look lovely, Maggie Ross. Don't you forget—I'm expecting you!"

John Fortune was a compelling man. Maggie found herself saying, "I know, I'm come. Tomorrow."

"Good, good. James, I'll drop in at the shop soon. Good night, children!" A final wink and a nod, and he walked away.

Laughing and shaking his head, Jamie sat down once more.

"How well do you know that man?" Maggie asked urgently.

"I know him very, very well." Jamie was smiling. "The question is, how do *you* know him, when you've been here such a short time?"

"No, you first." Jamie's smile relieved her somewhat, but she still had reservations. "Tell me about him, please, it's important."

"John Fortune was my first customer when I opened the bookshop, and he's still my best customer. He's the most intelligent person I've ever known, and more. John has taught me things, told me what to read. . . ." Jamie fell into a brief reverie, then roused himself. "I guess the reason John is so important to me is that from the very first he understood me, and nobody in my family ever did. Okay, so he's on the weird side, but in a good way. And he doesn't take to many people, though I'm not surprised he took to you. So now, tell me how you met him."

"My third day here, when the rain let up, I drove down to Rodanthe. . . ." She let her voice trail off, not wanting to finish what she had started to say. She didn't want the Golden Drum obsession to get hold of her again.

Jamie waited, and when the pause became awkward, he filled it by asking, "Why Rodanthe? There's nothing down there. Oh, you must have gone out on the pier, to see the wrecks."

"What wrecks?" asked Maggie, glad to think of something different.

"Old shipwrecks. Winter storms uncover them from time to time, and you can see them from the pier in Rodanthe."

"Oh. No, I didn't know about that, and looking at old wrecks is not my idea of a good time—I don't think I'd want to see them. Anyway, I did go there and I parked at that lifesaving place, Chick—chic—" Her tongue tangled.

"Chicamacomico. Great name, isn't it?" Jamie grinned.

"Yes. Chicamacomico. I parked there and went down to the beach, and there he was. John Fortune. We got into a conversation." She was determined to say no more, and thrust her chin up, a little defiant. "That's all."

"You promised him you'd see him tomorrow." Jamie studied her across the table. "There's something you're not telling me, something important."

Maggie sighed. She felt as if she'd been on an emotional roller coaster for the last hour, and she just wanted to get off. She surrendered, the best way she knew how. In a small voice she said, "I don't want to talk about it. Just take me home with you, Jamie. Please."

He took her home, to his tiny A-frame of weathered cypress on Croatan Sound. Jamie made love to Maggie with exquisite slowness, giving most graceful pleasure. She felt herself split apart from sheer joy, and he put her back together again with love. He did not take her back to the inn, he kept her with him. Maggie slept all night in Jamie's arms.

July 3, 1752

"Douglas! Douglas! Oh, Douglas, you've come!" cried Margaret, rushing down the cliff path to meet him.

"Aye, that I have," he said, opening his arms. When he closed them again, he held a full-grown woman. They were both eighteen, and he had not seen her for five long years.

After she'd fair squeezed the life out of him, Margaret stepped back. "You've grown taller," she said critically, "and broader, too. And your hair's too short. Have you become a Hanoverian then, with your short hair?" She wasn't serious, he could tell—her eyes were dancing.

"Never," he said, "and besides, you've got the wrong bunch. The ones with the short hair were Puritans, and I believe they're all dead now." He reached down to pick up the pack he'd dropped when she came rushing toward him. He peeled it back at the top, and gold gleamed out. "You see, Margaret, I still have the drum. I'm still a Jacobite and I work for the Prince's cause."

She rolled her eyes and tried to look exasperated, but she was too happy to achieve it. "I expected no less. It's a miracle you're still alive. Come, let's go up to the house. How long can you stay?"

"Not long." As he said the words he regretted them. In his memory of Margaret, she had always been beautiful, in body as well as in spirit, but now she was so lovely she took his breath away. In typical defiance she wore a dress of the bright red Macquarrie plaid, and her hair, no less bright, was tamed in a net upon her neck. She, too, was taller, and thinner, small-waisted yet full-breasted, and she moved with a woman's grace.

"I fear my father willna be glad to see you," she said over her shoulder.

"Some people are, and some people aren't," said Douglas philosophically. He traveled all the time now, on the run, for the English knew of his activities. He tried unceasingly as he ran from them to raise money for Bonnie Prince Charlie's return. He had not yet given up hope of seeing the Stewarts back upon the throne.

* * *

Margaret came to Douglas in the night, clad only in a thin white bedshift. She carried a candle, which made him think of his last night in her father's house, all those years ago. She placed the candle on the table near the bed and climbed in beside him.

Margaret said, "I'm a woman now, Douglas, and I've not been with any man. Take me, show me how, for I'll never love any but you."

He took her, trembling with happiness. She learned quickly.

The next night Margaret came to him again. He was waiting for her, already erect and throbbing with tense anticipation. She pulled off her shift without a hint of shame and stood naked, proud as any goddess, her perfect breasts and fiery red thatch glowing in the candlelight.

"Do you find me pleasing, Douglas Douglas?" she asked.

"You know I do," he growled, reaching for her.

Laughing, she fell into his arms and immediately thrust her tongue into his mouth. Now that she was no novice, Margaret made love the way she did most things: with ferocity and abandon. She wore him out with pleasure.

Toward dawn, Margaret shook Douglas awake. "We have to talk," she said.

He groaned but opened one eye. "About what?"

"You leave today."

"Aye. That canna be helped, you know."

"I know. I want you to take me with you, Douglas."

"What?" He was awake in a shot and pushed himself up on one elbow to look at her. "Are you daft, woman? Your father would kill me! And like as not, you, too!"

"He'd have to catch us first. And he won't, he wouldn't come after us, Douglas, and he won't kill us. Not if you marry me."

"Och!" exclaimed Douglas, falling back upon the pillow. He threw his arm over his eyes, unable to look at her and for a time unable to speak. Margaret snuggled against him, her head in the hollow of his upthrown arm.

In a small voice she whispered, "Please?"

For a dangerous while he allowed himself to dream: of a croft somewhere, in an isolated spot where no one would find them. A farm, some sheep, just enough of a place to eke out a living . . . But there was no such place, and he knew it. He stroked Margaret's hair and said sadly, his arm still shielding his eyes, "I canna do it, Margaret. I'm a hunted man, I must keep moving from place to place. I have no land, no home. I canna make a place for you."

"I'll run with you," she said. She sat up and coaxed his arm down, forcing him to look at her. Her beauty struck him to the heart.

"No."

"You don't love me, then."

"Of course I love you! I've loved you since we were no more than children. I doubt not that I will love you until the day I die!"

"And I love you. We belong together. It's very simple. So take me with you."

"Oh, lassie, my love, my love." Douglas lightly traced the contours of her face, her neck, her white sloping shoulder. Now touching her brought pain, worse than any wound. "Be patient. Stay here. I'll try to find a way for us to be together, but—"

"But what?" Margaret was getting angry now. He could sense her temper like a pulse beneath the surface of her skin.

"But you should not defy your father. He won't want us to marry, you know that. He will want you to make a better match, someone with money and property, and I have none. All I have is my life—"

"And the Golden Drum!" snapped Margaret. "Listen to me, Douglas Douglas. If you don't take me with you, I'll follow. I'll find you, and I'll stay with you. I'm not a child, and my father cannot force me to do anything I don't want to do!"

"Oh, Margaret, you're wrong. Alexander Macquarrie is feared and respected by many, and he's far, far stronger than any daughter. Even you. I fear you have too much pride, Margaret."

She tossed her head. Red hair flew. "I don't think pride is a sin. I think it's a virtue. And I will follow you, I swear it!"

Douglas was desperate with fear for her. "One year. Wait one year," he begged, and in his desperation made a rash promise. "A year is not so long. I'll come back then, I swear it, and perhaps things will be different."

Margaret's anger vanished like mist in the sun. She smiled and threw herself upon him, kissing him boldly and plunging her hands beneath the covers, reaching between his legs. She said in a low, arousing voice, "If I'm to wait a whole year, Douglas, then you must give me enough pleasure now to last that long!"

Maggie reached for Jamie; her hand between his legs made him instantly hard, and he awoke. He rolled toward her and saw that her eyes were closed, her breathing slow and regular. She was asleep, yet she stroked him, and in her sleep she smiled. Jamie was deeply, deeply moved. He let her stroke him until he could stand the arousal no longer, and then he began to touch her, too. He would wake her with his love.

February 13, 1993

Maggie found John Fortune's cottage with no trouble at all, for there was only one road—more of a track—opposite the lifesaving station, and only the one cottage on that road. Smoke curled from its chimney and was snatched up by the wind. She squared her shoulders resolutely, got out of the car, went up to the door, and knocked.

"I said I would come, and here I am," she said with a touch of defiance when he opened the door.

"Welcome, welcome, come in!" John stepped back with a flourish, and Maggie entered a room full of muted colors and warmth. Books were everywhere—on shelves lining the walls, on tables, chairs, and in piles on the floor. Antique maps filled what wall space was not already taken by books; a large, well-worn oriental rug with a geometric pattern covered most of the floor, and a fire burned in a fieldstone fireplace. It was impossible to feel uncomfortable in such a room.

She let him take her jacket, seat her on a soft couch, and

hand her a cup of steaming coffee. Guardedly Maggie looked at John. In a red sweater, baggy trousers, and argyle slipper-socks, he somehow matched the room.

"Thank you for coming," he said. "I sense that you didn't really want to."

"No, I didn't."

"What about the dreams—did you do as I suggested?"

"Yes and no."

John raised his bushy eyebrows in inquiry.

"I did what you said, and it worked. But . . ." Maggie turned her face away from him and gazed into the fire. She found no guidance there and could only proceed blindly. "But the dreams have been . . . disturbing. The one I remembered in detail, after talking to you that day, was terrible. Deeply upsetting, not the kind of thing anyone would want to recall. So—" Now she looked again squarely at John. "I have discovered that your prescription works equally well when employed for an opposite purpose."

"Ah!" He linked his fingers over his ample stomach. "In other words, you have chosen not to remember, and succeeded."

"Exactly."

"You have a very strong will, Maggie Ross."

She was surprised. "I wouldn't say that I'm strong-willed, no."

"That is because so much of your strength is tied up in self-deception. Just think what else you could do with all that strength if you would only let go!"

Zap! thought Maggie, but she sat up straighter. She knew how to take criticism: You don't listen, you think of something else, and above all, don't protest.

But John Fortune was a powerfully compelling personality, and she found herself listening to him.

He said, "Dreams come from the deepest part of the self. They cannot lie. Their truth is often veiled in symbolism that can be interpreted only by the dreamer or a highly skilled interpreter."

"And do you think you are such an interpreter, John Fortune?" Maggie challenged.

He shook his head. "No. For that I recommend the

Jungians." He turned his attention to a crowded little table beside his chair and rummaged around until he finally came up with a pipe. "Do you mind if I smoke?"

She shrugged. At the moment she was not disposed to feel kindly toward the man. "It's your house and your life, and pipes are supposed to be less lethal than cigarettes. So I guess I don't mind."

"Hum." He set about the lengthy business of getting the pipe filled and lit, saying casually, "And they are your dreams, and it's your life. I would be less than true to myself, however, if I failed to point out that your unwillingness to examine your own dreams is necessary to maintaining self-deception. By the way, if you want more coffee, there's a pot on the warmer in the kitchen."

"I'm fine." The polite lie. She wanted to leave but felt glued to the couch.

John leaned back with a sigh and began to puff contentedly. He did have a pleasant face, Maggie gave him that—like a large, pink-cheeked elf. He puffed a couple of smoke rings that rose, slowly spreading, to the ceiling. He said in an offhand manner, "I was able to get a little more information about that legend, if you're interested."

Maggie's mouth went dry. She decided to hear him out—after all, she was leaving tomorrow. What did it mater now?

He took her silence for assent and went on. "The year of the great hurricane in which the Golden Drum came ashore near here was 1757. The man whose life was saved stayed here on the Outer Banks, and in gratitude he gave the drum to the family who pulled him from the sea. Their descendants still have it. The drum has never been on display in a museum or anything like that. I was told they live in Wanchese now."

Wanchese! "It's—it's not Jamie's family, is it?"

"Jamie?" He didn't miss the Scots connection in the nickname—very interesting.

"I call him Jamie. Your friend, James Gentry."

"No, it's not his family."

Maggie looked disappointed.

"Have you told James about your interest in the Golden Drum?"

"No. In fact, I'm not interested in it anymore." Not realizing that she was contradicting what she'd just said, Maggie asked, "Did you find out the name of the man, the one whose life was saved by the drum?"

John Fortune relied a good deal on intuition, and his intuition told him now to keep the name to himself. So he shook his head. "There's one last bit of interesting information, though. The drum is said to beat by itself when anyone closely connected with it is in danger. I talked to people who swear that's true. For instance, a couple of years ago a hurricane was predicted to hit the Outer Banks in the fall. The drum did not beat then, and that hurricane skirted us, doing little damage. Then in the winter there was a huge nor'easter that the weather forecasters paid little attention to, but the Golden Drum made quite a racket. And that storm shifted sand dunes, ate up houses, blew out windows, and knocked out power for three days!"

Maggie smiled in spite of herself. "I'd like to have heard that racket!"

John puffed, beaming. "So would I, so would I."

He regarded Maggie through an intentionally created haze of smoke. He felt saddened, even disappointed. He supposed she was not yet ready. But there were things he could tell her that might make a difference; if she really wasn't ready, at least what he said could do no harm.

"Bear with me a little longer, Maggie, and then I'll let you go."

"I really should be going. This is my last day here, and there are things I want to do yet."

Her last day! Then what he had to say would probably be about as effective as spitting into the wind. But he persisted. "Do you know much about reincarnation?"

"No." She looked wary. "I never think about such things."

"Indulge me. Some people believe—*I* believe—that we are, all of us, individual souls living in physical bodies. When the body dies, the soul goes on, to another plane of existence. Then after a while the soul is born into a body again and lives another life. Our souls have an indwelling ideal of what is good—some would call God the ultimate good—and in each lifetime most souls choose to move in the direction of increasing goodness. Others may choose to go the other way, but we're not talking about them. Are you with me so far?"

"I guess so." Maggie was, actually, riveted.

"Okay. The personality traits we have—you know, stubbornness, kindness, quickness to anger, and so on—are soul traits, not body traits. They persist from one lifetime to another. They can trip us up or help us on in the progress of our souls. The more deep-seated the traits are, the more lifetimes we have carried them around with us. In the case of a negative trait, like quickness to anger, the entire purpose of a life may be to overcome that trait once and for all."

Maggie nodded. "That makes sense. I thought reincarnation was about something different, like if you're an animal abuser you might be born again as a helpless puppy."

John tapped his pipe out on the sole of his shoe, then put it aside. "There are religions that believe reincarnation goes up and down the entire scale of living things, from bugs to people, but I can't handle that large a scale—I'm concerned only with human beings. To go on: When a soul has been, shall we say, *hurt* in one lifetime, there is always an opportunity to repair the hurt in another. I'm sure you have noticed"—John winked, trying to lighten a heavy subject—"that people don't hurt or help themselves in complete isolation. So patterns occur, patterns of behavior, of souls relating to each other from one lifetime to the next, and the next. The same souls are reborn at the same time, over and over again, so that they will have a chance to work out their patterns together. To make progress from hurting, to helping, to loving. The goal is pure love, Maggie. Selfless love that expects nothing in return. That kind of love is the highest good in the universe. Which is why it has been said that God is love."

Maggie swallowed a lump in her throat. "I appreciate your telling me this. It feels right. But why—?"

John Fortune leaned forward and nailed Maggie with his

blue eyes. "Because you need to know. Because a woman does not leave her home and drive hundreds of miles in search of a legendary object that may very well not exist, without a very good reason. Because our dreams, dreams that come from the deepest part of ourselves, are a direct connection to our souls; dreams can link us to the other lifetimes we have lived. There are other ways to make the link—a certain level of meditation, hypnosis—but those require special skills, whereas anyone can take control of his or her dreams."

"The way you told me to do."

John's lips curved in a half-smile. "I tried, but you turned it around on me. I would bet every book in this room, Maggie, that you have dreamed about the Golden Drum. That you have lived a life in which the drum played a major part, and your soul remembers. That something happened in that lifetime and became a pattern. A pattern I surmise is troublesome, or you would not suppress the dreams. You would welcome them.

"And finally—I would not say this to you except that you've said you intend to leave here tomorrow—I believe there is another person, another soul in your troublesome pattern, and he's a friend of mine: James."

"Jamie!"

"Yes. James Gentry. When you met him, didn't you feel as if you'd known him before?"

Maggie shook her head. "I don't think so, but he—he did. He said he did, and it seemed to puzzle him. H-have you ever talked with Jamie about all this reincarnation stuff?"

"No. James is a man at peace with himself, which suggests that he has resolved many of the kinds of problems we carry with us from one lifetime to another. On the other hand, in all the years I've known him, he has never had a close relationship with a woman. I remarked on that once, and he said he was waiting for the right woman. Then, last night, I saw him with you. . . ."

"Well, this is all very interesting, but I'm afraid it doesn't matter, since I'm not likely to see either of you again after today." Maggie put her coffee cup down decisively, and John could see her mind snap shut, like a shutter closed behind her eyes. "Thank you for taking the time to ask around about the Golden Drum on my behalf. I should leave now. I have a lot to do."

Maggie extended her hand formally for a handshake, and John obliged. Her eyes were opaque, her face a mask. Never had he seen such perfect denial. He thought, as he helped her on with her jacket, that the hurt she had suffered in that former lifetime must have been very deep to produce a denial so strong. He felt a pang of empathy; he passionately wanted to give her the tools to heal herself.

John stood in his doorway and watched her go. When she was almost to her car, he called out, "Maggie!" She turned her head. "The man with the Golden Drum was named Douglas."

Maggie shrugged: it meant nothing to her. Her denial was complete. All her strength now went into maintaining it. From her car she waved goodbye to John Fortune, certain that she would never see him again.

"What do you have there, under your arm?" asked Jamie, ushering Maggie through the bookshop door at six P.M. He locked it behind her, then flipped the sign in the window to read CLOSED.

"Something I made for you. It's a going-away present." Maggie had spent the time since leaving John in assembling a frame-kit for her oil pastel of the sunset; it had been a struggle because the paper, which had seemed sturdy when she was painting, was delicate once torn from its pad. It was also large—two by three feet. She'd tied the framed painting corner-to-corner with a purple ribbon, no wrapping paper.

Maggie preceded Jamie to the back of the shop, then presented her gift to him. She felt suddenly shy, eager for his approval. "I hope you like it."

"You—*made* this?" An expression of wonder transposed to joy as Jamie studied his gift. "You mean you painted it? This is a Maggie Ross original?"

"Yes, I did." She began to glow.

"This is wonderful! I had no idea—you said you were a commercial artist, but this—my God, Maggie, you have talent! You should do more." Jamie carefully removed the purple ribbon and propped the painting against the wall, then stepped back to admire it.

"I have. I've worked every afternoon since I've been here. But the others aren't as finished as this one. They're more on the level of color sketches. I might use them as studies for oil paintings later. . . ." She let her thoughts trail off, knowing that once she was back in Atlanta she would do no such thing. Her oil paints were all dried and cracked in their tubes. She hadn't touched them for years. She'd need new brushes, and brushes were expensive. She'd never be willing to spend the money. . . .

"Maggie, this is really good. Why would you work as a commercial artist when you can paint like this? It's a waste of your talent."

"I told you, Jamie, I have to earn a living. I couldn't support myself painting pictures."

Jamie narrowed his eyes and stroked his beard, looking from her, to the painting, and back at her again. "I disagree. Maybe in some places you couldn't, but here on the Outer Banks, you can." He took her by the hand. "Come. I want to show you something. I didn't know you painted, or I would have shown you before now."

He unhooked the chain from across the flight of stairs to the art gallery in the loft and led Maggie up. He flipped light switches. There were bare patches, but still many paintings of different sizes hung on the walls. "There. You can paint like that. Better than that. Can't you?"

Maggie walked slowly around the room. Most of the paintings were landscapes. All were representational and had something to do with the sea or the beach or landmarks of the Outer Banks. "Yes, I guess I can. Most of these are watercolors, though, and I prefer to work in oils. I'm not all that good at watercolor."

"So what? One small oil will bring a higher price than a larger watercolor. I know this isn't serious art, Maggie, but it's a step above commercial. And if you can paint like this, I can sell your paintings to the tourists." Jamie came up behind her and took her shoulders in his hands, pulled her back against him. His beard was soft on her cheek, and his lips moved at her temple. "Maggie, Maggie, stay here. Paint. Stay with me." He turned her around. His face was incandescent. "I love you, Maggie. I feel as if I've waited for you for a very long time. Live here. Love me."

Maggie felt a sinking sensation in her stomach, as if she were falling. Blood pounded in her ears, and Jamie seemed very far away. "I can't," she said. "It's too big a risk."

Jamie drew her close, but she pulled back and he let her go, putting his hands in his pockets. "Then don't decide now. We'll go get some supper, and afterward we can talk about it some more at my place."

Maggie was in control again. She lifted her chin. "I'm not going to your place or out to dinner. Last night was perfect, and it was enough. I came to say goodbye, Jamie. The painting is my parting gift to you. I'm going back to Atlanta, and I don't expect that I will ever see you again."

On the other end of Roanoke Island, in Wanchese, the ancient drum—no longer golden—made a rat-tat-tat. Once only. No one heard.

1753—1756

A year passed, and Douglas did not come back to Margaret. A letter came instead: Douglas had gone to France, to take the money he and a few others had raised to Bonnie Prince Charlie. He was sorry, but he'd had no choice, he had to go. He would be back, and would come to her, as soon as he could.

First Margaret cried, then she became angry. The anger made her want to do something—anything! She got on a horse and rode to the other end of Skye to see her cousin Flora. Flora had survived her imprisonment in the Tower of London; she had returned home and married another cousin, Macdonald of Kingsburgh. So now Flora had a husband and a house, near to and not quite so grand as Armadale Castle, and she had bairns. A boy and a girl. Margaret now envied Flora as much as she admired her, but she also loved her cousin and knew she could confide in her.

Flora Macdonald had a baby in her arms and a toddler at her feet, and she listened to Margaret bewail the folly of

Douglas of clan Douglas—and his treachery, for had he not betrayed her by failing to keep his promise? She let Margaret wind down from her tantrum before saying quietly, "I understand how you feel, Cousin. I myself think that the Stewarts have become a lost cause, but I stay in touch with the handful of people who still support the Prince. They have been good to your Douglas, they've sheltered and clothed and fed him, and he could scarce refuse to go to France when they asked him. Can you not begin to think of Douglas as a friend, or even a lover, one you may see happily from time to time while you make your life—your real life—with someone else?"

The baby in Flora's arms began to whimper, and she opened her blouse and put him to suckle. Margaret watched the tiny mouth close upon the nipple, and a knife of longing cut deep, deep into her. "Nay," she declared vehemently, "I want Douglas, and I will have no one else!"

"Your father has other ideas, you know."

"I know, but I'll not marry until I can marry Douglas. My father can keep finding me husbands, and I will keep refusing them." She tossed her head.

"I fear you are too willful, Margaret, and too proud. One day your father will break you. I would not like to see that happen. I know from my own experience how it feels to have your pride humbled."

"My father will never break me! Will you not help me, Flora? You have contacts. You can find Douglas for me when he returns, and I will go to him."

Flora sighed and shifted the baby to her other breast. She had known Margaret since the girl was no bigger than the babe in her arms, and she had always been as passionately determined to have her way. "All right, I will help you. But I fear we will both regret it some day."

Another year passed before Flora told Margaret that Douglas was at Inverness. Flora said it was too long a trip, and too hard in the winter months for Margaret to attempt to join him; by the time she could get there, he would likely be gone.

Margaret set out alone on her horse, anyway. Alexander

Macquarrie's men caught up with her halfway across Wester Ross and brought her home. He confined her to her room for the rest of the winter.

But Flora smuggled a letter in to her, from Douglas, and Margaret took heart. Her father proposed another husband, and again Margaret refused. He ranted, reminding her that she was past twenty and soon would be too old to attract any man. Her love for Douglas was no longer a secret, since her flight toward Inverness—she flung it in her father's face saying, "I will wait for Douglas, and he will come for me! If I have to, I'll wait until I'm white-haired and snaggle-toothed and have one foot in the grave!" Her father growled that they would see about that, but when spring came, he let her leave her room.

In October of 1756 Margaret Macquarrie sailed from the tip of Skye to the Isle of Lewis and into the waiting arms of Douglas Douglas. He thought he had at last found a safe place and a home for them: a stone hut, once abandoned, that Douglas claimed by squatter's rights. The hut was on the western side of the island, not far from the Standing Stones of Callanish. On the first night of the full moon, Margaret and Douglas pledged eternal love for each other there, among the standing stones. The Golden Drum was their only witness.

They had three months together before Alexander Macquarrie found them. Like an old dragon, Alexander snorted fire and snarled a warning: If Douglas valued his life, he would leave Scotland forever—for if the English didn't have his head, the Macquarrie would, for dishonoring his only daughter!

Douglas promised to go and begged for a final moment alone with Margaret. Douglas kissed her for the last time and whispered, "As soon as I can get some money together, I will go to America, as many Scots have done. When I get there I will make us a place, much finer than this one, and I will send for you." Margaret, blinking back tears, believed him.

This time Alexander Macquarrie imprisoned his willful daughter in the old stone tower of Dunkellen Castle. He vowed he would keep her there until he broke her spirit. It took a year, but finally Margaret broke. She had not been able to bear the long confinement; she had all but gone mad. Her red hair was streaked with gray, though she was only twenty-three. Dimly Margaret remembered that she was supposed to wait for Douglas to send for her. She was docile now. She sat by the window in her old room, folded her hands, and waited.

In the meantime, Douglas and his Golden Drum were crossing the Atlantic Ocean on a ship that was soon to be wrecked off the shore of Hatteras Island, in the colony called North Carolina.

July 1993

Maggie Ross knew that she still dreamed about the lovers and the Golden Drum. The admonition she made to herself nightly—*I will not remember my dreams*—did not work perfectly. But it worked well enough, because on waking she would recall only shadows, and traces of emotions. She went doggedly on with her life. She worked, and worked hard, every day; but other than keeping faithful attendance at her job, she had become a recluse. Rita, who was her only real friend in Atlanta, got a better job with another firm, and Maggie was not all that sorry to see her go. She preferred solitude.

There was, however, something that troubled Maggie. She wanted to hear from James Gentry. She wanted this passionately, although she knew she was being irrational. She had told him not to write, not to call; she had made him promise that he wouldn't. Yet she wanted him to do it anyway. She grew angry, when there was no reason to be angry. Gradually her anger turned to something like despair.

Once she thought: *I'll go to him, I'll go back to the Outer Banks.* But as soon as the thought was fully formed in her mind, it frightened her. She was convinced that going to him would be futile. She was supposed to wait. He was supposed to be the one to get in touch with her—regardless of his promise. So she believed, no matter how irrationally. Maggie waited.

December 1757

Flora Macdonald came to Castle Macquarrie to see Margaret. Flora had seen her cousin only once since her father had released her from the tower. That visit had been a shock. Though Flora herself had cautioned Margaret, she had not really been able to imagine that her fiery cousin's spirit might be broken. The sight of a docile, submissive Margaret had been hard to bear.

Flora dreaded this present visit, because the news she had to impart was bad. In fact, it could not be worse. But Margaret had a right to know, and it was Flora's duty to tell her. For, while Margaret was locked in Dunkellen's tower, Douglas had come to Flora, saying that he had scraped together enough money for one passage to America, and he would soon set sail. He promised to stay in touch with Flora, and asked her to act as go-between for his messages to Margaret. But there had been no messages. Until now, and this one had not come from Douglas.

"Margaret?"

She sat, as she so often did, by the window in her room. She turned her head. Where once she would have cried out in greeting, and rushed to fling her arms around her cousin, now Margaret merely curved her lips in a wan smile and said, "Hello, Flora."

Flora knelt by her and took both her hands. "I have sad news, Cousin. Of Douglas."

"Douglas!" Her exclamation was only a whisper.

"I have had word, reliable word from North Carolina, across the sea. The ship that carried Douglas as a passenger was caught in a terrible storm, in a place where many ships go down. It is called Hatteras, an Indian name. The ship sank, Margaret. It would be foolish to hope that any survived."

"So Douglas is dead," Margaret said tonelessly. "He will never send for me."

"I'm sorry, Margaret. So very, very sorry!"

That night Margaret Macquarrie left her father's house. She climbed the path she had so often climbed with

Douglas. She stood on the cliff where they used to sit, side
by side. From deep within herself she summoned the last
spark of her old fire, and she raised her arms to the black
sky, threw back her head, and howled. The sound of her
anguish reverberated from rock to rock. And Margaret
threw herself down off the cliff into the sea.

October–December 1993

The letter was from Jamie! Her fingers trembling with
eagerness, Maggie tore open the envelope and read:

> Dear Maggie, I know you made me promise not to write
> or call, but I can't help myself. I think of you constantly.
> I have this fantasy that I'm a pirate and I sail down to
> Atlanta (I know it's not a seaport, but I'm a fair sailor, and
> anyway this is a fantasy), where I capture you and force
> you to sail back to the Outer Banks with me. Seriously,
> Maggie, I need you. I'm going nuts without you. I
> honestly believe you would be happy here on the Outer
> Banks, and I never saw any sign that Atlanta was making
> you all that happy. But I don't care where we are, as long
> as we're together. If you don't want to come here, I'll go
> there—I can always find some kind of a job. Please,
> Maggie, come back to me. Or let me come to you. All my
> love,
>   Your Jamie

Maggie looked at the last two words. She touched them
with a reverent finger: *Your Jamie.*
He had done it! Against all reason, against her every
soul-deep expectation, he had done it! Maggie read the letter
over again, and again, almost unable to believe her eyes.
Then she picked up the telephone and called him, and said,
"I got your letter. I'll come."

John Fortune was thinking that it might be time to admit
he was getting old—every day the quarter-mile walk from
his cottage to the Chicamacomico Station seemed to get
longer. One of these days he would give up and drive his car

up there, which would cut his daily fishing trip to the beach in half—

Uh-oh! As soon as he saw Maggie's car parked there, he got a sinking feeling in his stomach. He cautioned himself not to overreact. Other people drove Saabs—but not, he observed when he was close enough—with Georgia plates. It was Maggie's car, all right. His stomach sank all the way down to his toes.

No one in the world, not even James Gentry, knew better than John the courage Maggie had shown when she came back to the Outer Banks. For her to be able to break through that wall of denial . . . well, it was little short of miraculous.

They still had some things to work out, though. He could tell, even if James hadn't occasionally confided in him, just as he used to do. For instance, they weren't married. Weren't even engaged to be married (did people get engaged anymore? John wasn't sure). And though Maggie lived in James's house, she said it was only temporary, until she could get a place of her own. This frustrated James, and was the source of his confidences; James would marry Maggie tomorrow, but she was *afraid to commit.*

And now James was out of town on a buying trip, which left Maggie alone, and here was her car, which meant that she was down on the beach where John had first seen her. Right in a spot that was loaded with significance for her, because it was right about here that Douglas and his Golden Drum had been pulled to shore. Did Maggie know that? Had she, finally, remembered her dreams?

Maggie Ross stood ankle-deep in the cold surf. It was early December, and she had come out in one of her long sweaters over black leggings. No coat, no scarf. She had not taken off her shoes, she didn't even realize that she was standing in the water, and she did not feel the cold. All she knew was that Jamie was gone, and she was certain he would never come back.

Sure, he'd only gone on a buying trip—that was what he said, that he had to go for a couple of weeks every year at this time. But he had only called once, and Maggie could not be expected to understand that James, so long accustomed to life alone, simply did not think to call. *Patterns from other lifetimes* . . .

Maggie waded deeper into the ocean. The waves broke just short of her knees.

In Wanchese the aged, once-golden drum stirred upon its dusty shelf. The metal surface and the tight-stretched drum head gathered tiny, unseen particles of energy. The drum made ready to beat.

Maggie wanted to cry, but she could not, the tears would not come. She felt completely drained. Of strength, of will, of hope, of life itself. What she felt was despair: Jamie was gone. For almost three months they had been happy together in his little house, but now he was gone and he would never, ever come back. . . .

Jamie was gone, but the sea was here. Always, the sea was here, it never went away; the tides rolled in, the tides flowed out, on and on. Forever. Men make promises by the light of the moon, they swear for all eternity, but their promises are not eternal. The sea is eternal, vast, and mysterious, the source of everything. . . .

Maggie walked two steps forward. The waves broke upon her thighs.

John Fortune paused on top of the dune. He held a hand up to shade his eyes, for there was a high, white overcast that made a glare upon the sand and the water. At first he could not find Maggie, but then he saw her, hip-deep in the ocean, just beyond the breakers.

The Golden Drum began to beat by itself: rat-tat-tat, rat-tatta-tat, ratta-tatta-ratta-tatta, rat-tat-tat!

Maggie stood mesmerized by the waves around her. She felt the tide pushing, pulling, pushing, pulling; felt the sand shift under her feet. It was hard to stand, and in the sea was peace. . . .

*   *   *

John's first impulse was to shout, but he did not. His next impulse was to plunge into the ocean and pull her back, but he did not. He could feel the significance of this moment for Maggie, feel it as surely as if it were heavy smoke in the air. She was caught in that old pattern from her former lifetime, and if he interfered, he would rob her of her chance to break through. He could only stand and watch. And hope.

The Golden Drum beat furiously: RAT-TAT-TAT! *Hear me!* RATTA-TATTA-TATTA-TATTA-RAT-TAT-TAT! *Hear me!* RATTA-TATTA-RATTA-TATTA-TATTA-TATTA, *RATTA*-TATTA-*RATTA*-TATTA-TAT-TAT-TAT! *Hear me!* RAT-TAT-TAT-TATTA-TAT! RATTA-TATTA-TAT!

John Fortune saw the waves close around Maggie's waist. He couldn't bear to watch anymore. He picked up his fishing gear and turned his back, trudging home.

From far, far away Maggie Ross heard the sound of a beating drum. A wave, bigger than the rest, splashed her breast. She noticed how cold it was.

There! The drum again, louder now: rat-tat-tat! rat-tatta-tat! On and on; once she'd heard it, she couldn't get the sound out of her ears. And suddenly she knew its source: the beating of the Golden Drum.

Maggie turned around in the water—carefully, she didn't want to fall—and looked back at the beach. She saw someone she recognized: a tall young man, with very fair skin and black curling hair, and a slender yet muscular body—if she were close enough, she would see he had gray eyes, rimmed in black. She knew his name, a funny double name: Douglas Douglas—that was because he was of the clan Douglas, which made his last name the same as his first.

She still heard the drum, but more faintly now. She waded back a few steps toward shore, to get closer to the young man. She thought she felt sadness coming from him. . . . Yes, she felt his sadness as he gazed so intently out to sea. He was waiting for someone, longing for someone; that was because he didn't yet know that Margaret had drowned herself because she thought he was dead.

"Oh, my God!" exclaimed Maggie, and in that instant her mind-vision of Douglas vanished. So did the sound of the drum, for it had done its work. She looked around and was amazed to find herself standing knee-deep in a freezing ocean! Maggie pushed her legs against the water, making for the shore as fast as she could. When she stood once more on the wet sand just above the line of surf, she wrapped her arms around herself and turned back, looking out to sea.

"I am Margaret!" she said, marveling; then, "I *was* Margaret. And I was just about to do the same thing she did—drown myself in the sea!"

Maggie didn't have to try to remember anymore: The content of her dreams, which she had for so long suppressed, came rushing back to her, whole and complete. She knew she was Margaret, and Jamie was Douglas, and it all made sense, such beautiful, beautiful sense! She jumped in the air, shouting for joy, not realizing how much she sounded like Margaret Macquarrie: "He loves me! He really, really loves me! And I'm free, free, free!"

Back in the house she shared with Jamie, Maggie stepped out of a hot shower and thought, *I should call John Fortune. He deserves to know about this.* As soon as her hair was dry, she did. She told him everything, concluding, "Thank you, John. If you hadn't told me all those things about reincarnation, I don't know if I'd have been able to put this all together. But you know, this is some serious stuff—I could have drowned out there!"

On the other end of the line John chuckled. He sounded supremely happy. "Yes, you could have, but you didn't. And by the way, Maggie, did you hear about the Golden Drum? The whole town is talking. Three people have already called me about it."

"No. What about the Golden Drum?"

"This afternoon, oh, I'd guess a couple of hours ago now, the drum began to beat by itself. It made such a terrible racket that the family in the house came to see, and the people up and down the street came to see. There were all sorts of witnesses!"

Maggie murmured, "The Golden Drum beats when anyone who has been close to it is in danger. . . ."

There was a light tap on the door, and then it opened. Maggie looked up, startled, from the book she was reading as she sat on the couch. "Jamie! You're back!" She jumped up, not caring that the book fell to the floor, and flew to him. She wrapped her arms about him and covered his face with kisses.

"Whoa!" Jamie exclaimed, laughing when she finally let him go. He was immensely pleased—Maggie had never been so demonstrative before.

"But you weren't due back for three more days," she said, planting one hand on her hip. "Why did you come home early?"

"Well," he said, coming farther into the room, rubbing his beard, "you'll never believe this, but I had the strangest dream. There was this drum, called the Golden Drum, and it started to beat and it kept on beating until it just about drove me nuts, and somehow I knew it meant I should come straight home!"

"Oh, I believe it, all right," said Maggie, linking her arm in his and dragging him to the couch. "And have I got a story to tell you!"

Out of Place

Out of Time

Anna Jennet

1

"YOW! THE BLOODY bitch nearly bit my finger off!"

"Never mind that. She's getting away. After her!"

Sylvie Pentayne heard her pursuers and tried to run harder to outdistance the four thugs she had just escaped. Branches scratched at her flesh and the ground tore at her bare feet, but she paid little heed. All she cared about, all she could think of, was escaping from the hooting, shouting animals who chased her. This was the nightmare she'd been having night after night come true. This time however, she would not wake up safely in her bed, shaking and sweating with fear.

She should never have left her hometown in Maine and come to the coast of Cornwall. She certainly should never have left the hotel's grounds. It was pure madness. Her plan had been to banish the dream by walking—safely—across the landscape featured so starkly in her nightmare. Instead she was now living it, fulfilling whatever fate the dream had been trying to warn her of.

Fingers scratched across her bare back, and she cried out. They were gaining on her. Despite the adrenaline fear and self-preservation were pumping through her, she doubted she could produce any more speed, certainly not for any length of time. As she plunged through a thick growth of shrubbery, she glanced over her shoulder. Her attackers were no longer gaining on her, as she thought. In fact, they were scrambling to a stop. Suddenly the ground gave out beneath her feet.

This was the place in her dream where she had always woken up sweating and terrified. That horrible, chilling sense of falling did not stop this time, however. No bedpost

appeared in her hands, clutched tightly as she fought to
recover from her fear. Nothing but empty air surrounded
her. She could see the aghast yet morbidly fascinated
expressions of the four thugs who had assaulted her, torn her
clothes, and chased her. Laid out below her were the
sea-splashed rocks of the Cornish coast.

The rocks drew no nearer, yet her sense of falling did not
ease, and Sylvie grew even more terrified. Had she now
plunged into some kind of hell where she was to be
tormented for all eternity with a never-ending fall to the
rocks below? She could think of absolutely nothing she had
done in her short twenty years on earth that deserved such
a penalty.

A hazy mist, its swirling, oppressive smoke an eerie
mixture of blues and grays, began to wrap itself around her.
The foam-dotted water below her disappeared. She could no
longer see her tormentors. A tight, cold sensation of panic
gripped her as she realized that she could see nothing but that
mist. She could hear nothing but her own terrified thoughts.
Sylvie felt cocooned yet not safely—smotheringly. The mist
was alive with flashes of colors and energy. It made it nearly
impossible to breathe.

Sylvie opened her mouth in a desperate effort to pull
more air into her lungs, then closed it fast as she slammed
into the water. She plummeted down beneath the white-
flecked waves. As soon as she could get her arms and legs
to heed her commands, she tried to propel herself back to
the surface, but she was too weak. Escaping her attackers
had sapped her strength. Still she struggled, all her muscles
aching and knotted, unable to give up on life.

A shape loomed up in front of her in the cloudy waters,
and she tried to struggle past it. When a long muscular arm
curled around her waist, she curbed the urge to fight the
man. She needed help to reach the top, to reach the air. If
the man dragging her to the surface was an enemy, a threat,
she could do nothing. Sylvie hung limply in the man's hold
as she tried to recoup her strength.

She was tossed onto the cold, damp sand somewhat less
gently than she had anticipated. She opened her eyes. She
was flat on her back, feeling distinctly nauseated. Two

strong, well-shaped legs straddled her, water threading down their lightly haired length. She looked up and up and was wondering just how tall her rescuer was when she finally saw his trim hips. Or, she mused, she assumed they were trim beneath what looked unsettlingly like a big white diaper. Her eyes still stinging from the seawater, she narrowed them as she skimmed a glance over his taut stomach, sleekly muscled chest, and broad shoulders. The man had a body like a Chippendale dancer—not too pumped up, but nicely lean and strong.

Sylvie carefully looked up a little higher, bracing herself in case his face was not as handsome as his magnificent body. What she found was thick gold hair dipping below his shoulders and framing a face that nearly made her gape. His face had the lean dangerous cut of Clint Eastwood's, but he had rich green eyes, fine, heavily lashed eyes the color of malachite. She could not fully suppress a sigh when she saw that he had a mouth just like Peter Weller's. The man embodied everything she had ever liked in a man, despite his strange taste in swimwear. It was highly depressing since she knew he would never take a liking to her. He would assure himself that she was unhurt, pat her on the head, and go on his way. Scrawny women with black hair and cat's eyes never attracted men like him.

"Hell, you sure are something even with the diaper," she said. Sitting up a little, she held out her hand. "I am Sylvie DeLorenzo Pentayne. Thank you very much for hauling me out." A look of astonishment crossed his face, but he did not respond. "Can't you speak English?" she pressed. "One of those German tourists, are you?"

Barric Tremayne studied the mysterious woman he had pulled from the sea. He was not a particularly superstitious man, but he felt the old fears well up inside him for a moment. Then reason quelled any doubts. She was only a too thin, too wet girl. Although her copper-colored eyes hinted at something otherwordly, it would appear, he thought, that Mad Annie was not so mad. The old woman had said that he would pull a woman from the sea, a woman who spoke a strange yet not strange tongue, and had eyes like a feral cat. He would not, however, immediately assume that the rest of the old crone's prophecy would be fulfilled.

Looking closer he decided that more than her wide eyes were strange. The remnants of her clothes made it difficult to know exactly what she had been wearing, but he was certain she dressed as no one he had ever seen before. The materials and the fashion were unrecognizable. He had never seen clothes in quite that shade of blue and red, either.

What *was* easily recognizable to him, and of immediate interest, was her lithe body. The torn strips of her upper garment exposed a great deal of her slender body and an exquisite pair of small but beautifully formed breasts. Her waist was tiny, her hips slender yet curved, and her legs were long and slim. He was pleasantly surprised at how pale her complexion was: a smooth white which any lady of court would envy. He continued to stare. . . .

Sylvie finally withdrew her hand when he made no move to shake it and then rose to her feet. She decided he had gawked at her long enough.

"Now that you've had a good look"—she tried to brush the sand off her wet clothes—"maybe you'd tell me how you lost those creeps who were chasing me." She swallowed hard, trying to will away a lingering wooziness.

"Some men were chasing you?"

Oh, Lord, she thought, the *coup de grace*. Mr. Universe has a voice just like James Earl Jones. She took a deep breath and forced herself to be mature, calm, and discreet— none of which she felt. What she wanted to do was jump him. She almost smiled. He certainly had taken her mind from all the horror preceding his gallant rescue.

"Yeah, four dirty creeps," she answered.

"I have been here for an hour or more and have seen no one."

"That's impossible. They were right behind me. They chased me off this cliff."

"Nay, not this cliff, mistress." He looked up at the cliff behind them. "If you had fallen from these cliffs, you would have fallen onto the sand and rocks. You might have fallen on me. Howbeit, you would not have safely fallen several yards out into the sea."

Already unsettled by his manner of speech, Sylvie looked

around her and felt her heart lodge in her throat. They stood on a small beach. There had been no beach at the base of the cliffs she had run off. Had there? No. And there was no way she could have run off one cliff and landed at the foot of another. Yet, such an incredible thing would be easier to accept than what she faced now. Though she had fallen off the cliff, somehow, as she fell, it had changed.

Sylvie became short of breath, and a throbbing began in her head. She rubbed her forehead with her palm and realized that something was very wrong, and—worse—it was something incomprehensible.

"I think I need to get back to the hotel," she muttered. "I think I'm going to be real sick."

"Hotel?" Barric could see that she was becoming agitated, but he was not sure how he could help her. He hurried to put his clothes back on in case he needed to act. "That is not a word I know."

"Not a word you know? I am speaking English here and so are you—a weird English, but still English. What part of the word do you find difficult? Oh, man, this is getting just too strange," she said as she watched him get dressed. For a moment she was shocked out of her sarcasm.

Her rescuer was donning clothing she had never seen except in a movie or a play. He was looking far too historic for her comfort. If he was part of some theatrical production, he was meticulous in choosing his attire. He laced on his clothes—no buttons, zips, or elastic. He dressed in a gray hose, a gray shirt, and a short black tunic top. Then he yanked on a pair of soft boots, which he laced onto his legs. She took a step back when he buckled on a sword. What she considered most unsettling as he tugged on a pair of black leather gauntlets and watched her was that he did not look ridiculous. The whole outfit suited him.

"You're in a play or something, right?" she demanded as he took her hand in his. He towed her along behind him as he began to climb a rough path to the top of the cliffs. "You're playing Henry the Fifth in some Shakespearean festival, is that it? I saw the movie." When he glanced back at her, she did not find any comfort in the way he looked at her.

"A *fifth* Henry? You are amiss in your counting. We have had but one, and he has been dead for two years. The land now bleeds beneath the squabbling over the throne. Matilda of course claims the throne, while Stephen sits on it."

"Matilda and Stephen?" she whispered, and he nodded as he helped her up the last few feet of the path.

A dull knot formed in her stomach. By some fluke she knew about Matilda and Stephen. Matilda's story had been in a book detailing the lives of strong female figures of the past. Matilda and Stephen had squabbled in the mid-twelfth century. That the man holding her hand spoke of the pair as if they were alive and well meant one of two things—he was playing a strange joke on her or he was an utter looney. There were also two other possibilities, but they were too much like script ideas for *The Twilight Zone*.

What she found at the top of the cliff made her head throb more and her stomach churn even more violently. Yet again things were recognizable, but different, and not simply because there was now a horse tethered there. It was the same headland she had run over, but altered. The path running along the cliffside was narrow and faint, not wide and trampled hard by many feet. Even the foliage was slightly altered, being thicker, wilder, more unkempt. Sylvie could see where she had been wrestled to the ground, where she had broken free, and the path she had taken, which had led to her fall, but they were changed. It was as if someone had let the public footpath go to seed, as if no one made regular pleasure strolls through the area anymore.

Or hadn't yet.

Sylvie used her free hand to massage her temples as the man pulled her along by her other hand. It was not until he grasped her about the waist and started to heft her up into the saddle of his horse that she found the strength to resist. She scrambled free of his hold and met his look, which was an equal mixture of concern and irritation.

"I don't go anywhere with a man who can't even tell me his name," she said.

"Ah." He bowed slightly. "I am Barric Tremayne, a knight in the service of King Stephen. I am Baron of Penmoorland." He stretched out his hand toward the castle in the distance, then reached for her again. "I will take you there so that Mad Annie and the women of the castle can tend to you. You will come to no harm there, m'lady."

Since she could think of no real alternative—and he *had* saved her life—Sylvie decided to accompany him. She let him set her up on the saddle and drape a heavy woolen cloak around her. He mounted behind her, and she fought the sense of being overwhelmed by him when he wrapped his arms around her and grasped the reins.

Nothing was right. He was not right, the place was not right, his English was not right, not even the saddle was right. It did not look like any saddle she had ever seen, having what appeared to be a high pommel at each end. Sylvie clenched her hands into tight, white-knuckled fists and took several deep slow breaths to ease her rising panic, but it did not help very much.

"You must not be so frightened," Barric said as he nudged his horse into motion.

"Just get me back to the hotel, Mr. Tremayne. Oh, I mean sir, I guess. I'm not sure how to address a baron."

"It does not matter. And I still do not know what you mean by hotel."

"It's a place where people pay to spend the night, or a couple of nights. Where did you learn your English?"

Barric ignored that last remark. "Ah, you mean an inn. So, you were at the inn on the road to the village. Well, that is no place for you now. You have been through an ordeal and will need care. 'Tis best if you reside at Penmoorland. I will send someone to gather your belongings and bring them back to the castle."

"All right. Fine."

She decided not to argue with him. Except for a small part kept as a private residence, the castle was not livable. The man had to know that, had to know that his little game would be exposed once they reached it. All the things she could not fully understand and recognize so far would be explained away. There was no way the man could change the castle from the crowded tourist attraction that it was. Everything would be back to normal in just a few minutes

and the police would go after her assailants. She relaxed a
little as she concentrated on what to tell the police.

As they drew nearer to the castle Sylvie began to feel less
and less sure of herself. Where was the highway? The
parking lot? The noise of a large group of tourists? None of
those things appeared. All she saw was the occasional
person with a few farm animals and wearing the same sort
of museum attire her rescuer was; although the "Baron's"
clothes were nicer. A few thatched-roofed hovels had
replaced the quaint cottages she had seen as she had rattled
away from the hotel.

By the time the castle was in full view, Sylvie could
hardly breathe, her head throbbed deafeningly, and the
stinging bile of an increased nausea burned the back of her
throat. Normality was nowhere in sight. The things she
needed to see to restore her equilibrium were not there.

Yet again, everything was recognizable but not quite
right. The castle, however, caused her true alarm. The moat
should have been a grass-covered depression in the ground,
but it was full of algae-greened, foul-smelling water. Someone bellowed a greeting to the baron, and Sylvie looked up
to see the glint of armor and spear points on the walls.

"Where is the ice cream stand?" she muttered in a
shock-weakened voice as they rode over the drawbridge.

"Mad Annie said you would speak oddly, but I am not
sure even she knew just how oddly. Come, you need not be
so afraid. No one will hurt you," he reassured her as they
rode into the courtyard of the castle.

At the moment, *physical* threat was the very least of
Sylvie's worries. She sat on the horse and stared around her
in growing horror as the baron dismounted. People in
archaic costume walked around, farm animals scurried
underfoot, and a number of lean-tos encircled a central stone
building. She recognized the castle despite the lack of
gardens, benches, and plaques. She recognized it even
though what was once in ruin was now whole and that there
were none of the newer additions to the main stone keep.
The castle her rescuer presented as his own was exactly like
the small pewter replica on sale in the gift shop of the castle

she had toured earlier—a replica of the twelfth-century Penmoorland. Sylvie heard herself groan as a loud rushing noise filled her ears and blackness engulfed her mind.

2

"COME, MY PRETTY Silkie, time to wake up."

Something hard and slender poked Sylvie in the arm. She swatted her hand in the direction of the raspy voice, but the only response was a dry cackle. A bad smell curled up her nose, and she coughed. It was an obnoxious mixture of dirt, body odor, and bad breath. Placing her hand over her nose and mouth, Sylvie cautiously opened her eyes. She quickly sidled away from the person leaning over her.

The smell Sylvie found hard to tolerate emanated from a wizened, greasy-haired woman at her bedside. When the woman grinned, Sylvie saw blackened, widely spaced teeth. The woman reached out a filthy bony hand, and Sylvie sidled even farther away.

"Don't you touch me," she warned, then, when the old crone hesitated, she looked around the room.

She felt weak, her head still ached, and her stomach still roiled. Looking around her did not help. She was in a massive but simple bed, and someone had taken her ragged clothes. The sheet she clung to was not as filthy as the old woman, but it was not clean and fresh, either. A long narrow window was the only source of natural light, and it allowed very little in. The dim illumination there was provided by smoky candles stuck in candelabras of varying heights plus two smoldering torches stuck in sconces either side of the crude fireplace. There was a dull haze in the room and a smell which told Sylvie that the candles were not the nicely scented kind or even of wax. She had once read of the smell of tallow candles and suspected she was getting a little firsthand experience.

She could not shake her fear. Two young maids at the foot of the bed were dressed in archaic clothes and stared at her in mesmerized terror as if she was the one who was odd and out of place. On the bed was a heavy coverlet of stitched-together sheepskins. Other animal skins were scattered over the stone floor. Hung on the wall was an arrangement of brutal medieval weapons that made her shudder.

What troubled Sylvie most was the dirt and, even more so, the way it was accepted. She could convince herself that some strange elaborate farce was being played out, but, for the sake of some joke, would anyone allow themselves to get that dirty? Would the owner of the property allow it to be so soiled? Would the actors be able to act so naturally in such a foreign setting? Everything she saw implied the impossible—that she had fallen back in time, that she actually was in the reign of Stephen. Sylvie shuddered and shook her head. It was a dream, nothing more.

"Come, child, a fine Silkie like yourself should not be afraid of me," cooed the old woman.

Sylvie cringed away when the woman reached for her. "I'd really prefer it if you didn't touch me—at least until you cleaned up some."

"Cleaned up? Ah, of course. Being a creature of the sea, you would find us somewhat dirty."

"Somewhat?" Sylvie muttered and shook her head. "And what do you mean—a creature of the sea?"

"A silkie. You are a silkie."

"I am a *Sylvie*. My name is Sylvie DeLorenzo Pentayne."

"Aye, aye. Sylvie. Very good. 'Tis a fine name for a silkie."

"What the hell is a silkie?" Sylvie snapped and saw the two maids at the foot of the bed cross themselves.

"You are a silkie, a creature who crawls out of the sea and takes on human shape. I am called Mad Annie . . ."

"Now there *is* a surprise."

". . . and I saw your coming in my dreams. You are to be Lord Tremayne's mate."

"Am I now?" Sylvie found that prediction dangerously alluring. "Not likely. This is some strange cult thing, isn't it?"

At that moment Lord Tremayne entered the room. Sylvie was both relieved and alarmed. He could answer a lot of the questions she had, but he could also say a lot of things she did not want to hear. She wanted him to be a rock of sanity but doubted that he would be. She also feared that she could be lulled into inaction by his good looks.

"I am glad to see that you are awake, mistress," he said as he walked to the side of the bed. Then he frowned at Mad Annie. "Have you been frightening the girl?"

"Nay," Mad Annie denied. "I was just telling her about my dreams. She does not seem to know what she is or why she is here. 'Twill make it very difficult to get her to do as she must."

"Enough, old woman. Now is not the time for that." Barric signaled the two young maids to leave, then nudged Mad Annie after them. "Go, and take those two cowardly girls with you. 'Tis time to soothe this poor woman, not afright her."

"But matters must be settled soon," Mad Annie argued as Barric shooed her out the door.

"They will be, but not now."

Barric gave the old woman one last gentle push out of the room, then shut the door and barred it. He turned to look at Sylvie and sighed. She looked painfully beautiful sitting in the middle of his bed, her waist-length, rich black hair tousled around her shoulders. She also looked frightened as she watched him and clutched the linen sheet to her chest. He tried to approach the bed carefully without even the hint of a threat, but she still cringed. Barric wished he knew how to ease her fear.

"You must not be so afraid," he said. "No one at Penmoorland will hurt you."

"It's not really the people here who frighten me."

Although he sat down on the edge of the bed in a completely unaggressive manner, Sylvie tensed. There was such strength in him, such barely leashed power in his every gesture. She briefly frowned as she realized that, for the moment, what she had been wearing was unusual, and his attire was quite in fashion. It was a fact she wished she could ignore.

"Are you still concerned about the men you said were chasing you? I saw no one, but I could send some of my men to search my lands."

"Don't bother. You don't really believe you'll find anybody, and they're probably long gone anyway." She combed her fingers through her hair and tried not to be too enthralled by the look in his fine green eyes: A look of sympathy touched with interest.

"As you wish. You appear unhurt. When Mad Annie undressed you, she found no injuries."

"So, Mad Annie undressed me." Sylvie was just about to breathe a sigh of relief when she noticed an odd expression briefly pass over his face. "She did, didn't she?"

"With some help, for she is a frail old woman. You shall require some new clothes."

Sylvie had to admire the way he admitted to helping strip her and then went on to a new subject. She fought her embarrassment over being seen naked by a man she did not know. And a man who could well be crazy, she mused, for if he isn't—I am. She decried the possibility that, due to the trauma of her near rape, she had lost her grip on reality, but it was something she was finding harder to ignore.

"Look, sir, can you just give me something to wear, and I'll go back to the hotel." She grimaced and muttered, "Wherever it's disappeared to."

"My men returned from the inn and said there was nothing of yours there. In truth, they said no one had seen you—ever. There is another inn nearly twenty miles away. Could you have come from there?"

"I came from the hotel, a hotel you could see from the castle gates. That's why they called it the Castle Gate Hotel. Are you sure you didn't take me somewhere after you pulled me out of the water?"

"Nowhere except to drag you up onto the sand. There is also no place called the Castle Gate Hotel. Surely you saw that as we rode here. I would like to help you, but, I confess, you confuse me. Mayhaps if you tell me what happened to you to cause you to fall into the water, I can better understand."

With a tremulous sigh Sylvie slumped back against the

pillows. How could she make him understand if she was unable to understand herself? Then, too, there was the chance that he was a player in some elaborate scheme, although that theory was beginning to seem too much like intense paranoia. It would be easier to accept that she was caught up in some delusion brought on by trauma or some dream she was having while lying in a hospital bed.

She started to tell him her story, beginning with the nightmares that had driven her to come to Cornwall. Simply speaking of the attack upon her brought back the terror, the wrenching sense of helplessness and the revulsion. When Barric reached out and took her hand in his, she did not pull away. The silent strength and comfort he gave her helped. As she continued, she could tell that he did not fully believe her, but he at least sympathized with her trauma whether it was born of a real or an imagined terror.

"You ask me to believe a great deal," Barric said, looking at her hand in his and idly thinking of how small it was.

"I see it a little differently," she said. Or at least I am trying to, she added silently. "I think you're all playing some elaborate trick."

"From what you have just told me, it would have to be a very elaborate one. Why should anyone wish to play such an intricate jest on you?"

That was a question to which she had no answer. "Then you are some strange cult I have had the misfortune to stumble onto. This"—she waved a hand around to indicate the room—"is just some new, warped, alternative lifestyle."

Barric sighed and shook his head. "I am trying to understand you so that I can help, but 'tis nearly impossible. So many of your words are strange to me. I cannot give you answers when I do not understand what you are saying or asking."

Sylvie thought he sounded sincere. He looked honestly perplexed. The problem was she needed him to be guilty of some great fraud, or she would have to start believing everything she saw around her. She eased her hand out of his, determined not to trust him.

"Perhaps the thing to do is to ask particular questions." She sat up straighter. "You saw no sign of my attackers?"

"None at all. I even returned to the place to see if there was any sign of them or your battle with them to be read upon the ground." He shrugged his shoulders. "I found nothing."

"But you saw me fall into the ocean. Where did I come from?"

"You appeared in the air over the water, then fell into it."

"I appeared?"

"Aye." He gave her a faint apologetic smile. "A heavy mist covered the sea, then it parted and there you were. It was as if something held you there, in the air, for a moment, then released you."

"Are you sure there wasn't some big boat out there? That maybe this heavy mist hid the boat from view? I wasn't in the air, but held out over the ship's railing, then dropped."

"Nay, there was no boat. The mist cleared abruptly. No boat could have moved so fast. There was just you."

"Do you know how foolish that sounds?"

"Aye, I do, but 'tis the truth."

"All right, I won't argue with you. Next question—are we really at Penmoorland?" He nodded. "In Cornwall?" He nodded again. "Not far from Land's End and just a wee bit west of the A30?"

"The A-what?"

"The A30—the highway. Oh, hell, the motorway?" The blank look on his handsome face made her very nervous, and she grabbed him by one shoulder, giving him a little shake. "We're about two hundred thirty miles from London, west of London—right?"

"Ah, aye, that is right. We are about a fortnight's ride from London."

"A fortnight's ride? Two weeks? What are you talking about? It's a half day or a day's ride. Just depends on whether you go by train or bus or car."

"I fear you have begun to speak of things I do not understand again."

Sylvie had the strongest urge to hit him, as if all that had happened to her was his fault. She knew that was idiocy. Even if it was all his fault, pounding on him was not going to change anything. She needed to hit something, however, so she slammed her fist against the mattress a few times. It did not resolve anything, but it did ease some of the tension she had felt tightening her insides.

"Then how do you get to London?" she asked, instinct telling her she was not going to like his answer.

"By horse and cart. Some folk have tried to go by sea or river, but I have ne'er liked traveling on the water by barge or by ship." Barric stood up, walked over to a table in the far corner of the room, and poured himself a tankard of wine. "Would you like some wine?"

"No. What I want are some answers, and you aren't giving me any I want to hear." She took a few deep breaths to calm herself. "Every answer you have given me is either a lie or—"

"I do not lie, Mistress Pentayne."

"Well, if you *do not lie,* then that means the world I know is gone, and you must see how hard that is for me to tolerate. All right, here's a question you'll probably think is stupid, but I now feel compelled to ask it—what year is this?"

"What year?"

"Yes, what year? Please, just answer it before I chicken out and withdraw the question."

"'Tis 1145, the tenth year of the reign of Stephen." He frowned when she turned ghost white and collapsed against the pillows. "Some wine?" He poured her some and brought it over to her.

"Yes, I think I need some now." She downed the wine as fast as she could without choking on it, then thrust the tankard back at him. "A little vinegary, but it'll do in a pinch." After making sure that the sheet was drawn up beneath her armpits, she vigorously massaged her forehead. "Y'know, there's a very big part of me that wants to believe I have somehow tumbled back in time. It's absurd, of course."

"Sometimes the absurd is all there is."

"Or the absurd is the more palatable of your choices. But a person can't go back in time. I couldn't fall off a cliff in 1992 and land in the ocean in 1145."

Barric did not like the increasingly high note in her voice. It hinted at a growing hysteria. He sat down on the edge of

the bed and took one of her small, cold hands in his. She
tensed a little and eyed him warily, but he ignored it and
lightly rubbed her hand between his. He wanted to banish
the wild ideas from her mind, yet he was not sure what to
say or do to accomplish that feat. Her presence was as great
a puzzle to him as it was to her.

"Is it not better to land in the wrong time or place than to
land on the rocks or drown?" he asked and decided that her
smile, weak and shaky though it was, was enchanting.

"Yeah, I guess I could look at it that way. I was headed
straight for the rocks." That realization comforted her in a
small way. "There was no way I was going to survive that
dive.

"I've heard that God moves in mysterious ways, but this
is just a little too strange." She yawned and decided that the
wine had been a lot stronger than she had thought. "I need
some clothes."

"By the morrow you shall have some."

"Good, then I can start looking for some of my own
answers."

"You cannot do that alone. 'Tis too dangerous."

"Are you trying to keep me a prisoner here?"

"Nay, mistress. I but mean to keep you alive."

"Well, I can't argue with that." She yawned again. "I'm
sorry. I don't mean to be rude. 'Tis just that I'm feeling very
tired."

Barric nodded and stood. "Rest. I begin to think that you
will need a great deal of strength in the days to come."

Sylvie stared at him for a moment before her eyelids grew
too heavy to keep open. Although he was part of the trauma
she was entrapped in, he gave her comfort. She prayed that
he would not turn out to be one of the enemy, for she knew
that, already, even after such a short acquaintance, such a
betrayal would really hurt her.

3

SYLVIE TRIPPED OVER her skirts and stumbled to her knees. She finally ceased to hold her breath, greedily sucking air back into her starved lungs. It was a relief to find that the air where she squatted was a little fresher. It was her first time out of bed since being brought to the castle the day before, and she could almost wish to be back in her bed. She was going to have to find some way to eradicate the stench in the garderobes. It could permanently damage her system if she had to hold her breath each time she had to go to the bathroom.

She tried to stand up, tripped on her skirts, then righted herself. The clothes were going to be a problem, she decided, as she brushed dirt and bits of rock from her skirts. Though she could see that having three or more layers of clothing could have some distinct advantages to it in the colder months, she could also see that they could prove to be far too much to endure in the heat of the summer. Taking a deep breath she told herself to stop whining, that these people could easily have chosen an archaic style that was far more torture to wear. Sylvie was determined, however, to get herself some undergarments.

"Aha, there you are, my pretty Silkie," rasped an already familiar voice.

"Annie," Sylvie muttered as the old woman scurried over to her. "You were looking for me?" She stepped back and held her hands out. "Look, Annie, I have nothing against you—not yet anyway—but I'd just as soon you didn't touch me until you've had a good scrubbing."

"You mean—bathe?"

"Yeah, I mean bathe. I'd think that your total lack of any sense of personal hygiene was why they called you mad, but I've only been out of bed for an hour or so, and I've realized that cleanliness isn't a priority around here. All I ask is that you clean up a little first, then you can touch me."

"Clean up? Ah, 'tis because you are a creature of the water. I forgot that for the moment." She gave Sylvie a sly smile. "I will give it some thought. Now, you must come along and break your fast. If you do not hurry, there will not be anything left for you to eat."

Sylvia was not sure she wanted to eat anything these people had to offer, but her hungry stomach immediately disagreed with her. She hurried after Mad Annie as the woman started toward the great hall. As she went she studied her surroundings, looking for something that could tell her that she was being tricked, that she was still back in the twentieth century. She had found nothing, and that was very hard to accept. The facts she was slowly gathering were asking her to believe the unbelievable—that she had fallen through some hole in time. She should have died, should have been broken on the rocks, but instead she was stuck in 1145—a time she knew little about except that it was bloody and violent.

"And unbelievably dirty," she mumbled as she followed Mad Annie into the great hall.

The rushes strewn across the floor had clearly not been changed recently. They were dull, matted down with dirt and food scraps as well as the occasional patch of dog waste. She nervously eyed the three huge wolfhounds sprawled around the baron's chair. Mad Annie had to give her a little shove to get her to sit on the end of the bench next to Barric. Sylvie returned his nod of greeting, then cautiously eyed the food set in front of her.

Her plate was a shallow wooden thing, roughly made. On it were placed several thick slabs of bread, a piece of what she suspected was fried fish, possibly sautéed, and two different sorts of pie. She warily picked up one of the slices of pie and blushed a little when she caught Barric staring at her.

"That is a brie tart," he said. "Cheese, egg, pastry, and saffron, I believe."

"You know your food." She took a tiny bite, decided it was all right, and began to eat.

"I was a temperamental child. I would eat nothing until I knew exactly what was in it. For a moment there you had the same look of distrust. That is simply dried fish heated in a sauce of wine, vinegar, and spices. The other is a baked herbed egg dish. Nothing unusual in it. 'Tis a heartier meal than usual, for we have already been at work and will now return to it."

"Work? What sort of work?"

"I am trying to strengthen our defenses." He relaxed in his seat, watching her as he sipped his cider. "These are dangerous times. A lot of blood is spilt when a crown is fought over. This land has suffered terribly. It forces a man to dance about and try to take no vows for he cannot be certain he has chosen the right one."

"So, which side have you chosen?"

"For the moment—Stephen. He sits upon the throne. I use possession of the throne as my measuring stick. If you hold the throne, then you are my king—or queen—and I try not to join in the battles. So far this ploy has worked. I swear myself to no one and I rail against no one."

"Ah, I get it. You sit on the fence."

"Pardon?"

"You sit on the fence, balance between the two, favor neither one nor the other."

"Aye, 'tis what I do. I care little for such a game. The choice should be clear. I should not have to play the sweet-tongued courtier who says what everyone wishes to hear yet makes no promises and takes no true actions."

"Sometimes the choice isn't clear, and a little balancing is all that will keep you and yours alive." She shrugged as she started to eat her bread. "A bit of tiptoeing is no great sin."

"All you say is true. I just feel it is not very honorable."

"Well, it's called survival. Sometimes it's the only thing to do," she murmured and wondered if she would have the strength and will to remember that particular tidbit of wisdom.

"You are still worried about having some answers." Barric sat forward and covered her hand with one of his. "Mayhaps there are simply no answers."

"There are a few possibilities for which there are no

answers, but I'm still hoping for one that can be explained, then rectified."

"I am ready to escort you around the castle, the grounds, the fields beyond the walls, and even the village if you wish."

"In other words—to keep a guard on me." She pushed her half-empty plate away and drank some cider.

"Nay, mistress, not as you mean. I have no wish to keep you as a prisoner at Penmoorland."

Barric took a hearty drink so that he would not have to meet her gaze. What he had said was not exactly a lie but not the full truth, either. He did not really wish to imprison her, yet he intended to do everything but that to keep her at Penmoorland. Several times during the night he had crept in to watch her sleep. She fascinated him. Although he had never fully believed in Mad Annie's dreams, or wanted to, the old woman's prediction that he and Sylvie Pentayne would be mates was growing more appealing by the hour. He was not sure what she was, who she was, or where she was from, but he was certain that he wanted her.

"Then why do you feel you must tromp around after me?" Sylvie demanded. "You don't even know what I'm looking for. You can't help me search for answers when you don't even know the questions."

"I intend to 'tromp' around after you to protect you. 'Tis dangerous to wander about alone."

"Surely not inside these walls?"

"Aye, here, too, for you do not know this place. The first time you walk around it, you should have a guide. As for stepping outside of these walls—aye, you will be guarded, for two reasons. The first is that I do have an enemy or two. And the second is that there is a lawlessness which is running rampant in the land. All manner of rough, desperate men roam the country. I believe you should also be aware that many people here find you curiosity enough to be afraid of you. That must be very closely watched."

"All right. You're the boss." She more or less agreed with him, but, as she stood up, she decided not to openly confess to that fact. "Shall we begin our tour?"

When Barric stood up and took her by the hand, Sylvie

almost yanked it free. A pulse of pure heat went up her arm at his touch. The man was dangerous, she thought as she stumbled along after him when he strode out of the great hall. He was a threat in ways he could not possibly understand. If she found that she was caught up in some hoax or trapped in a cult, a man like Barric could make her actually consider staying. If it was all some delusion she suffered from, a vision like Barric could make her reluctant to be yanked back to reality. Sylvie sighed as they began their tour of the castle. She could not believe that she had often bemoaned her dull life in Maine and wished for some adventure.

Buffeted by a strong wind from the ocean, Sylvie stared at the ground and cursed. The tour of Barric's lands was proving as fruitless as the tour of the castle. Not only could she not find any proof that things had been changed just to fool her, but she could find no sign of the twentieth century at all. Now she was back at the site of the attack upon her and her fall, but there was no sign of the traumatic event. Sylvie shook her head.

"There must be something here," she grumbled and started to walk the path of her panicked flight again.

Barric sighed and, leading his horse, ambled alongside her. "There is nothing, mistress. Not an overturned rock, not a broken piece of brush, not any trampled grasses . . ."

"I get the point," she snapped, glaring over her shoulder at him, before continuing on. "Just allow me my follies, please. Can't you see how hard it would be to accept what's in front of my eyes? If I can't find some clue, some hint that I was here, then I have to accept your explanation—that I suddenly appeared in the sky and it's 1145. I'm sorry, but that's too damn much strangeness for me to handle."

"I understand."

She whirled to face him, abruptly halting their stroll over the headland. "You understand? You understand? Hah! You *don't* understand. You can't possibly understand. Not ever! One minute I'm in a land with ice cream stands and flushing toilets, and the next I'm in a hygienist's nightmare having to eat food I don't even recognize, let alone trust. I've got some foul-smelling old woman running around talking about silkies, creatures from the sea, and all sorts of other gibberish." She started to poke him in the chest to stress her complaints. "People cross themselves when I pass. I'm dressed in clothing I can barely walk in. Everything I recognize is gone, yet enough of it remains to make it the same place that I left. It'd be very interesting to see your face if you went to bed in your castle one night and woke up the next morning in some Saracen's dungeon. I wish I knew more history so that I could give you a much better example than that. But, believe you me, you don't understand and never could understand. So don't keep telling me that you do—got it?"

"Aye."

Barric stared down at her flushed, angry face and nearly smiled. He did not understand half of what she said, but that no longer troubled him. There was no glint of madness in her eyes. She simply looked furious, and at that instant, with her long, slender finger poking into his chest, he decided that he wanted her.

"Are you done here now?" he finally asked.

Sylvie took a step back and looked at him. She did not think she had altered his opinion of anything. The man was like a rock. A very attractive rock, but an immovable, cold rock nonetheless.

"Yeah, I'm done here. The question is—now where else do we go?"

"The village."

"No, no. I wouldn't remember enough to make it worth my while. Or yours. Is there a little church nearby? I did go to a church, and a nice old rector took me on a tour around the place."

"Why do you keep on looking?" he asked as he mounted, then helped her swing up behind him.

"I need one clear sign. Just one. I can't really say what it might be until I see it."

She wrapped her arms around his trim waist as he nudged his mount into a slow, even gait. She just prayed that she could find that one thing she needed to prove to herself that she wasn't insane.

It did not take them long to reach the church, which was at the castle end of the village. Sylvie felt a sudden thrill of fear and wondered why. There was absolutely nothing frightening about the medium-size stone building. It did not make sense to her, but as Barric dismounted and helped her down, she had to admit to herself that she was indeed afraid.

"Maybe we could come another time," she mumbled and resisted when Barric tugged her toward the church.

"Why? The weather is fine and Father Donner is here. I can hear him scolding someone just beyond the corner here."

Although Sylvie continued to allow him to pull her along, she felt her fear increase. She did not know why, but she did not want to see the priest or the church and certainly did not want to go where Barric was leading her. Sylvie fought all of that. She saw all those feelings as even more reason to go. There must be some explanation for those emotions, and it could be because she was about to find one of those answers she sought. Sylvie was not about to turn away from the truth.

As they stepped up to the modestly rounded priest and the man turned their way, a young boy fled toward the town. Sylvie calmed herself enough to smile at Father Donner as Barric introduced her. Then the priest began to chatter about people in the village, the crops, and the wine. Sylvie eased her hand out of Barric's grip. Before the boy had run off, he and the priest had been looking at the lower corner of the building. She moved to look at what had so interested them—and froze, slowly sinking down onto her knees.

Sylvie was not sure how long she knelt there, mesmerized by what she saw, before she heard Barric sharply call her name. She could not force herself to answer, shock and dismay freezing her tongue. Even when he grasped her by the shoulder, and gave her a little shake, she had to struggle to speak.

"What is it, Sylvie?" Barric demanded, alarmed when he saw how pale she had become.

"I found my answer."

"Here?" Barric frowned as he studied the lower corner of the stone wall that she stared at so fixedly. "This foolish

scratching by a naughty village boy? 'Twas an error to gift
the boy with such skill. Few have it."

"I fear it *is* this foolish scratching, as you call it." She
reached out an unsteady hand and traced the words the boy
had etched into the stone.

"Father"—Barric looked at the priest—"I think a goblet
of wine would help. She is still unwell after her near
drowning. You understand."

"Of course, of course. Be but a moment," the priest said
as he hurried away.

"You just lied to that priest." Sylvie did not make any
attempt to pull away when Barric put his arm around her
shoulders and held her close to him.

"I will do a penance. What about this marking here?"

"Ah, that. Well, where I came from it was inside a room,
a meeting room used by the church. It was also under glass.
This kindly old man who showed me all around was quite
proud of it, pointing it out to me as a spectacular piece of
ancient graffiti—our fancy word for scratchings. Yup, they
figured it'd been put there some time in the twelfth
century." She looked at him. "You haven't been lying."

"Nay. And this tells you that?" He slowly smoothed his
hand over her long thick braid.

"It does. There's no ignoring the fact that it's new and that
this building is already old. The thing I was studying as a
cute antiquity only yesterday morning has just been done by
that boy. There is one funny thing," she whispered, still
numb from her discovery.

"And what is this funny thing?"

"Oh, this silly thing is the subject of much study and
speculation. It's faded and my people can't read it correctly.
I'm now probably the only one who knows what it truly
says. It says 'Father Donner is a fat friar.' It's such a stupid
thing, such a childish thing, and yet it's the epitaph for all
my hopes. I am *not* home, and I can probably never get back
there."

4

"DO YOU MEAN to do more than gaze off toward the cliffs and sigh?"

Used to that deep, rich voice and the way Barric could creep up on her, Sylvie gave only a slight start. She turned and leaned against the parapet she had been staring over. The truth she had discovered at the church still rocked her. In the week since, she had done little more than stare out over the walls, walk to the cliffside, and stare out over the ocean. She also kept snarling at Mad Annie, who still had not taken a bath and kept insisting that Sylvie was a silkie. When she was not feeling sorry for herself, she was trying to clean up Penmoorland and meeting with more resistance than she thought reasonable.

She frowned up at the baron. He was the one bright spot in her life at the moment. He was always kind, always ready to listen, and often just a simple pleasure to look upon. At the moment, however, the too strong scent of horses and sweaty male covered him. She sighed. It was obviously too much to hope for that, unlike everyone else at Penmoorland, he would value cleanliness.

"I've been doing other stuff," she said in her own defense. "I'm trying to earn my keep."

"Your keep?"

"To pay you in some small way for the bed I sleep in and the food I am eating."

"'Tis my bed and I have gifted you with the use of it, and you eat very little. Too little. 'Tis why you are so scrawny."

"Scrawny? I'm not scrawny!"

"Slender."

"That's better." She narrowed her eyes when she caught the glimmer of laughter in his, revealing that he was just

163

teasing her. "I believe in doing something to help, in doing my chores. I think I've found a job, too."

"If what I have been told is truth, then you have been scrubbing nearly everything and everyone or insisting that it be done."

"Well, yes. I've overstepped myself, have I?"

"Nay, 'tis just that your insistence leaves many of us at Penmoorland very puzzled."

"Your inclination to stay dirty puzzles *me*."

"'Twas very clean where you came from, was it?"

Sylvie crossed her arms beneath her breasts and half smiled at him. She was beginning to like him far more than was wise. He was so different, so good-looking, and oddly endearing in the way he tried to understand her. The way he lived was a little too macho for her liking, but she was beginning to see that he was surprisingly liberal for a twelfth-century knight. She struggled to fight the allure he had for her, however, for she knew enough history to know that he could not marry anyone of her ilk. In truth, his lack of a wife was a bit curious, but she knew she would get no information out of his people about that, and she was determined not to even look at Barric, let alone look into his family's past.

"You have no idea where I come from," she answered with a hint of amusement, quickly trying to turn her thoughts away from his marital state. "However, yeah, it's clean. There are dirty places, but most people keep pretty clean. It's considered to be better for your health."

Barric reached out to smooth his hand down her large black braid, which was draped over her right shoulder. "I want to know where you came from."

"You won't believe me."

"You have never allowed me the chance. You elude any queries."

"Even with all I have seen, all of the proof, I can't believe it all. If I told you the whole story, you would think my wagon wasn't toting a full load." She sighed when that faintly confused look came over his face, the one she knew meant he did not understand her words again. "Um, I have moonsickness? I am a looney?"

"Nay, I do not truly believe you are mad. I saw you fall out of the sky. I have watched you and listened to you. You do not speak like one who is mad—even if what you say is oft incomprehensible and sounds impossible. And if you are mad, you are harmless. So, too, do I think I share some of that madness, for I do not completely disbelieve what you say or what I know has happened."

"All right, so maybe you do believe *something*. But exactly what? And even if you're ready to believe everything I say as gospel, it wouldn't make much sense to you. I am over eight hundred years from my land, my life, my people. Even as I say it, I still find it hard to take in. Besides, according to every science fiction or fantasy story I have ever read, I shouldn't tell you anything or it could change history." She frowned and rubbed her chin. "But then, my being here should do that anyway. I should try to get back."

"Nay!" He suddenly grabbed her by the arms but ignored her startled look. "You are to stay here. If what you said about *how* you came here is all true, then—"

"—to return is to die, to smash upon the rocks I was plummeting toward. I know it. It does make it all very puzzling. I've been trying to figure it all out, but it's not going very well."

"Good, then you will stay." He moved closer to her, pinning her against the parapet. "This is where you belong. You would not have been flung here if you did not belong." He touched a kiss to her cheek.

Sylvie really wanted to enjoy his gentle seduction. She had never had such a good-looking man try to kiss her or tempt her. Unfortunately, even when the light brush of his lips across hers caused a ripple of heat in her stomach, his scent was a little *too* manly. She put her hands on his upper chest and forced him back.

"While I'll admit I really like all this charm, I'm afraid I've got to tell you to go and take a shower first." She gave him an apologetic smile when he stepped away from her.

"Take a shower?" he asked.

"Clean up. Wash. Bathe."

"Bathe? But it is only a little o'er a week since I dove into the water for you. A swim is as good as a bath."

He looked so stunned, so confused, and slightly insulted, that Sylvie almost laughed, but to hurt his feelings was the very last thing she wanted to do.

"It's one of those things about me that you probably won't ever understand. You smell like horses."

"Aye, I have been riding hard and working hard."

"Well, in my world a man would go wash that smell off before he came looking for hugs and kisses." She wondered what was behind those narrowed green eyes when he stared at her as he took a long sniff of his arm. "Have I insulted you? Because I really didn't mean to."

"Nay, I am not insulted." He bowed slightly and started toward the narrow stone steps that led down from the walls. As she moved to follow him, he glanced briefly over his shoulder. "Be careful coming down off these walls. You are very clumsy in those skirts."

Sylvie stopped short and gaped at his broad back as he continued on his way. "Low blow."

His Lordship's pride had been stung, she thought as she cautiously made her way down off the walls. She felt a twinge of remorse. And she was not sure she wanted him to return bathed and ready for a kiss. Considering how her body had reacted to the light touch of his mouth, he could prove to be nearly lethal once he was clean and sweet-smelling.

Barric tugged on his jupon for the tenth time as he stared at the door to his bedchamber. He heard a dry cackle and glared at Mad Annie, who scurried away. The last thing he needed was that old woman advising him on how to handle a woman. He straightened up and rapped on the door.

A soft cry of surprise escaped Sylvie, and she dropped the fine bone and bristle hairbrush she had been using on her hair. She realized she had been lost in a lovely daydream about herself and Lord Barric. Now that she was out of it, she remembered enough to see that it resembled an Errol Flynn movie too much for her comfort. Shaking her mind free of the last vestiges of it, she scrambled off the bed and hurried over to the door.

"Ah, Sir Barric," she greeted him after opening the door.

"Have you come to escort me to the meal in the great hall?" she asked.

"Nay." He moved her out of the way simply by stepping toward her a few times, then shut the door behind him and bolted it.

"Then why are you here?"

"For my hugs and kisses."

"Excuse me?"

"But one hour ago, when we stood together upon Penmoorland's walls, you said that a man would wash that smell off before he came looking for hugs and kisses. I have washed off the smell you found so troublesome." He wrapped his arms around her and lifted her up against his chest.

Sylvie gave another soft cry, more of surprise than alarm. "Well, I don't believe I meant it the way you've obviously interpreted it."

So great was her astonishment when he walked over to the bed, dropped her down on top of it, and then sprawled on top of her, she did not make a sound. Then she decided she did not really want to complain. For the first time in her short life she was deeply and fiercely attracted to a man. The feel of his lean hard body pressed against hers had her breathing faster. There was a heat in his green eyes that flowed straight into her veins.

"You do smell a lot better," she whispered, then grimaced. "Dumb. Very dumb."

"When you told me about what other men in your world do, was this knowledge gained from a woman or a man?" He slowly ran his hand down her side, his gaze fixed upon her face so that he could more certainly judge her reaction to his words and his touch.

"Mostly from sources other than men themselves, although I have had my share of kisses."

"Have you." The wave of jealousy that gripped Barric took several moments to push aside.

Sylvie saw the flare of anger brighten his eyes and said, "Oh, I see. This is the age of pure women and impure men. Of what is sauce for the gander better not get anywhere near the goose. That's incredibly unfair, y'know." It was very hard to maintain a sense of outrage when such a gorgeous man was nibbling her ear, Sylvie decided.

"I have considered that." He cupped her small face in his hands and smiled down at her. "I am not an unreasonable man. I know you are from a different land where the customs are different from ours. I shall not fault you for what has gone before." As he kept his gaze fixed upon the hollow of her throat, Barric prayed he could hold fast to that fine sentiment and overcome the intense jealousy he felt over the mere thought of another man touching her.

"Look at me," Sylvie demanded, and she nearly laughed when he did. Barric looked positively sullen. "Boy, you're choking on those words, aren't you?"

"I have said them, and I will hold to them."

"Oh, I don't doubt it for a minute. I was just meaning that it was hard for you to say them at all. It's not surprising. It's the twelfth century. I might not know much history, but I know you guys weren't the most liberal lot of people in the world. It's probably a good thing that I'm not terribly enlightened, or so I was often told."

Barric sighed and briefly touched his forehead to hers. When she talked as she was doing now, it left him confused. Worse, he sometimes felt stupid, and he knew he was not. Some of the differences in her speech he had learned quickly, but whenever she spoke on what her world was actually like, he simply could not follow her.

Logic and all he had been taught in life told him that he should consider her sadly beset by delusions, use her body to sate his lusts, then discard her. They also told him that what she believed and the things she said were pure madness or, worse, the machinations of the devil. But he could not believe it. Although he questioned Mad Annie's insistence that Sylvie was some mysterious creature from the sea, he knew Sylvie was from some place he had never seen. He wondered if there was any chance that they could find some common ground. As he stared into her heavily lashed copper eyes, Barric realized that he already wanted that to be possible.

"Every time you speak, I am left to wonder if we have

anything in common," he murmured. He sounded almost sad.

Sylvie rushed to contradict him. "We have a great deal in common. In fact, I am astounded at how *much* we have in common." She gave in to the urge to slowly move her hands across the strong breadth of his chest, and the intense look that came across his face made her feel very excited. "True, customs are different, there are none of the comforts I am used to, and I'll need to do a lot of learning, but there are lots of other things that I recognize and can do. I can clean things." She frowned when he chuckled, then shivered as he touched his warm lips to the hollow in her throat.

"So I know from the complaints of all my people."

"Oh, yeah. Well, it really is for their own good. Maybe, after a little while, there'll be fewer grumblings. They'll start to notice the advantages. There really are some."

Sylvie's eyes widened as he lifted up her arm and the wide pleated sleeve of her undertunic fell back, exposing her slim arm up to the elbow. She had left off the tight-sleeved undertunic many others wore because it was too hot. The way he trailed kisses from the inside of her wrist to the hollow of her elbow and back again made her head swim.

"Aye, mayhaps you are right," Barric murmured as he kissed her palms. "You do taste better. And smell better."

"Better than what?" she whispered.

"Better than most anything."

He brushed his lips over hers, and she curled her arms about his neck. Even though most of his body was against hers, she felt a need to be even closer. When the press of his lips grew even stronger, she welcomed it, for the weight of his body also increased.

She gave him no resistance when he touched the tip of his tongue to her lips, asking entry. Sylvie opened her mouth and greedily accepted the stroking of his tongue. Never before had a kiss affected her so completely. There was not one single part of her body that was unmoved. Sylvie shifted beneath him until she was able to twine her legs around his trim hips. She echoed his hungry groan as their bodies settled into an intimate position which mimicked the act she and Barric now ached for.

Barric forced himself to break the kiss, although it was the very last thing he wanted to do. He stared at her flushed face, a pinch of jealousy inching up through the passion knotting his insides. "You kiss very well for one who has only had a few kisses."

"One only needs one or two to learn the trick of it. *How* one does it depends on whom one is kissing." She found his touch of jealousy intriguing. "You are very good yourself."

"Then we are a fine match. Mayhaps Mad Annie is not so mad after all."

"What are you saying?" It was hard for her to concentrate when he was sliding his big hands up and down her sides. "I'm sorry, but I don't think many people would argue that Annie is a little odd."

"True, but sometimes she is right in what she has to say."

Sylvie was not particularly interested in Mad Annie. She wanted to do some more serious kissing, but Barric was not cooperating. One moment he was kissing her with a rough hunger that curled her toes. The next he was nibbling at her lips in a way that stirred her yet frustrated her by denying her the harder, more demanding kiss she was craving more and more.

Then, suddenly, he shifted his position a little, moving his groin rhythmically against hers. There was no question that the man wanted her, and Sylvie found that heady knowledge indeed. What further astounded her was the way her body reacted—greedily. Her body was eagerly demanding something it had easily, even adamantly, refused for twenty years. She briefly wondered if this was what she had unwittingly been waiting for, then harshly told herself not to be such an idiot.

"Are you going to kiss me or not?" she finally demanded in a hoarse whisper.

"I will when you say aye to what I am about to ask you."

"Bribery, huh? Well, what are you going to ask?"

"Will you fulfill Mad Annie's prophecy and become my lady wife?"

Sylvie gaped at him. "Marry you?"

He nodded and she could not think straight for a full minute. She held his steady gaze as a hundred different thoughts whirled through her mind. One clear thought repeated itself over and over—she was completely alone in his world, and he made her bones melt with his kisses. She then briefly considered the fact that her life expectancy had been effectively halved when she had fallen through that time slip. Then he trailed his tongue across her lips, and she did not puzzle over the matter any longer.

"Yeah, I'll marry you." She thoroughly enjoyed the swift hungry kiss he gave her, but it was short-lived. He ended it far sooner than she wanted him to, left her arms, and started toward the door. "Where are you going?"

"To speak to the priest." He winked at her over his shoulder. "If I stay here much longer, I may act with less than honor."

"Who cares?" she muttered, but he was already gone.

Sylvie shook her head and softly cursed. She was now faced with two new problems. One was having a blind hunger for a man who had the strength to practice restraint. The other was agreeing to marry a man she had barely known a week and who could still turn out to be a figment of her imagination. It was clear that when she had tumbled through that gap in time she had left her mind back in the 1990s.

5

AS SHE GINGERLY suckled on her finger, Sylvie decided that needlepoint was not her forte. She had spent most of the morning in with the other women of the castle, struggling to learn the simplest of stitchery only to fail miserably. Sylvie suspected the other women had been glad when she had excused herself. It meant that they could cease mouthing polite words about her utter lack of skill. In the week since she had blithely accepted Barric's proposal, it was just one in dozens of chores and skills she had tried and too often failed at.

Sylvie forced a smile when the young maid Jane entered to tidy up the bedchamber. The timid brunette was growing a little less timid, but was not yet daring enough to be friendly. The fear born of deeply rooted superstition was still glinting in the girl's blue eyes. Sylvie could not help but wonder if she would ever be accepted at Penmoorland.

"Maybe being accepted here isn't what's supposed to happen anyways," she mumbled as she hopped off the bed. "Well, it'd be nice if someone would give me some kinda sign to tell me just what the hell I'm doing here."

"Pardon, m'lady?" Jane paused in cleaning out the fireplace to cast Sylvie a nervous glance.

"Nothing, Jane. I'm just grumbling. It's time for lunch? I mean, the midday meal?" When the wide-eyed girl nodded, Sylvie took a quick check of her appearance in a long, dull mirror, then headed off to the great hall.

The moment Sylvie stepped into the hall, she met Annie. Sylvie promised herself that she would start to keep a closer eye out for the woman. She was growing fond of Annie in an odd way, but she did hate to hear the woman talk of dreams, fates, and silkies. The last thing Sylvie needed was to start believing in any of the woman's many superstitions. There was also the small problem of the woman's refusal to bathe. When Annie fell into step at her side, Sylvie struggled not to breathe too deeply.

"The guests for the wedding will soon be starting to arrive," Annie announced.

Sylvie thought of the weak, hesitant reaction of Barric's people when he had announced their betrothal in the great hall, the very night he had proposed. "I hadn't thought that there would be any guests."

"A few. Sir Barric is not a man of the court or an intriguer, and so few people endure the travail or risk to come here to Penmoorland. And you are alone, so no one will be coming for you."

"Nope. No one." Sylvie found that depressing because it was not due to where she was, but the fact that she had no family or close friends. She doubted she was even being missed.

"Nay, I thought not. Such mystical creatures like you are often alone. I have ne'er heard of silkies traveling in a herd, or whatever they might call it."

"Don't look to me to give you an answer. I'm *not* a silkie. And I'd appreciate it if you'd stop talking about me as if I were. It's making it very uncomfortable for me, and I might be stuck here for a long time."

"But you knew that. 'Tis what you want. 'Tis why you agreed to marry Lord Barric."

"I agreed to marry Lord Barric because he kissed me until my brains turned to mush."

Annie giggled in a way that was a little obscene. "I knew you two would be well matched. Ah, such fine sons you will breed."

The thought of having babies under the conditions she now found herself in made Sylvie cringe. "Losing my wits over a fine bod is not a good reason to get married. I'm beginning to have second thoughts about all of this. Maybe I'm not stuck here. Maybe I can find a way to leave if I look real hard."

Annie gave her a quick sharp look as they approached the doors to the great hall. "You will be here forever. This is where you are meant to be—where God and fate intended you to be."

"If God and fate intended me to be here, then why'd they stick me somewhere else for twenty years?" she demanded as she held the thick iron-studded door open for Annie. "Don't have an answer for that, do you."

"I, a mere old woman, would never presume to understand the workings of God and fate."

Sylvie looked Annie square in the eye and had to smile. The old woman's rheumy gray eyes had an irrepressible gleam in them. "Of course not," she murmured and shook her head when the old woman cackled softly and hurried away with a group of elderly women. "Sly old witch."

"Sylvie," called Barric as he stood up and held his hand out to her. "Come and sit down."

"I'm coming." She was a little surprised to find a heavy

oaken chair now placed on his right. "This is new," she said as she walked over to it and he held it out for her.

"My wife should have a seat of honor at my side."

Heady stuff, she mused as she sat down and he retook his own seat. She would have to keep reminding herself that power corrupts. Barric was born and raised in his position of power, but being boss was very new to her. She had to remember never to misuse her position.

Then again, she thought, maybe she could use it for the benefit of all. One look at the greasy meat and heavily buttered bread only strengthened that possibility in her mind. If the people in this age did not die of so much else first, Sylvie suspected heart disease would be a real concern.

She picked up her goblet, sniffed the dark liquid inside and sighed. "Is there anything else to drink besides ale, wine, and hard cider?" Sylvie was certain that alcoholism had to be a serious problem.

"Aye, but they are not as safe to drink," Barric answered. "Some people water it down."

"Er, no, I don't think so. Not with your water anyway." She took a sip and briefly pondered the chance of keeping a supply of well-boiled water on hand for herself. "I don't know, Barric. The more I see of your world the less certain I am that I'm suited to it."

Barric took her hand in his and raised it to his lips to press a long heated kiss to her palm. He kept the twist of fear he felt to himself. It not only surprised him, but he did not yet want her to fully realize the hold she had on him. There was only one thing he was certain of, and that was that he would do everything within his power to make her stay with him.

"I wish I could ease your qualms, little one," he murmured and kissed the inside of her wrist. "Is there someone you are eager to return to?" He leaned closer to her, talking softly so that no one could overhear them. "Do I have a rival?"

"Well, Mel Gibson will be heartbroken. Only kidding." She stared into his warm green eyes and felt captivated. "No, no rival at all."

"Then, has my wooing been lacking?"

She thought of all the heated kisses, the flowers, and the

attention he lavished on her. The only answer she could give to that question was a no, and she shook her head. Although she had never really been "wooed" before, she was sure that no man in Barric's time or her own could do a better job of it.

"Then put your concerns at ease, dearling. Eat your fill, and we can go for a ride if you wish."

When all she did was nod, Sylvie inwardly cursed. She was totally ensnared by the man, she decided as she turned her attention back to her meal. Despite the unappetizing appearance of the food in front of her, she began to eat. It occurred to her that she would need to eat to keep her strength up and that she was going to need all the strength she could muster to hold her own against Sir Barric Tremayne, Lord of Penmoorland.

"Your skill at horsemanship will soon improve," Barric assured Sylvie as he helped her dismount after their afternoon ride. "You are not as poor a rider as you think you are." He could not fully suppress a chuckle over the fulminating look she gave him.

"Next you'll tell me that I don't feel as bad as I think I do, either," she muttered and subtly rubbed her aching backside. "The people here obviously kill all feeling in their butts at a very young age."

"In their whats?" Barric signaled to a stableboy to take his and Sylvie's horses away.

"Their bottoms," she whispered and softly cursed when he laughed. "Now that I have entertained you for the day, I believe I'll go to my room for a while." She frowned faintly when he placed an arm around her shoulders and held her back. "Is something wrong?"

"Nay, loving." He touched a kiss to the tip of her nose. "I but wished to kiss you."

She did not resist as he tugged her closer, but she nervously looked around. "It isn't very private here."

"There is no shame in a groom kissing his bride." He gave her a short but slow and inviting kiss.

Sylvie sagged against Barric, clutching the front of his soft leather jupon as she stared up at him. The man made her

feel positively weak-kneed. It was a little alarming and
somewhat embarrassing. The only sign she had that she was
reaching him in any way at all was that his breathing grew
a little faster and the green of his eyes became an enticingly
warm color. Sylvie wished for just a little more equality.

"Ah, my friend, I had not realized that your bride was
such a pretty woman," drawled a cool voice from just
behind Sylvie, and she felt Barric tense a little.

Barric kept his arm around her shoulder as he tugged her
to his side, tuning her toward the man who had just spoken.
"I thank you for those kind words, Lord Denton. Allow me
to present my bride to you. Sylvie DeLorenzo Pentayne,
meet our neighboring landholder, Lord Simon Denton,
baron and a knight in King Stephen's service."

As carefully as she could, since she was still new at it,
Sylvie curtsied when the slim Lord Denton bowed. Inexpe-
rienced though she was, she recognized his bow as barely
polite and felt Barric tense even more. She had a very bad
feeling about Lord Denton, and the flat look in his hazel
eyes did nothing to ease her qualms.

"I'm pleased to meet you," she said and prayed that the
man could not tell that she was lying. "I hope you will
forgive me for excusing myself so soon after our meeting,
but Barric and I have only just returned from our ride. I was
about to go and tidy up."

"Of course, m'lady. Do not feel hindered because of me,"
Lord Denton said with another tiny bow.

After one last look at an expressionless Barric, Sylvie
headed into the keep and straight to her bedchamber. Lord
Denton gave her the chills. For the first time since Sylvie
had dropped in on Penmoorland, she had truly sensed the
underlying violence so common to the time period, and it
frightened her.

One thing that worried her was the way his eyes had
narrowed as she had spoken to him. She had been practicing
her speech, trying to make it sound more like everyone
else's, but Lord Denton's look made it clear that she had not
done a very good job. That flat Maine speech, that distinc-
tively Yankee flavor to her words, was impossible to
eradicate completely. What she was not sure of was—what

could Lord Denton possibly do with such information? All
she could do was pray that there would not be any trouble
because of her.

"A strange young woman," Lord Denton murmured as,
after freshening up, he sat in the great hall with Barric and
sipped at a goblet of wine. "Very pretty, and endearing, but
odd."

"What do you mean—odd?"

"Unusual. Her speech is strange to my ear. I have never
heard anything like it."

"'Tis from a remote place in Ireland."

"Ah, Ireland. One of our allies, I pray." Lord Denton
faintly smiled at Barric.

"Of course. You ask many questions about my wife."

"Very true, but 'tis also the king who asks. These are dark
and dangerous times, my friend. When news reached the
court of your impending nuptials, there was no one who
recognized your bride's name, and you offered up no
knowledge. Did you expect no one to be at least curious?"

"Curious—aye. Howbeit, you insinuate some wrong, and
that approaches an insult."

Lord Denton held up his hands. "Nay, calm yourself,
m'friend. Have pity on my poor position. I shall be sorely
questioned when I return to the court."

"When you return to the court, you may tell anyone who
asks that the nuptials went smoothly. If our king wishes to
inquire about my wife, you may tell him that she and I are
at his command. He but needs to summon us, and we will
come and reply to any questions he may have."

"As you wish."

It was nearly time for the evening meal before Barric saw
Mad Annie. The woman hurried up to him as he walked to
the great hall. As he stopped to face her, Barric smiled
faintly at the woman who had been his nursemaid. Sylvie
was right—Mad Annie was sorely in need of a good
scrubbing. He quickly sobered, however, when he saw how
worried the woman was.

"Is something amiss with Sylvie?" he demanded, uttering the first concern that entered his mind.

"Nay, the child is fine. She should soon be coming down to dine. I left Jane braiding her hair."

"Then what is concerning you, and do not say 'tis naught, for I can see it in your face."

"Sylvie is fine now, but she may not be if you do not get rid of that man."

"What man? Lord Simon Denton?"

Mad Annie vigorously nodded her head. "Aye, that man. Ah, lad, he is a bad one, a very bad one."

Barric touched a finger to his lips as he glanced around. "Softly, woman. The man has the king's ear. I have no wish to anger him and have the words whispered to my liege in a twisted and tainted fashion."

"Aye, aye. Sometimes I can be a foolish old woman. I should at least peek around a corner or two ere I say too much. 'Tis just that I fear for our little silkie. That adder Denton wishes to strike at you, m'lord, and he sees how to do that now. He will use that pretty bride of yours. Send him away, m'lord. Send him far away."

The woman's agitation infected Barric, and he combed his fingers through his hair. "I would like to send him away, but I cannot. He is the king's man. He is my closest neighbor, my only possible ally for miles about." Barric struggled to think of more than just Sylvie's safety.

"That man will never be your ally. He hates you."

A soft curse escaped Barric as he nodded. "I know it well though I do not understand why. Many a time I have pondered this hatred he holds for me, and I find no reason for it. None. When he rode into Penmoorland today, I could see that his hatred for me now reached out to soil Sylvie. I ached to cut him down on the spot, but that is not possible. Unless the man strikes at me or one of mine, I can do nothing but treat him with courtesy."

"Then at least try and keep that cur away from our Silkie."

"Aye, that I will do." He shook his head as the old woman hurried away. "And her name is Sylvie."

By the time Barric entered the great hall, Sylvie was

already there. She sat stiffly in her chair to his right, and he
did not have to look far for the source of her tension. Seated
directly across from her was their unwanted guest—Sir
Simon Denton. The man only glanced Barric's way briefly.
Barric hurried to his seat, putting himself between Denton
and Sylvie. He prayed that such tactics should be enough to
divert trouble, but one look at Denton's face told him that it
would not suffice. Simon Denton scented blood, and the
man would cling to the trail until he was defeated or
victorious.

The questions the man asked revealed that he had spent
his time at Penmoorland efficiently. Denton knew every
small detail of Sylvie's unusual arrival at Penmoorland.
Barric was heartily glad that he had tossed her rags into the
fire before anyone besides Mad Annie could look at them.
Denton clearly wanted to feed people's superstitious fear, to
turn those of Penmoorland against Sylvie, and stir up
trouble in that way. Nothing Denton said was openly
insulting, thus inviting a challenge. All Barric could do was
reply politely and hope that his people would not pay the
man heed. He did not question his people's loyalty, but they
had not had the time to come to know Sylvie.

Sylvie listened to the men talk and tried not to squirm too
much beneath Lord Denton's steady, cold stare. He and
Barric were bandying words in a way she did not really
understand, following rules of honor and etiquette that she
had not yet learned. What she did understand, however, was
that she was in danger and, through her, so was Barric. The
thought that she could be the source of a threat to Barric
upset her so much that she knew she cared deeply for the
man. After facing that fact she could do nothing else but ask
herself how she could ease the threat against Barric no
matter what it might cost her.

6

A HEAVY ROCK in each hand and her skirts tucked up beneath her girdle so that she would not trip over them, Sylvie started on her third fast walk around the keep. For the first time since she had arrived at Penmoorland she was painfully aware of how closely the people watched her. In the three days since Denton had arrived at the keep, he had done a very skillful job of stirring up everyone's fears. Mad Annie and Jane were the only women who really talked to her. Sylvie suspected that the only thing keeping her safe and holding open rebellion at bay was the people's loyalty to Lord Barric.

She avoided any contact with Denton. The man gave her the willies for two good reasons—he was a threat to Barric, and he hated her. That hate stung, for it was totally unearned, but her greatest concern was for the trouble she was bringing to Barric. She could see that, by whatever rules the game was played in twelfth-century England, Barric could not simply throw the annoying Denton out on his conniving backside.

As she stepped up to the water bucket that marked the start and end of a complete circuit around the keep, Sylvie tossed her rocks onto the ground. She quickly rinsed her hands in the cool water, shook them, and then wiped them on her skirts. Then she turned to go back inside the keep only to confront a slyly smiling Denton and half-a-dozen Penmoorland men-at-arms. The men with Denton looked more curious than dangerous, so Sylvie concentrated on Denton himself.

"A good walk aids the settling of a meal," she said, explaining the exercise ritual she knew people at Penmoorland found strange.

"You ate very little," Denton murmured.

"It's also good exercise. I am accustomed to doing more than gossiping and needlework. Perhaps I will grow used to the softer life here, but until I do, I end the day too restless to sleep." She noticed several of the men nod faintly in agreement. "Lord Barric prefers me slender."

"One wonders why that is."

The way Denton eyed her made Sylvie feel briefly ugly, but she shook that away. She had no doubt in her mind that Barric desired her. When a man like him eyed her with interest, it made a very strong shield against any insult.

"I never bothered to ask." Sylvie decided she had had her fill of his spite. "The hour grows late, sirs. I bid you good night."

She nodded to all the men and started to walk past them. Lord Denton reached out and grabbed her by the shoulder. Sylvie did not really think of what she was doing. Ever since the day Lord Denton had entered the walls of Penmoorland, she had been made to feel threatened, afraid, and angry. Sylvie reacted to the man's touch with one of many moves she had been taught in her self-defense class. Since His Lordship was caught completely by surprise, it was easy, despite his height and a hundred-pound advantage. While the men with Lord Denton watched in openmouthed astonishment, she neatly flipped the aggravating man over her shoulder. It was not until he was sprawled in the dust at her feet that Sylvie realized that it might not have been the wisest thing to do, no matter how satisfying it was. The look Lord Denton gave her as he got to his feet was murderous.

Lord Denton called her a vicious name, and Sylvie reacted too slowly to avoid the full force of his blow. She was sent tumbling backward by the slap he gave her right across the face. The men with Lord Denton were Barric's soldiers and instinctively acted as they knew their lord and master would want them to. They grabbed Lord Denton before he could strike her again. Her face stinging and the warm salty taste of blood in her mouth were all the incentives Sylvie needed to make a swift retreat. She scrambled to her feet and ran, not stopping until she was inside her bedchamber with the heavy door shut behind her.

Slumped against the door for a full minute, Sylvie

struggled to calm herself. She hated violence of any kind, yet it was constantly in evidence in some form at Penmoorland. The rough side of life was not hidden by layers of refinement and invention. There was no subtlety. There was no hesitation by the men with Denton; they had acted immediately to stop him because they had no doubt he would have hit her again and probably gone further than that.

A throbbing pain and a tickling dampness on her cheek roused her from her lingering shock. She walked over to her mirror and studied the spot where Denton's blow had connected. It was already faintly swollen, and there was a small gash oozing blood, marring the high bone line of her right cheek. She suspected she would have a vivid rainbow of color over at least half of her face.

Sylvie was just wringing out a cloth to wash her injury with when the door to her bedchamber was slammed open. She gave a high squeak of surprise and fear. When she saw that it was Barric, she gave him a cross look and returned to carefully washing her cut. He stepped up behind her, and when Sylvie finally met his gaze in the mirror, she shivered. The man was furious, so furious it made her afraid. Suddenly, despite feeling that Denton ought to be punished in some way, Sylvie could only think of placating, of soothing.

"It's just a little cut. Don't think it'll bruise badly." She grimaced beneath the look he gave her. "Someone told you what happened?"

"I saw most of it, but could not reach you in time. One of the men told me the rest."

"Denton's obviously an important man. You said as much yourself. I don't want to cause you any trouble."

"Denton believes he is more important than he is."

"Can't you just report him to the police? I mean, the sheriff, or a judge, or even the king? Let them do whatever must be done."

"They would think me a base coward and tell me to see to my duty myself. 'Tis my place to protect the honor and person of my betrothed."

"Yeah, yeah, but there are times when it's best to push that macho crap aside and try for peace."

Barric crossed his arms over his chest and studied her. "Have you come to care for Denton then?"

"Care for that creep? I think you have caught Annie's madness." She started to walk away only to have him gently, but firmly, enclose her in his arms. "I just don't want any trouble. Now, I know I'm probably going to hate the answer to this, but what's going to happen next?"

"On the morrow Denton and I will face each other, sword to sword. We have agreed to forego all armor save for our shields. He has grossly insulted you and must pay for that."

Even the way he traced the shape of her mouth with soft kisses could not banish the chill that ran down her spine. "You're going to kill him, aren't you?"

"I should, but, nay—not unless he forces me to it."

Sylvie pulled free of his hold, walked over to the bed, and sat down. "The fact that I can't stomach blood being spilled because of me won't make any difference, will it?"

Barric walked over to stand in front of her. "Nay. Howbeit, this concern for life is a compliment to your womanhood. . . ."

"Oh, boy, there's sexism. Never mind," she said when Barric frowned in that way which told her that he did not quite understand her. "I'd like to think that my reluctance is due to more than my being female. I'll admit that there's a big part of me that'd like to repay Denton but that doesn't make it right." She studied him for a moment, then sighed. "I can tell by the look on your face that I might convince you of the correctness of the sentiments, but it won't change your actions."

"It cannot." He sat down next to her and put his arm around her shoulders. "I have come to accept that you come from a place very different from here. If it is a place where calm and peace rule, then it must be a fine place indeed."

"We have our share of violence, and I think a lot of it would seem very senseless to you. It's just that most of society doesn't accept it as a way of life anymore. There's always the simple fact that when violence is met with violence, the one in the right doesn't always come out the winner."

A slow smile erased the solemnity of Barric's expression, and he touched a kiss to her forehead. "So, this is all because you fear for me. There is no need. I can easily defeat a man like Denton. His skill is in sly intrigue, not in honorable battle."

"But he hasn't needed to be skilled in honorable battle, has he? You yourself said he is a king's man. Even if I felt as sure as you do that you could fight the man and win, there's still the question of who he is. Will your king understand? Can you be sure fighting with Denton won't be seen as a slap at the king?"

Barric was not sure at all, but he did not voice his own concerns, for they were not very big ones. He concentrated on trying to make Sylvie understand why he had to face Denton, how the rules he lived by left him no choice in the matter. "The man has insulted you and struck you. This becomes an attack upon me as well. If I do not act, I add to the crime done to you and tell every man in England that he is free to treat you as he wishes. You cannot throw every man to the ground as you did Sir Denton. And I mean to discover how you did that as soon as this trouble is cleared away."

Sylvie waved her hand in a dismissive gesture. "Just a little trick I learned in self-defense class. You're telling me that if you don't react swiftly and strongly to Denton's attack on me, then others will see me as free game?"

"Aye, they will see you as unprotected yet not untouchable."

"A dangerous combination if the tone of your voice is any indication."

"Very dangerous. Then there is the matter of my honor. If I turn from a fight with Denton, I will be seen as a coward, as unworthy of my title and my spurs, the symbol of my knighthood. I would become a broken, scorned man. I would lose all power, all right to have my voice be heard. I could even lose Penmoorland. No one would trust me or wish to be allied with me, and a man alone soon sees the carrion birds gather overhead. The rules and customs I must live by may not be the best ones, but unless I find a near army of men ready to change them, I will continue to follow them. There are too many people who depend upon me and Penmoorland for their lives. I cannot fight some blind crusade I know I can never win."

What he said made sense and fitted what meager knowledge of history she had acquired. It was a stark revelation of his world that both alarmed and saddened her. He spoke as if he was totally helpless to change anything, but she knew he was being modest. Within the confines of Penmoorland she knew he was quite liberal in his views and actions. The question she needed to answer was—could she live by the same rules he was forced to live by? And did she have any choice in the matter? When she met his gaze, she suspected she didn't.

"No, and I don't think I'd want you to try some suicidal crusade, either." She reached up to trace the strong arc of his cheekline. "Maybe it was more of a curse than an act of fate that brought me here. I seem to be nothing but a source of trouble for you."

"Nay. 'Tis not you who causes the trouble."

Sylvie was about to argue when he neatly caught her up in his arms and lay on the bed with her sprawled on top of him. It was a neat, efficient move and, she decided with a half smile, quite seductive. She made no protest when he laced his fingers through her hair and tugged her mouth down to his. Sylvie met his kiss with a slow greed to equal his. When they finally broke off the kiss, her hair was completely undone and tumbling around her shoulders.

"You do that real well," Sylvie murmured after briefly glancing at her now unbraided hair, then meeting his warm gaze.

"Your hair is too beautiful to keep so tightly bound. I say that, yet I would be fiercely jealous if any other man saw it loose or had the privilege of threading his fingers through its midnight depths."

"Are you trying to distract me from the trouble with Lord Denton?"

"Are you distracted?" He rolled slowly until she was

lightly pinned beneath him, then kissed the hollow of her throat.

"Very much so."

She curled her arms around his neck and brushed her lips over his. He did make it easy to forget all that was wrong with the world she now found herself in. The dirt and smells were mostly curable, and she had been allowed to do her best. Even the garderobes had been improved. Of course, the way all the drains emptied into the sea through the underground tunnels was an environmental disaster, but she could not be expected to solve every problem. The culture, however, was not able to be changed much, and she knew that could prove to be a very real obstacle, if not even treacherous. After all, she mused, the consequences of breaking the rules were very harsh.

"You look saddened, dearling. There is no need to worry."

"So easy to say." When he started to say something else, she pressed two fingers against his lips. "There is no sense in talking about it. There could be a major change in our lives, yours and mine, come the morning. We've both said what we think and recognized that there's no complete agreement to be reached and certainly no changing anyone's mind. So"—she traced the shape of his ear with her finger—"I think we could find better things to do with the night, don't you?" She blushed faintly over the boldness of her own words.

He took her hand in his and pressed a kiss into her palm. "Aye, we could, but we should not. We will be wed in but a few days."

When he started to lift away from her, Sylvie firmly held him close. "You could lose tomorrow. I don't even like to say it, but the possibility is there. There is one thing I certainly don't want to be regretting. I was considered a little odd in my world because I believed in abstinence. Maybe there were more reasons for that than I knew. Now is the time to end that restraint. What do you say to that?"

"What could any man with a drop of blood in his veins say? Aye, aye, and aye again."

Sylvie groaned softly with welcoming pleasure when he

kissed her. She curled her body around his as she opened her mouth to his stroking tongue. Disease and unwanted pregnancy had been good reasons to practice celibacy, but she now saw that there had been another one. Somewhere in her heart and mind she had known that she was waiting, waiting for the one man who could curl her toes with one kiss.

She helped him when he began to take off her clothes while also trying to shed his own. It was not until she was completely naked that her modesty returned enough to briefly dim her passion. Then she looked at Barric, who knelt facing her. The man was so beautiful he took her breath away. He also stole all nervousness over doing what she had never done before. She leaned forward and touched her mouth to his. Sylvie echoed his growl of need as he held her close and then pressed her back down on the bed.

Barric's kisses kept her fears and natural shyness from making her hesitant. She matched Barric touch for touch, kiss for kiss. His lovemaking was skilled yet unrestrained. The touch of fierceness underlying it fed her own passion. When he penetrated her body, she was ready for him, her cry more of satisfaction than pain. She wrapped her body around his, welcomed and met his every thrust, and knew this was the union she had saved herself for.

"I will make sure that you do not suffer for this early wedding night," Barric said, holding her close in his arms as he stared up at the ceiling. "You are mine now, Sylvie DeLorenzo Pentayne. By giving yourself to me in this way, you have told me that you will stay with me."

"What I told you was that I didn't want to lose a chance to enjoy this," she murmured, slowly rubbing her cheek against his chest as she trailed her hand up and down his side.

"You are just trying to appear strong. We will talk about that when I am done with Denton."

Sylvie held him a little tighter. It was tempting to tell him exactly what she felt, to pour her heart out to him. She kissed him instead and prayed that she was not letting an irretrievable chance slip away.

7

SYLVIE BIT THE inside of her cheek until it bled, but it did not help much. She had her hands so tightly clenched that her nails bored holes into her palms. The raucous noise of Barric and Denton battling each other did not really penetrate her misery. She was both terrified for Barric and appalled by the violence.

Barric and Denton had stripped down to their braies. They each wore only a light helmet for armor and held their shields and swords. Right up until the moment the heavy swords had first crashed together, Sylvie had hoped that the battle would be called off, that some other way to punish Denton would be found. Her wishes had not been granted. She had to stand and watch the man she now knew she loved engage in a sword fight, and over something she still saw as her fault. A quick glance around her told her that a great many of the other people of Penmoorland thought it was all her fault, too.

A subtle swing of Barric's sword left a bleeding welt across Denton's somewhat thin chest. Sylvie discovered that the sight increased her fear as well as left her chilled and horrified. Here was the true unadorned violence directors so often tried to portray in their movies. Here was fierce hand-to-hand combat, where each man could actually look his opponent in the eye.

Denton delivered a neat jab and cut Barric's side with the tip of his sword. Sylvie had to clap both hands over her mouth to keep from screaming when she saw the blood seeping over his skin. The battle went on and on until both men were so smeared with sweat, dirt, and blood, they were barely recognizable. She could see that Denton was faltering, but Barric also looked weary.

One swift lunge and a fierce parry by Barric brought

Denton to the brink of surrender. Sylvie gasped along with the others when the man refused Barric's offer of clemency. What happened next left Sylvie so shocked that she was unable to think straight. There was a frenzied counterattack by Denton, and it was met skillfully by Barric, but it all moved too swiftly for Sylvie to follow. Then Denton screamed. Sylvie watched in numb horror as the man staggered back, away from Barric, and fell to his knees. Blood poured from a wound in Denton's chest as he slowly collapsed facedown in the dirt.

Sylvie could not take her eyes from Denton's body. She had never witnessed a violent death before. What chilled her most about the fight she had just watched was that it had not been done in the heat of the moment; it had all been planned out—coldly, calmly, and by a firm set of rules. But what terrified her most was the knowledge that it could be Barric's body sprawled in the dirt.

"Sylvie?"

She finally met Barric's gaze as he stood in front of her. "You won."

"I told you I would." The odd, almost distant look in her eyes made him nervous.

"Yes, you did. You had better get your injuries seen to. You don't want that dirt to get too settled." She forced a smile when he kissed her on the cheek.

With several of his men surrounding him, Barric walked into the keep. He looked her way only one more time before he entered the castle, and she waved. Then she stood, feeling as if all the life and warmth had drained out of her, watching as two men-at-arms callously dragged Denton's body away. She could also see that Denton's men were not going to stay to see if they would be made to share in their late master's punishment. It was a stark, unpleasant view of the world she had been thrust into and, by accepting Barric's proposal, agreed to stay in.

She took two steps toward the keep and stopped. She could hear the whispers of the people, see their sly accusatory glances. And before those had been Denton's lies and insinuations. Superstition had a strong grip on the people of Penmoorland, and everything about her plucked at their fears. Denton had used her to strike at Barric. Because of what she was, that had been an easy thing to do. And it would continue to be easy. She might win over the people of Penmoorland, but the stories about her would never disappear. She would always be Barric's greatest weakness, and one day that would get him killed.

Sylvie stared down at the bloodstained dirt. One day it could be Barric who was so callously dragged off, his blood turning the dirt into a gruesome mud. Just the thought of it was enough to make Sylvie nearly cry out in frantic denial. It was clear that if she truly loved Barric, then the only right thing to do was to remove herself from his life.

One more wary glance from a Penmoorland man-at-arms decided her. Sylvie started toward the open gates. She knew where she had to go. Just as she started to walk faster, she heard a familiar raspy voice call out to her. Sylvie sent Mad Annie one frantic glance and started to trot, knowing the woman would hold her back. A sharp tone entered Annie's voice, and Sylvie knew that the woman had guessed her intentions. Sylvie yanked up her skirts and started to run, right past the startled guards at the gates and straight for the cliffs.

Barric shook the water from his hair. He stood in a large tub in the guardroom while his squire fetched another bucket of water to pour over him. A sense of urgency gnawed at his insides. Although he was not sure why, he felt an intense need to see Sylvie. There had been a look on her pale face that deeply troubled him. The last thing he wanted was for the passionate night they had spent together to become an ending instead of a beginning. When his squire tipped a second bucket of water over him, Barric could see the rail-thin frame of Mad Annie scurrying toward him. He was out of the tub and drying himself off by the time she reached him.

"Something is wrong," he said as he hurried to dress and his squire quickly moved to help him.

"Aye." Annie leaned against the cool stone wall and wheezed as she struggled to catch her breath. "Our little silkie has fled back to the sea. I could not stop her."

"If she goes back the way she came, she will die."

"And she believes that if she stays here, she will be the cause of your death. She does this for you, and you must be the one to stop her."

"What? No prophecy? No dream this time?"

"Nay, nothing, you ungrateful boy. All I know is that she plans to return to the sea and that she must not. All I know is that this is one silkie who cannot return to the sea."

"It would help if you would cease to call her a silkie," snapped Barric as he yanked on his boots, and he saw his squire listening closely. "That just feeds people's fears. 'Tis true that I have no idea where she came from, but she is no mystical creature. Nay, 'twas a woman I held in my arms all night. She cried out, she sighed, and she sweat just like any other woman except that her noises were sweeter to my ear. 'Twas a woman I tussled with all night and not some watery fish turned female."

Annie was shocked. "You bedded her and you are not wedded proper yet?"

"She feared I would meet my fate when I battled Denton and did not wish to lose her chance of spending a night with me." He winked at his chuckling squire and knew, in that one exchange of glances, that the man would now be willing to mute any superstitious gossip about Sylvie. He looked at Annie as he buckled on his sword. "So, no more talk of silkies. I have no wish to keep chasing after my woman." He hurried out of the guardroom.

"Tell her that if she comes back, I will bathe. Maybe e'en more than once."

Barric only fleetingly smiled. He was too worried about Sylvie. Now he understood the pale look of hurt and sadness in her golden eyes. She had been thinking of leaving him. He raced to the stables and mounted the first horse he reached, curtly shooing away the stableboy who wanted to put a saddle on the animal. Bellowing a warning to the people in the bailey, he galloped out of the stables and through the gates. He had to catch Sylvie before she could try to go back to wherever she had come from.

Sylvie stared down at the rocky beach and decided that

the shock of watching a man killed had stolen her brains and every ounce of her common sense. She could not go back. If nothing else, she could not recreate her fall. Her point of entry into Barric's little kingdom was out over the water now. It was possible that she could swim out and find that the time doorway reached down to the water itself, but she did not see much point in doing that, either. Going back meant only death. She could not make herself believe that that was what was supposed to happen.

She peered over the edge, a little nervous about falling, but was distracted by the sound of a horseman approaching at a breakneck speed. Straightening up, she nearly gaped as she watched Barric race toward her on an old mare. Sylvie was just wondering what had possessed the man and if she should get out of the way when the horse thundered by her. Barric came hurtling off the back of the mare and tackled her to the ground, rolling them both away from the edge of the cliff.

"What the hell are you doing?" she rasped as she lay beneath him and struggled to get her breath back. "You could've knocked us both off the cliff!"

"I was trying to stop you from going off that cliff." Barric winced as he shifted his weight off her and realized that he had hurt himself when he had struggled to shelter her from the force of their fall.

"Oh." She cleared her throat and blushed a little. "Well, I had changed my mind."

"You did not look as if you had changed your mind. You looked ready to hurl yourself onto the rocks."

It suddenly occurred to her that Barric thought that she was about to leave him. He had made that wild ride to try and keep her at Penmoorland. Sylvie smiled faintly as she slipped her arms around his neck and kissed the tip of his nose.

"I wanted to save you from any more trouble," she said. "I saw myself as your weakness, something your enemies could use against you, and I decided that I had to get rid of that weakness."

"You are not my weakness; you are my strength."

"That's very kind, Barric, but I am trouble. I wanted to be

so noble. I was just going to get out of your life. Then I got here, and, well, I guess the shock of seeing that fight wore off and I got a little more sensible. I don't think I can go back even if I really wanted to. To go back I'd have to fall just like I did to get here."

Barric slowly sat up and looked out over the water. "And that is impossible."

"Well, I certainly can't figure out how to do it," she answered as she sat up and looked at him. "And you rode out here to stop me from trying it, to hold me back?"

He wrapped his arms around her and held her close. "Aye, I did. I was not being kind when I said you are my strength. You are. I need you. 'Tis strange, for you are an odd creature." He kissed the top of her head.

"Thank you." The sarcasm she tried for was lost, for she was simply too happy as she listened to him.

"Ah, Sylvie, I do not know what you are or where you have come from, but I do know that you belong here—with me. I knew it from the moment I pulled you out of that water."

"I think I knew there was something very special about you right from the start." She sighed and lightly rubbed her cheek against his chest. "I am just so afraid."

"Nay, you need not be afraid. I will protect you."

She glanced up at him and briefly shook her head. "I think we're going to have to have us a talk about women's rights and machismo." She reached up and touched her fingers to his cheek. "The superstitions I rouse will never really fade away. It could plague you for years. I could force you to face more Dentons than you can manage. So, although I can't go back to my old world, perhaps I should still leave." She gave a soft cry of surprise when he abruptly hugged her more tightly.

"Nay. God's beard, you are going to force me to bare my soul. Sweet Sylvie, I do not understand you at times," he began as he cupped her chin in his hand and turned her face up to his, "but I do love you."

It was hard to speak, but the soft uncertainty she could read on his handsome face told her she had better hurry and blurt out something. "I love you, too." She grimaced. "Not very clever or original, was it."

"It does not matter," he whispered against her lips and then gave her a hungry, slow kiss.

Sylvie felt a little groggy when he finally ended the kiss. The soft loving look on his face only added to that feeling. It was hard to believe that such a man could love her. She was torn between demanding that he say those three beautiful words over and over, and not wishing to be foolish.

"Mad Annie says that she will take a bath if you stay," he murmured and smiled when she giggled. "Mayhaps e'en more than one."

"Oh, my, there is sacrifice."

"And I will bathe before I come and ask for hugs and kisses."

"Barric, I have nothing to bring to this marriage. I know enough history to know that a dowry of some sort is required. I don't even have my own shoes. Oh, and I'm not of the aristocracy."

"You need none of those things. I only require that you love me. And that you will not try to run off a cliff again."

Sylvie laughed. "I intend to keep my feet planted firmly on the ground."

"So, my pretty Silkie—are we to be wed?"

"Oh, yes. It seems we're fated, my fine knight. Even time couldn't keep us apart."

Echoes of Love

Elaine Crawford

1

BRENN RYAN BLEW into the coffee shop on a blustery March gust. While taking a moment to rake her fingers through the long length of what she termed her straight-and-streaked-model look, she searched the green-clad tables for Angie Giannelli.

From the rear of the narrow brick room framed in rich mahogany, her friend waved to her with one of those pert frowning smiles meant to reprimand her for being fifteen minutes late. Again.

Brenn returned a helpless shrug and started toward Angie in long leggy strides. She'd always prided herself on her punctuality. But recently her schedule had become overly crammed. And after the call she'd just received from her mother, she might just as well take every one of her lists to the top of the Empire State Building and sail them on the winds like so many paper airplanes.

Reaching Angie, who'd been her closest friend since their freshman year at Harvard, Brenn took a seat across from the tiny girl whose opinions were always as blunt and practical as her precisely cropped jet-black hair. "Sorry. I hope you already ordered lunch for me."

"Don't I always?" Angie picked up her cup of coffee. "What was it this time, your boss or that endless stream of wedding plans?"

Brenn dropped her overstuffed shoulder bag to the floor beside her and sighed. "I wish you hadn't mentioned the wedding. You know the china pattern I chose the other day? I showed Ron the brochure, and he wants me to change it. He doesn't feel it makes the right statement."

Angie's dark eyes sharpened beneath her thin brows. "'Right statement'?"

"You know, for the whole image he wants us to create. And he's right. I can't imagine why I selected some innocuous floral pattern."

"You picked it because you liked it."

"Yes, but after we've so meticulously selected every piece of furniture, every fabric. Everything has to make just the right impression. You know how important entertaining is if you really want to get to the top."

"You mean like that no-nonsense brown suit you have on?"

"I thought you said it had good lines."

"Oh, it does if you're running for banker of the month. Come on, let's talk about something a little more romantic." Angie leaned forward with an impish grin. "Have you decided where you're going on your honeymoon yet?"

All that girl ever thought about was sex, Brenn thought, like it was the most important thing in the world. To hear Angie talk, it was as if Brenn had never quite grasped the concept. Not true, of course. Whenever she and Ron could spare the time away from all their pressing commitments, she enjoyed it as much as the next person. But listening to Angie rave, it was supposed to be as steamy and all-consuming as the movies made it out to be. The girl really needed to get her mind out of fantasyland and onto her future.

Brenn stared pointedly, not speaking until Angie's stupid smile disappeared. "Ron had settled on Bermuda for our honeymoon. But I think that's all changed now. And originally we planned to take two weeks, but things have gotten hectic where he works, and my boss has been giving me those 'you're-really-not-taking-your-career-seriously' looks. So last night we decided to cut it to one week. But now it looks like I'm even going to have to steal some time from that."

"Jeez, Brenn." Angie slumped back into her chair. "*Now you're too busy even for your honeymoon?* Look, I realize Ron has your every move planned out for the next fifty years, but don't you think you could add a tiny note to those lists of yours once in a while? Like, break for romance?"

Smiling, Brenn shook her head. "Well, you're going to hate to hear this, then. Just as I was leaving to come meet you, I got a call from my mother—that's why I was late. And now I have no choice but to ask for the next couple of days off. I can hear Mr. Sidman groaning now. Just this morning he dumped a pile of orders on my desk that's at least three inches thick."

"So, what's the emergency?"

"It seems I've inherited a ranch in California, and I have to fly out there immediately, like tomorrow. An attorney called Mom this morning and said I had to sign the papers. *Now.* And make some long-overdue decisions. He said there were some problems that couldn't wait."

"A ranch in California? You never mentioned anything like that before."

"You think you're surprised?" Brenn caught a flash of movement behind Angie. "Oh, good. Here comes our food." Brenn waited until their meals had been placed before them and she'd taken a couple hurried bites of her ham and cheese before continuing. "You remember my mother's aunt Sarah? The one who invited us over for dinner a few times when we were at school outside of Boston? Well, it seems she's been holding this ranch in trust for me since before I was born. Can you imagine that? Out of all the cousins— just me."

"You're kidding."

"My great-grandmother Martha Hampton specified in her will that her family's ranch was to go to the first girl child born in the family after her death. And that's me."

"That's a good one. But how come your grand-aunt didn't tell you before now?"

"Mom wondered about that, too. She called her before phoning me. Aunt Sarah said she kept it a secret because she didn't want the other kids to be hurt. Anyway, it was supposed to be turned over to me six months before I wed or on my twenty-fifth birthday, whichever came first."

"Obviously, she's a little late. You're getting married in five weeks."

"Aunt Sarah's been sick a lot lately and hasn't kept in touch. She didn't know about the wedding until she got her invitation yesterday."

"Did your mom say how big the ranch is? What it's worth?"

"That's what Ron wanted to know, too. I called him as soon as Mom hung up. He's really very excited about it. Says ranch land in California can be worth a lot, especially if it's within thirty or forty miles of a city. He says the way to go is to subdivide it into small parcels."

"I'll just bet he did."

"Now, Angie. Ron just wants the best for us. He wants me to call him as soon as I check it out. Then, if it looks promising, we'll go back there on our honeymoon so he can see for himself."

"Whoop-ti-doo. Life with Ron Egan begins."

"You just love to make fun of him, don't you? Well, twenty years from now we'll be—"

"Frozen. Solid."

Brenn burst out laughing. "If we are, it'll be inside the best freezer money can buy."

"I think it's time we talked about something besides Ron. You know I don't trust that holier-than-thou act of his. Now what about this old gal? Martha Hampton, did you say? Those are some pretty strange stipulations. The first girl born after her death?"

"That's what I thought. Mom doesn't remember much about Grandmother Martha—except she'd only fly in for the holidays. She left Boston to return West to her family's ranch when her husband died. Mom was only six or seven at the time. From what I've heard, Grandmother Martha was a quiet woman, but in her own way a bit of a rebel. She rarely agreed to attend the usual round of social functions. It seems the family's standing in Massachusetts meant nothing to her."

"Well, at least one of your illustrious relatives had enough sense not to want to become *frozen solid* with the rest of them."

Brenn ignored Angie's last jibe. "It gets stranger. Aunt Sarah said she spent her last years mooning over some lost love of her youth. And worse, just before she died, she became obsessed with the hereafter. Reincarnation, that sort of thing. Mom thinks she probably left me the ranch because she thought she could come back as me and, who knows, maybe find her old heartthrob again. Is that weird or what?"

"Hey, at least the old gal knew what was important." The mischievous glint in Angie's eyes returned.

The girl was a wonder, Brenn thought as she glanced down at her watch. Angie could retrack any subject back to sex as if it were the beginning and end of everything. "I'd better stop talking and start eating. I want to return to the office a few minutes early. I have a million calls to make before I leave. I have to confirm with the photographer, make airline reservations, and . . ." She hoisted her bulging bag onto her lap and opened it wide. "Where is that list?"

Bakersfield, California, was a real surprise. From all the cracks the media had made about it, Brenn had expected to see nothing but tobacco-chewing cowboys hanging out in front of honky-tonks. Instead, as she followed the directions to the lawyer's office given to her by the girl at the car rental agency, she drove along West California, a clean, broad thoroughfare bordered on either side by immaculate lawns spread around office buildings that were architectural masterpieces. Reflected in the cleverly angled walls of tinted glass, she caught flashes of trees and flowerbeds already in the full bloom of spring. And April was still two weeks away. She rolled down her window to enjoy the balmy midafternoon air.

Finding the address, she parked the small white rental car in a lot adjacent to a multistoried structure gleaming with sheets of aqua glass. As she passed between tall palms bordering the entrance, she had visions of legendary Malibu, with the sun dancing off waves and bronzed surfers. Although she knew she was a hundred miles from the beach, the hypnotic image caused her to slow to a more relaxed stroll. A tension in her neck she hadn't noticed before dissolved as she walked through the door and rode the elevator up to the law office of Phillip Turner.

"Hello," Brenn said to an older blonde, sitting behind a desk in the peach and powder gray waiting room.

"I have to go now," the secretary's red-lipsticked mouth said into the phone she held. Replacing the receiver, she looked up with a smile that didn't reach her eyes and spoke with practiced courtesy. "May I help you?"

Brenn's buoyant mood vanished, and she found herself wanting to smooth the creases from her tight black skirt beneath the houndstooth checked jacket she'd worn on the five-hour flight. "My name is Brenn Ryan. I don't have a set appointment. Mr. Turner told me to come by as soon as I arrived. I just flew in from New York."

"Yes. Concerning the Norwood Ranch." She whirled her chair around to a filing cabinet behind her and pulled out a thickly stuffed manila folder, then turned back. "I'm sorry, but Mr. Turner was called away to a hearing in L.A. He won't be back until day after tomorrow. He asked me to give you a set of keys and a map to your place. He was sure you'd want to drive up and see it while you were here anyway."

Two days! She didn't have time for this. "Look, I don't—"

"Of course. You don't have transportation." Her long nails clicked against the phone as she reached for it. "I'll arrange something."

"No. I have a car. What I don't have is time. I can't wait around here till he comes back. Can't I just sign the papers, take a look at the place, and go?"

"I'm afraid not. There are a number of matters that need to be dealt with."

"Like what?"

"I'm not at liberty to divulge that. But I can say it concerns the running of the ranch. Your aunt hasn't taken the interest she should have for some years now."

"But I'd planned to take care of my business today and fly out of here again tonight, tomorrow at the latest. You really should've called and rescheduled."

The plastered smile vanished, and the secretary's tone lost all warmth. "Mr. Turner is a very busy man. Legal matters come up, and these little inconveniences can't be helped."

She fished a set of keys out of an envelope clipped to the folder and handed them to Brenn along with a photocopied map. "And besides, you've obviously underestimated your allotment of time. The ranch is a good forty miles up in the Sierras, and it covers five or six square miles. I suggest you drive up there this evening, spend the night—I understand the main house is old but in excellent condition. Then tomorrow have Pascoe Dill show you around. By the time you get a feel for the place, Mr. Turner will be back."

"Who's Pascoe Dill?"

"One of those problems I mentioned. The couple that used to take care of the place retired to Idaho. Mr. Turner hired Dill and his wife to stay there until you decide what you want to do." The smile was propped into place again. "Good day, Miss Ryan. Have a pleasant drive. Oh, and by the way," she said, her voice turning syrupy, "if I were you, I'd pick up some groceries before I left town. I'm afraid you'll find the ranch rather isolated."

Brenn took what seemed a rather obscure road out of Bakersfield to the northeast. Soon it began to slow climb into treeless rolling hills blanketed in the startling green of new grass marred by an oil field. Pumps sitting in their own cleared and black-splotched patches moved slowly up and down, some emitting gaseous odors. A vast network of large pipes snaked through the gullies, connecting the pumps to large storage tanks. Eyesore though the oil field might be, she was certain Ron would appreciate the sight—it bespoke the area's prosperity.

Several miles up the winding road, she left the marred landscape behind and ascended into higher hills splashed with a spectacular palette of oranges, yellows, and purples. The unexpected beauty thrilled her as she recognized long-stemmed lupines strutting above shiny-petaled poppies. Tiny baby's breath filled the empty spaces, creating an unending bouquet. Ground squirrels flitted across the road, and, out on the range, scatterings of cattle feasted upon the bounty. An occasional tiny calf, the white markings on its russet coat startlingly bright and clean, looked adorably huggable.

Rugged oaks began to appear, each with its own unique shape to add to the verdant landscape. Sometimes when she topped a rise, she saw the craggy Sierras in the distance, still white with the snows of winter—a gorgeous contrast.

Every few miles she drove by a set of corrals and occasionally glimpsed a house perched atop a knoll. But, except for the rare passing pickup—invariably driven by someone in a cowboy hat—she was as alone as the secretary had predicted. But by no means was she lonely. She felt as if she were on a Sunday drive headed for someplace very special. Someplace she now owned.

"Damn, I wish I had my camera. Should've put it on my list."

Entranced by the panorama, she almost missed the street sign that read Norwood Flat Road. She slammed on the brakes and wheeled onto a narrow unlined road that meandered up a wooded hill and around a curve. An irrepressible smile curled her lips at the thought of traveling along a lane with the same name as her great-grandmother's family, and an impatience to reach her ranch overtook her. She had to force herself to drive at a safe speed around the unfamiliar curves.

After a couple of miles Brenn crested a rugged ridge where scraggly pines now joined the oaks. She rounded a sharp bend, and the road took a steep dive, with a dangerously sheer cliff dropping away on one side.

Then she saw it.

Hundreds of feet below lay the floor of a small valley surrounded on all sides by mountains. A stream cut a winding swath of darker green through meadows run wild with flowers.

Brenn stopped the car, got out, and walked to the edge. Drinking in the sight, she had no doubt that all she surveyed belonged to her. Joy and anticipation like none she'd ever known spread through her, warming her to the very depths of her being.

Home again. At last.

2

"HOME?" BRENN GAVE herself a mental kick. "Get real." She'd never been anywhere near Norwood Flat in this lifetime or any other. It was obviously the kind of place anyone would want to claim. And for all she knew, the valley below might not even be hers.

But it was. She just knew it. Almost.

She returned to the car and checked the map. A circle encompassed a large area approximately three miles from the main road. That very spot. She looked out the window again in amazement. This time she also noticed a cluster of structures in a grove of trees near the center of the valley. "No wonder Grandmother Martha wanted to come back here. It's beautiful. *And it's mine.*"

Grinning like a five-year-old on her birthday, Brenn started the engine again. "I can't believe it." Then, after a sobering glance at the steep road and a quick prayer that the brakes would hold, she shifted into low gear and eased the vehicle slowly downward to the first switchback.

In a matter of minutes she reached the bottom but not before her palms were slick with sweat and her hands and arms ached from gripping the steering wheel so tightly. A sigh of relief escaped as she viewed a straight stretch leading to the buildings a mile or so away. She floored the gas pedal and let the car eat up the remaining distance.

Fenced pastures on one side of the road held young steers, of which almost as many frolicked as grazed. On the other side cows and some of those darling newborn calves, along with a couple of massive bulls, ambled through the meadow in a more leisurely manner.

"If Ron thinks I'll let this valley be cut up and paved over . . ." An uneasiness washed over Brenn. Their honeymoon could be ruined over the dispute. "But I can't give in. Not this time."

She spotted a few horses standing in the shade of an oak, and it suddenly struck her that all the livestock probably also belonged to her . . . and she knew absolutely nothing about their care. Aunt Sarah should've forewarned her, so she could've prepared herself for the responsibility. But apparently her grandaunt had never seen the need or, more likely, hadn't placed enough value on the place to be concerned. As far as Brenn knew, the matronly lioness had never ventured this far afield from her social territory. In the past if a problem had arisen here at the ranch, she'd probably just picked up a phone in her bejeweled fingers and called her lawyer. Brenn could hear Aunt Sarah's breathy but commanding instructions now.

"Do be a dear, Grant. Call that Turner fellow out in California. Have him handle it. After all, isn't that what we pay him to do?"

Nearing the buildings, Brenn noticed a red pickup parked by a small house behind a much larger one. She turned in on a dirt drive lined with cedars. After crossing a grating of long pipes across a ditch that she assumed was a cattle guard, she drove alongside a sturdy picket fence. It enclosed a parklike yard. In its middle sat the main house, a white two-story with pale green shutters and an inviting railed porch that ran the length of the front. After spending most of her life in a closed-in townhouse in Boston—no matter how elegant it may have been—then the last couple in a cramped Upper East Side apartment, the spaciousness of the grounds was intoxicating.

A little past the main house and yard Brenn braked to a stop beside the smaller one-story cottage also surrounded by a sturdy fence. As she parked behind the dust-covered pickup she'd seen from the road, a man, then a woman banged through the screen door. Brenn got out of the car and walked around to meet them as they stepped outside their gate. "Mr. and Mrs. Dill?"

"Are you Brenn Ryan?" the freckle-faced woman asked. Her straw-colored hair pulled into a ponytail made her look far more youthful than her well-rounded body attested.

Wearing a snug T-shirt and even tighter jeans, she moved closer, waiting for Brenn's answer.

"Yes."

Both she and her skinny, raw-boned companion burst into instant grins—an unbelievably warm welcome.

"You show her around," the deeply browned young man said to the woman, "while I hitch the trailer to the pickup." He turned to Brenn. "Nice to meet you. But we really have to get going. But I guess Mr. Turner told you all about it." Striding past before she had a chance to answer, he jumped in his pickup and started the engine.

Get going? Brenn stared after him. She must've misunderstood.

"Miss Ryan." The blonde touched her shoulder as the man drove past a shed and a large unpainted barn in a swirl of dust. "Sorry he was so short with you. But Pascoe's been climbing the walls. Mr. Turner promised to have a replacement for us by the first. And here it is, the sixteenth. Pascoe told him he always drives a cattle truck for Morosa Brothers every spring and fall. The dispatcher called just last night, threatening to give his spot to someone else. We were so relieved when Turner's secretary called this morning."

"Are you telling me you're leaving now? For good?"

"I'm afraid we have to. But, look, I have a list of possible replacements in the house. Come on in while I get it." She opened the gate and waited for Brenn to precede her.

Brenn didn't move. "Surely, you're not just turning it over to me. There must be someone else here, isn't there?"

"Not really."

Brenn spread her arms. "In this entire valley?"

"Don't worry. The cattle will be okay for a few days until you hire someone else. Brandings don't start for another week or so, and we haven't had any problem with the wells or water troughs. There's plenty of grass, and most of the cows have already calved."

"Most?" They were just going to drive off and leave her here, alone, to midwife some pregnant cows?

"Really, they usually have them without any trouble at all."

"No trouble?" And what the hell else was the woman babbling about? "Brandings? Water troughs?"

The woman wrapped an arm around her. "This is all going too fast for you, isn't it? My name's Judy. Judy Dill. Why don't you come in, and I'll get you a soda or a cup of tea or something. And we'll take it a little slower." She smiled and winked good-naturedly. "Okay?"

All Brenn's stunned mind could think of as the couple drove away pulling a small camper trailer behind them was the flip remark she'd heard in one of those car-chase movies Angie had dragged her to—*eat my dust.* Standing in the driveway, she continued to watch the Dills' departure as they turned onto the pavement and sped along the straight stretch until they started snaking up the mountainside.

Gradually Brenn began to notice a sharp pain in her hand. She looked down and found she was clutching so tightly the large ring of keys Judy Dill had given her that they were digging into her palm. Easing her grip, she hesitantly turned the other way and scanned the shadows engulfing the shed, the dilapidated old barn, and a couple of other outbuildings, then looked beyond to the sun sinking behind a ridge. It would be dark soon, and she was alone. Except for the livestock and a couple of cats she'd seen skulking about, she was utterly alone.

Her gaze settled on the back of the main house standing beneath the high canopy of several tall elms, then she focused on a trellis arched over the back gate that virtually dripped with wisteria blooms. A stone walkway meandered from it to a door with budding lilac bushes posted at either side. It looked incredibly cozy, like a beloved old greeting card. All her fears vanished, taking her tension with it.

Unlatching the slatted gate, she passed through and picked her way in spiked heels across an uneven slate walk to the door. As she tried several keys in the lock, she unaccountably had the clearest picture of what lay just beyond—a library with a gray stone fireplace that rose up at an angle in the corner. At last a key fit. Turning it, she heard a click, then took a stilling breath before opening the door. Would it be as she'd imagined? Or would it be merely a kitchen—a far more logical choice?

She swung the door wide. Only the dim light of dusk invaded the draped room. She reached inside. Finding a light switch, she flipped it on, and a lamp sitting on a big desk near the entry illuminated the room in soft green light, revealing a wall of book-filled shelves and the massive fireplace. The only difference from her vision was the presence of two leather recliners and an old television instead of overstuffed tweed chairs.

She should be frightened—get the hell out of there. Yet she felt like that same five-year-old birthday girl again, but this time she'd just opened her first present.

Then she realized she'd merely been letting her imagination work overtime. The heavy drapes at the window and the chimney at the side of the house had been obvious clues. What in the world would Ron think of her airhead imaginings? And Dad—she didn't even have to guess. She could easily see his withering scowl, his staunchly folded arms, the slow wag of his head while he pinned her with one of his authoritative stares. "Haven't I told you often enough? If it doesn't compute, it isn't real. Dig deep enough, and you'll find some con man's get-rich-quick scheme behind all that hocus-pocus bunk."

Still, it was fun to think something mystical was happening, that the crazy reincarnation story Mom told her had some validity. Brenn giggled like a naughty child as she walked through the room and into a central hallway. She stepped past a staircase to an opposite doorway and found the kitchen. Daisy-yellow covered the walls of the large square room with knotty pine cupboards and older but serviceable-looking appliances.

She crossed matching yellow linoleum to a side entrance. She needed to unload the car and get a fire going before dark, because the temperature always plummeted with the sun around here this time of year.

"At least I think it does," she said with a nervous laugh as she unchained the door and hurried out.

Due to the three-hour time difference between New York and California and the excitement of the day, Brenn could

barely hold her eyes open by the time she'd cleaned up after
her quick meal of canned stew. She picked up her overnight
case and the shopping bags containing the casual wear she'd
bought before leaving Bakersfield, then headed upstairs.

When Brenn reached the top landing, she bypassed the
first doors on either side. Choosing not to analyze her
choice, she went directly to the second one on the right.
Going inside, she dropped her burdens and walked across a
thick rug to a nightstand beside the bed and switched on a
hurricane lamp.

Warm colors wrapped themselves around her—from the
rose-print chintz and lace covering the windows and four-
poster, to the lacquered glow of knotty-pine walls rising up
from the wine-colored carpet. Rich cherry-wood furnishings
added the perfect finishing touch. Charming. Absolutely
charming. Everything was exactly as it should be.

Ron, of course, would hate it.

She pushed the unpleasant thought from her mind.
Tonight she just wanted to enjoy sleeping in this coziest of
havens.

From out of the clouds she came, circling the emerald
valley, surveying this jewel of a gift, her new domain. She
soared on the breeze with the ease of a great-winged bird,
light and airy as an ostrich feather. With a thrill tickling her
belly, she swooped down until she skimmed the tops of the
trees shading the ranch buildings . . . down . . . until
she sighted a tall slender girl hoisting a saddle atop a
reddish-colored horse with a golden mane. The girl re-
minded her of herself, the leggy figure, the long hair. Even
pulled back in a braid, Brenn could see streaks highlighting
the rich brown. She floated nearer, but not too close—she
didn't want to frighten the young woman . . . or was it for
herself she feared . . . ?

A gunshot rang out.

"What the—? There shouldn't be anyone within miles."
Marty Norwood let go of the cinch strap on Terra Cotta's
saddle and stepped away from her sorrel filly to look past

the barnyard. She thought the shot had come from the north, but she couldn't put a fix on the exact location. "I know Daddy never gave anyone permission to come hunting. He would've told me before he and Mother left for Sacramento."

A second sharp crack reported and echoed across the flat. It came from the area of the big pond at the head of the valley.

She glanced behind her to the ranch foreman's house. "Lands, of all days for Lula to get sick and have to be taken into town." Ben Cauley wouldn't be back with his wife till sometime tomorrow, if then. "I'll just have to see about these trespassers myself."

Leaving her mount hitched to the corral fence, she charged to the house and fetched one of her dad's rifles from his gun cabinet. Returning, she slammed it into her saddle's scabbard, then flipped back her long braid and grabbed the cinch strap with both hands while ramming a knee into Terra's side. "I don't have time for your games, girl. It's probably some fool town dandies with no more sense than to shoot up the place. *Suck it in.*"

For once, on command, the rebellious animal relaxed and stopped bloating its belly, allowing Marty to sufficiently tighten the leather lash.

Grabbing the horn, Marty swung up and heeled the horse into a gallop before her bottom had hit the seat. It wasn't unheard of for some of the so-called sportsmen up from the valley to mistake a cow for a deer. She leaned low over Terra's neck and sped along the side of the white picket fence surrounding her house, then raced out across the meadow.

Scattering cattle as she rode, she felt exhilarated by the power and freedom of having a swift, surefooted animal beneath her, by the heat of the sun as it warmed her wind-braced cheeks, by the scent of the flowers and tender grass.

Then, just as suddenly, the deepest sorrow tightened her chest, constricted her breathing, as tears of self-pity formed.

As if Terra could feel her eagerness ebb, the animal slowed.

She spurred the horse onward, but the thrill was as lost as she surely would soon be. How could Mother and Daddy make her leave all of this to marry some distant cousin in Boston? Couldn't they see if she was locked inside a city of brick and stone she'd wither like a plucked poppy? And what if she hated her husband-to-be? What if his touch made her skin crawl? No matter how much they argued it would be for the best, it wouldn't. Couldn't.

Her nails cut into the palm holding the reins, returning her awareness to her immediate purpose. She took a big gulp of air, and blinking away her tears, she scanned the slightly rolling landscape for the trespassers. Spotting no one, she didn't slow until she reached Poso Creek a hundred or so yards downstream of the largest pond on the ranch. She pulled Terra to a halt and searched the heavily wooded area near the pool.

Hidden somewhere behind the brush, a horse nickered.

Her blockheaded filly answered.

It could be just one of their own herd, but Marty wasn't taking any chances. She pulled out her rifle and nudged Terra forward at a walk. Moving along the edge of low-hanging willow branches, she reached a sandy clearing that slanted down to the still water. The heavy scent of wet earth filled her nostrils as she eyed several mallards floating undisturbed among a stand of reeds, the only sign of life.

Wheeling Terra away, she nudged the filly out of the trees again, then heeled her into a gallop as she circled the dense foliage blocking her view . . . and saw a saddled buckskin with bulging sidebags and a bedroll. Obviously its owner hadn't ridden up here for just one day's sport.

The gelding grazed about fifty yards to the north. But where was the rider?

Goose bumps ran up her arms as she glanced all about. She slowed Terra to a walk and raised her rifle.

Suddenly, from out of a shallow gully beyond the buckskin, a good-size man emerged, his back to her. He didn't turn.

Marty reined to a stop and zeroed in on a spot between his broad shoulders. She took a heart-stilling breath while convincing herself the trespasser couldn't possibly know she was out here alone. And, besides, it wasn't as if she couldn't handle herself. Even if she had spent most of the last four years away in San Francisco at that confounded finishing school, she could still shoot the tail feathers off a blue jay at a hundred paces.

Just as she started to yell at him, the stranger, dressed in a plaid workshirt, stooped out of sight again.

She kneed Terra a few paces closer until she saw the sun glint off his hatless flaxen head. She pointed the rifle barrel at it and spoke with the deadly calm her father always used on trespassers. "Afternoon."

He came up in a fast spin to face her.

At his abruptness her index finger came within a thread of pulling the trigger before she saw he held a newly birthed calf instead of a rifle.

Covered in blood, he, along with the newborn, looked gruesome. His stunned expression transformed almost instantly into the grandest, friendliest smile.

And with her Winchester pointed at him, no less.

"Howdy. Name's Cal Williams. Just passing through on my way to Five Dog Ranch." He lifted the wiggling birthling higher on his chest. "This your place?"

She nudged Terra a little closer. "What are you doing with that calf?"

She caught him glance briefly at her weapon, but his grin didn't waver. "Suppose you heard the shots." He turned and motioned behind him with his curly blond head. "I come across your cow, here, dying, so I put her out of her misery."

Lowering her rifle but still maintaining her vantage point astride her mount, Marty guided Terra to the edge of the depression and saw that the stranger didn't lie. Blood matted the grass at the rear of a blaze-faced Hereford, indicating severe hemorrhaging. More dripped from a spot just behind her ear. "I guess it was lucky you happened by when you did. You said you were on your way to Five Dogs?"

"Yeah." The strapping young man climbed up the embankment still gripping the calf with big square hands. The sleeves of his gray plaid shirt were rolled up exposing muscled forearms that were as deeply tanned as the face she couldn't help staring at. His eyes seemed unbelievably blue beneath a rangy swath of bleached brows.

He couldn't be from around here. She would've remembered meeting that smile. Those eyes.

"I met Jim Snow, the foreman, at the stockyards south of Visalia. He told me to ride on up here, and he'd keep me busy till June."

Three months. It sounded like an eternity compared to the ten days she had left. Ten days and she'd be gone . . . *forever*. The thought slashed at her with renewed pain. She tried not to let it show in her tone. "Well, I'm afraid, Mr. Williams, you've taken the wrong turn."

"Are you sure?" His eyes sparkled as they roved her face in a very flirty manner. Seemingly oblivious of his bloody appearance, he stepped closer. "Snow drew me a real good map."

With the suddenness of a slap in the face she realized she was presenting herself in jeans and an oversize, faded shirt to the handsomest man she'd seen in ages. She could just crawl in a hole and die. Worse, her braided hair hung down her back like a cow's tail. Feeling heat creep up her face, she shoved her rifle in its scabbard and pointed up the steep, winding wagon tracks that climbed out of the valley. "About four miles up that path you'll come across the stage road. Take it south until you get to Granite Station. Ol' Walt, he'll tell you how to get the rest of the way. Tell him I sent you."

"I'll be only too glad to if the lovely lady would be willing to part with her name."

Lovely lady? Perhaps she didn't look like such a tomboy after all. "Norwood. Marty Norwood. My father owns this flat."

"It's real pretty, like everything else around here." Those laughing eyes never strayed from hers. "Like I said before, my name's Cal. Cal Williams from over Salinas way."

Uncomfortable, she dropped her gaze . . . and noticed the messy newborn in his arms. "Oh, how thoughtless of me. Please, hand me the little leppy."

"It'll ruin your clothes."

"Naw, these old things don't matter. I'll take the calf over to the pond and clean it up."

"If you're sure." His smile diminished only slightly as he gave her a doubtful look.

Nodding, she patted the spot in front of her.

His brawny arms barely flexed as he lifted the slimy animal and placed its wiggly body across the saddle.

That strong metallic odor associated with birth wafted up as she secured the warm little thing to her. She looked from it back to him and found that though his eyes still beheld her, his smile had disappeared. Her day again darkened considerably . . . and in another few seconds he would be gone! Was he disappointed, too?

Suddenly she thought she wouldn't be able to bear it—not along with everything else she was being compelled to forfeit. "You could use some cleaning up, too. You're welcome to join us."

The sun returned with his smile, and this time she noticed how the deep dimples softened his square jaw. Rashly, she wondered if he'd be just as affected by her own smile if she, too, dared.

But she couldn't be that forward. Her impulsive invitation, along with her unladylike attire, was already enough of an embarrassment. She could hear her mother's sharp censure echoing in her ears this very second. *"Mark my words, young lady, you'll rue the day, rue the day. No true gentleman would look twice at anyone in such hoydenish trappings."*

"You sure I wouldn't be a bother?" he asked, mounting his horse.

At the earnestness in his expression, warmth spread all the way to Marty's toes. Maybe a "gentleman" wouldn't see past her practical clothes, but a hardworking cowhand might quite easily. "Of course not. If it weren't for you, this little leppy probably would've died, hidden down in that ditch like it was. In fact, it would be most un-neighborly of me not to at least invite you up to the house for a bite to eat before you go."

"Neighbors. I like the sound of that."

And Marty liked the soft raspiness in his mellow voice when he said it.

She led the way back to the secluded sandy bank. And although she knew they were utterly alone in the valley, not until they drew within the cover of the draping willows did she feel the intimacy of it, especially since this was the very spot where she'd so often sneaked away in the summer to bathe in the raw. Pushing the thought from her mind, she quickly averted her gaze from the luring water. Her attention shifted to Mr. Williams as he dismounted. While his back was to her, she nakedly admired the fluid movement of his lithe yet commanding physique as he swung his leg over the buckskin's back and lowered himself to the ground. From some heretofore untapped recess of her mind, the vision of the two of them swimming together, *unclothed*, flitted before her. A strange tingle plucked her heart, then seared to her lower region. It jolted her to her senses just in time as the young man strode to her horse's side.

"Here, let me take the leppy while you get down."

Even if she wasn't staring straight at him, she would've known he was smiling—it was so evident in his voice and in his touch when his big calloused hand brushed across hers as he took the calf. She wondered if the contact had made his heart skip a beat as it had hers.

But it couldn't have. His attention immediately centered on the calf. He murmured gently to the little orphan while placing it on its feet, then knelt beside it and cozied it to him.

For heaven's sakes, she scolded herself silently as she swung down from her horse. You're starting to twitter worse than some of those scatterbrained schoolgirls at the academy. Get hold of yourself. The man's just being a good Samaritan, and because he's cheerful doesn't mean he has designs on you. Even if you do keep falling headlong into that smile of his. "I'll take the calf now. You'd better do something about your shirt before it's permanently stained."

Grasping the newborn at its neck and hindquarters, she urged it forward until its tiny hooves were immersed, being careful not to soak her boots.

As she stooped and began scooping water over the calf's

back, Cal Williams dropped to his knees beside her. His soiled shirt clung to him and his heavily muscled chest expanded considerably as he straightened to untuck the tails.

She couldn't keep from sliding glances his way as he leaned over the pond and splashed water onto the fabric. The muscles across his shoulders and back rippled, enticing some very earthy visions of what he'd look like without that shirt. "You really should take it off. You'll never get the blood out that way." *Good heavens! Had those words actually come out of her mouth?*

He must have been equally shocked. His hands froze midair.

Hers certainly didn't. With her eyes trained solidly on the calf's back, her fingers worked feverishly to sluice it off . . . until he spoke.

"If you're sure my state of undress wouldn't offend you."

She shot a glance at his serious expression, then frantically began working on the orphan again. "Of course not. It's the sensible thing to do. Besides, it's not as if the men around here don't ever work without them."

"You're right." He unbuttoned and stripped it off.

And she really did keep her eyes diverted from his flexed muscles as he scrubbed the plaid . . . most of the time. In fact that little blaze-faced calf was becoming the cleanest newborn she'd ever seen. Then, when Cal straightened and began rinsing his chest, she definitely kept her attention where it belonged since she now felt the weight of his hot bold gaze upon her.

When it became too heavy for her to bear, she quickly rose. "Guess I'd better go find a cow willing to adopt this little critter."

Wringing out his shirt, he came to his feet so close to her, she could count the curly golden hairs on his bronzed chest.

She forced her eyes to raise to his face and met that toothy grin again.

"You'll have your hands full, hanging on to the calf while trying to rope some cantankerous mama. Wait for me to put on a clean shirt, and I'll help you. I sure wouldn't want to be un-neighborly."

3

MARTY CUDDLED AND quieted the leppy as she slowly followed after Cal Williams. At a trot he crisscrossed the oak-shaded meadow ahead of her, searching for a cow that had calved within the last two days. In a freshly donned shirt the same soft shade of blue as his eyes, his hair seemed lighter, brighter, and his complexion was burnished to the warmest gold. She caught herself literally sighing at the sight of her cowboy Adonis. She could just imagine the hoard of young ladies in Salinas who'd mourned his leave-taking. She was surprised none of them had managed to throw a rope over him before now. But, then, there was a lot she didn't know about him. In fact, everything.

A short distance ahead, Cal wheeled his horse and rode back to her. "I've found a likely prospect over there." He pointed to a cow beneath the crusty limbs of an old tree. "Wait here, and I'll bring her to you." Unhooking a coiled lariat from his saddle, he gently nudged his horse toward the Hereford and her spindly-legged calf, all the while he widened the loop.

The russet-and-white animal watched him with wary eyes.

Marty heard him murmuring to the animal in a soothing stream as he gradually circled within a few feet.

The cow bolted.

Cal and his horse became one in their pursuit. As he spun the lasso overhead, his buckskin matched the Hereford's every veering tactic. On the first toss Cal managed to rope her.

The horse immediately skidded to a halt and started slowly backing up. Cal hauled in the slack as the bawling cow thrashed about.

But within seconds the defeated cow stopped struggling

and followed peacefully along as if she were a dog on a leash.

Her calf caught up and tailed its mother.

Watching Cal return with his offering, the deepest sense of well-being filled Marty. She allowed herself to pretend he was her man, that the two of them were working the range just as she'd always dreamed it would be for her one day. The way it should've been.

If only her mother had tried, even a little, to become a part of the land, to cherish its beauty and harmony as Marty and her father did. If Mother could've seen the rightness of it all, instead of forever complaining of the boring isolation she'd been forced to endure *for her husband*. Mother just wiled away her afternoons, reading in her sitting room until she could cajole Daddy into taking her on yet another trip. And this one had been incredibly untimely. She must have done some intense wheedling to pull him away during calving season, Marty thought with a grimace. No governor's ball should've been that important.

But if Mama wanted something badly enough, Daddy always gave in, more out of guilt for depriving her of her family and life in Boston than love. And marrying their only child off to Mother's second cousin had proved no exception. Marty was sure that her mother's most pressing motive had not been to secure a successful future for her daughter, but to guarantee more visits back East for herself. As usual Daddy wouldn't deny her anything within his power to give. Even at his or Marty's expense.

"Miss Norwood."

Startled, she jumped.

Cal had dismounted and was standing beside her. Mischief sparked in his eyes and in his lax grin. "I do hope you allowed me to play at least a small part in your daydream."

Oh, the man was a charmer, possibly even a rogue. Feeling reckless herself, Marty favored him with the beginnings of a smile as she handed him the orphan. "I doubt, Mr. Williams, that you could ever imagine yourself relegated to a minor role in any young lady's dreams."

A chuckle rumbled through him as she dismounted, and it didn't die completely away until she'd captured the other calf. Then he turned unnervingly quiet as he placed the orphan beside the slightly bigger calf and helped Marty rub its scent onto the leppy.

His hand collided with hers.

It was like touching fire and ice. She very nearly jerked away as the impossible combination sent the wildest sensation from her fingertips to her heart. Breathing grew more difficult, and she became grateful for his silence, grateful that she didn't have to keep up her half of a conversation. Even if she could manage to put two intelligent words together, they'd surely come out in a croak.

"That should be enough," he finally said in a hoarse whisper. Straightening, he picked up the orphan and carried it to the cow, which was still being held taut by his well-trained cutting horse. Cal held the leppy up to her nose.

Without hesitation, the cow stuck out her big tongue and licked its head.

"Well, looks like we fooled the old girl." Cal stepped back toward her hindquarters and placed the calf beneath her udder.

The mother's eyes showed a considerable amount of white as she strained against the rope to watch. But, thank goodness, she stood still while Cal nuzzled the little one's mouth to a teat until it took one and started nursing.

Born and raised on a ranch, she'd seen calves suckle thousands of times, and never before this very minute had it embarrassed her. Feeling her cheeks begin to burn, she veered her gaze away until it settled on Cal's mouth and, especially, his fuller bottom lip. Her attention drifted upward . . . *and found him staring back at her.*

Cal rose slowly to his full height. "I didn't think anyone's eyes could be more beautiful than a calf's. Yours are the richest brown I've ever seen." His words poured through her like warm honey.

Regaining her senses, she quickly retreated a step. "I— uh—I didn't mean to—"

"Neither did I," he said, saving them both. A trace of a smile returned as he took a ragged, chest-expanding breath and glanced around uneasily. "I think the calf will do fine now, don't you?"

"Yes. No doubt. Certainly. Absolutely." Knowing she sounded like an idiot, she swung away to her horse, mounted, and heeled it into a walk.

Cal did the same and caught up with her within seconds. Long moments passed before he broke the silence. "This sure is a nice spread. How many acres do you have?"

Grateful for the change of topic, Marty relaxed. "There's only about twenty-two hundred down here in the valley. But including the surrounding hills, it comes to almost thirteen thousand."

"How many head do you run?"

"A couple thousand."

"That's a fair-size herd. Must take quite a few hands."

She got the distinct idea he was thinking of asking to hire on. But by the time Daddy would need extra help, she'd be gone. But the thought that he might be interested pleased her, nonetheless. "We don't have to hire as many as Five Dogs. Mostly just at branding time and when a herd is driven to market. You see, we don't have to move our cattle several miles up to the mountains in the summer like they do. We're higher up and have better grass. And, as you can see, our mountain pasture is all around us."

"Yeah," he said, gazing about. "It is perfect for cattle, isn't it?"

"Yes." She sighed. "And I'm going to miss it more than anything."

"You're leaving? When? For how long?" His intent look turned to one of hesitation. "I'm sorry. It's none of my business."

"No, that's all right. I'll be leaving for Boston in a matter of days. I'm to . . . My parents have decided that—" She couldn't bring herself to say the words. Not to him.

"They think you need some *culture*, do they? I know how it is. I've spent my whole life watching my mother trying to turn my five sisters into acceptable young ladies."

"Five sisters!" No wonder her dashing knight knew how to be so charming.

"Yeah," he said on a chuckle. "All older, and all bossy. And with me being the only boy, it's a wonder my ears aren't stretched three feet long, they've been yanked on so much."

Marty burst out laughing at the picture of a yelping little towheaded boy being hauled along after he'd committed some outrageous prank, which she had no doubt was merely one of a long string.

He joined in until their horses started prancing nervously from the raucous noise.

Taking a firm grip on her reins with one hand, Marty clamped the other over her mouth and muffled the sound until it died to a giggle.

Cal's laughter also faded away. Even his smile disappeared as he stared fixedly at her lips with eyes that had grown achingly darker, hotter.

Marty felt herself melting like wax in the sun, and she couldn't stop the sensual sensation any more than she could tear her eyes from his face when it so clearly showed that she affected him in the same way.

Finally his tempting mouth moved, and he spoke in little more than a whisper. "You're incredibly beautiful when you laugh."

She had the most ardent need to feel his lips upon hers. To feel the soft pressure, to taste him. Almost unconsciously, she reined Terra closer.

The horse stumbled over a rock, jostling her out of her addled state.

She stiffened abruptly. She'd heard of moonlight madness before, but this was broad daylight, for heaven's sake. She slammed her heels into Terra's sides, and the filly leapt forward into a full gallop. Hugging the animal with her knees, she yelled over her shoulder, "Race you back to the house."

In a wild dash she cut across the grassy field, frightening scores of ground squirrels as she dodged past their honeycombed hills. Soon she heard the thunder of a second set of hooves narrowing her lead. Not daring to look back for fear of losing the advantage, she spurred her swift young filly to greater speed.

By the time she reached her fenced yard and charged around to the back, she didn't have to turn to see the powerfully built buckskin's nose edging alongside. But not quite far enough. She'd won. She reined Terra to a sliding halt in a swirl of dust. As Cal did the same, she wheeled her winded filly and faced him triumphantly. "Bet you're not used to being beaten by a girl, are you?"

Grinning as usual, he slowly shook his head. "Especially one who announces a race after it's begun."

She tilted hers and flaunted her own dimples. "I thought the weaker sex was always allowed a bit of a head start."

Cal patted his spent gelding's lathered neck. "Tell that to Dusty." He glanced at her own sweaty horse. "That's one long-legged little filly you got there. Takes after her mistress." His gaze gravitated to thighs covered by jeans so tight that they held few secrets. Then, abruptly, he snapped his head up and glanced around. "Your folks in the house?"

Marty dismounted and hid her face behind Terra before she answered in her most nonchalant tone. "I don't think so. They were both gone when I left." She heard the creak of leather and knew he, too, had swung down to the ground. She walked in front of her sorrel, looping the reins over its head as she went. Cal came into view, and she handed him her horse. "Why don't you unsaddle them and give them some grain while I go in and cook us up something."

"Are you sure? I wouldn't want to put you in a compromising position."

"Nonsense. Just because no one's in the house doesn't mean I couldn't holler up someone in a hurry if I wanted to." She glanced toward the ranch hand's cottage as if he or his wife were inside.

"You're sure it's all right, then?" He still sounded doubtful.

Marty whirled away, letting her long braid fly, then sauntered toward her back gate. She slowed only long enough to toss over her shoulder, "Do you want your potatoes fried or mashed?"

Never in her most fanciful dreams had she thought she could be this brazen. But, heaven help her, this would probably be her one and only chance for a little romance before she was buried alive in Massachusetts. And, besides, the miracle of this jaunty young rake happening along on

the only day she'd ever been left here alone had to be fate.
If it wasn't, she didn't know what was.

She'd no sooner closed the back door behind her than she
began ripping at the buttons of her soiled and smelly shirt as
she ran through the library to the hallway and up the stairs.
She simply had to get into something more presentable. She
slowed, pulling her braid over her shoulder and swishing the
ends across her cheek, then smiled wickedly. Perhaps she'd
wear her breezy white dress with the ever-so-generous
gathers across the bosom. Even mama said it made her look
much more womanly.

The scantest minutes later, she rushed back down the
stairs certain she was putting her best foot forward—or
shoe, she mused as the soft kid slippers made hardly a sound
on the steps. The high lace neck and the exaggerated puffs
of the leg-of-mutton sleeves were especially designed along
with the accordion-like upper bodice to create the illusion of
the tiniest waist, which was assisted, of course, by a tightly
cinched corset. The deep rose of her satin sash, she knew,
drew attention to her waist as much as its bow did to the
abundant gathers clustered at the back of the trailing skirt.
And even if her mother and the instructress at the academy
always scolded her for exposing her complexion to the sun,
she thought the smooth kiss of color added to her appearance, especially against the pristine white of her gown. And
the gold streaks in her otherwise boring brown hair added
zip.

But, she had to admit, her hair's casual styling did mar the
otherwise sophisticated picture. She simply had not had the
time to do more than brush it out and secure it at the nape
of her neck with a wide ribbon that matched her sash.

Reaching the bottom of the flight, she shrugged. It
couldn't be helped. Then, remembering the meal she'd
supposedly started the second she entered the house, she
hurried into the kitchen and snatched a bibbed apron from
off a hook beside the door.

Marty needn't have worried about the lost time—the
potatoes were cooked, mashed, and placed on the kitchen
table along with yesterday's roast and gravy and the last
jar of asparagus spears, yet Cal still hadn't come in.

While rushing about, she'd checked out the rear window several times to reassure herself his horse was still in the corral.

She pushed aside a yellow organdy curtain to look again while getting the bread from its box on the worktable just below. She didn't think she could stand it if he changed his mind and rode away without even a goodbye after he'd . . . He'd what? Undoubtedly she'd made far too much of his casual flirting. Her desperation over her impending marriage was lending an exaggerated importance to his every glance. She quickly sliced some pieces off the loaf, placed them on a plate, then carried it, along with a mound of butter, to the table across the room.

She took a moment to study the daisy-trimmed china that went so well with the sunny kitchen. Normally, when the family had guests they ate in the dining room at the big table, but she preferred the coziness in here. Satisfied, she stripped off the apron. Then, smoothing down her skirt with fingers that she noted were trembling almost as much as her insides, she went out to call her new friend to supper.

She searched the clearing, but he was still out of sight. Refusing to do anything as unladylike as to yell, she started for the gate.

As she walked beneath the latticed archway cascading with lavender wisteria blooms, Cal Williams emerged from the barn. He'd changed into a white shirt, clean jeans, and some highly polished oxblood dress boots. The dampness of his blond curls attested to the fact that he'd done his best to tame them. And that big warm smile, of course, was splashed across his face. But strangely, it faded more with each of his long strides as he approached. It completely vanished by the time he slowed to a stop before her.

Marty's confidence crashed in around her as she numbly swung open the gate for him. He was obviously anything but attracted by her metamorphosis into femininity.

A frown creasing the bridge of his nose, he stopped close enough to lend the fragrance of his cologne to that of the wisteria. "Miss Norwood? And I thought you were beautiful before."

Nervously she smoothed an errant tendril at her temple. "Umm—supper's ready."

"You're a vision. A golden angel in a cloud of white." Taking her hands into his, he looked down at them, then up to her face again. "You're so . . . I—uh—" He dropped his hold and shifted his weight.

Marty thought she saw a tinge of red color his face, but she couldn't be sure, since she was too nonplussed, herself, to speak.

"Since no one else seems to be around," he continued, blessedly filling the awkward silence, "I fed the animals in the barn and brought in your Jersey cow and milked her. I left the pail in the springhouse."

Marty had the hardest time concentrating on those last sentences. "That was kind of you." Her words came out all breathy. She cleared her throat and tried again. "I'm sure Ben, our ranch hand, will appreciate it. He already has his hands full today." Then, not giving Cal a chance to ask the missing man's whereabouts, she whirled around and led the way into the house, in an absolute flutter of excitement.

Taking him through the kitchen, she invited him to sit while she took the blue-speckled coffeepot from the stove and poured them each a cup. She could feel the warmth of his gaze on her even as she replaced the pot, and it took all her effort not to rush as she walked back to the white enameled chair opposite him.

His gaze dropped away, and he suddenly seemed quite timid, which seemed out of place for a man big enough to dwarf the small table.

"Don't hang back," she said, placing her yellow checked napkin in her lap. "Fill your plate. Dig in."

His shyness persisted as they scooped out their portions and began to eat. She was sure he was thrown off by the idea that they were alone, but could be interrupted by her parents, which she'd led him to believe could happen at any minute.

"You say you're from Salinas. Good farming country, from what I hear," she chatted, trying to ease his discomfort. "What business is your family in?"

"My pa owns a feed and farm supply store."

"And you say you're his only son? I'm surprised he hasn't insisted you stay and help him." If she'd been a boy, she was sure her own father would've stood up for her, let her follow in his footsteps.

An endearing sheepish grin brightened his expression. He picked up his napkin and wiped his mouth. "Yeah, he's not real happy about me roaming around, cowboying for a while, but we made a deal. He's giving me three years to 'sow my wild oats' as he puts it. Then he expects me to return home for the Turn of the Century celebration, then take up my responsibilities."

"I'm sure running a feed store would be very interesting. Being at the center of things with all the farmers and ranchers dropping by with the latest news."

He seemed to have regained his confidence as he swallowed a bite of potato. "Yeah, but you have to spend so much time inside. I like seeing the open sky."

"I know what you mean. I just returned from school in San Francisco two weeks ago. Terrible climate. Nothing but fog. I never felt so closed in in my life."

"One of my sisters lives there with her new husband. From the sound of her letters, she doesn't seem to mind it at all. But when you're young and in love, I don't think it much matters where you live."

"No, I suppose not. *If* you're in love." Noticing the direction their conversation was taking *and* how quickly it had gotten there, Marty began eating again with pretended earnestness.

They ate in silence for a few minutes, then, after taking a sip of coffee, Cal spoke. "How many brothers and sisters do you have?"

She looked up from her plate. "None, actually. It seems there were complications after my birth, and my mother hasn't been able to have any more."

"That's too bad. Must've been lonely for you growing up here all alone."

"Not really. I had a wonderful dog for a playmate until he died last year. And my dad always let me ride with him."

Cal chuckled. "And he taught you real good, too."

She couldn't help grinning, knowing he referred to the

wild race to the house. "Much to my mother's dismay, I'm afraid."

"Mothers. They're always trying to clip our wings, aren't they?"

"You, too?" Marty found herself leaning closer, no longer just noticing the gorgeous exterior of the man, but his easy-mannered pleasure in the tomboy side of her.

He snorted. "If my ma had her way, I'd already be wed to the daughter of the local granary owner. The fact that every time the girl opens her mouth a whine comes out hasn't slowed Ma one whit in her matchmaking."

"Oh, I know how you feel," Marty said, rising to get them a refill from off a hot plate on the wood stove. "My mother has a husband picked out for me, too." As she replaced the coffeepot and rejoined him, her gaze wandered to the curls that refused to stay in place at his temples. An aching tenderness swelled within her, and she yearned to reach over and rake her fingers through them. Reluctantly she forced the thought of his hair and his bewitching blue eyes from her mind. "Mother's choice for me is so starched up, I swear, the one time I met him, he made cracking sounds when he walked."

Chuckling, Cal leaned back in his chair and picked up the fragile china cup in his oversize hand. "Reminds me of the time I was forced into my first stiff collar. . . ."

As he regaled her with an animated tale, replete with a humorous display of hands at his throat and exaggerated frowns, Marty knew this was not only the type of man, but the exact one she would've picked for herself if she'd been given a choice. By the time he finished his story, the deepest realization of this profound loss stole every vestige of her joy.

His smile also died, and he rose to his feet. "Guess I'd better get going. It's almost dark."

Oh, dear. He must've thought she'd grown tired of him. Marty jumped up. "I won't hear of it!" Suddenly aware that she sounded desperate, she sank down again and folded her hands. "I mean, Daddy would be very upset if I let you leave this late in the day. You might fall off a cliff in the dark, or worse. Stay the night. Then tomorrow we'll send you safely on your way."

Indecision showed in his wavering gaze. "It does make sense. But your father's not here. You're alone."

"But he should be soon."

"I guess it would be all right if I slept out in the barn."

"With a perfectly good guest room upstairs? Besides, it can turn really cold here at night. In fact," she said, giving a little shiver and rubbing her arms beneath the thin fabric of her lace-trimmed sleeves, "it's already getting chilly. Would you mind starting a fire in the library while I clear off the table?" She couldn't believe the outrageousness of her own duplicity, but at the moment she refused to feel guilty. She would not give up this one measly evening fate had offered her.

And from the good humor returning to Cal's countenance he was looking forward to it as much as she. "A fire. Whatever the lady wants," he said, unbuttoning a cuff. He turned and started rolling his sleeve as he headed for the hall door.

"The woodshed's at the side of the house. Oh, and while you're out there, you might as well get your saddlebags."

He stopped and came slowly around, displaying a nodding smirk. "If you promise to hide me when your father comes after me with a shotgun."

She cocked her head to the side, unable to resist knocking that smug expression off his face. "Did I mention my dad is seven feet tall and weighs three hundred pounds?"

It did the trick. "No, you didn't."

"That's probably because he isn't." She turned toward the table, hoping to hide the giggle trying to escape.

"You know," he said, his chuckling voice diminishing with his retreating footsteps, "you're as full of the devil as I ever was." Going out the back door his last words were almost indiscernable, but she desperately wanted to believe he said, "What a pair we'd make."

4

MARTY WILED AWAY the hours with Cal, basking in his warmth and that of the softly glowing fire. Cosseted in overstuffed armchairs with equally plump footstools, they spoke of everything and nothing with the ease of ones who'd known each other all their lives, yet the space separating her from him was charged with unspoken excitement.

He'd been a complete gentleman the whole evening, his manners without fault. But their time together was spilling away, and like watching water pouring into sand, it only made her more thirsty for him.

She desperately wanted to move across that forbidden territory, so distant, yet only a side table away. But the fear of what secrets might be unleashed if she did stopped her. She cursed herself for her lack of courage as only their words were allowed to bridge the gap. Only their voices touched, intertwined.

The grandfather clock in the entry hall had already intruded by chiming the hour four different times since they'd come into her father's cozy library, and now the impatient contraption bonged out the count of eleven.

Marty felt something akin to panic as she faced the fact that she couldn't stretch this precious interlude any longer. She'd have to allow the poor man to retire. It was the only decent thing to do, since he'd been on the trail since early morning.

Even while her heart pleaded with her not to end it, she steeled herself and stood. "It's getting late. I'd better show you to your room." On reluctant legs she stepped to the fireplace and picked up a piece of kindling. She lit it in the embers, then brought it up to flame the wick of a kerosene lamp on the mantel.

Without hearing or seeing, she knew Cal had come to stand behind her. The heat from his body branded her back and carried with it the heady scent of his maleness. He reached past her and took the lamp. "Let me."

If only she had the courage to turn and face him, she would be within his arms. If she did, she was certain he would understand and give her what his eyes and the soft, low music of his voice had offered, promised, from the first.

A full five seconds passed as her desire battered at the walls of propriety.

He remained behind her. Still. His hand must not have been too steady, though, for the lamplight cast a quavering shadow.

Her rigid upbringing won out. With a sigh she moved away and started for the hall doorway. "Follow me. I'll show you to your room."

"Are you sure? Your folks haven't returned."

She looked back at that handsome sun-bronzed face, that virile cowboy's body, and tortured herself with a comparison to the thin, pasty-skinned man she was to marry. The crush of dismay nearly closed her throat. "There's no need for concern. My parents have ample proof of my compliance to their wishes."

Marty caught a flicker of disappointment in his expressive eyes as he picked up his saddlebags propped against the desk and followed her up the stairs to the first door on the left. Opening it, she stepped aside. "You'll find we have a modern bathroom at the end of the hall. If you would like, I can start a fire beneath the hot water tank for you."

"No, I'll be fine." His words came out even quieter than hers had.

"Then I suppose I'll bid you good night." She started away.

He caught her hand.

His touch sent a shock up her arm, straight to her heart. Her mouth sprang open as she turned to face him.

He instantly dropped his hold. "I—I just wanted to say thank you for tonight. It's been . . . I won't ever forget it. Or you." He stepped closer. "I may not have the chance in the morning, so I'd like to ask you now."

"Yes?" *Oh, yes, please say something, anything that would bring us together. Here. Now. Can't you see the desire in my eyes, hear it in my every yearning breath?*

"If I'm not being too presumptuous, I'd like to come calling before you leave for Boston. Would Sunday be too soon?"

Foolish hope budded. "I would enjoy that very much."

His flash of a grin faded. "You don't know how I hate the idea of you going so far away when we've just begun to know each other. How long will you be gone?"

She couldn't bring herself to say forever, for a lifetime. No longer able to meet his eyes, she dropped her gaze. "I'm not quite sure. But let's not dwell on that. Let's just think about Sunday."

"Yeah, Sunday. Good night, pretty one. Sweet dreams."

Pretty one. She thought her heart would break as she walked down the hall to her own room, knowing all the while he watched, since the lantern he held continued to light her way. Opening her door, she turned back and tried her best to cover her raw emotions with a smile. "Sleep well."

Sleep for her, however, would not come. Long after she'd slipped into the thin batiste of her pink nightgown, brushed her hair until it fell in abundant waves down her back, and blown out her light, she tossed about in her four-poster bed, trying to ignore this strange new hunger that gnawed to her innermost core. She'd heard one of the girls at school talk about being kissed by an overeager suitor, a real grown-up kiss. Emma had said it had made her knees go weak and had stolen her breath, but no one had ever told Marty about this fevered craving.

Each time the covers tugged across her restless body, every inch of her skin they touched flamed, and her breasts peaked into hard little buds, begging for attention, pleading to be taken into the big square hands of a cowboy she didn't even know.

She tossed the blankets off her burning body. Every instinct told her to go to him, confess her need for him, only him.

But she knew she couldn't.

The clock downstairs chimed twelve.

Frustrated, Marty opened the drawer of her nightstand and found a match, then lit her lamp. She plucked a book of American verse off her stack of school texts. Plumping her pillows against the headboard, she leaned against them and opened it. Maybe some soothing verse would take her mind off what could not be. She peered down at the page and found a poem she'd always enjoyed, had even memorized. Edgar Allen Poe's *Annabel Lee.*

Unable to concentrate on the words, she glanced instead to the door, willing Cal to come through it. If he would but make the first move, she knew she wouldn't have the willpower to resist.

But there was no sound, no presence. She forced herself to return to the book.

It was many and many a year ago,
In a kingdom by the sea,
That a maiden there lived whom you may know
By the name of Annabel Lee;—
And this maiden she lived with no other thought
Than to love and be loved by me.

She was a child and *I* was a child,
In this kingdom by the sea,
But we loved with a love that was more than love—
I and my Annabel Lee—
With a love that the winged seraphs of Heaven
Coveted her and me.

Tears blurred Marty's vision, and she slammed shut the volume. She couldn't bring herself to finish this poignant lyric that spoke of a young man's eternal longing for his lost love. With trembling fingers she returned the book to the stack and blew out the light.

As she lay back and closed her eyes, other lines from the poem stole into her mind:

. . . her highborn kinsmen came
And bore her away from me,

To shut her up in a sepulchre
In this kingdom by the sea.

The words, always touching, were now almost unbearable in their prophecy. "My kinsmen, too, will be taking me
away from my new love and shutting me up in a tomb. A
cold lonely tomb with a jailer just as lifeless."

No, she mustn't think about that tonight or in the
morning. Not until after Sunday. This small slice of time
was all she had, she mustn't spoil it. Think about something
else. . . . The lovely last lines of the poem. Yes.

For the moon never beams without bringing me dreams
Of the beautiful Annabel Lee;
And the stars never rise but I see the bright eyes
Of the beautiful Annabel Lee;
And so, all the night-tide, I lie down by the side
Of my darling, my darling, my life and my bride,

The remaining lines were forgotten as she recited that last
phrase. " 'I lie down by the side of my darling, my darling,
my life and my bride.' " The whispered words poured
through her, body, heart, and mind, like molten lava. His
bride, how she needed to be *his* bride. Not some haughty,
gaunt stranger's. His.

An ache within her womanhood became intense. She
rolled over and clutched a pillow to herself in an effort to
crush the pulsing pang. It didn't help. Thrashing onto her
back, she tossed the pillow aside and sprang to her feet.

Her gaze bore into the door until, no longer able to
restrain herself, she ran recklessly to it and flung it
open . . . and crashed into a hard chest.

"Marty!" Cal caught her shoulders, then placed her a
discreet distance from him. "Please don't be scared. It's not
what you think. I was just coming to tell you I think it's best
if I ride on out of here. I really can't—"

"But I thought you were staying the night," she said while
straining to see his face more clearly in the dark.

"I know, but your folks haven't returned, and, well, I have
to. I know you trusted me—and I really appreciate that.

But, you see, men have, well, needs. And the truth of the matter is, I can't trust myself with you sleeping just down the hall. I tried, I really did, but I have to go." Abruptly he released her and spun away.

"No!" She ran after him, grabbed his arm. "You don't understand. When I leave for Boston, I won't be coming back. My mother's forcing me to marry that"—a shudder ran through her—"that cold fish I told you about."

Cal reached for her, capturing her face in his hands. "You're not going to, are you? Not after today—I mean—I know this is sudden, but by the time we left the pond this afternoon, I was already hoping . . . Please say you won't go through with it until you've given me a chance."

Marty's heart lurched painfully. She turned her face into his palm and kissed it, then covered his hands with hers. "I wish I could, but I have no choice. I'm only seventeen."

"We'll find a way. There has to be a way." He raised her fingers and brushed his lips across them.

The tenderness of his touch took the strength from her knees. She began to sag.

He caught her and pulled her flush against his chest. Only the thin material of her nightgown and his shirt separated them.

She felt her nipples harden.

One of his hands found its way to the nape of her neck, and he buried it in her hair. "When I come back Sunday, I'll speak to your father. I'll make him understand how we feel."

"It won't do any good. My mother has been set on this merger for years now."

"Merger? You're not a piece of property—you're a person with feelings."

"Mother says I'm too young to know what's good for me. She says I'll learn to love him. But I know I won't." Marty could hear herself whining, the very thing Cal had said he disliked about that girl in Salinas, but she couldn't help it. "Please don't leave me tonight. This may be the only chance I'll ever have to be with someone I love."

"Oh, Marty, you'd hate yourself in the morning. And me, too, for stealing your innocence."

"No. Don't you see, it was meant to be. I lied to you before. My parents are in Sacramento, and Ben Cauley took his wife to the doctor down in Bakersfield this morning. He won't be back until sometime tomorrow or the day after. For the first time in my life, I've been left here alone. And, like out of a fairy tale, here you came, my knight in shining armor to save me . . . to—to give me . . ."

His mouth captured hers with a fierceness.

Startled, she stiffened and tried to pull away.

In the space of a heartbeat he loosened his hold and raised his lips from hers. "I—I'm sorry. I forgot myself for a minute. I'll be more gentle." Then, as if to prove it, his hands returned to her face, and as he rubbed his thumbs slowly across her cheeks, he rained kisses on her closed eyes, her temples, before moving down to brush her lips.

Her hands found their way to his chest. Feeling the powerful telltale pounding of his heart, she had no doubt how difficult it was for him to control his passion. As his mouth left her lips and began a sensuous slide down her neck, the girlish nervousness she experienced earlier vanished. She had nothing to fear from him. She looped her arms around his neck and tipped her head back while reveling in the mind-stealing tremors racing through her body.

His tongue circled a spot just below her ear, and her blood stormed hotter. Her breath came faster, and a moan escaped.

With a groan of his own he swooped her up in his arms and carried her into her room.

The moonlight coming through the window turned his golden hair to fairy silver, and his eyes shimmered darkly with a desire she knew was only for her as he lowered her to her feet beside the bed.

"You're so beautiful." His whisper feathered across her ear as he lifted the hair draped across her shoulders and moved it to the back. "I love that you're tall and carry yourself straight and proud. I love that I don't have to bend so far to kiss you, that your eyes make love to me even when you don't realize it." His hands meandered down to her breasts, which thrust freely beneath the thin fabric.

So sensitive were they to his touch that she lost her breath.

He halted.

"No. Don't stop." She made herself exhale. "Touch me. Anywhere it would please you."

"Everywhere would please me." His hands slid to her sides, then beneath her breasts, cupping them. The thumbs that had caressed her cheeks only moments before began rubbing back and forth across her nipples.

With every trip, sharp delicious shocks exploded, then streaked down to her intimate sheath. Marty had never experienced anything so exquisite in her life . . . until he slid his hand through a gap in her nightgown, exposing a mound . . . *and took it into his mouth.* His tongue swirling around the crest. Tasting. Sucking.

The sweet torture was almost too much to bear. Her breaths came in jerky spurts as he untied the ribbons below her throat and unveiled the other one.

He bent to it and gave it the same tantalizing treat.

She could bear no more without touching him, too. She ran her hands around his neck, inside his collar, and down his back in frantic forays.

Suddenly his head came up, and his hands moved to her bottom and lifted her tight against him. The swollen manhood trapped within his jeans pressed against her soft belly in an unmistakable proclamation of his own desire.

With a gasping sigh, she clung to him as he moved her across his iron-hard need. "Yes, oh, yes. Don't stop. Don't ever stop."

Without slowing, he raised his mouth to hers. "I won't, sweet one. Not until I make you mine." He nibbled at her lower lip, then his tongue traced between her lips until they parted, and he took full possession of her mouth, entering, exploring.

Her heart fluttering like the wings of a sparrow, she tentatively followed his lead, then with more boldness when she felt his own heart kick against her breast.

His hands released their grip and began a languorous trip up her back.

No poem, no romantic tale, had ever prepared her for the

trilling shivers racing ahead of his gliding touch. Such
ecstasy. She'd been so right to ask Cal to stay. Even if they
could never be together again, she would have tonight. For
the rest of her life she could draw on this time and know
what it was like to love and be loved completely, purely.

His caress stopped at her shoulders. Then, abruptly, he
tore his mouth from hers and eased away.

Her eyes flew open. Had she been too brazen? Shocked
him? Was he rejecting her?

No, she realized as he slid the gown off her shoulders and
watched it glide to the floor.

His breath caught.

She knew the eyes roving her nakedness should turn her
shy. But they didn't. Instead that same hungering ache
carved through her, rendering her damp with desire.

He reached out and ran his palm across her belly.

She froze with anticipation as it descended lower.

But he stopped. Slowly his dusky gaze traveled back up
until it met hers. "You're even more perfect than I imagined."

Her body clamored for more, much more. "Please." She
reached for his shirt button.

As if he was emerging from a trance, a slight smile curled
the corners of his mouth, and he pulled out his shirttails and
started unfastening buttons from the bottom up as hastily as
she did from the top down. Within seconds his shirt was off.

While Cal unbuckled his belt. Marty could not, would
not, stop her hands from exploring the molded contours of
his chest. Her palms slid downward across a furry field to
the ridged muscles of his abdomen that rippled beneath her
touch. When she reached farther to the tender white skin just
above where he unfastened the last button of his jeans, she
felt the vibration of his low moan. Knowing with some
primeval sense the pleasure she gave him, she smiled.

He grabbed her hands and rasped, "You think driving me
crazy is funny?"

Her smile widened. "I am?" She loved the idea of sending
him into the same frenzy as he had her.

His chuckle came out on a shudder. "Trust me, I really

need to get my boots off before we get any more carried away."

"Then what's taking you so long?"

Releasing her, he sat down on the bed.

When he bent down into the shadows, she didn't like that. How could she remember every nuance of this night if she couldn't see him? "Do you mind if I light the lamp?"

He stood, his hands poised at the flared waist of his denims, and stared through the faint light at her. "I'm sorry, what did you say?"

"If you don't want me to, I won't. I just thought . . ."

Although his words were a bare whisper, they sang with tender passion. "I'd like that a lot."

And as they would at a poignant melody, a swim of tears came to her eyes as she lit and adjusted the flame to a low glow. She brushed them away and came around to find that Cal had discarded the last of his clothes. This time it was her turn to gasp.

The evidence of his desire was far more than she'd expected. She couldn't believe there would be a place inside her for that much of him . . . until she gauged the depth of her craving. She must've stared too long.

"Don't be afraid," he said, moving to her. He pulled her into those big powerful arms.

The heat, the scent of desire, the intimacy of skin touching skin, and the smooth, hot, hardness of his man-hood pressed between them. "Oh, my, this is so incredible." The words poured forth from her. "You're so beautiful, and you feel so good. Thank you. Thank you."

His chuckle sounded embarrassed as he gave her a quick hug and drew her with him to lie on the bed. Pillowing her head on his arm, he brushed some long silken strands from her face. His expression grew serious as he peered with eyes that had turned shades darker. "If this is a dream, don't ever wake me. I'm so filled with need for you. I never knew it could be like this. I hope I can help you feel even a little of the wonder that I do."

Hadn't he been listening to her? Marty pulled out of his hold and rose to her knees. She took his hand and urged him up until he faced her. Placing her fingers at the sides of his throat, she felt the pulse of his surging blood as she looked deeply into his eyes. "You . . . are the wonder. That you would come to me when I thought all was lost. Come to me with such life, when I saw only years of emptiness stretching before me. When . . ."

Her words died on her lips as his hands poured over her with the same gentleness as the gaze that held hers.

Trembling with emotion, she moved to play in the curls feathered across his brow, curls cast in the silvery-gold aura of the lamplight. His magnificently sculpted shoulders, too, were washed in the warmest hues as the glow subtly played over them. She wanted to memorize all of him, but when his hands brushed the soft outer sides of her breasts, her eyes fell shut, as all her senses but one gave way. She felt his hands, gentle but sure, moving down to her waist, over her hips. Moving closer to . . . Her knees lost strength, and she dropped down onto her heels.

Cal did the same, one of his knees resting between hers. His manhood pulsed against her inner thigh as his hand found its way to that place that longed desperately for him. A finger moved inside, then upward in a flaming probe.

Jolting pleasure snapped open her eyes, and she beheld him staring at her languorously, his mouth slightly parted. Her vision glazed over again as his passionate assault began a rhythmic entreaty.

Her own body responded, meeting his every foray. She wanted to give him the same pleasure. She reached down and circled him with her hand.

He gasped.

Her excitement mounted. Her breath came in short pants as she caressed the smoothness of the skin over the throbbing corded hardness.

He drove his finger deeper into her, and at the same time thrust himself through her palm.

"Oh, yes," she murmured as he withdrew and repeated the exquisite torture again and again, taking her into realms that never before existed.

His mouth sought hers, and she opened to him. His tongue entered and retreated, matching the erotic tempo of their engaged bodies until tension in her screamed. With all her strength she drove at him, around him, across him—tongue, hands, and her thrusting sheath, in a fiery frenzy. Faster. Harder.

Suddenly she spilled into an explosion of stars. Her whole body turned to flame, until, on the longest sigh, she melted against him.

Barely conscious that he'd withdrawn from her, she gave no resistance as he lay her down and moved over her.

"I love you, Marty Norwood," he whispered as he guided the smooth rounded tip of his hardness into her.

Lushly warm and ready, she spread herself to welcome his fullness, praying that she would be able to take all of him.

But he only slipped in partway, then started to retreat.

She clutched at his back, trying to hold him.

He halted. "Am I hurting you?"

"No. But don't leave me."

Chuckling, he lowered his body farther over her until his chest was close enough to rub across the tips of her breasts. "I'm not going anywhere." He moved within her again, a little deeper this time, then, as before, slowly withdrew.

The walls of her sheath clamored for more. She arched against him.

His mouth claimed hers, and he met her with a more powerful thrust.

It smothered her gasp as she stiffened with pain.

He must've realized he'd hurt her, because, though his shaft remained fully buried, he relaxed over her until his body completely covered hers. "I'm sorry," he whispered, his lips moving softly across hers. "I was told there's pain with the first entry. I wish I could've suffered it for you."

"Will it hurt like that again?"

"It shouldn't." He withdrew gently. "Does that?" His eyes held the same concern as his words.

She smiled to reassure him and lifted her hands to his ruffled hair. "Not really. Everything else I'm feeling far outweighs a little tenderness." She lifted her thighs, inviting him to return again, which he did several times with such agonizing slowness, only to remove himself with the same deliberation until she thought she'd go mad with the desire to be taken, swifter, harder. She wrapped her legs around him and with her impatient hands pressed down on his hips.

He needed no more encouragement. He took her with far more force. Then, his own urgency building, he impaled her again and again with all the conquering power he, alone, possessed. Vanquishing her every aching, throbbing sensation, while creating new ones so intense she thought she would die. Gasping, panting, she returned what he gave. She heard his own heaving and groans as he grew so large within her, she thought he'd burst.

He did! His shaft convulsed and exploded.

She, too, flew into a million pieces.

Hours later . . . or was it moments? . . . she floated down on a warm lazy sigh.

Collapsing onto her, Cal sprinkled her face with moist kisses as he murmured, "I love you," over and over, but never too many times for her raptly listening heart. His breathing gradually calmed, and he began to withdraw.

"No," she begged, unable to keep the panic from her voice as her hands shot to the small of his back to keep him there. "Not yet. Stay just a little longer. I can't bear the thought of losing you yet."

He relaxed and dropped his head alongside hers, brushing his lips across her ear. "You couldn't drive me off with a bullwhip. We're one now. Nothing will ever change that. I promise."

5

BRENN CAME INTO consciousness, instantly feeling the loss of Cal's body, the loss of heat, his weight no longer pressed over hers, yet she still felt hot beyond belief. And the deepest gnawing tingle raged where he'd just been.

Just been?

Kicking off her blankets, she swept a hand across the

sheet just to make sure he really wasn't there. And was devastated when she found him gone. "*Damn.*"

Taking a deep breath in an effort to slow her wildly banging heart, Brenn brought a hand up to it . . . and grazed a breast, sending a fierce jolt downward, magnifying a need that throbbed with each heartbeat. She squeezed her legs together, tight.

It did little good.

She sprang off the bed and stepped to the window, shoving it up all the way.

Icy air washed over her face and arms. She lifted her nightshirt, exposing the rest of her. She hadn't felt this hot and bothered since . . . since when?

Since never. With Ron she'd never felt anything even remotely so powerful.

She stayed at the window until her pulse slowed and the chill breeze began to cool her, all the while becoming more amazed at the incredibly real, incredibly erotic dream. . . . By far the most staggering adventure her subconscious had ever taken her on.

Climbing back into bed, she pulled up the covers and noticed that her skin was still so sensitized she could feel the very weave of the sheet spread across her. Its coolness quickly warmed to her own temperature.

She lowered her lashes and tried to blank her mind, but all she could see was Cal's eyes as they ate up the very sight of her. *No,* she thought. Marty was the one he'd looked at, not me. I just somehow crawled inside her skin, felt everything she did.

And, jeez, did that girl know how to feel.

Brenn's eyes sprang open again. What's the matter with me? she asked herself. I'm an educated, knowledgeable woman of the nineties—not some naive child experiencing her first taste of life. *But why hasn't Ron ever aroused me that way?*

She eased into a sitting position. And why haven't I ever seen raw passion in his eyes, felt it in his touch? My God! All of Angie's not-so-subtle hints are true.

Suddenly chilled, Brenn drew up her legs and hugged them to her. I may be the one he plans to marry, someone who'll give all his dreams of the future a big boost—me and my family of bankers. But he doesn't lust for me. He's never been the least pushy. He's always been perfectly content with an evening once or twice a month. And now he even wants to turn our honeymoon into a business trip.

But it'd been as much her fault as his, hadn't it? She'd never given him any extra encouragement, never gone out of her way to dress sexy for him. But should that really matter if he loved her? Cal had said it so simply. *A man has needs.* And if Angie was right, Ron was taking care of his elsewhere.

Stop it, she ordered herself sternly. I sure am letting my imagination get the better of me. Brenn slid down onto her pillow again and rolled over. We're just too preoccupied right now. I'm sure on our honeymoon when we're more relaxed, I'll feel all the things Marty did.

Her eyes fell shut, and she smiled languorously as she drifted into her dream again . . . Oh, my, yes.

"Cal, if you don't stop," Marty said, giving a halfhearted push to the hand sliding across the bodice of her full-skirted dress, "I'm never going to get these dishes done."

From behind, Cal chuckled in her ear as his other arm reached around her waist and pulled her against him. "You know, now that I've had something to eat, I'll bet I could take you upstairs and really show you how much I love you this time."

Dipping the last plate into the rinse water, she could feel the evidence of his capability growing as he snuggled her closer. She laughed. "And I thought our bull, Target, was full of vinegar. Here it is, after eleven, and we're just now getting breakfast over with."

"I take my job just as seriously as ol' Target. And just to prove it, why don't we head on upstairs again."

"Job! That reminds me." Marty dumped the dishpan in the sink and turned to face him. Feeling mischievous, she ran her wet fingers through his springy blond curls. "If Ben and Lula got an early start, they could be getting back anytime now. So I think any more of your bedtime stories will have to wait for another time."

"Is that a promise?"

A sudden pall shadowed her joy, and she drank in all the love in his eyes as if she were dying of thirst. "At least we'll have Sunday. I'll wait for you on the road at the top of the ridge. I don't want to have to share you with anyone on our last time together."

His expression hardened. He grabbed her arms. "What do you mean? I thought it was understood. You're staying here. I'm coming courting. And don't worry about your mother. I'll bring her tons of candy and flowers. And when I hand them to her with my boyish grin, how could she refuse?"

"You don't understand. Mother doesn't find cowboys the least bit charming." Attempting a smile, Marty ran a finger along his cheek. "No matter how cute his dimples are."

Cal caught her hand and brushed it across his mouth, his hurt gaze nearly melting her into tears. "She has to," he said in a harsh whisper. "I can't give you up."

Marty couldn't bear to look at him any longer. She turned around. "Let me finish up here. Then would you like to come with me to check on our little leppy? Make sure its new mama is still letting it nurse?"

His hands dropped away. "Sure. But we *will* talk about this again." Cal retrieved a cup off the drainboard, poured himself some more coffee, and took a seat at the table behind her.

And, although he didn't utter another word while she dried the dishes, she knew he watched her every move. But he just didn't understand. How could he? His father had given him three years of freedom before he had to take up his responsibilities. With a father as considerate as that, Cal would find it hard to believe that some parents didn't love so unselfishly.

Finished, she rolled down the sleeves of her buttercup yellow dress and walked to the side door. She looked back and attempted a brave smile. "You coming?"

He stood up and followed her out into the full light of day. "You're not going up to change into britches first?"

"I thought it would be nice to walk for a change."

"Well, dang. I was really counting on getting you upstairs again." He grinned, but it didn't erase the sadness in his eyes. "I'm a whole lot more convincing when I've got you in bed."

She took hold of his big calloused hand. Giving it a squeeze, she led him along the stone path to the side gate. "See that knoll over there?" She pointed to a distant rise with a giant water oak shading most of it. "From there we should be able to spot the new little family."

As she started for it, Cal matched his steps to hers. He tucked her arm in his, drawing her closer. "Did I tell you how beautiful you look in yellow?"

Marty felt a blush creeping into her cheeks. He'd told her she was beautiful any number of times since last night, but somehow, under the bright sun, the compliment seemed so much more potent.

"Of course," he said, leaning down, "nothing will ever surpass how you look after I've just made love to you."

That did it—she was turning flame-red. She broke free and, snatching up her skirts, sprinted away. "Race you to the top!" she shouted without looking back to see if he was game—she had no doubt he would be.

She'd almost crested the top of the grassy hill when, despite her laughter, she heard his nearing footsteps. But it was only a few more feet to the tree. With a last surge of energy, she stretched out her hand.

He caught her around the middle and swung her away from it. "Not this time," he said, chuckling, almost as out of breath as she. With slow deliberation he placed his palm against the bark. "And this is the exact spot I'm going to carve our initials."

As he lowered her to the ground, she wrapped an arm around him and nestled close. "Do it now. Do you have a knife?"

"Sure." He drew it from his pocket and opened the blade. "How do you want it—M.N. loves C.W. or the other way around?"

"The other way. It'll be proof. A hundred years from now, I'll know that this day really happened. That on this very day, Cal Williams loved me."

He pulled her around to face him and untied the yellow ribbon holding her hair, then catching up a handful, he drew her face to his. "On this day and every one from now on."

His lips crushed down on hers, already swollen and tender from the hundreds of kisses that had preceded it. But she couldn't help being just as hungry for him this time as all the others. She wrapped her arms tightly around his neck and answered his every quest with her own until, heart pounding and breathless, she broke away. "Oh, Cal," she said, her fingers going to his face, memorizing every curve. "How am I ever going to give you up?"

He swallowed hard and his eyes glittered. "*You're not.*" He wheeled around and brought his knife up to the trunk. But the other hand, Marty noticed, rubbed across his eyes.

At the thought that he'd been near tears, some of her own began to well. "While you're doing that," she said, placing a hand on his back from a need to touch him once more before she walked away, "I'll look around for our calf."

Marty spent as much time glancing at Cal as she did scanning the lounging Herefords. While Cal carved, the muscles across his shoulders mesmerized her. They corded and rippled in a wondrously sensual display of his power—a power that had given her such a sense of wholeness when he had become one with her. Even now she could feel that very strength swathing her in love and safety. She'd never felt so alive. Waves of excitement coursed through her. At the same time she felt as contented as a sated cat.

Unable to concentrate on her chore, it was purely by accident that she spotted the calf. About fifty yards to the east it rose out of the grass and, on slightly wobbly legs, tottered over to its adoptive mother. Stepping under her big round belly, it bumped and nuzzled until it found a teat to nurse.

The mother bent around and watched with big gentle eyes that seemed to be filled with an abiding love for the little leppy.

Hugging her own bosom, Marty could almost feel a pink and cuddly infant in her arms, drawing from her own breast—Cal's baby, only Cal's.

Suddenly arms enfolded her from behind, and Cal pulled her into his embrace. "It would be so right. Nothing could be more right." He was so attuned to her, he'd read her thoughts.

She rubbed a hand across his forearm and leaned her head against his chest. "I know."

"I'll speak to your parents Sunday. I'll make them understand."

The spell was broken, and all the torment crashed in on her again. "They won't. I told you, my mother is determined."

"So am I." He kissed the top of her head. "If it's a prosperous son-in-law they want, I'll tell them how successful our mercantile business is."

Turning to face him, Marty clasped her hands around his neck. He was still hers for now. "I'm sure it would impress me to no end, but I'm afraid my mother comes from an Eastern banking family. She only met my father because he'd gone back there to pick up a prize bull from England. He was a houseguest of a cattle broker friend of the family. They met at his summer place on Martha's Vineyard. Mother told me she was in a silly rebellious stage at the time and thought it would be utterly romantic to run away to the 'Wild West' with a cowboy. Although she loves Daddy, I know she bitterly regrets leaving all the wealth and glamour behind."

"Is that why you agreed to go? Do you want it, too?"

"Good heavens, no. But, try as I might, I can't convince her."

"Then do as she did. Run away to the Wild West. Come with me now to Salinas." His earnestness was evident in the pressure of his hands at her waist. "I'll start work for my father right away."

Marty searched Cal's eyes. "You'd do that for me? I thought you hated the idea of being cooped up all day."

"We'll save our money, buy some land in the hills behind the store, run a few head of cattle so we'd always have an excuse to go riding. It'll be a good life. I promise. When we're in the mood for a little sea air, it's just a couple hours' ride to Monterey—and San Francisco is less than a hundred miles away."

"But what would your family say? Bringing home a girl you've known less than twenty-four hours."

"My folks'll love you even more for being the one who brought me back. Besides, what's not to love about you? You're . . . everything. We could cut across the valley to San Luis Obispo and get married there before starting north." He pulled her against him, surrounding her with his will—his strength. "*Say yes. Please.*"

But could she dare? Fear gripped her from the inside. When her parents found her gone, they'd track her down. Daddy would skin Cal alive.

But how would they know where to search if she didn't tell them? She could leave a note so they'd know she was safe, but just not tell them Cal's name or where he lived. Then, later, after she and Cal were married and settled, and her parents had a chance to cool down, she could write them and tell them where she was. It would work. It really would.

"Marty?" The vulnerable expression on his face gave her that last push.

"Yes!" she cried and rose up on her toes until she was within inches of his mouth. "Oh, yes."

The passionate kiss she expected didn't happen. Instead, he released her and laced his fingers in her hair. After a shaky breath he brushed her lips with the utmost tenderness. "You'll never regret it."

"I know." Feeling a little weak herself, she sank back down, then remembered that the Cauleys could return home at anytime. "I'd better hurry and pack before our ranch hand comes back. He'd be a problem."

Cal smiled, displaying those darling dimples. "I'll go saddle our horses."

Moving out of his arms, Marty noticed the carving on the tree. Lovingly, she walked to it and traced her fingers over their initials.

He stepped up beside her. "Someday, when we come back for a visit, I'll put a heart around 'em."

"Yes," she said, her confidence building. Eventually her parents would accept their marriage and invite them to return. In the meantime, she'd be living out *her* dreams . . . *not her mother's.*

She felt such a rush of exhilaration, she burst out laughing and spun away, sending her full skirts soaring. Then, catching up the hem, she took off down the hill, stretching into a long-legged sprint. "Bet you can't catch me this time!"

She heard him chortle, then let out an uninhibited whoop, giving her even more of a lead before he started after. She flew across the meadow. She'd beat him this time for sure.

The sharp crack of a rifle resounded.

Marty came to a halt and looked around as the noise echoed through the valley.

A couple hundred yards to the west, Ben Cauley came riding at top speed, his rifle in hand.

Marty swung back to Cal. For a second she didn't see him. Then she saw the white of his shirt, the blue of his jeans as he sprawled facedown in the grass among some poppies and baby's breath. He lay incredibly still.

An icy chill drizzled down her spine.

He lay still as death.

"Cal?"

He didn't move.

"Cal!" Marty raced to him. Dropping down, she grabbed his shoulder and rolled him over.

Red soaked the right side of his rib cage.

She pressed a hand to it and looked at his face.

Those wonderfully expressive features were blank. His eyes stared up without seeing.

"No!" It couldn't be. Marty threw herself over his chest and pressed an ear against it, listening for a heartbeat. Any small hope.

"Marty."

She was being lifted away.

"Marty."

Ben's face was before her.

"Are you all right? Did I get him before he hurt you?"

"Hurt me?" What was Ben talking about? Couldn't he see? She tried to pull free.

The lean older man's grip tightened, and he gave her a shake. "Are you hurt?"

"He's dead."

"Yeah, I know." He shook her again. "Are you all right?"

Pain ripped across her breast. Her heart plummeted, and she turned to water. Cal . . . Everything . . . It was all gone. Tears poured from her eyes, down her face, and she knew that she, too, was draining away as surely as Cal's blood flowed from his lifeless body, taking him away from her. Tears, a blessed river of tears, flowed out of her. They would take her to Cal. . . . She had to find him before he got too far. She couldn't lose him now, not before they'd even begun. . . . *"Cal, wait for me. Please. Wait . . ."*

A cold wind blew across Brenn's face, cooling her tears, turning them to ice. Swiping at them, she saw the chintz curtains billowing and felt a cold spray of rain coming through the window. She lay unmoving and let the shocking wetness revive her until she'd convinced herself this overwhelming sense of loss had been caused by nothing but another dream.

Nonetheless, she felt emotionally shredded, and it was several minutes before she could trust her legs enough to get up and close the window.

As soon as she did, she turned on the bedside lamp and picked up her watch lying next to it.

Seven-ten.

It couldn't be, it was still dark. Then she remembered she hadn't reset it for the time change. In New York, Ron should be getting ready for work about now. She could give him a call. Touch base with reality.

Remembering she'd seen a phone in the library, she practically ran downstairs to it and switched on the light.

He answered on the third ring. "Yes?" He sounded a little irritated.

"Hi. It's me."

"Are you home already? How'd it go?"

"No. I'm still in California. The lawyer's out of town and won't be back until tomorrow. So, I drove up to the ranch and spent the night."

"That's great. All the better to look the place over. What do you think so far? Is it worth anything?"

Brenn recalled her first reaction to the valley. "It's really quite beautiful."

"Is it close enough to Bakersfield for subdividing?"

"Ron, could we talk about this later? I just woke up from the worst nightmare of my life. I really just wanted to . . . to know that you're there."

"Of course I'm here. I thought we trusted one another."

"You don't understand. I dreamed that . . . someone was . . . I guess I just needed to hear another voice."

On the other end he chuckled. "You can be such a child sometimes. Now, getting back to the ranch—how many acres is it?"

By the time Ron ran out of questions about the property and Brenn could hang up, she was more upset than before she'd called. Not only had he not acknowledged her need for comfort, all he wanted to do was desecrate her valley.

Desecrate? She frowned at the odd choice of words. But the more she considered it—and the dream—the more she realized that was exactly how she felt about his idea.

Perhaps she should call Mom. Maybe her mother could give her some answers. She picked up the receiver again and dialed.

From the husky, "Hello," at the other end, Brenn knew she'd awakened her.

"Sorry. I thought you'd be up."

"Is that you, Brenn?"

"Yes. I'm here at the Norwood Ranch. I spent the night."

"Hmm. Is it a nice place?"

"Yes. Great. Wonderful. It's in its own little valley. And the house—it's old but well-maintained. Very homey."

"Sounds charming. Maybe I should've gone with you. Get a break from all the problems I've been having with the wedding reception. And now your father, the old skinflint, will not even *try* to understand the need to hire an electrician. I'm sure if Ron came from a more . . . Oh, you know—a more substantial family. Well, it is still *our daughter's wedding*, and I absolutely refuse to have a bunch of gaudy orange extension cords strung out all across the grounds."

The wedding was the last thing Brenn wanted to talk

about now. "Mom? Listen. What exactly did Aunt Sarah tell you about Grandmother Martha? You said she lived here during the last years of her life. Did Aunt Sarah or Grandma or any of the other relatives spend time here with her?"

"No, I don't think so. Sarah said Grandmother Martha had always been a very private person and grew even more distant after her husband died. She asked to be left in peace and to not be disturbed unless there was an emergency. Before Mamma passed away, I remember her saying once that when Grandfather Winston died it was as if she'd lost both her parents. The strange part was, Martha and Winston rarely spent any time together at all."

"If Grandmother Martha was so private, I'm surprised she told Aunt Sarah about this lost love of her youth and her quest to find him again."

"Oh, believe me, she didn't. When Aunt Sarah went out to California to have the body shipped back here, she ran across a journal of some sort."

"Is it still here?"

"Grandmother Martha had already given everything pertaining to her life in Boston to her children before she went out West. When Sarah returned she said nothing at the ranch would be of comfort to the family. She'd been quite adamant about it. Said she'd left everything there untouched, as she'd been instructed in the will. I'm sure that includes the journal."

6

BRENN REPLACED THE receiver on the desk phone and turned to face the room. Its massive fireplace filling the corner and the wall of books were just as they'd been in her dream. But that was easily explainable since she'd seen them when she came in last night. Yesterday's recliners were there, though, instead of the overstuffed chairs. The

drapes and wall-to-wall carpeting were also different from
in her dream, not to mention the addition of the television
and electric lights. But, in her fantasy, she'd cleverly replaced
the more modern furnishings.

Nonetheless, the dream had been so real, she felt as if
she'd really spent last evening here with her young man.
And she'd been so innocently enthralled. So desperately in
love.

No. It was not she. She had to stop transporting herself
into Marty. She was *not* that recklessly free girl. She never
had been. It was impossible.

But she had dreamed her up—she couldn't deny that.
Maybe Marty was just the unfettered spirit she wished she
could be sometimes. Taking chances, being adventurous.
But, as Dad always said, if you take your eyes off the goal
for even a second, you could lose all you've gained.

Quite obviously the dream had just been the result of
some latent pre-wedding jitters. Yet, drawn by the pair of
chairs separated by that same oak tree, Brenn walked up
behind one and ran her hand over the oxblood leather—*the
same shade as Cal's boots.*

Dream or not, it had been an evening of such fragile, yet
awesome, first awakenings. An innocent age—a time before the movies and TV had stolen the wonder of first love.

Becoming aware of the cold predawn air, especially down
at her bare feet, Brenn noticed some kindling and logs
stacked on the grate, ready to light. How thoughtful of the
Dills, she thought, and pulled a long match out of a copper
container. Then, after flipping her straight hair out of the
way, she bent to torch it.

Once her feet and backside were warmed, Brenn went
into the kitchen to make coffee. The sunny yellow walls
surprised her when she switched on the light—they'd been
white in her dream.

"*So what,*" she said aloud as she hurried across the icy
linoleum to reach the throw rug in front of the sink. So what
if the stove, double sink, and tiled counters replaced the
more primitive ones. And so what if there hadn't even been
a refrigerator. She had to stop thinking it was a big deal

just because everything had been so flawlessly nineteenth century.

Lifting a can of grounds out of one of her grocery sacks, she spotted an electric percolator on the counter. "It's not as if I haven't seen my share of western movies."

While waiting for the coffee to get done, she wandered through another door into a large oblong dining room, switching on the light as she went. A mahogany table with a dozen graceful chairs dominated the space while tall velvet-draped windows lined one side and the front, and a huge china cabinet covered most of the back. A fringed Persian rug covered the hardwood floor, and a crystal chandelier above reflected its splendor on the highly polished table. The total effect created an elegance the old-monied back East would appreciate. Obviously, the decorating had been that of Marty's mother.

"Damn, there I go again. Acting like my dream is how it actually was." She noticed dawn peeking through slightly cracked coral drapes and walked to the nearest window. "The light of day, that's what I need." She pulled them open.

Looking out the front corner window, Brenn noticed rain-kissed flowers and leaves, and the rising sun streaking across the meadow beneath receding storm clouds. Then, peering past a porch swing, she saw a knoll rising in the field across the road—*the one with the giant water oak.* She suddenly had no doubt. *Marty and Cal's initials would be etched into it.*

As if on a mission now, she walked through the wide archway to the central hall. The tall grandfather clock she'd heard so often in her dream stared silently back. She paused and ran a hand over the elaborately carved wood that framed the glass. Later, after she had some answers, she'd wind and set it. Turning away, she hurried to the rear of the house and into the library. Grandmother Martha's journal was probably among the rows of other books.

She easily found the narrow red volume, since it was the only one without a title on its spine. After pouring herself a cup of coffee and adding a log to the fire, Brenn settled before it and opened to the first page.

In all these years, Cal, I have never spoken of you to a living soul. Our time together was too precious. And it belongs to us alone.

Cal. There was his name in black and white.

But I went to the doctor today, and he said it will not be long now. The foolish man made such an effort not to frighten me. I couldn't help smiling. If he only knew how much I have been looking forward to finally going to you. All the lonely years. A lifetime of emptiness.

Brenn quickly scanned more pages. It was all there . . . how Marty's parents had whisked her away to Massachusetts before any hint of scandal could attach itself to her, the hollow marriage, and how in her final years she'd read everything she could find on the hereafter and rebirth. The little mention Marty had given to her life in Boston left Brenn feeling almost as disturbed as the aged woman's obsession with finding a path to her young lover again.

Grandmother Martha had taken no comfort in the years she spent with her husband and little joy in her three children. She'd cared for them, but mourned more the love she would have felt for them had they been Cal's.

Only a dozen or so pages of the journal were filled, and when Brenn finished, she closed her eyes in despair and leaned back. Small wonder Aunt Sarah had chosen to keep these findings from the rest of the family. Once Marty had experienced the fullness of love and passion with Cal, she'd been unable to take pleasure in anything less from that time forth.

Brenn swallowed down the last of her now cold coffee and walked to the bookcase again. At eye level she found an entire shelf of volumes on every religion and several that pertained exclusively to reincarnation. "The old gal was covering all her bases. Even left her personal estate to me in case she could return again in me."

Suddenly enraged, Brenn spun around. "How dare she try to steal my life." Retrieving her cup, she went to the kitchen to get a refill. "And dumb. Simple arithmetic should've told her that Cal had a good seventy-year head start on her. Did she really expect me to go out and look for some dried-up old cowboy?"

Laughing at the idiocy of scouring the hills for a dottering old coot with a head of silver curls and a set of dimples hidden among a road map of lines and creases, Brenn started upstairs to get dressed. Reaching the bedroom, her smile collapsed. The memory of every spot Cal had touched her hit with full force. She felt his hands exploring, the weight of his body spreading across her. Hot, seeking. The power of his thrust as he drove into her. Again and again. The whispered words, the very smell of him, of their lovemaking.

Throbbing, flaming desire melted her insides and her legs turned to jelly. She grasped onto the doorjamb for support. The sight of the bed, that same rumpled chintz spread, the pine walls, all seemed to pull her into this insane yearning.

Either she was losing her mind or the room was haunted.

Her breath coming in jerky spurts, she ran in and scooped up all her belongings, then raced downstairs as if she truly were being chased by ghosts.

Down by the fireplace, she tossed off her nightshirt and put on the jeans, a loose-fitting jade-green sweater, and running shoes she bought the day before, then found a half bath beside the stairs. She'd just have to make do without a shower since she had no intention of going upstairs again. At least, not alone. She'd drive back into Bakersfield, get a room there for the night.

After finishing with an abbreviated version of her morning ritual, Brenn passed the ominous staircase again on her return to the library. Spotting her overstuffed handbag on the nearest recliner, she was propelled by a fresh spurt of panic. She spread it wide and began ripping through the accumulation of bills, receipts, and letters for the car keys.

Her notepad fell in a flutter of pages onto the floor.

Retrieving it, she noticed it was opened to the list of names and addresses Ron had given her of some business associates he'd especially wanted invited to their wedding.

Damn, she'd forgotten all about them. Ron would be

furious. "Great. Just great. I can hardly wait to tell him when I get home." She began flipping through more pages. "What else is being left undone while I'm here letting my great-grandmother take over my life?"

The doorbell chimed.

She jumped at the sound. Who in the world could it be? She was in the middle of nowhere. She stuck her head into the hall and looked toward the front door with its intricately etched oval pane. She saw movement beyond. Someone was definitely out there. But how could they possibly know she'd arrived?

The chimes bonged again.

"Well, genius, the obvious way to find out is to answer it," she muttered to herself in an effort to build courage as she strode to the front entrance. After turning the deadbolt knot, she swung open the door to a man who literally filled it. He was at least six-four.

And a calf dangled from his arms. A modern day Cal?

"Hi. I was just driving through. I . . ." His words died away as he stared back at her. Obviously, he hadn't expected to see her, a total stranger. "I have a cabin up on Greenhorn Mountain. . . ." He seemed to lose his train of thought again. Then he shifted his gaze away, but just for a second. "Anyway, I noticed this little one. It was bawling next to a cow that's all bloated and stiff-legged."

"Bloated and—*what*?"

"You know, dead." He shrugged shoulders that no doubt looked even broader in his shiny blue windbreaker. "A good two days, anyway. This baby's sure to be real hungry by now. So I thought I'd better bring it to you. Here."

Suddenly a calf that must have weighed thirty or forty pounds was dropped into her arms. She staggered back a step before getting a firm grip. Looking up, she found him still staring. Was he waiting to be thanked? Or, perhaps, tipped?

Just as she was about to speak, the man turned away, and she noticed SLATER CONSTRUCTION printed across the back of his jacket as he trotted down the porch steps. *He was leaving.* "Wait!"

At the bottom he wheeled around and grinned. A deep

dimple dented each cheek. "Oh, guess I forgot to tell you.
The cow's just north of the road before you cross the creek.
Just follow the buzzards."

Not only did he have dimples, but Brenn noted the bounty
of short chestnut curls lapping up the sides of his baseball
cap. There was something almost criminal about someone
being that virile and that cute at the same time. Then his last
words sank in. "*Buzzards?*"

"Yeah." He grinned wider. "They're making a real feast
of it."

Brenn's stomach curdled at the conjured picture.

"Well, I guess I'd better get going." He didn't sound all
that certain, even his slowness in turning away seemed
hesitant.

The calf squirmed.

Brenn panicked. "No! You can't!"

As he turned back, the smile had vanished, leaving faint
lines along either side of a generous mouth on an evenly
proportioned, deeply tanned face.

Noticing so much about his looks under the circumstance
impressed her enough to cause her to soften her tone. "You
can't just walk away and leave me here with this calf."

"I don't understand. It belongs to you, doesn't it?"

"Yes, I guess. I mean—I just inherited the place. I flew
out here from New York only yesterday. I haven't the
foggiest notion what to do with it."

"Where's the couple that runs the place? They'll know."

"They quit when I came. Mr. Dill had another job to go
to. They said I'd have to hire someone else. So you see—"

"But, lady, I don't know the first thing about cattle. I'm
just passing through. See the back of my pickup?"

Brenn glanced past him to the tan truck parked on the side
of the road beyond the picket fence. Red-flagged boards
stuck out over the tailgate.

"I'm on the way up to my cabin to do some repairs. I'm
a contractor. I build houses."

"And *I* work on the sixty-second floor of a high-rise. You
can't just drive away and leave me alone here with a
starving calf." Lowering the little fellow to the floor, she

vaguely heard the pages of her forgotten notepad crunch as she pressed the calf against her legs.

The man shifted his lean athletic frame into a slouch that would rival the sexiest male model's and pushed back his ball cap. "I see. What we have here, then, is your actual damsel in distress. Well, at least, maybe I can now say I have a reason for buying that rundown shack of mine last year—it's not worth the spit and glue holding it together. I only bought it because it gave me an excuse to take a drive up through here every few weeks. There's something about this little valley."

"A building contractor, you say? I suppose what you see is all the money to be made by cluttering Norwood Flat with tracts of houses. Just like someone else I know."

"Hell, no." He strode back to the bottom of the steps. Beneath a wide swath of brows, the green in his gold-fringed eyes hardened. "Tell me you're not going to do that."

She resisted the urge to flinch. "No. I'm not." And she'd never meant anything more. Ron or no Ron.

The tension in his expression relaxed, and he rubbed his left hand across his jaw—a long, strong hand, Brenn noted, that was ringless. He eased into a sheepish grin. "Sorry. It's just . . . I really can't explain it. A couple years ago I got lost trying to find a job site and stumbled across this valley. And, like I said, there's just something about it."

"I know. I felt the same thing from the first moment I saw it yesterday. I love everything about it. And this old house is wonderful."

"That's good to hear. At least I know I'm not the only one."

"Surely the rest of your friends feel the same way."

"Truth is, I've never brought anyone up here. Couldn't bring myself to . . ." He straightened and spread his hands disarmingly. "Sounds like I'm some sort of weird loner. But I'm not. Really. I have plenty of friends, and I run three crews. I have more business than I can handle. The name's Steve Slater. It's just that I haven't wanted to share how I feel about the place. It's hard to explain. Sounds crazy, but I have the strongest feeling I'm supposed to . . . Never mind. Like I said, it's crazy. You say you just inherited this ranch? From what I understood, the owner died twenty, twenty-five years ago."

"That's right. It's been held in trust for me until I was old enough to inherit. It's just that no one bothered to tell me."

The little creature against her legs tried to buck free of her grasp.

Dropping to her knees, Brenn laughed as she slung an arm around its neck. "If they had, I would've at the very least read a book on animal husbandry. Anything to prepare myself."

Slater climbed up the steps, shaking his head. He sat down on the top one and rested a steadying hand over the calf's haunches. "All this was going to be yours, and nobody informed you?"

He was suddenly incredibly close, that manly weathered face level with hers, his gaze wandering across. She almost forgot to answer. "Hard to believe, isn't it? I'm still trying to get used to the idea."

"Did you know your eyes are the same color as the calf's?" There was an unmistakable intimacy in his soft tone.

Brenn had never been any good at small talk. She smiled nervously. "Is that supposed to be a compliment?"

"After seeing this baby's, you have to ask?"

Looking from the calf's big brown eyes back to his, Brenn had the strongest feeling of déjà vu. She could see Cal's expression, could hear *I didn't think anyone's eyes could be more beautiful than a calf's.*

A sudden gust whipped a strand of hair across her face, blocking her view of him. She flipped her head, but the wind held it. Then she felt, more than saw, Slater's hand as he reached across the calf's back to brush it behind her shoulder.

The trace of a smile flickered at his mouth. "Now that you've finally come, you do plan to stay, don't you?"

Finally? Was he aware of more than he was saying or how his slightest touch had shot shivers through her? "I don't know. I . . . ."

He abruptly glanced away. "If you'll hang on to the little

fella, I'll go out to the barn and see if I can find some nursing bottles."

"Steve?" She moved her hand over his, and he returned a look that telegraphed that he was equally aware of her. But, undoubtedly, all they were feeling was the closeness of two healthy young bodies. Yet her overactive imagination kept telling her there was more . . . far more. "Did you know I'd be coming?"

"No. I mean, I . . ." He pressed his lips tightly together, then took a deep breath and exhaled. "Last night I woke up in the middle of the night from a . . . dream. Strange dream. And I just couldn't stop myself from coming up here today. A Twilight Zone kind of thing, I know, but . . ." He raised his brows in a self-conscious gesture. "Anyway, I called my secretary at dawn this morning and told her to cancel everything. And since I never take off unless I'm dying, she thinks I've lost my mind." Chuckling, he shrugged and rose to his feet. "I threw that bunch of boards in the back of the pickup just to give myself a bona fide reason."

Looking up at him, Brenn laughed, too. "I know just how you feel. I've been working both sides of the rainbow, myself, since last night."

"Really?"

"Yes, but I think it's going to be okay now."

"Then I know it is." His gaze held hers far longer than should have been comfortable, but it only made her feel more at ease. Then his attention shifted and he reached down. "Here, let me put your notepad up on the railing. It's getting all mangled."

"Thanks, but nothing in it's important . . . anymore." Handing it to him, Brenn couldn't resist the urge to rub her cheek across the soft fur of their little captive.

"Yeah, I know what you mean." He dropped to one knee in front of her. So close. His eyes offering so much.

This was crazy, her every sense told her. Could she possibly think of turning her back on a lifetime of training, her family, Ron, all her goals, because of one night's dream and the promise in a stranger's gaze? But, my God, the open sincerity in it was enough to die for. No—*to live for.*

"I do need to know one thing, though," he continued. "What's your name?"

"Brenn. Brenn Ryan."

"It's as beautiful as you are." He took her face in his hands. "There's an oak tree someplace across the road I want to go see later. If it's still there. But right now, I'm going to kiss you, Brenn Ryan. It's been a long time. Way too long."

"I know."